SOMEONE I USED TO KNOW

PAIGE TOON

PAIGE TOON PRESS

Paige Toon Press 2021

Copyright © 2021 by Paige Toon

All rights reserved.

ISBN 13: 978-1-913341-52-7 (paperback edition)

This book is a work of fiction. The characters, incidents and dialogue are drawn from the author's imagination and are not to be construed as real. Any resemblance to actual events or persons, living or dead is fictionalised or coincidental.

This book was first published by Simon & Schuster UK in 2021.

Feel it all with Paige Toon

The Minute I Saw You
2020
'Gave me that gorgeous, glowing happy feeling you get at the end of a truly uplifting read'
Beth O'Leary
'So unique and moving, I adored every lovely word' **Josie Silver**

————

If You Could Go Anywhere
2019
'Heart-warming, wistful and full of joy'
Lindsey Kelk
'Warm, inspiring, like a holiday mood in book form' **Mhairi McFarlane**

————

One Perfect Christmas and Other Stories
2018
'Paige introduces us to characters old and new in this witty, heartfelt and romantic collection of short stories' *My Weekly*
'Like a delectable Boxing Day buffet, this tasty collection reunites some much-loved characters from Toon's fifteen novels in nine never-before-printed short stories' *Heat*

————

Five Years From Now

2018

'Filled with warmth and poignancy, *Five Years From Now* is a page turner and a delight' **Catherine Isaac**

'Full of living-in-the-moment and what-might-have-been contrasts, this tender read pulls at the heartstrings' *Fabulous*

———

The Last Piece of My Heart

2017

'Wonderfully heartfelt... Her best book yet!' *Heat*

'A gorgeous, warm novel' **Adele Parks**

———

The One We Fell in Love With

2016

'You'll love it, cry buckets and be uplifted' **Marian Keyes**

'I blubbed, I laughed and I fell in love... Utterly heart-wrenching' **Giovanna Fletcher**

———

The Sun in Her Eyes

2015

'Paige really ratchets up the tension. You'll be in a reading frenzy by the end' **Lisa Jewell**

'Paige Toon's epic bestseller shows how life can change in a heartbeat' *Glamour*

———

Thirteen Weddings

Pictures of Lily

2010

'An absorbing and emotional narrative – brilliant!' *Heat*

'Another perfect summer page-turner by Paige Toon' *Mirror*

———

Chasing Daisy

2009

'A fast-paced and funny read... with great jokes and a thoughtful heart' *Daily Express*

'Laugh-out-loud funny and touchingly honest' *Company*

———

Johnny Be Good

2008

'Pacy, highly enjoyable insight into life in La-La Land!' *Closer*

'All the warmth and fun I've grown to expect from the talented Ms Toon' **Freya North**

———

Lucy in the Sky

2007

'I loved it – I couldn't put it down!' **Marian Keyes**

'A fab debut and a great summer read' *Elle*

ALSO BY PAIGE TOON

In order of release...

Lucy in the Sky

Johnny be Good

Chasing Daisy

Pictures of Lily

Baby be Mine

One Perfect Summer

The Longest Holiday

Thirteen Weddings

The Sun in Her Eyes

The One we Fell in Love With

The Last Piece of my Heart

Five Years from Now

If You Could Go Anywhere

The Minute I Saw You

Someone I Used To Know

Novellas:

Johnny's Girl

One Perfect Christmas

A Christmas Wedding

Young Adult:

The Accidental Life of Jessie Jefferson

I knew You Were Trouble

All About the Hype

For every Child Looked After and everyone who cares...

And for Ian and Helga Toon, who have been showing me Yorkshire's gems for over half my life. I couldn't have asked for better parents-in-law.

PROLOGUE

Neither then nor now...
...but sometime in between

The farm is visible as soon as the taxi crests the brow of the hill.

'There it is,' I say to the driver.

'Hard to miss,' he responds good-naturedly.

When I left at five thirty this evening, it was still light, but now, at almost eight, the fields are blanketed in darkness, save for the occasional glowing window from neighbouring farmhouses – and our place, which is lit up like a giant Christmas tree.

Jamie really went all out with those fairy lights, I think with a mixture of guilt and envy.

I wish I'd done more to help him set up. This is my parents' joint seventieth birthday/retirement bash and I haven't even managed to stay for the duration of the celebrations. The party kicked off at three, but I had to take Emilie back to the Airbnb in Harrogate after only two and a half hours and she took ages to settle. Hopefully she'll stay asleep until we return. The babysitter, Katy, seemed competent, but I wouldn't wish our screaming fifteen-month-old on anyone.

'Would you be able to come back for my husband and me later?' I remember to ask the driver.

'Afraid not, I'm clocking off after this. My mate could probably do it, though. What time are you thinking?'

'Midnight? Could he also take our sitter home afterwards? She lives a few minutes away.'

I wait until the return journey is arranged before getting out of the car, wincing a split second before my black high heels connect with mud. But the soles of my shoes hit only grit because, as I now remember hearing, '*Jamie was out here all morning, sweeping the whole courtyard and the length of the drive.*'

Jamie, Jamie, Jamie...

My brother, more of a son to my parents than I am a daughter, it often seems, yet he is not my blood.

He *has* done an incredible job, I acknowledge, as I pay the driver and get out of the car. This place has never looked better.

Festoon lights criss-cross from one side of the courtyard to the other, reflecting in the darkened glass of upstairs windows and casting a warm glow onto the sandy stone walls of the farmhouse and barns. Tealights in lanterns sparkle atop brightly painted metal outdoor tables, and colourful bunting sways overhead, dispersing the ribboning smoke from cigarettes below.

A scan of the crowd confirms that my parents have retreated inside along with their friends. They never were

ones to outstay their welcome where the younger generation was concerned.

My gaze comes to rest on Theo, who is sitting at a sky-blue
table with Jamie and a girl I don't recognise. His dark hair
falls just shy of the collar of his black shirt and a lit cigarette is
resting all-too-familiarly between his long slim fingers. He
brings it to his lips and inhales deeply, his face flaring briefly
to reveal a sharp jaw and a perfectly straight nose.

I'm snapped to attention by the taxi doing a U-turn.
Moving out of the way, I track its headlights as they sweep
across the field, illuminating the small wood in the lower
paddock. The white trunk of a solitary silver birch tree
shines back like a beacon before it's enveloped once more by
darkness.

Technicolour synths and drumbeats explode from the
outdoor speakers as Cid Rim's 'Repeat' featuring Samantha
Urbani kicks into gear.

Jamie has hijacked the music.

I smile and set off towards the courtyard.

Jamie sees me first, bouncing to his feet and almost
bumping his head on an outdoor heater. He's fairly tall at
five foot ten, but his hair – black, short at the sides and wild
and curly on top – adds at least another three inches to his
height.

Arms open wide, a huge smile lighting his face, he
hollers at the top of his voice, 'SNOW WHITE!'

It's the nickname he gave me years ago in the dead of
winter when my skin was, admittedly, as white as snow –
especially compared to his warm brown complexion. That
was as far as my resemblance to the fairy tale princess went:
my hair back then was long and light brown, not ebony, and
my eyes are hazel rather than brown. But at the time, before

I could rustle up any sort of comeback, he warned, with a perfectly straight face, 'Careful, don't be racist.'

Theo shoots his head around to look at me – along with every other person in the courtyard, thanks to Jamie bellowing – and quickly stubs out his cigarette. He gives me a cheeky, guilty grin as I approach.

'*I quit! Absolutely-one-hundred-per-cent-for-good this time!*' I mimic his words of only a few months ago.

'I only had one,' he replies in a huskier voice than usual.

'Sure,' I say drily.

'Okay, maybe this is my second.' He smiles up at me with his best puppy-dog please-don't-be-mad impression. 'You've been gone ages!'

'I know,' I reply grumpily, indulging his change of subject.

The girl at the table freezes theatrically, her big bright eyes boggling up at me from behind a thick coppery fringe. '*Leah*?!' she asks.

Out of the blue, I'm hit with a memory of a mousier, plumper, younger version of her.

'Hello!' I cry as she jumps up to give me a hug.

I rack my brain wildly for her name.

'*Danielle*,' Jamie mouths helpfully at me over her shoulder.

How could I forget?

'Danielle!' I exclaim, drawing back to study her as Theo grabs a pastel pink chair from nearby and swings it around to face the table. 'I need a drink,' I murmur meaningfully.

'I'll get you one,' he replies.

'What took you so long?' Jamie demands as I sit down.

'Emilie was *wired*. I swear someone fed her a bag of sugar.'

'She did eat two pieces of birthday cake earlier, plus all your dad's leftover icing,' he tells me casually.

'Bloody hell! Why didn't he stop her?'

'I don't think he noticed.'

'Why didn't *you* stop her?' I think to ask.

'She looked happy,' he replies laughingly, palms up.

I roll my eyes long-sufferingly at him and smile at Danielle. 'How *are* you?'

Danielle, Jamie, and many of the other twenty- and thirty-somethings here tonight were fostered by my parents at some point in their lives. I left home for university in London when I was eighteen and made the city my home, so there are people here that I hadn't met before today. Others are more familiar to me, like Shauna, who was with us for two years and who still lives locally.

Some flitted through briefly: Danielle stayed only a few months while her mum was in rehab. And then there's George, who left a scar on my heart that still takes me by surprise, considering the relatively short time I knew him.

But Jamie hurtled into our lives at the age of thirteen and never left. He turned thirty recently and although he hasn't lived at the farm in almost a decade, he turns up nearly every day to visit my parents. They'd be lost without him.

Mum and Dad have finally retired from fostering, but they will never retire from parenting, and that's what they consider themselves to be to every young person who ever walked through their front door: parents. Those who came to them left knowing that this place would always be open. Fostering wasn't a job to my parents, it was a vocation. It's why they've stayed in touch with so many of their former charges, why so many of them have made the effort to travel here tonight.

Of course, there are exceptions.

'I should check on Mum and Dad,' I say to Theo when he returns with my drink.

I find them in the living room, in the midst of their friends. My parents are fit, healthy and active, but neither looks young for their age. Dad is head down and deep in conversation with some of his fellow stallholders from Masham market, his hair now entirely white and as wild as ever. Mum appears more polished with her make-up still intact and her neat light-brown bob clipped back at the sides. She's been dyeing her hair for years, but the lines around her eyes and mouth betray her age. They seem to have expanded even in the few months since I've seen her.

She's talking to Veronica, our closest neighbour and the mother of Becky, my old school friend.

'Have you only just got back?' she asks me with surprise.

I nod reluctantly and raise my glass to chink hers and Veronica's before taking a sip.

Mum tried to convince me to put Emilie to sleep in their bedroom, but the thought of waking up a teething toddler in the dead of night and expecting her to transfer to her cot after a twenty-minute taxi ride... She would have kept us awake for hours.

We *could* have stayed here, but... *nice solitary Airbnb vs full house*... No contest. It seemed worth sacrificing the return journey time for the peace and quiet.

'Never mind, you're here now.' Mum pats me on my arm.

She doesn't do 'I told you so', *Supermum* that she is.

I'm not even being sarcastic.

'I hear you're moving to Australia?' Veronica chips in as my father excuses himself from his friends and comes over.

'That's the plan,' I reply with a smile at Dad as he throws his arm around my shoulder.

'As long as neither of them gets a criminal record before their visa application is sent off,' Dad teases, repeating Theo's joke from earlier.

He gives me a kiss on my temple, the smell of whisky on his breath. The weight of his arm is familiar and comforting.

Oddly, I miss him, even though he's standing right next to me. Is this what anticipatory homesickness feels like?

'How's Becky?' I ask Veronica, feeling bad that I don't already know the answer.

'She's really well,' Veronica replies warmly as Dad lets me go again. I shoot him a smile, hoping he doesn't stray far. 'Did you know she's expecting?'

'No!' I feel a pang at my ignorance. 'When's the baby due?'

'Late August, so he or she will either be the youngest in their year, or the oldest if they don't grace us with their presence until September. Becky doesn't mind either way; she's just glad it's not Christmas.'

'I bet,' I say with a laugh.

Becky's own birthday is overshadowed by Christmas. Emilie was also born in December, but she was an accident, so her date of arrival was down to the luck of the gods. I have no idea if Becky and her husband were trying for a baby or not.

'She was so sorry she couldn't be here,' Veronica continues. 'She would have loved to have caught up with you. She and Robin are in Canada at his sister's wedding. I have a horrible feeling Becky's going to like it there so much that she'll also decide to emigrate.'

'Oh, no, she *won't*,' Mum says dismissively, trying to reassure her old friend.

Her reaction makes me feel guilty: my parents are gutted that we're moving abroad.

'I would have loved to catch up with her too,' I say, and it's true. Once, my high school bestie and I were inseparable, but now an entire year can go by without us exchanging a word. It's not that we meant to grow apart, we just did.

'She and Robin sent a lovely card.' Mum nods at the crammed side table.

'Jamie read them out earlier,' Veronica adds.

'You missed the telegrams!' Mum realises with dismay.

I stare at her and she has the grace to look awkward.

So, not only did Jamie read out all the messages sent by those who couldn't make it – something that surely should have been my responsibility – but I wasn't here. Did anyone even notice my absence?

'There was one from George,' she adds, and my jealousy is immediately scrubbed out by another emotion I couldn't even begin to describe.

'George Thompson?' I ask with barely contained disbelief.

Mum nods, blissfully ignorant of what this news is doing to me.

In a daze, I walk over to the side table and pick up card after card until his handwriting leaps out at me, immediately recognisable with its small neat letters and left-handed slant.

Dear Carrie and Ivan,

I saw the article in the paper and felt compelled to write. I'm sorry it's taken me so long to get in touch, but I wanted to say thank you for all that you did for me. I've thought about you often over the years. I'm doing okay and hope you are too. You look well in the picture.

Wishing you both a very happy birthday and a (hopefully) relaxing retirement.
George Thompson

His handwriting has hardly changed in almost thirteen years, yet he sounds completely alien.

Suddenly I see him clearly inside my mind: long legs, high cheekbones, chestnut curls, dark eyes...

Every hair on my body stands on its end.

George saw the article?

The local rag ran a piece about my parents and it was picked up by one of the nationals. But where did he see it, the local or the national newspaper? Somewhere online? Where *is* he?

I turn the card over, searching for a return address and finding nothing.

'Hey.'

The sound of Theo's voice causes me to spin around. He looks at the card and then at me, with my rabbit-caught-in-the-headlights expression.

'Oh, yeah,' he says flatly. 'Jamie read it out earlier.'

'I heard.' My hand is shaking as I return the card to the side table.

'Thought he was gone for good.' His tone is quiet, uneasy.

'I thought so too.' I swallow hard and turn back to him.

'Theo Whittington!'

We both start as Alfred, an elderly farmer from the surrounding area, interrupts from a nearby huddle. The old man hobbles over to say hello, unaware that we're having a 'moment'.

'Now then! How are you, lad? I swear you look more like your father every time I see you.'

'Hello there,' Theo replies amiably, somehow managing to sound cheerful.

I step closer to his side and take his cool hand in mine as Alfred persists in making small talk.

If there's one thing Theo hates, it's being compared to his father.

He squeezes my hand, *hard*.

Later, in the taxi, I take the middle seat because I want to be close to my husband.

He climbs into the car beside me and buckles up, slipping his arm around my waist as we leave the party lights behind us.

He's on edge until we pass by the imposing stone gateposts and gatehouse of his former home, but once that obstacle has been cleared, he relaxes and pulls me close.

'You look so beautiful tonight,' he murmurs in my ear. 'I like this dress on you.'

It's black with long sleeves and a hemline that skims my knees.

I tilt my face up and he dips his head, giving me a gentle kiss. I lean into him, wanting more, and he doesn't disappoint. The smell of his cigarettes lingers as he kisses me, deep and slow, but I don't mind the taste on his tongue as much as I did the last time he started smoking again. Maybe it's something to do with the nostalgic feelings that the evening has dredged up. The past seems closer somehow, more tangible, within reach.

I push my fingers into his dark hair, feeling heady. I've consumed so much wine in the last couple of hours in my attempt to make up for lost time that I realise I'm actually quite drunk.

Theo's hands slide along the curve of my waist and I breathe in sharply, a thrill darting through me.

The car jolts to the left and right in quick succession as the driver corrects his line.

Theo tenses and breaks away, giving the rear-view mirror a black look. He takes his arm out from behind my waist and places his hand on my knee.

I'm figuring that's the end of our make-out session for now. These winding country roads are dangerous enough without giving our voyeuristic driver additional distractions.

We're staying on the outskirts of Harrogate, a few miles away. I've been checking my phone intermittently throughout the evening and Katy has obliged me with repeated 'all is quiet' texts. I let her know we're on our way back and she opens the door straight away to our light *rat-a-tat-tat*.

'Hello!' she exclaims in a loud whisper, her long blond hair swinging in a thick high ponytail as she steps out of the way. 'Did you have a good night?'

'Yes, thank you. How was she?'

'Perfect!' she replies to my relief, hopping on one foot as she pulls on a trainer. 'Not a peep! I checked on her a few times, though,' she adds hurriedly, shoving her toes into the other shoe.

'Thank you.'

Theo plies her with the wad of cash we counted out on the return journey. 'I'll see you to the taxi,' he says. 'We've already paid the driver.'

While Theo walks Katy outside to the waiting car, I kick off my heels and go to look in on Emilie. Our daughter is fast asleep, sprawled out on her back with her arms spread-eagled like a starfish. It's hot in here – it's only March, but the heating has been turned up too high – and a few strands of her dark-blond hair are plastered to her forehead. I can't resist carefully brushing them aside, holding my breath as she stirs. She falls still again so I crack open the window to let in a whisper of cold night air and quietly leave her room.

Theo is standing inside the front door, looking uncertain.

'You okay?' I ask.

'Yeah,' he brushes me off.

'What is it?'

He hesitates, shifting on his feet. 'I didn't like that taxi driver.'

'Why? Because he was perving on us?'

'No, more than that. I have a bad feeling about him.'

'Are you worried about Katy?' Now I'm concerned. Theo's instincts are usually correct, and although he can be overprotective, Katy is only seventeen. The thought of anything happening to her...

He frowns and then shrugs. 'I'm sure it's fine. I asked her – in front of the driver – to text us as soon as she got home, so he knows we'll be checking up on her.'

'Good thinking.'

'Emilie okay?'

'Out cold.'

He gives me a small smile, his twilight eyes framed by dark lashes.

I slide my hands up and over his toned chest to rest on his shoulders. It's more of a reach than usual – he's still got his shoes on. I'm tall at five foot eight and Theo is a little under six foot, so when I'm wearing heels, we're almost the same height.

He leans down to kiss me.

George was taller...

I push out the thought and focus on the feeling of Theo's hands skimming my waist. He pulls me against him as our kiss deepens and I want him, like I haven't wanted him in ages. I'm tugging his shirt out of his trousers when he stills my fingers.

'Let's wait until we hear back from Katy.'

I sigh, but nod in agreement, resting my head against his shoulder. I like that he cares. When I first met him, it seemed as though he cared about nothing and no one, but how wrong I was about that. It's *because* he cares that he had to build a fortress around himself.

My heart hurts for the boy Theo used to be. And once again my thoughts are pulled towards another boy and the pain *he* suffered...

'You okay?' Theo asks, sensing the shift in my mood.

'Fine,' I reassure him, lifting my head and nodding at his pocket. 'Any word yet?'

His brow furrows and he digs out his phone to check the screen. 'No. She'll probably text you though, right?'

I hunt out my phone from my clutch but that, too, is silent.

'How about a drink?' Theo asks.

I smile at him. 'I don't think I need another one, do you?'

'Tea?'

'Go on, then. You don't seem that drunk,' I note as I follow him into the kitchen.

'I'm not. I slowed down when you got back to the party. Sorry I smoked.' He shoots me an apologetic look as he fills the kettle and switches it on. 'I won't start up again.'

'You'd gone without for so long this time,' I point out gently.

'I know.' He rests against the counter, facing me. 'I love you.'

'I love you too.'

'You really do look so beautiful tonight,' he murmurs, reaching up to tuck a lock of hair behind my ear. 'I'm sorry you missed part of the party. You know I would have been happy to bring Emilie back here myself.'

'I do know. Thank you.'

It was only that she tends to nod off faster when I do bedtimes. I didn't want her to be unsettled for her first time with a babysitter.

The kettle boils and Theo makes us tea, but we're both preoccupied.

He checks his watch again. 'Katy should be home by now,' he mutters. 'She's only in Killinghall.'

The village is less than two miles from here.

'I'll text her,' I say, typing one out.

We wait, but there's no reply, and no notification to show us that the message has been received.

'There might not be any phone reception,' Theo speculates.

I dial her number. 'It's ringing,' I tell him, waiting on tenterhooks.

The phone rings out and goes to voicemail.

'Shit,' Theo exclaims, his anxiety building. 'What about your dad – can you get her parents' number from him?'

Katy is the daughter of one of Dad's market buddies.

'Her parents are away,' I remind him. 'Otherwise they would have been there tonight.'

'You could get her home number, though,' he points out.

'And wake the whole household? Her nan's there, looking after Katy's younger brothers.'

Theo gives me a helpless look. 'Better than the alternative,' he says simply.

Reluctantly, I ring my dad, but he doesn't answer his phone. I try the home phone, but that also goes unanswered. The party was still in full swing when we left, so I doubt anyone can hear it ringing.

'She's probably forgotten to call,' I rationalise as Theo tries Katy's number again.

He shakes his head, his lips drawn into a thin line. 'I'm going to drive to her place,' he says at last.

'Theo, you can't!' I exclaim with alarm. 'You've been drinking!'

'I feel fine!' he insists. 'It's only a few minutes away. You may be right and she has forgotten, but I'd never forgive myself if anything happened to her.'

'Let me call Dad again,' I say hastily, but Theo is already reaching for his car keys.

'I'll be back in two secs,' he says simply, giving me a kiss.

'Theo, wait!' I grab his wrist.

'Honestly, Leah, I feel totally sober!' He laughs lightly and detaches himself, opening the door. 'I'll be back before you know it.'

The door clicks shut behind him.

1

NOW

'Y ou have to sit really quietly, okay?' I remind Emilie in a whisper.

'Where's Gramps?' she asks in a tiny voice that shatters my already fragile heart.

'He's in the coffin, sweetheart,' I tell her again, dragging a sodden tissue across my nose.

She peers towards the front of the church. 'In the brown box?' she asks curiously, glancing sideways at me with her big hazel eyes.

'Yes, darling.' I take her hand as the minister starts to speak.

Mum reaches for my other hand. She's trembling.

Emilie wriggles on her bottom, looking up at the cream stone archways and the high oak beams overhead.

Perhaps it was wrong of me to bring a three-and-a-half-year-old to a funeral, but the thought of leaving my daughter today was more than I could bear. In some ways it's good to have a distraction. It means I *have* to hold myself together.

'Is that a dragon?' she asks, her high-pitched voice piping up over the sound of the minister's solemn address.

'Shh, baby,' I repeat softly, imploringly.

'Look,' she insists, pointing past my shoulder to the left-hand wall of the church.

I indulge her, following her gaze to a stained-glass window that does indeed appear to feature a large golden-red dragon being slain by St George, but before I can say anything in agreement, I see him.

My George.

Shock detonates my insides.

His head is bowed and his burnt-caramel-coloured hair is riddled with familiar-looking curls. Coupled with the strong shape of his jaw and his high cheekbones, he's instantly recognisable.

Mum lets go of my hand and I quickly face forward again, my heart pounding against my ribcage. I realise with a start that Mum is standing up along with everyone else, so I hasten to do the same, my fingers fumbling with the Order of Service as the opening chords of 'Jerusalem' surge from the church organ.

The congregation begins to sing, but I can't find the words, and then Mum is holding the right page in front of me.

Her voice is weak, wavering and full of emotion. This is one of Dad's all-time favourite songs and I want to do it justice – do *him* justice – but I can't catch my breath.

Emilie climbs up onto the pew so once again I'm side-tracked, making sure she doesn't fall. I feel an overwhelming, *overbearing* surge of longing for Theo. I've grown used to coping alone, somehow, but there are times when I really need him, and this is one of those times.

George is here. The realisation slams into me.

After all these years.

I feel the presence of him, prickling over my skin. He's two rows behind me and it's hard to not turn around.

Have you seen me, George? Have you noticed Emilie? Do you know about her, about Theo?

Jamie is speaking. I was asked if I'd like to say something, but how could I get up and talk at a time like this? I don't understand how Jamie can. He sounds so strong, so composed. I force myself to concentrate.

'He never raised his voice, he never lifted a hand in anger. He persevered when things got tough, and he always listened with empathy and patience. He gave so many children and young people stability and consistency, and above all that, he gave them love. I would not be the man I am without him.'

Jamie continues to speak, but my mind is all over the place. A murmur of laughter disrupts the sound of the other mourners' sniffling, but I don't know what Jamie has said to amuse them. I'm numb, in shock from so much more than my beloved father having a fatal heart attack out in the fields. After living his life for others, how could he die alone?

At that thought, grief swallows me whole. Mum clasps my hand again, her own body giving way to shuddering sobs, and Emilie clambers onto my lap and loops her soft little arms around my neck.

Jamie catches my eye from up at the altar and his face crumples. He breaks off and hunches over and it suddenly sounds as though the whole congregation is falling apart with us.

.   .   .

The funeral reception is being held at Dad's favourite pub, by the church in Masham where he used to religiously drink a single pint with his pals after each of the town's two market days: Theakston's Old Peculiar on Wednesdays, Black Sheep Bitter on Saturdays. He refused to choose between the town's two breweries, unable to do favourites, even when it came to beer.

There are more people here today than there were at Mum and Dad's party a couple of years ago, but I haven't seen George. He wasn't at the graveside when Jamie and the other pallbearers lowered Dad into the ground, or if he was, he stayed out of sight.

I wonder how he knew about the funeral.

I take Emilie to the bathroom and, while she's washing her hands, catch an unfortunate glimpse of my reflection in the mirror above the basin. I was pleased with my hair when I had it done a few weeks ago – it made me feel somewhat human again – but now the lighter shade looks too bright against my red, splotchy face, and the new shorter length seems limp as it falls somewhere between my chin and shoulders. I'm wearing black for the first time in over two years – the same dress I wore that evening I'd give anything to forget. Theo told me I looked beautiful in it and I couldn't bring myself to throw it away.

I don't feel beautiful now. I've shrunk inside the fabric, smaller in every way, and not merely physically.

Averting my gaze, I perfunctorily dry my daughter's hands and lead her out of the bathroom.

'...*drunk-driving accident.*'

I jolt to a stop at overhearing this shred of conversation.

There are three women of about my age, standing by the bar. They're huddled together, having a good old chinwag.

'He only got five years,' one of them says.

'That's outrageous! Five years for getting two people killed?'

'Three if you count the fact that the woman was pregnant,' the third girl chips in.

'Apparently, he could be out in two and a half...'

Their gasps of disapproval are audible, but I can no longer see them because Jamie has stepped in front of me. He turns around and loudly says to them, 'Oi. Time and a place, yeah?'

The group falls silent. One of them peers round my foster brother and her eyes widen. I recognise her now – we went to school together – but we weren't friends.

'Sorry,' she mumbles.

She and her friends collect their drinks and handbags and scurry outside to the patio.

'You okay?' Jamie asks, cupping the side of my face with his hand.

I nod shakily.

'Pick me up, Uncle Jamie!' Emilie chirps.

'You want me to pick you up?' he asks with mock astonishment. 'You want me to pick you up and break my back?'

She nods up at him eagerly, beaming.

'You're so big now, I don't know if I can.' He bends down and groans, making a huge deal out of heaving her into his arms. He pretends to drop her, she bursts out laughing, and some of the pain is eased from my heart.

Jamie looks past me and his eyebrows jump up, and when I glance over my shoulder, George is ducking under the door frame on his way into the pub. He straightens up and his eyes lock with mine and then everything else becomes blurred around the edges.

I thought he was tall before, but he was a boy compared to the man he is now: six foot four at least, and perfectly proportioned, with long limbs and broad shoulders encased in a well-fitted dark-grey suit.

'George!' Jamie says, and George's dark eyes move away from mine to meet his.

'Jamie,' he says in a slow, deep voice that seems even slower and deeper than it used to be. He extends a hand.

Jamie shakes it. 'Good to see you.'

George nods at him and, again, his gaze returns to me.

'Hello, Leah.' The greeting resonates through my whole body.

I swallow and stare up at him, and after all these years, after everything I've wanted to say, words elude me.

'And this is Emilie,' Jamie fills the silence. 'This is George,' he says to my daughter in a chirpy voice. 'George used to live with us at Gramps and Nanna's.'

Jamie was almost eighteen at the time, on the verge of 'ageing out' of the care system. We already had a full house: two young sisters plus thirteen-year-old Joanne squeezed into one bedroom; and Preston, age fourteen, with Jamie in another. Then there was me, of course, in my box room that was tiny, yet the envy of Joanne, who hated having to share.

There certainly wasn't room for George, but the social worker was desperate, as I overheard Dad telling Mum.

'She asked if he could have the study until Preston's bed becomes available.'

'Did you tell her we would've liked a longer grace period for Preston?'

The boy was soon to be reunited with his mother, but

my parents weren't at all convinced that it would work out long term.

'I did, so she asked about Jamie,' Dad replied. 'I said, "He may well be about to turn eighteen, but that doesn't mean we'll be kicking him out."'

'How old is George?' Mum asked.

'Fifteen, so he'd be in Leah's year.'

'Mm, not ideal.'

'This would be his fourth placement,' Dad added. 'She thinks he would benefit from being out of the city.'

'Don't say no to him on my account,' I snapped, entering the kitchen and hunting out a bag of microwave popcorn from the larder cupboard. 'What's one more?'

My parents were silent until I left the room.

I went to Becky's soon afterwards. It was the last day of the Easter holidays, a bonus teacher-training day that we'd forgotten about. It was also the last day I'd know life without George. My parents bowed predictably under pressure from his social worker and he was there by the time I returned home.

Little did I know how important he'd become to me. In the months that followed, I would give him my heart and he'd break it.

And now here he is again, and I feel as open and exposed and as raw as I did when he left.

2

THEN

'See you on the bus!' I call to Becky as she waves me off from her bedroom window.

'Bye!' she calls back with a grin, waiting as usual until I've gone through the field gate before ducking inside to get ready for school.

It's a stunning morning. The birds woke the two of us up with a dawn chorus that was so loud it sounded as though they were in the room with us. They certainly had something to sing about: the skies are cornflower blue and the low April sunshine is casting my shadow four storeys high across the frost-encrusted hills. The weather forecast claims it'll be twenty-two degrees today and my spirits are soaring after such a grim Easter. All we've had for weeks is grey skies and perpetual drizzle.

Last night was so much fun. I've never stayed over at someone's house on a school night before. In fact, Mum had actually messaged to ask me to come home early – they'd agreed to take in that boy I'd overheard them discussing and she was preparing a special meal.

'Oh, for goodness sake!' Becky had exclaimed when the text came in. 'You're always having welcome dinners!'

I wanted to stay at Becky's house. I knew that, if I went home, everyone would be on edge, this new arrival would probably throw things or break things or refuse to eat and there would be a horrible atmosphere hanging over everyone and everything.

So I caved and called Mum. 'Can't I skip this one? I'm having a really nice time with Becky and I'd like to end the Easter holidays on a high note.'

Rather than the low note it was sure to end on if I came home.

I left that last part unsaid, but Mum heard it, loud and clear.

She relented – I don't ask for much – and I went on to spend the rest of the evening trying to forget the trace of disappointment in her voice.

It's not as though I don't go out of my way for my foster siblings, but sometimes, just sometimes, I'd like to come first.

Crunching through the frosty paddock in my wellies, I swerve around thawing cow pats and squelch through boggy, muddy patches created by too many hooves. Becky's family own the neighbouring cattle farm and their herd is way more destructive than ours.

When we moved to North Yorkshire from London eight years ago, my parents bought seven alpacas. That herd has expanded to twenty-six, but thanks to their soft, padded two-toed feet and an inclination to go to the loo in the same spot, our animals don't wreak havoc on the land.

I can see some of them now, grazing on the top paddock. Around the other side of the farm are the boys – even my parents can't bring themselves to call them studs, or *machos*, which is their Spanish name. They're boys and girls to us, although we usually call their babies by their proper title: *cria*.

I smile up at our girls with affection. They're so pretty. I can never understand why some people go to the trouble of dyeing their fleece. Their natural colouring is gorgeous: white, beige, fawn, grey, brown, black and several shades in between.

Marigold is larking about with Mistletoe, her snowy white fleece glistening under the sun and contrasting with the glossy black of her playmate. They were born last June, along with Marshmallow, who's rose grey. He's in with the other boys now and seems to be settling well. Males and females have to be kept separate once they reach a certain age to avoid unplanned matings, but I always hate to see the young taken from their mothers.

Crossing into our land, I carry on walking, gazing up the hill to the point where the green grass of our fields gives way to a rugged, rockier terrain. We live on the outskirts of Brimham Rocks in an 'Area of Outstanding Natural Beauty', as my dad never tires of telling us. The main outcrop of rocks is a bit of a trek away, but I prefer it at the edge, away from the tourists. Sometimes I head up there to escape from it all.

'I'm back!' I shout as I come through the kitchen door, but I doubt anyone hears me over the sound of Nia wailing. I assume she's making the fuss rather than her older sister. Ashlee is three, but she's a mouse. I dread to think what she's suffered to make her that way. My parents tend to spare me the details, and, for my own sanity, I try not to ask.

I jog upstairs, hoping the bathroom I share with the girls is empty because I *really* need to wash my hair. Typically, it's not.

'Are you going to be long?' I call through the door.

There's no answer from inside, or if there is, I can't hear it over the sound of Nia crying.

'Joanne!' I shout, presuming the thirteen-year-old is the culprit. 'How long will you be? I need to wash my hair before school.'

'*I'm* washing my hair!' Joanne shouts back angrily.

I bet she's using my favourite shampoo too. *And* the water will no doubt be cold by the time I get in there.

I should have had a shower at Becky's. My friend's older brothers have both left home and she has a bathroom all to herself. I could kill her for it.

'Use our en suite,' Mum interrupts, appearing at the door of the girls' bedroom with Nia in her arms. She's rubbing the eight-month-old baby's back soothingly and the crying seems to be lessening in volume.

I stomp into my room and grab my things, as well as the spare towel I've learned to keep in here, then head down the corridor to my parents' bedroom.

'*Nice to see you too,*' I mutter under my breath. '*I had a great time, thanks for asking.*'

I'm late by the time I come downstairs, too late to have breakfast. I didn't have time to dry my long hair before I plaited it, so it's trickling droplets of water from the light-brown tips onto my blazer.

It's chaos in the kitchen, lunches being thrown together, school bags being emptied and repacked. Joanne and Preston are fighting over the last packet of salt-and-vinegar crisps and my dad is in the thick of it, buttering sandwiches and trying to cool the argument before it escalates. Jamie is bouncing a now-smiling baby Nia on his knee while encouraging Ashlee to eat her porridge. I look around for Mum and spy her on her knees in the adjacent living room.

'I'm sorry, George,' I hear her say. 'You're so much taller than Jamie. We'll go shopping this afternoon.'

She gets to her feet. 'Okay, everyone!' she calls out as she comes into the kitchen, looking harried. 'The bus will be here in one minute! Outside.'

'Leah, have you eaten?' Dad asks as some toast pops up and Jamie passes Nia to Mum.

'No, but I'm fine.'

'Quick, take this,' he insists, smearing butter and homemade blackberry jam onto the slice.

'Thanks, Dad,' I reply gratefully, easing my rucksack onto the crowded wooden countertop as the older kids noisily exit the kitchen into the courtyard. With the toast clenched between my teeth, I shove my lunchbox and water bottle into my bag, zip it up and turn around to face the room, swinging my rucksack over my shoulder as I do so.

A tall skinny boy is standing in the kitchen.

'Do you need some help with your tie, son?' Dad asks him.

It's hanging around his neck, but hasn't been done up.

George shakes his head.

Dad pops a sandwich, a can of Coke and a packet of crisps into a white paper bag and offers it to George. 'In case you don't fancy a school dinner,' he says.

As George takes the bag from him, I inadvertently glance down and realise what Mum was doing in the living room: George is wearing Jamie's spare school uniform and his trousers are at least three inches too short for him, even though Jamie is almost three years his senior. Mum has let down the hem, but they're still not long enough, and now they also have a visible crease running around the rim.

When I look up again, George is staring straight at me. No, not staring, *glaring*. His jaw is set and there's hatred in his dark eyes.

My stomach drops.

'Oh, George, this is Leah!' Mum exclaims, jiggling Nia on her hip. 'Off you go, you two, you can chat on the bus.'

And with that, she shoves me out the door.

I shoot a sideways look at George, but he stalks off ahead of me in the direction of the others.

The bus comes around the corner so I shove the rest of my toast into my mouth and step up my pace. I'm last to board, but Becky always saves me a seat. She grins and waves as I follow George on. He slides into the first vacant row he comes to, only one row ahead of my friend. I try to catch his eye as I pass, hoping I can offer him a friendly smile to make up for noticing his too-short trousers, but he's already turned to stare out the window.

I sigh and flop down next to Becky.

'Newbie?' she whispers.

'Shh,' I hiss.

'Pretty hot.'

I gape at her sideways, my eyes wide in warning.

She giggles at me. 'What? Sorry, but he is.'

'He's angry,' I whisper.

'Nothing new there.'

'Nope,' I reply drily.

'It's all right, he's putting his music on,' Becky points out, and through the crack between the seats in front of us, we can make out a white headphone lead trailing up to his ears. 'What's his story, then?'

I shrug. 'Wouldn't have a clue.'

Becky Norton and I have been best friends since we met, aged seven, shortly after my parents and I moved here from London. She was a right little ragamuffin back then, always seemed to be splattered with mud and God knows what else. We met during the summer holidays when she'd go days without brushing her hair. It was as long as it is now, dark-chocolate-brown, thick and unruly. Back then it got wilder and more tangled as the holidays went on so I barely recognised her when school started and she looked so polished and put-together.

Becky's parents, Veronica and William, were one of the few local families to extend the hand of friendship after we arrived. My parents had already caused a bit of a stir by selling off the sheep that came with the farm and investing in alpacas instead. As far as the local farmers were concerned, we were hobby farmers, not to be taken seriously. Frankly, we were a laughing stock, but none of them found it remotely funny when my parents started fostering. I remember Mum saying that, overnight, her babysitting options shrank to almost non-existent. My playdate and birthday party invitations suffered as well.

It didn't help that the kids my parents took in were almost always angry, troubled teenagers. They knew from their experience of working within the field – Mum used to be a social worker and Dad was a family court clerk – that the younger teenagers were the hardest to place. Easier were the older teens who would 'age out' of the care system before long, and little ones who were considered generally more manageable. There was a distinct lack of foster families who were willing to take in younger teenagers with their hormones and angst, not to mention explosive tempers – and that's without even considering the unimaginable emotional trauma they'd endured. That trauma naturally manifested in unpredictable behaviours, which many foster parents struggled to handle, resulting in countless young people being moved on and on, often ending up in children's homes.

So my parents decided to focus mainly on these kids, resolving to provide long-term stable foster care that wouldn't crumble at the first hurdle.

I admire them for that decision, respect them for it, but there have also been times when I have really resented them.

The teenagers who come here need my parents more than I do. That's a fact. But sometimes I need them too and they're not always emotionally available to me. It's hard sharing them.

'Has the bus broken down?' Becky asks with confusion as we come to a stop outside a familiar gatehouse, nestled amongst large laurel bushes and tucked behind a high wrought-iron fence. I lean past her and glimpse tall cream stone gateposts.

If you head through those gates and follow the winding road for about half a mile, past rolling green fields punctuated with mature oak trees and roaming deer, you'll come to one of the nicest country houses in the area. I know because I visited it once with my parents.

The bus doors whoosh open, but before we can find out what's up, a boy appears, wearing our school uniform.

His jaw-length hair is almost black, his eyebrows are

dark slashes on his pale angular face and his eyes are the deep blue of oceans.

'What the hell?' Becky says under her breath as he flashes his bus pass at the driver and makes his way down the aisle.

She's not the only one wondering what wealthy, stuck-up, boarding-school boy Theo Whittington is doing on our state school bus.

Theo ignores the whispers and drops his slim frame into the vacant seat directly in front of me. Why he chooses to sit there is a mystery – there are serious don't-fuck-with-me vibes coming off George in the seat next to him.

The bus trundles off again, but the chatter increases in volume.

'Oi!' comes a shout from down the back. 'Oi, you!'

'Here we go,' Becky says with a sigh.

'Fancy boy!' the shout comes again.

In the crack between the seats, I see George throw a quizzical look at Theo, but the other boy is facing straight ahead.

'What're you doing on our bus?' comes the shout again.

'Leave it out, Pete,' I hear Jamie say wearily.

'What's up with you?' Pete asks. 'I only want to know what Posh Lad is doing on our bus.'

'Nowt to do with you, is it, fella?' Jamie replies.

That shuts Pete up.

For now.

Theo is the first one off the bus, on his feet and moving towards the front of the vehicle before it even comes to rest in the bay. The driver grumbles, but Theo doesn't say a word of apology as he waits for the doors to open. I watch him through the window as he heads for the school building. I'm so distracted that I bump into the back of George as he's sliding out of his seat.

'Sorry!' I gasp as he stiffens and freezes.

'After you,' he says pointedly, *sarcastically*.

'No, go on.'

My tone is neutral, but there is no way I am moving until he does. Perhaps he senses my determination because he unfolds his long body without another word and straightens up. His blazer is too short for his arms as well – my parents really need to sort that out.

George lopes off the bus with his head bowed and his shoulders bunched together. A few paces later, he hesitates, looking ahead at the wide squat building stretched out in front of us, starkly grey against the vibrant green grass of the hill behind it.

'I can take you to the office,' I offer as I come to a stop at his side.

'Just point me in the right direction,' he mutters, not meeting my eyes.

'I'll take you,' I insist, hoping for a fresh start. 'It's this way.' I walk towards Reception, expecting him to follow. 'Will you let Mr Balls know what I'm doing?' I call over my shoulder to Becky.

'Will do,' she replies.

I glance at George in time to catch his smirk.

'Whatever you're thinking, he's heard it all before.'

'Poor guy.'

'See if you still feel that way when he's droning on in History.'

We walk the rest of the way in silence, but I feel better after our light-hearted exchange just now.

Theo is at Reception when we arrive. I'm about to leave

George to it, but Miss Chopra, the school administrator, spies me. 'Ah, Leah!' she says brightly. 'Could you take Theo with you to Mr Balls?'

'Sure,' I reply with a nod, hoping for similar camaraderie from Theo at hearing our form tutor's name. Instead I receive only cold detachment.

'Oh, and is this George?' Miss Chopra asks, noticing who I'm with.

My parents will have called ahead.

'Yes,' George and I reply at the same time.

George grimaces, not appreciating me answering for him, I suspect.

'Could you wait a minute and take him too?' Miss Chopra asks me.

'Sure,' I repeat, albeit weaker this time around.

Theo looks thoroughly pissed off as he slings his bag over his shoulder. Not a rucksack, like the rest of us have, but *a brown leather satchel*. Are those his initials stamped onto it? *TW*. I think of Pete and realise it's only a matter of time before this perfect boy gets the shit kicked out of him.

And he *is* perfect. Smart black blazer that looks as though it's been tailored to fit, black trousers with hems that rest lightly on polished, expensive-looking shoes, a pristine starched white shirt and a red-and-grey striped tie, hung at exactly the right length. I've seen my dad knot enough ties to know that this takes practice. George's effort is a case in point.

I meet Theo's eyes and realise I've been staring.

'Hi, I'm Leah.' I force the words from my mouth.

He exhales heavily and averts his gaze, not even dignifying my introduction with an acknowledgement.

Still as much of a tosser as I remember him to be, then.

. . .

I've caught glimpses of the Whittington family a few times over the years. Theo has an older brother called Acton who looks as though he has a rod shoved up his butt, and his mum, Sylvie, is even more comically haughty. But Theo's dad Edwin is the worst of them, having once snubbed my parents at a local charity ball, an offence I only heard snippets about later.

None of this could deter Mum and Dad from visiting the Whittington residence three years ago when it was featured on the Open Gardens calendar. It was the first time the gardens had been opened to the public since we'd moved to North Yorkshire and my parents were keen to turn the day into a fun family outing.

There were five of us in total as well as my parents: Shauna, who was seventeen; Tara and Brandon, both fourteen; fifteen-year-old Jamie; and me, age twelve. We travelled there in our battered old army green Land Rover which had had seat belts fitted to the rear bench seats. I remember the journey clearly because Brandon had refused to shower since his arrival two days earlier and he stank of putrid old sweat, greasy hair and sharp, fresh body odour.

I felt nauseous, even with the windows open, jiggling around next to him on the slippery wooden bench. I'm sure I wasn't the only one struggling to breathe, but unspoken etiquette made us all hold our tongues.

Others had no such qualms.

A temporary café had been installed in one of the barns and after exploring the gardens, we headed there for afternoon tea. Theo and his brother were inside, helping to serve tea and cakes as part of an initiative to raise money for charity. Neither looked happy to be there.

Acton towered over Theo at the time and still does, a strawberry blond beefcake of a young man who, at the age of eighteen, was the spitting image of his father. Theo's supermodel-tall mother also has fair hair, which was partly why Theo fascinated me when Becky first pointed him out to me in Harrogate the year before. With his slightly pointy features and dark satiny hair, he looked like he didn't belong in this family of blond giants. He was the Dark Prince among them, a fragile, beautiful boy.

So, despite the grim set of Theo's face, I felt a small thrill at being close to him.

And then he spoke.

'What is that *smell*?' he asked his brother distastefully in a high, reedy voice.

The whole family was born and bred in Yorkshire, but they didn't sound it. At twelve, Theo's warm Northern accent had already been knocked out of him at boarding school.

'Oh, dear God, they *reek*!' Acton scathingly agreed.

'What is it?' their mother asked plummily from nearby, scuttling over as my oblivious parents reached the counter.

Sylvie's face contorted into ugly disgust.

'Oh no,' she said, waving her finger at us. 'Oh no, no, no, no, no. You'll put people off their food.'

'Have you no decency?' my dad asked in a low voice, his face brightening with rage and indignation.

'Sit outside if you have to, but not in here,' she snapped, and I remember catching Theo's eye and wanting to disappear through the floor.

So yeah, I remember Theo Whittington. But I'm not sure he remembers me.

3

NOW

'Hello, George,' Mum says with affection, joining our gathering at the wake. Her voice sounds subdued, but there's no surprise to be found in her greeting.

As George bends down to give her a hug, it dawns on me that this is not the first time in fifteen years that they have seen each other. Nor is it the first time George and Jamie have crossed paths. I was too shaken a moment ago to realise.

'Thank you for coming,' Mum murmurs.

'Of course,' George replies, his hand dwarfing her shoulder as he gives it a tender squeeze.

Of course?

Of course?

At what point did it become a certainty that '*George Thompson: Missing*' would attend my father's funeral?

'I'm sorry about Ivan,' George says as Jamie ducks away to speak to a friend.

'He was so happy to see you again.' Mum's voice wavers, but she forces a smile onto her face and swoops down to pick up Emilie. 'Have you met my granddaughter?'

'I have,' George replies, and I feel him glance my way, but I can't bring myself to look at him.

'And Leah? You remember Leah, I'm sure.' Mum indicates me.

If she knew what had transpired between us, she wouldn't doubt it for a second.

'Can I have apple juice?' Emilie interrupts, her small hand gently patting her grandmother's cheek to ensure her full attention.

'Yes, let's go find you some,' she says, heading off to the bar.

Nervous energy pulsates through me. We're alone.

George speaks before I can ask a question that has preyed on my mind for so many years.

'I'm sorry about your dad.'

I nod.

'And Theo,' he adds.

'What are you doing here?' I sound unintentionally prickly.

He lifts his shoulders. 'I came to see your parents a few weeks ago. Remembered how much I liked it, so decided to stay.'

'You stayed?' I ask with disbelief, now staring at him openly.

'At least, for the time being.' He shrugs again. 'I work at a pub in Ripon. I'm renting one of their upstairs rooms.'

'You're in Ripon?' My voice has jumped an octave. I realise I'm repeating everything he's saying to me, but what the actual fuck? George, who walked out of my life without a backwards glance, leaving me utterly devastated, is now calmly telling me that he lives in a town less than twenty minutes away from my parents and he didn't think to get in touch?

'I was going to write to you.'

'Were you now.' My voice is laden with sarcasm.

He looks taken aback at the abrupt change in my tone, in my demeanour. I am too. Gone is the self-consciousness of strangers. Fifteen years has dissolved into thin air and I'm talking to him how I used to.

'I guess we have some catching up to do,' he says uneasily.

'You *think*?'

His eyes snap to mine and the look in his dark-brown depths quells my anger: there's remorse, guilt and sadness in his expression. These emotions transfer to me in the same way that they used to, filling me up from the inside out.

My body always responded to George's pain in a way that it didn't with my other foster siblings. With them, I had a protective barrier, a distance that I tried to maintain for my own self-preservation. But with George, there was none of that. When he hurt, I hurt too.

I can feel his pain now and it wrecks me. We're still linked to each other.

The realisation scares the living hell out of me.

'Did you find her?' I ask in the smallest of voices.

He shakes his head, his eyes full of regret.

So it was all for nothing?

I do the only thing I can do, which is walk away. But I'm being torn in two.

4

THEN

My parents give George a few days to settle in before mentioning the tree-planting ceremony.

'You'll have to have a think about what tree you'd like, George,' Dad says casually over dinner on Friday night.

There are eight of us around the dining room table: Mum, Dad, Jamie, Preston, Ashlee, Nia, George and me.

Joanne is having a self-enforced Time Out in her room. Her social worker paid her a visit at school today and she's still raging about it. There aren't many teenagers who enjoy being made to feel different in front of their classmates.

George stares at Dad blankly.

'You haven't heard about the tree planting ceremony?' Dad asks with surprise. He's acting. He knows Mum won't have spoken to George about it yet and it's unlikely any of us will have mentioned it – we've hardly seen him leave the study. He's sleeping on the sofa in there until Preston goes.

'Everyone who comes to live in this house has one,' Dad says grandly, bigging it up.

'Basically, you have to dig a hole and bung a tree in it,' Preston interrupts.

Preston is fourteen, and is, like Joanne, a bona fide teenager. He's short for his age with bleached curly blond hair. I suspect he has foetal alcohol syndrome – I've learned to recognise the signs in children whose mothers drank during pregnancy. They can have a certain look about them: a smaller-than-average-sized head, distinctive facial features, like small eyes, a thin upper lip and a smooth area between their nose and mouth. They can also suffer from behavioural problems and learning difficulties, all of which is true in Preston's case.

'You make it sound so bland, so boring,' Dad chides him gently.

'It *is* bland and boring,' Preston replies.

'Oi,' Jamie says sharply. 'Mind it.'

'What? It's just a—' Preston catches the look on Jamie's face. 'Whatever,' he gripes, shoving a couple of chips into his gob.

There are two dinner rituals we've followed ever since I can remember, long before my parents began fostering. On Sundays, we have a roast: beef, chicken, lamb or pork, Yorkshire puddings, crunchy roast potatoes with fluffy insides, rich gravy and cauliflower cheese – the works. And on Fridays, anything goes. The table is laden with options: pizza, fish fingers, sausages, burgers, chips, garlic bread... It's junk food night and everybody loves it.

I feel a pang of pity for Joanne. No amount of cajoling by my dad could convince her to join us.

'So you want me to plant a tree?' George asks.

He has an unhurried manner about him, but I don't think he's 'slow', as such. His voice is quiet and deep.

'You don't simply *plant* a tree; first you *choose* a tree,' Dad says as Nia lets out a loud shout and starts to bash her spoon against her high-chair tray. The spoon goes flying, ketchup streaking the dark wooden floor. Mum and Dad don't even look down. We no longer have carpet to worry about, thankfully.

'Here you go, honey,' Mum says patiently, passing Nia a clean spoon. Her big brown eyes widen as she takes it. She has the longest lashes I've ever seen on a baby.

'There's a tree nursery not far from here,' Dad continues. 'We go, you choose a tree you like the look of, and we plant it with the others in the lower paddock. We've got a bit of a wood going on now, haven't we, kids?'

I think the only child who *doesn't* have a tree is me.

My parents would be horrified if they knew that this bothered me, but the fact that I know they'd rectify it if I asked them to helps.

The next morning, Dad takes Preston and Joanne with him to the market in Masham. Mum has her hands full with the little ones so she asks Jamie and me to give George a tour of the farm.

The weather has held out all week and it's a cool clear day with barely a cloud to be seen. April has always been one of my favourite months. The skeletal tree trunks of winter are beginning to show signs of life, bright splashes of sunshiny colour from the daffodils break up the monotonous green of the verges, and the blackthorn blossom is out, its frothy white flowers dominating the thorny branches.

'Where are you from?' Jamie asks George as we trudge uphill.

'Leeds.'

'Me too. Which part?'

'Pudsey.'

'Ah, right. I'm from Hunslet.'

Jamie is good at talking to the teenagers who come here. His casual, friendly manner relaxes them and gets them to open up. I've always thought he'd make a great counsellor, but he has other plans.

'How long have you been here?' George asks him.

'Since I was thirteen, so almost five years.'

'When do you turn eighteen?'

'Couple of months, but Carrie and Ivan have said I can stick around.'

We reach the field gate and Jamie goes to open it, squelching through the mud that's thick at its base.

'After you,' I say to George, smirking at his boots.

He didn't fit into any of our spare wellies so Mum bought him some new ones. They're black and shiny and oh so clean.

'No, go on,' he replies to me, and his dry tone makes me wonder if he's purposefully mimicking our exchange on the bus.

'I insist,' I say sweetly, feeling gratification at the sight of his lips twitching as he turns away.

He walks forward and I'm seized with an impulse to jump into the puddle behind him. Mud splatters up his boots.

'*How* childish?' George remarks, pressing his lips together as I hoot with laughter.

Jamie chuckles with amusement and holds the gate open for us to pass through, securing it again after us. He's carrying a red bucket full of a fine grey dust called diatomaceous earth, and as soon as the alpacas spot it, they come running, their fluffy tails waggling excitedly like long-limbed oversized puppy dogs.

Alpacas don't wash – they're naturally dirt repellent – but there's little they like more than rolling around in this dust. That and having the sprinkler put on them when it's thirty plus degrees and they're baking.

'It's all right, they don't bite,' Jamie assures George, who's gone rigid. 'They've only got bottom teeth.'

This makes eating certain things difficult. My mum will stand up here, hand-feeding them apples. I have no idea how she finds the time.

George watches as Jamie shakes the bucket's contents into the hollows in the ground. The alpacas take turns rolling around, bodies wriggling this way and that with as much excitement as a toddler in a ball pond. I watch as Hazel puts her right foot in and out, does a bit of a bum wiggle, gets down on her knees and stands back up again. A proper hokey-cokey routine.

George is now watching with amusement, which is the best reaction we could hope for under the circumstances.

We've long since learned that most of the children and young people who come here have never heard of alpacas, let alone seen them in the flesh. If they have, they often mistake them for llamas, but alpacas are smaller, with stubbier noses and shorter ears.

Jessamine spreads her legs and does a massive wee, setting the others off. They love a synchronised wee.

'It's their spit you need to worry about,' I tell George as

he backs up against the drystone wall. 'Right, Jamie?' I flash him a mischievous look.

'Don't know what you're laughing at, Snow White, she got you too,' he points out.

'Yeah, but at least I was wearing a hat.'

George frowns at us. 'What are you talking about?'

I indicate a white female whose hair has grown so long on her head that her big dark eyes are half hidden behind crimpy white fleece.

'That's Daisy. Last year, her cria, Lily, got pneumonia, and when she came home from the vet, she had to have daily injections. Jamie administered them and, the first time he did it, Daisy stood behind him and spat green goo all over his head. She thought Jamie was hurting her baby. I got caught in the crossfire when I tried to cover him with a towel. You moved further away from her the next day, didn't you, bro?'

'Too right I did,' he replies.

'*You* gave her the injections?' George seems surprised. 'Not the vet?'

Jamie shrugs. 'Carrie and Ivan would've normally done it, but they let me. They obviously knew I had it coming,' he adds with a grin.

'Jamie wants to be a vet,' I explain. 'Nothing fazes him when it comes to animals.' If I sound proud, it's because I am. 'You even stuck around to watch a couple of castrations recently, didn't you?'

'Ouch,' George says.

The operation *is* totally grim. It *must* be harder to watch if you're a boy.

Wethers – castrated boys – have nicer, softer fibre than 'intact' boys. They can no longer be used for breeding, but the two in question were being overly aggressive, so it was an easy decision to make.

Iris, a medium fawn beauty with golden highlights, wanders right up to us.

Alpacas don't generally like to be petted, but they might tolerate it, and in some cases, like it. Ours are very tame so they tend to oblige us.

Iris's fleece flattens beneath Jamie's hands as he runs them down her thick soft neck. It's been almost a year since the herd was shorn, so they're especially full-bodied and fluffy.

'Why do you keep them?' George asks as a breeze flows down the hill and rustles the brown curls on his head.

I draw my cardigan around myself. The sunny day had me fooled – the temperature has dropped again.

'We farm them for their fibre,' Jamie explains. 'They're shorn once a year in May and their fleece is super soft, light, warm and worth a lot more than sheep wool.'

'Is that what Ivan sells at the market?'

Jamie nods. 'He sells yarn, but we knit stuff to sell too.'

'We?'

'Carrie, Joanne, Preston, Leah and me. We all make gear: scarves, finger puppets, hats... Carrie has a whole other group of people who do blankets, gloves and headbands – all sorts, really.'

'Wait.' He looks dubious. '*You* knit?'

'Yep. Carrie will have you learning too. And don't get all snarky like I did: "*I'm not doing any of that shite. What is this, child labour*?"' Jamie mocks his younger self.

I remember it well.

'You keep every penny you make,' he continues. 'Carrie and Ivan charge next to nowt for the fibre, so it's almost all profit. That's why there was no moaning from Preston and

Joanne earlier. They love going to the market to sell their crap.'

I grin at Jamie and he mirrors my cheeky look.

Often the produce *is* a bit questionable. Mum can sometimes be found staying up late into the night on Fridays, trying to fix flaws and get products to a saleable state. But luckily there are a few kind locals and plenty of tourists who support the stall.

'Come on,' I urge, shivering. 'I need to walk to warm up.'

'You ain't going to ride Daisy?' Jamie asks, deadpan. 'George, you take Marigold; I'll hop on Mistletoe.'

He points out the two youngsters, who are playfully pronking, all four feet lifting off the ground at the same time as they spring into the air.

'Hands off Mistletoe, she's mine,' I warn jokily as George snorts with amusement.

Mistletoe's black fleece is tipped with brown and, when she's shorn next month and her fibre is eventually spun into yarn, it'll be the luxuriant dark colour of liquorice. My parents have promised I can make myself wrist warmers out of it.

Mum calls to us as we cross the courtyard. She's standing in the kitchen doorway, her light-brown hair falling half free of her high ponytail. Nia likes to tug at it.

I can hear the baby inside, crying, but Ashlee is peeking out from behind Mum's legs.

'Can you take Ashlee with you to see the hens?' Mum asks.

'Sure.' I walk over and hold out my hand to the three-year-old. 'Do you want to come with us to Chicken Island?'

She stares up at me with big dark eyes and then looks at my hand, tentatively reaching out to take it. Her tight black curls are barely long enough, but somehow Mum has managed to secure them in pigtails on either side of her face. She looks super cute.

'Let's put on your wellies so you can splash in the stream.'

Ashlee's face lights up and she stomps her feet with excitement.

Mum disappears back inside and George and Jamie stand by while I sit the child down on the bench seat under the kitchen window and retrieve her boots from the nearby row of pegs. She watches George warily as I release the velcro straps on her pink trainers and remove them from her feet, placing them side by side under the bench.

When Ashlee first came to us, she was terrified of white men: the milkman, the vet, other farmers – most of the men around here, to be honest. If any of them paid us a visit, she'd make herself scarce. She even avoided my gentle, kind dad, and once, when Preston lost his shit about something, she fled from the room and hid in my mum's side of the wardrobe. It took us ages to find her.

On the whole, social workers try to find placements with foster families who live in the same area as the child needing care – ideally, there shouldn't be any need to change schools or leave behind friends. Our place, being so rural, is a bit of a last resort.

But Ashlee and Nia were moved away from their local area for their own safety following the death of their mother and the disappearance of their father. The police still haven't tracked down their dad – he's wanted for questioning – but neighbours have alleged that he was a very violent man.

Ashlee and Nia's father is white and their mother was black. I don't know if the girls suffered physical abuse at the former's hands – as I say, I try not to ask for the details – but the fact that they gravitate towards Jamie, while avoiding any man with pale skin, I think, speaks volumes.

Thankfully Ashlee is fine with Dad now – it helps that he never raises his voice. She's okay with Preston too, but she's unsure what to make of George. He's still an unknown quantity.

'There you go,' I say when she's ready. 'You look like a mini superhero.'

She's wearing bright red boots, sky-blue leggings and a red hoodie.

'Aah, but can she fly?' Jamie asks meaningfully. He walks over and holds out his hand with a grin.

'You want to swing?' I prompt in a whisper.

Ashlee smiles and lets Jamie take her hand, stretching her free one out to me.

'One, two, three, *swing!*' we say in unison, laughing as an eruption of giggles carries across the farmyard.

The sound is so addictive that we carry on all the way down to the stream, and my arm is aching by the time we pause on the small wooden bridge. Below us, the cool clear water bubbles over the pebbles on its way to the River Nidd.

'Can you point out Chicken Island to George?' I ask Ashlee.

She gives him a guarded look and edges slightly behind me, but obediently extends her finger.

George glances down at her and nods, but doesn't engage further.

The stream widens out at this point and is so shallow that a sandy mound has formed in the middle of the water. A couple of years ago, Jamie laid a plank of wood across from the bank for the flock of chickens to use as a bridge. A few hens can usually be found pecking about in the grit there.

We make our way down to the water's edge. The flock pays us no attention, too busy scratching around for grubs.

Ashlee nudges her toe into the shallows, not fully trusting that her boots will keep her dry.

'Where's the Little Red Hen?' I ask, crouching down so I'm at her level.

She looks around, her eyes darting from one bird to the next. 'There!' She points at a chicken with a reddish hue to her brown feathers.

'Well done!'

'We don't think she'd ever even heard a nursery rhyme until she came here,' Jamie says to George. 'Now she'll actually sing if you get her started.'

From the look on his face, I think the chances of George instigating a singing session are incredibly slim.

Ashlee takes a careful step onto the plank bridge and holds out her hand to Jamie. He helps guide her across to the island.

When Ashlee and Nia arrived five months ago under an emergency court order, they were supposed to stay only until a long-term placement could be found. My parents' focus was on teenagers, but over the course of several long sleepless nights, Mum formed a bond with the little girls and asked to keep them until they could be adopted. She's so hands-on with them that she no longer has much time for Joanne, Preston and Jamie – and now George.

Let alone me.

But I'm not resentful. Looking at Ashlee and seeing how far she's come, I feel only a sense of pride. My mum has worked wonders with her, and we've all played a part.

George has ventured into the stream and is watching the water surge over his boots, washing away some of the mud from the higher paddock. He glances up and catches me staring, but doesn't look away. A strange feeling flutters inside me. And then he *stomps*.

Water splashes up towards me, the chickens all around us squawk and flee in a cacophony of panic and I squeal in shock as my jeans are drenched from my knees to my thighs.

'You git!' I yell, going after him.

He strides into deeper water, the sound of his laughter doing lovely things to my stomach. I scoop up ice-cold liquid and send it hurtling towards him, cracking up when he flinches and yelps. All too late I remember that Ashlee doesn't cope well with chaos, but to my delight, when I glance at her, she's beaming.

Water hits the side of my face, shock wiping my smile clean off it. I'm still staring at Ashlee, dumbstruck. Then she lets out a squeal and flops over at her waist into full-on belly laughter.

Jamie and I lose it. I catch George smiling, before he abruptly frowns and wades off in the other direction.

My amusement wanes.

'Want to go see if your tree has grown?' Jamie asks Ashlee.

'Yeah!'

We head out past the coop to the lower paddock where the male alpacas are grazing. The land falls away again to the right of their paddock and there's a short, steep stretch of long grass to navigate before reaching the young wood we've created around a central oak tree. There are almost two dozen trees now, each one symbolising the life of a child who has come to live here.

Ashlee runs down the hill towards her sapling, shouting over her shoulder. 'This one's mine!'

She must be saying it for George's benefit because Jamie and I know, of course.

'What is it?' George asks Jamie and me as we follow at a more contained pace.

'An oak,' Jamie replies. 'Nia's got the same.'

'Mighty oaks from little acorns grow,' George says drily.

My hackles rise at the sarcasm in his voice, but Jamie chuckles good-naturedly. He points out his tree. 'I've gone for walnut cos I like nuts, but you can choose what you like: peach, pear, anything.'

'I'm not doing a bloody tree ceremony,' George snaps.

'Ah, come on, fella,' Jamie chides. 'I know it seems a bit odd, but it makes them dead happy.'

'Why is it my job to make them happy?' George retorts.

I shoot a quick look at Ashlee, but she's wandering between the trees, oblivious to his raised voice.

'They only do it to make themselves feel good; a reminder of how many kids they've tried to save,' George continues. 'It's egotistical.'

'That's not it at all.' I sound defensive, but Jamie merely shakes his head, dismissing George's comment. 'There *is* a point,' I state. 'It's about being a part of something that's lasting, something permanent. You can come back in the future and see how much your tree has grown.'

'Or you can stick around and watch it grow,' Jamie gently interjects. 'Every kid who comes to live here gets a tree, whether they're staying for weeks or years. There are no exceptions. You can choose, or Carrie and Ivan will choose one for you. Either way, you have a place here. We don't know your story, lad, and we're not asking you to tell us, but if you end up going back to your mam or your dad or whoever and it all goes tits up again, Carrie and Ivan will do what they can to bring you back to the farm instead of letting you get bounced around the system again. They hate that so many kids get moved on.'

George blinks, and I realise he's holding back tears. He stalks away from us a few paces, leaving us rooted to the spot. Jamie and I share a mutual look of concern.

It's not as though we haven't heard others complain about the tree ceremony, but I don't think either of us expected him to show emotion following his outburst.

'What about you?' George asks me out of the blue. 'Which one's yours?'

'I don't have one.'

'I thought you said every kid...?'

'Leah is Carrie and Ivan's bio,' Jamie enlightens him.

George turns around to stare at me properly. 'Are you? I wouldn't have guessed.'

I shrug. 'My parents try to treat us all the same.'

Mum and Dad believe every child deserves to be loved unconditionally – they don't agree with labelling. When asked by ignorant strangers, 'Which child belongs to you?' They reply, 'They all do.'

George stares at me for a long moment before glowering and averting his gaze.

I have a feeling he wouldn't have said any of that stuff about my parents if he'd known I wasn't in a similar situation to everyone else here.

My heart sinks at the realisation. I doubt he'll ever be as relaxed around me again.

5

NOW

After leaving George standing in the middle of the room at my father's funeral reception, I go off in search of Emilie. She's no longer with my mum, but has instead wandered off to an adjoining room where she's sitting on the floor, building a tower out of brightly coloured plastic blocks. Her face is fixed in concentration, so she doesn't see the blond boy toddling over to her until it's too late. He sends her blocks flying, delighting in the act, then regards her with surprise when she squeals at him with righteous indignation.

'Hey you.' I kneel beside her on the grubby carpet, hoping to avoid World War Three. 'It's okay, I can help you build it again.'

She gives the toddler a look of furious distrust and I follow her gaze, studying him. He seems familiar. Who does he belong to? And then I remember the picture I was sent last autumn, and the year before that, shortly after he was born. I search for my friend and spy her in a nearby huddle.

'Becky!' I exclaim, getting to my feet.

She glances over at me and a moment later I'm being squeezed half to death. 'Oh my God, Lee, I'm so sorry about your dad.'

'Thanks.' My voice is muffled against her shoulder.

She withdraws to look at me. 'I wanted to come to the service, but Robin's away for work so there was no one to look after Hayden. We headed straight here – I was about to hunt you out. Emilie, you've grown so big!'

While Becky fusses over Emilie, I crouch down beside Hayden, scarcely able to believe that the last time I saw him he was a tiny baby.

'Hello, Hayden.'

He ignores me, knocking over another pile of blocks.

'MUMMY!' Emilie wails, outraged.

'Hayden, no!' Becky says firmly, waggling her finger at her son. Hayden picks up one of the blocks and hurls it across the room. Becky sighs as he tears after it. 'I'm so sorry, Emilie,' she says to my daughter. 'He's a terror.' We stand back up and she rolls her eyes at me. 'That's a nice way of saying he's a little shit,' she whispers conspiratorially.

I giggle. 'The terrible twos have come early?'

She nods. 'You could say that. I've heard the effing threes are even worse?'

I shrug and glance down at my daughter. 'She's doing all right.' *Considering…*

Becky winces, hearing the unspoken addition to my sentence. 'How are *you* doing?' Her tone is gentle, but then she snaps, 'No, don't answer that, it's a stupid question.'

I smile at her.

Becky and Robin stayed in Edinburgh after university

while Theo and I remained in London. We've lived so far apart for years, but I love that when we do catch up, we're able to pick up where we left off. She may look a bit different these days – her thick, dark locks have been expertly thinned into a feathery bob, and, in a role reversal of our teenage selves, she's now the curvy one while I'm too thin – but she's still the same funny, loveable, outspoken girl that she used to be.

'How's Canada?' I ask.

Turns out Veronica's fears were warranted: Becky did indeed fall in love with Robin's home country while attending his sister's wedding – I remember her fretting about this scenario when we spoke at Mum and Dad's party over two years ago. They settled in Canada soon after Hayden was born.

I feel an unwelcome pang at the reminder that *our* emigration dreams never came to pass.

'We moved back!' Becky replies with surprise. 'Didn't your mam tell you? We're converting the old stables.'

'Wait, you live at the farm?' I ask with astonishment.

'Yes! We're living with Mam and Dad until the conversion work is done. I was going to call you – we've only been back for a few weeks. Robin's away loads and I was so homesick in Canada. I wanted to be closer to my parents. I could do with their help, frankly,' she adds as an aside.

The news has cheered me up, which is quite a feat today.

'What about you?' she asks. 'You still enjoying city life?'

I hesitate. If I answer truthfully, it will be the first time I've spoken the words out loud. 'I've been toying with the idea of moving back here too.'

'Really? Oh, go on! It'll be like old times!'

'Here's trouble,' Veronica, Becky's mum, says with mock dread, coming over to us. She gives me a rough, affectionate kiss on my temple and when she pulls away, I see that my mum is with her.

'Did you know Leah's thinking about moving back too?' Becky tells Veronica with excitement.

Mum baulks at me. 'Are you? I thought you were glued to London?'

I shift on my feet uneasily, shrugging off Becky's silent apology. 'I haven't made up my mind yet.'

Mum takes the hint and moves on, but I know we'll revisit this topic later. 'You heard that Rebecca and Robin are converting the Nortons' old stables to live in?' she asks, reminding me that people tend to call my friend Rebecca these days.

She'll always be Becky to me.

I nod. 'Becky told me.'

Another thing my mother failed to mention.

I'm intensely aware of George's presence throughout the afternoon, but when it's time to leave, he's nowhere to be seen. I feel nonsensically dejected, considering the lengths I've gone to in order to avoid him.

Emilie is spent, a heavy lump in my arms. Mum and Jamie are still saying their goodbyes, but I was craving fresh air so I've come out to the front to wait for them. I lean against the wall of the pub, trying to sustain my daughter's weight. I feel light-headed as I breathe in the scent of the rose climbing the sandstone beside me. When was the last time I ate? This is becoming a habit, and not a good one.

Across the square, people are queuing up for the chippie and drinking pints on the pavement outside another pub beneath the glow of fairy lights. I envy them and their ordinary Friday.

There are more cars than usual parked in the square tonight, but tomorrow it will be filled with market stalls. Was Dad really here only the weekend before last?

George comes out the front door, lowering his head to fit under the frame.

'Oh, hey,' he says as my stomach flip-tumbles. 'You okay?'

'Yep. Do you know if Mum and Jamie are on their way out?' I ask bluntly, shifting the weight of Emilie in my arms.

'Your mam is inside, waiting for Jamie,' he replies. 'I think he's having a bit of trouble with Dani.'

Dani – Danielle – is Jamie's girlfriend. They hit it off at my parents' party and have barely spent a day apart since.

'Is she wasted?' I ask.

George nods reluctantly.

Jamie doesn't drink. Dani drinks too much. It's the only way in which they seem less than perfect for each other.

'Do you need a lift anywhere?' he asks.

I shake my head obstinately and turn to look at the door. 'We'll wait for Jamie.'

George shifts awkwardly, but he doesn't walk away. A few moments of strained silence later, Jamie comes out, supporting his very wobbly girlfriend. He looks harried. Mum is trailing behind them.

'I'm sorry, I'm sorry,' Dani mumbles. She reaches behind her and tries to pat Mum's shoulder, but misses, her arm falling heavily to her side. 'I'm so sorry,' she says again, tearfully gazing up at Jamie, looking back at Mum, foggily staring ahead at George, Emilie and me.

Dani has coppery coloured mid-length hair with a thick blunt fringe, and she always looks so cool with her smokily-made-up, piercing blue eyes peeking out from beneath it. But right now, her eyes appear ringed with bruises.

'It's all right, it's all right,' Mum soothes, rubbing her back as my daughter raises her head from my shoulder to see what the commotion is. She's in time to witness her uncle's girlfriend throw up on the pavement.

My immediate instinct is to walk away with Emilie, but I force myself to stay put, turning my child so she's facing in the other direction.

Jamie scrubs his hand over his face and crouches down beside Dani.

'I can take her home,' George offers.

Jamie glances up at him, but his hopeful expression fades. 'We couldn't do that to your truck, fella.' He sounds weary.

'Perhaps George could give *us* a lift home?' Mum suggests, glancing at George who nods his assent. 'You should be with Dani tonight,' she tells Jamie.

Jamie hesitates. I know he wants to see Mum and me right, but his loyalties are divided. Dani works weekends at the museum in Pateley Bridge – a job she adores and won't want to jeopardise. Jamie will help sober her up tonight and make sure she gets there on time in the morning.

'If you're sure?' Jamie asks, supporting Dani as he straightens back up.

George nods, pointing towards a tree in the middle of the town square. 'My truck's parked over there.'

I feel weak and giddy as I carry Emilie across the road. It's only when we reach George's truck – a dark-grey pickup with a double cab – that I remember Emilie's car seat is still with Jamie.

He's already on it. 'I'm coming!' he shouts from across the square, striding towards us with the bulky contraption in his hands. 'I'm sorry about this,' he mumbles to me, panting as he fits the seat into the back.

'It's fine. Honestly,' I reassure him.

He hovers while I secure Emilie. 'I really wanted to be there for you both tonight,' he mumbles.

'We'll be okay,' I insist, turning to face him.

He pulls me into his arms.

'You did well today, Jamie. Dad would have been proud.'

He hugs me tighter.

'He was so proud of you,' I add, vividly recalling the look on Dad's face when Jamie graduated from veterinary school. I bet he got a kick out of each and every one of Jamie's work visits to the farm.

'He was proud of you too,' he replies gruffly, and when he lets me go, we're both crying. We automatically reach up to brush each other's tears away, a gesture that makes us laugh a little. Jamie's face is warm and rough under my fingertips, stubble beginning to push through. I remember the sparse black bristles he had when we were younger and how they would clump together in tufts. I'm hit with a flashback of my dad teaching him how to shave and have to let him go before I break down again.

Mum sits in the front of the truck with George, but they don't speak much on the way home. I notice that she doesn't give him any directions, and there are a couple of times when I'm on the verge of calling out instructions myself, but he always flicks on his indicator before I can become a back-seat driver.

Midsummer is only a couple of weeks away and it's not quite dark by the time we arrive at the farm. I carry a sleeping Emilie to the kitchen door and wait for Mum to unlock it. A warning call from one of the alpacas makes us all turn and look towards the high paddock.

'Probably a fox,' Mum says, opening the door and then hesitating at the sound of a second screech piercing the night air.

'Do you want me to take a look?' George offers.

'Would you?' Mum replies. 'I'll get you a torch.'

I take Emilie upstairs to what used to be my room. My parents did it up for her a couple of years ago and it has a woodland theme: light oak furniture, pale green walls, a white bedspread printed with woodland creatures and a yellow rug shaped like a flower. It's lovely.

Emilie doesn't even stir as I change her out of her dress and into a nightie. I'm back downstairs in under five minutes.

Mum is raiding the liquor cabinet.

'Is George still outside?'

'Yes, do you want to check on him?' Mum replies, extracting a bottle of sherry.

'Okay.' I want it more than I'm willing to admit.

I swap my heels for wellies and grab another torch, then head outside to the farmyard. Up on the hill I can see the white light of George's torch chasing the path of a rabbit in flight.

Rabbits tend to huddle close to alpacas when they hear a warning call. It usually means that predators are about, which the more dominant herd members will see off. Back in their native lands of South America, a predator might have been a mountain lion, wolf or bear. Here it's mainly foxes, which aren't dissimilar to baby wolves in the eyes of an alpaca. The animals are also not generally fans of cats and dogs for the same reasons of resemblance.

It's a mild, dry night so I shine my torch towards the middle of the field where I know the herd is likely to be. In bad weather, they sleep in their stone shelter.

I find them clustered together, facing outwards. Typically, the young, weaker animals will be in the middle, the stronger on the outside. Dahlia – the large light silver grey female who's making all the noise – is standing off to the side. They take turns being sentry.

George comes back down the hill towards me, his flashlight jerking with the motion of his steps. I deliberately shine my torch at his face as he approaches, getting a kick out of him flinching and shielding his eyes with his hand.

Some of us never grow up.

'I forgot that they sleep with their eyes open,' he says, coming to a stop on the other side of the drystone wall.

'That used to freak you out.'

'Still does.'

'Any sign of a fox?'

'No, they must've scared it off.'

I take a step backwards and feel instantly faint. My vision goes fuzzy, red and then black. I clutch onto the damp mossy rocks in front of me, trying to steady myself as George says my name, but I can't resist succumbing to the pull of oblivion, and I'm only vaguely aware of him vaulting over the wall as I fall.

THEN

I wake up to the sound of Joanne flipping out. She's full-on screaming – something about Nia and Ashlee keeping her awake in the night. My stomach is taut with anxiety as I lie there, listening to my mum trying to calm her down. She doesn't want to go to school today. She claims she barely slept.

'It's Friday,' I hear Mum tell her soothingly. 'Only one more day until the weekend. You're doing so well.'

'When the fuck are they going?' Joanne asks angrily. 'Because I can't put up with this for much longer!'

Nia lets out an almighty scream.

'Come on, now.' My dad has joined the fray, using the same gentle cajoling tone he always uses when dealing with Joanne. 'How about an omelette for breakfast? You can get ready for school later. Let's go downstairs and I'll make you a hot chocolate too.'

I drag myself from bed. Nia is still crying.

'It's all right, it's all right,' I hear Mum saying over and over, then suddenly her repetition is broken with an abrupt: 'Do you need to go to the bathroom, Ashlee?'

I open my door and walk groggily across the landing to the girls' bedroom doorway. 'I'll take her.'

'Thank you, Lee-Lee,' Mum says gratefully, using her pet name for me.

I hold out my hand to Ashlee, forcing a bright smile onto my face. 'Shall we go do a wee?'

She looks up at me, her lip trembling. She shakes her head at the same time that an awful smell clouds the air.

'It's okay,' I say softly, trying not to wrinkle my nose. 'Let's get you cleaned up.'

Ashlee has recently started toilet training, but she still wears a nappy at night in case of accidents. I peek inside her pyjamas bottoms and see immediately that this is a job for the shower – there's only so much a baby wipe can do.

By the time I've washed and dried Ashlee, Joanne is back upstairs and barging into the bathroom.

'Hurry up, I need to get ready!'

'Tell me about it,' I mutter under my breath, wrapping Ashlee in a towel.

Joanne barely moves aside as I carry the child out of the bathroom. The door slams behind me, making me jump, even though I was anticipating the bang.

Mum is changing Nia's nappy and the eight-month-old is chattering away nonsensically. 'I'll take over with Ashlee,' she says, her hands steadying the wriggling body on the changing mat. 'Can you put her in her dressing gown?' She nods at the fleecy garment hanging behind the door. 'I'll get her dressed in a bit.'

I do as she asks, passing Ashlee her favourite cuddly toy – a teddy bear called Dolly, bizarrely – and giving her a quick kiss on her cheek before leaving the room.

My day takes another nosedive when I check my phone and see a message from Becky telling me that she's ill. I don't have time to reply.

Joanne is chewing Dad's ear off when I get downstairs. 'George has his own room and *she* has her own room,' she says, pointing at me. 'Why do *I* have to share with the babies?'

Her green eyes are flashing with fury. She's so pretty when she smiles, but the sight is rare. I have to remind myself – often – that she has every right to be angry. All the children and young people who come here have been harmed in some way, whether physically, emotionally or both. Joanne is no exception.

George follows Joanne's gaze and meets my eyes, but the contact lasts only a second.

He's been like this all week, cold and distant and keeping to himself as much as possible. I've tried to strike up conversations with him when we've been in the same room, but while I've heard him talking to Jamie and the others, he's resisted my attempts to be friendly. It's been making me feel quite dejected after Saturday when I thought I might've found an ally in him, a friend who'd have my back at home and at school. It's a novelty for someone my age to be here – my parents have always avoided it, not wanting me to have to share my school day with a person who is already sharing my parents and my home. It's why I've always had my own room, tiny though it is. It's my haven.

'Why can't *she* share with them?' Joanne asks, her light-blond ponytail whipping her face as she turns to glare at me.

'Come on now, love, you're going to be late for school,' Dad says gently. 'We'll talk about this later.'

My insides lurch. But he wouldn't ask me to give up my room.

Would he?

There should really only be two to a bedroom in foster-care situations, even though Joanne, Ashlee and Nia's room is plenty big enough for three. When the little ones came to us, it was only supposed to be a temporary measure. Since they've stayed, it would make more sense for them to take *my* bedroom and for *me* to share with Joanne, but the thought of that is... is... *unbearable*.

I can't stomach breakfast, which is just as well as I don't have time to eat anyway.

Dad doesn't even notice. I think Joanne has sapped all his energy this morning.

It's a cold, damp day, with a thick low-lying fog coating the land like a blanket. We can't see more than ten metres in front of us. It's not raining, but the grass on the verges is soaking wet and water is clinging like teardrops to the twiggy branches on trees and bushes.

Joanne baits me as we walk towards the bus stop. 'That's that, then. You can share with the babies.'

'I am *not* moving out of my room,' I reply firmly, wishing Jamie was here, together with his mediation skills. He's having a revision day today so is studying from home.

'Why, because it's your house and you're special?' she spits.

'No, because I'm two years older than you and that's been my bedroom for eight years!'

'Oh, well aren't you jammy?' she asks sarcastically. 'Maybe it's time you knew what it felt like to be shoved around!'

'Leah!' Dad shouts from the doorway.

I look over my shoulder to see him pulling on his boots. I turn back and run to meet him halfway across the courtyard.

'Don't worry, love. Everything will be okay,' he says, pressing a piece of buttered toast into my hand and giving me a kiss on my forehead.

'Thanks, Dad.' Tears prick my eyes and I blink to dispel them as I hurry back to the others.

'Your parents had better not get any more brats in after those two, that's all I'm saying,' Joanne says bitterly, eyeing my breakfast with disgust. 'They can't be gone soon enough.'

'Are they going back home?' George asks as the bus appears at the end of the lane.

Joanne acts as though she hasn't heard him and Preston is similarly noncommunicative. Finally, George's gaze travels to me.

'No, they'll be adopted,' I explain, relieved that my invisibility cloak has momentarily slipped. 'Nia has a family who want to adopt her, but they're still trying to find people for Ashlee.'

His eyes widen. 'They're not going to the same family?'

I shake my head, my last mouthful of toast lodging in my throat.

This subject is a source of incredible pain for all of us, but especially my mum.

The girls were initially going to be separated straight after leaving their emergency placement with us, so they should already be used to life apart, but my parents hoped they might stand more of a chance of being adopted by the same family if they were kept together. Unfortunately, Anita and Ollie, the couple in line to take Nia, want a baby; a clean slate. They don't want an older child with all of the baggage it would bring. Once children turn two, their chances of getting adopted are much slimmer.

I wish I could feel angry at Anita and Ollie, but no other emotion can compete with my sorrow.

George clenches his jaw. The action causes hollows to form in his cheeks, making his cheekbones seem even more pronounced.

'None of us want them to be separated,' I say hastily.

He ignores me, angrily stalking off towards the bus.

I sigh heavily and board in time to see Joanne settling herself into the row I usually share with Becky.

She sneers, thrilled to get one over on me, but I'm too shaken by my brief exchange with George to feel annoyed. Without reacting, I slide into the only other vacant row near the front.

Doesn't George have any idea how hard it is to be a foster family? We *care* for the people who come here and we grieve for them when they leave. I can't even bear the thought of saying goodbye to grumpy Preston, let alone cope with letting Ashlee and Nia go.

As the bus rounds the bend near the Whittington residence, I see Theo leaning against one of the tall stone gate posts, his feet casually crossed at the ankles and the thumb of one hand hooked into his trouser pocket. His other hand is holding a lit cigarette.

When I escorted him and George to the classroom last

week, Mr Balls enlisted the help of two students to look after them. Martin and Steven are decent lads – in fact, the former is Becky's current crush – and they will have made George and Theo feel welcome. But while I've seen George with Martin several times – in the lunch hall, passing by in corridors, and even once on the football pitch – Theo seems to have shirked all offers of help and friendship, avoiding Steven and the rest of us like the peasants that we are.

Outside of the classroom, he's hardly ever to be found, although I did spy him yesterday up on the field, all alone and as far away from the school building as he could get. I wonder what his deal is.

Everyone on the bus has been wondering too.

Mum and Dad couldn't shed any light on why he's no longer at boarding school – or any other private school, for that matter. Nor could Becky's parents.

Despite his lack of interest in any of us, Theo Whittington has all of us talking.

He brings his cigarette to his lips and inhales deeply, seemingly in no rush whatsoever, and as the bus pulls to a stop, he stares straight at me through the window. I don't know what compels me to, but I hold his gaze. His blue eyes penetrate mine for several seconds, and then the bus doors whoosh open and he throws his cigarette to the ground, breaking eye contact as he watches it fall. He boards the bus to the sound of unimpressed tutting from the bus driver.

'Morning, Pretty Boy!' Pete calls from the back.

Theo ignores him as he always does.

Good manners command me to drag my rucksack onto my lap, freeing up the seat next to me, but whether Theo considers the action an invitation or even notices, I don't know: he sits down beside me all the same.

I continue to stare out of the window, but I'm tense. Out

of the corner of my eye, I see him unzip his army green rucksack, and I realise then that he *has* a rucksack – a rucksack like the rest of us instead of a monogrammed leather satchel. Maybe he *does* want to fit in.

He pulls out a packet of Spearmint Extra and nudges a shiny white nugget out of the end, popping it into his mouth.

His fingers are filthy, not only stained with nicotine but grubby around and under his fingernails. Sensing me watching, he offers the packet of gum to me.

'Ta,' I mumble, taking one from him, my cheeks warming at being caught looking, even if for a different reason to the one he's maybe assumed.

He puts the packet back into his rucksack and goes to zip it up, then hesitates.

'Oh shit,' he mumbles.

I glance at him sideways as he rummages around in his bag, rifling through his textbooks. I spy an intricate-looking pencil drawing on the back of one, but he's moved on to the next before I can see it properly.

He groans and his shoulders slump in defeat as he stares straight ahead.

'You all right?'

He glances my way. 'Forgot my Maths homework,' he deigns to explain, his dark hair swinging forward as he dumps his bag at his feet.

'It was due yesterday,' I point out.

We're in the same class: top set.

'I know. Which means I'm getting a detention today.'

'Oh.'

We fall silent. I kind of want to keep him talking, but I don't know what to say. It's not like he wants to talk to me anyway—

'Where's your friend today?' he interrupts my train of thought.

'Becky? She's not feeling well.'

He jerks his head in Joanne's direction. 'You're not in your usual seat.'

'Nope,' I reply sullenly.

He slides his eyes away from mine, his jaw working away on the gum. The air is pungent with warm, cigarette-smoke-infused mint.

The bus trundles on, taking corners at speeds that should be reserved for lighter, faster vehicles. I stare out of the window as the fields flash past and the bus fills up. Drystone walls, brown and white spotted cows, grassy verges alight with daffodils, newborn lambs frolicking with each other...

'Oi, Pretty Boy,' Pete calls as the bus squeals to another stop.

Theo sighs. Pete stomps down the aisle and slides into the seat opposite him while the driver is distracted.

Pete is heavyset and solid. He has a face full of freckles, small wide-apart eyes, and a reputation for acting up in lessons. He's always been decent to me, but I don't go out of my way to spend time in his company.

'Oi, Pretty Boy,' Pete says again, looking at Theo directly. 'Can I scrounge a cigarette?'

Pete's friend Dave has followed, flopping into the seat behind us. He's taller than Pete, but lankier. There's something about the pair of them together that reminds me of naughty goblins.

'Come on, Fancy Pants, I'm sure you can spare a couple.' Pete reaches over and scuffs up Theo's hair.

'Fuck off,' Theo snaps, glaring at him.

'Ooh, it speaks!' Pete says with cruel delight, grinning

around at others in the vicinity. 'Where'd you get your accent, Posh Lad? Why aren't you at boarding school anymore? I'm talking to you,' Pete says nastily, ruffling Theo's hair again.

Theo angrily slaps him away. 'I said, *fuck off*,' he warns menacingly.

'What's going on back there?' the bus driver shouts.

Ice trickles down my spine at the murderous look on Pete's face.

He glances at Dave and, a second later, nods as if in silent agreement. The tension is unbearable for the rest of the journey.

At lunchtime, there's talk of a fight. Theo is nowhere to be seen. It's hardly unusual as he's kept to himself since he arrived, but Pete is incensed, all worked up with nowhere to expend his energy.

We have Art together as last period, and Pete, Dave and a couple of their mates keep making clucking noises.

'Hiding out at lunchtime, were you? *Chicken*,' Pete spits at one point when the teacher is out of earshot.

It occurs to me that Theo was probably serving his detention, rather than purposefully trying to avoid an altercation, but he doesn't explain himself.

When the final bell rings, I assume he will get up and make a dash for the bus, but instead he takes his time packing away his things, looking as though he hasn't a care in the world.

Unable to tear myself away from the car crash waiting to happen, I slow down the packing of my own bag and am one of the last to walk out of the classroom behind Theo.

Pete and his cronies are waiting in the otherwise empty hallway. There's a scuffle, Theo's rucksack is torn from his back and upended on the floor. Pete, grinning, reaches down and swipes the packet of cigarettes. As he goes to pocket them, Theo launches himself forward and shoves Pete's chest.

Pete stumbles backwards, almost falling over. The look of surprise on his face is comical, but it quickly transforms into rage.

It all happens so fast. One minute they're apart, the next Pete and Theo are flying at each other, a mass of fists and fury. I've seen punch-ups before, but the violence of this one shocks me.

They're so entangled that the punches they land are mostly on each other's arms and torsos, but then Pete wrestles some distance between them and thumps Theo squarely on the face. The raw starkness of fresh blood is startling – Theo's lip has split, right down the centre: an oozing crack of glossy red.

All motion ceases – even Pete is frozen for a couple of seconds – and then Pete seems to deflate, the fight visibly going out of him. I feel a spark of relief as he takes a step backwards – it's over.

But then Theo does something unexpected.

His white teeth rimmed with scarlet, he laughs.

Pete stares at him.

'You punch like a pussy,' Theo says.

He's grinning. Like a madman.

'Watch it,' Pete warns, but he no longer sounds so full of himself.

Theo spits blood out onto the floor.

'Come on, try again,' Theo goads him, beckoning him with both hands.

'Leave it,' one of Pete's friends interjects. 'Walk away,' he urges Theo.

Theo's expression slowly sobers. 'You're *all* a bunch of fucking pussies,' he says deliberately, looking at each of Pete's friends in turn.

'What's going on here?' Mr Edwards, our mild-mannered Art teacher, emerges from the classroom doorway, coming all too belatedly to the party.

'Nowt, sir,' Pete answers quickly.

He and his cohorts make themselves scarce while Theo bends down to pick up the contents of his rucksack, hiding his face in the process.

'Leah?' Mr Edwards asks, and Theo shoots me a surprised look – he didn't know I was here, but now there's a warning in his eyes.

'Theo dropped his bag,' I reply, covering a drop of blood on the floor with my shoe. 'Don't worry, I'll help. See you later, sir. Have a good weekend.'

'Oh, okay, then. You too.'

Mr Edwards walks away as I swoop down to pick up the same textbook that I saw in Theo's bag this morning. A lead pencil drawing of a maze takes up the entire back cover, complete with tiny, exquisitely detailed gargoyles at several of the dead ends. Their postures and expressions all differ, whether they're standing, sitting, flying, screaming or grinning evilly.

'Cool,' I murmur, pausing to look.

Theo stands up and snatches the book from my grasp, stuffing it into his bag. He stalks off, angrily zipping up his bag as he walks.

I run to keep up with him. 'Are you okay?'

He doesn't answer. He doesn't even acknowledge my presence. There's no humour on his face, mock or otherwise. The blood on his lip has darkened in colour, already starting to scab.

We turn the corner of the building to see that a small crowd has gathered near the bus, a huddle of boys getting the lowdown on the scrap. Pete and Dave are amongst them, but both seem more frazzled than victorious. Pete's stance is non-combative as Theo approaches, and then he holds up his hands, as if in a peace offering. Theo steps right up to him and gives him a hard push.

'What the hell?' Pete asks with outrage as he stumbles backwards. 'Have you got a death wish?'

'Maybe,' Theo replies. 'Give me my fucking cigarettes.'

This time when Theo shoves, Pete shoves back. But before the fight can escalate, George puts himself between them, his hands and arms raised in a bracing position.

'Hey! What's going on out there?' the bus driver shouts, finally paying attention.

No one responds.

'Give him his cigarettes,' George commands Pete. 'Now.' He's holding Theo back with force.

Pete digs into his pocket and pulls out the now-crumpled packet. George passes them to Theo, who takes a step backwards, out of George's reach. He calmly gets out a cigarette and proceeds to light it.

'Oi! No smoking on the bus,' the driver calls.

Theo inhales deeply, eyeballs Pete like a lunatic, and then walks away from all of us in the direction of town.

'Flipping 'eck,' Pete grumbles, picking up his bag and boarding the bus along with Dave and the others.

But I stand and stare after Theo.

'Are you two coming or what?' the bus driver prompts.

You two?

I glance over my shoulder to see that George is standing

with me. He meets my eyes, his expression serious, uncertain. We stare at each other for a strange, meaningful moment, and then I shake my head at the driver and set off after Theo.

A few seconds later, I hear the sound of George's footsteps following.

7

NOW

W hen I come to, I'm in George's arms, being carried like a baby across the farmyard.

'Are you all right?' he asks.

'Yes,' I reply weakly, lifting my head and then deciding against it. I rest my cheek back against his broad shoulder. He smells clean, of washing powder, deodorant and shaving gel.

'You fainted,' he says.

'I haven't eaten much today.'

'Fucking hell, Leah, there's nothing left of you,' he snaps, but his voice is racked with anxiety.

A thrill darts through me at hearing him speak to me like this: so familiar, so protective.

'I've halved in size, you've doubled,' I point out, feeling giddy with misplaced amusement.

'It's not funny.'

We reach the house and I look up at George's face, cast in gold from the light spilling through the kitchen door and window. His rich brown hair has fallen down a little across his forehead and his eyes are partially obscured beneath curling shadows. I resist the urge to reach up and run my fingertips over his sharp cheekbones.

He shifts my weight to open the kitchen door and continues across the threshold.

'Carrie?' he calls towards the living room. When there's no answer, he cranes his neck to look down at me. 'Where's your mam?' His dark eyes are serious, and I'm suddenly acutely aware of how close he is.

'She was getting a drink when I came outside.'

George kicks off his boots with some difficulty and I know I should instruct him to put me down, but I can't bring myself to formulate the words. He carries me through to the living room and carefully lays me on the sofa, not even slightly out of breath as he removes my boots.

A moment later, all contact between us is broken. Disappointment surges through me, disconcerting in its intensity. He straightens up and stares down at me.

'I'll get you something to eat.'

He disappears back into the kitchen with my muddy boots in hand.

I feel light-headed as I listen to the sound of cupboard doors opening and closing, the jangle of cutlery and the whoosh of the fridge door. After a while, George returns with a sandwich.

Gingerly swinging my legs off the sofa, I sit up, accepting the plate with a thank you.

'Did you make yourself one?' I ask.

'No.'

'You should.'

'I ate at the wake.'

I nibble a corner of bread, my tastebuds coming to life at the contact with tangy cheddar and pickle.

George looks around. The living room isn't that different to how it was when he lived here. It has the same dark wooden beams spanning the ceiling, the stone lintel above the fireplace, the big picture window, currently hidden behind the same heavy cream-coloured curtains. The grey sofas are new, as is the cream carpet, but even that has the familiar well-worn footpath created by too much foot traffic between the kitchen, dining room and hallway.

His eyes take in the wooden coffee table and its current, new position, pushed up against the wall.

'The funeral directors brought Dad home yesterday,' I explain flatly, recalling my numb shock at seeing the coffin resting in the middle of the living room. Mum wanted him here for one final night, and the memory of Jamie, Shauna, Preston and the other pallbearers carrying him out to the hearse earlier today makes my heart shatter all over again.

George sits beside me and rubs my back as I begin to cry, but it's not enough: I miss being held.

My thoughts jerk violently towards Theo and I imagine how he would feel seeing me in George's arms. Guilt wallops the grief out of me, just as Mum returns.

'Oh, Lee-Lee,' she murmurs with sympathy, her own eyes fresh from weeping. She must have escaped upstairs to cry in private. She comes to sit on the other side of me and takes me into her arms. 'Thank you, George,' she says over my shoulder.

She's giving him permission to go.

I feel him hesitate, but the thought of Theo keeps me from lifting my head. By the time I gather myself together, he's long gone.

8

THEN

'Theo, wait!' I call.

Theo looks over his shoulder, his surprise transforming into a scowl at the sight of George and me.

'What do you want?' he asks as we fall into step beside him.

'We wanted to check you're all right,' I reply, slightly out of breath.

'You're going to miss the bus.' He takes a long drag of his cigarette.

'We've already missed it.'

He laughs humourlessly. 'Excellent. What fun.'

'Stop being a dick,' I say as he flicks ash onto the pavement. 'It doesn't have to be this way, you know.'

'What way?'

'You don't have to be all on your own.'

'I prefer my own company.'

'Bullshit.'

Theo frowns at me, then returns his attention to the path ahead. 'No, you're right. My company sucks as much as yours does.' He looks up at the sky as it starts to rain. 'Great,' he mutters.

The heavens open as we reach the park so we make a dash for the bandstand. I slip on the steps, my heart leaping into my throat as I go down, but George grabs my elbow and pulls me upright before I can hit the ground.

'Thanks,' I say shakily.

There are no walls around the bandstand, only black-painted metal pillars that hold up the octagonal roof above our heads.

George's face is glistening with raindrops, his dark eyelashes stuck together like the points of a star. He rakes his fingers through his rain-damp hair and sets the curls back from his face.

Theo narrows his eyes at us. 'I didn't know you two were *friends*.'

'We're not,' George replies bluntly, and even though it's true, it stings.

'Aah,' Theo says with a knowing smirk, coming to his own conclusions about our relationship.

'He's my foster brother,' I cut off the direction of his thoughts. 'Jamie, Joanne, Preston... On the bus? They're all my foster siblings.'

'Oh.' He shrugs, his disinterest apparent.

Something inside me snaps.

'You don't remember, do you?'

'Remember what?' he asks in a bored voice.

'Me. Us. Open Gardens Day. "What is that smell?" "Oh, dear God, they *reek*!"?'

Theo's eyes flare with recognition before he averts his gaze. 'I don't recall much of that day,' he mumbles uncomfortably, shrugging off his rucksack and dropping it on the floor.

'Must be nice to be able to forget.'

George raises a questioning eyebrow at me, but I ignore him and get out my phone. 'I'd better ring Dad and ask if he can give us a lift.'

Neither of the boys speaks to each other as I make the call. Dad doesn't question why I'm putting him through this inconvenience. That's one thing about my parents: they put a lot of trust in me.

As they should.

I don't drink, I don't smoke, I don't do drugs. I'm not aggressive or violent and I don't steal or break things.

I don't mean to sound flippant, but all that has got to count for something.

'My dad will give you a lift too if you need one,' I tell Theo. I didn't mention him on the phone, but Dad won't mind. 'We go past your place anyway.'

'I figured I'd call Bart, but I forgot he was off work today,' he replies, as though we should know who he's talking about.

'Who's Bart?' I ask, reminding him that we don't.

'Our groundskeeper.'

'You have a groundskeeper?' George asks with a frown.

'You've seen his house, right?' I interject.

'The one by the fence?' he asks.

'That's his *gate*house. Does anybody even live in there?'

'Bart does.'

I hadn't intended to leave Theo enough time to answer, but he managed to slip one in anyway. 'He lives in a mansion,' I tell George. 'A huge country house. My parents took a group of us there when the gardens were open to the public. We weren't made to feel very welcome,' I add significantly.

'Look, what can I say?' Theo erupts. 'My brother is a tosspot. I didn't mean anything by what I said – I genuinely didn't know what the smell was – but Acton... Acton is something else.'

'Your mum was even worse,' I point out.

'*Step*mum,' he corrects me. 'My real mother was *kind*. She wasn't like that.'

Abruptly, he turns his back on us. My anger dissolves. I glance at George, feeling helpless, but his attention is fixed on Theo.

'What happened to her?' he asks, but I'm not sure Theo hears him over the sound of the rain thundering down on the roof.

'Cancer,' he replies eventually.

'How old were you?'

'Six.'

George goes and stands beside him, leaning his back against the metal railing, but facing inwards rather than outwards.

'That's rough.'

Theo gives him a sidelong look. 'What about your parents?'

To my surprise, George answers.

'My mum was killed in a car crash a bit over a year ago, and my dad's in jail for armed robbery.' He could be relaying what he did at the weekend, he sounds so blasé.

'Jeez,' Theo murmurs. 'Don't you have any other relatives? Anyone else you could've gone to?'

'We went to my aunt's for a while, but that didn't work out.'

'We?' Theo hears the pronoun too.

'My sister and me,' George replies, and this time his voice cracks.

'You have a sister?' I ask with surprise as he turns to face the wall of rain, gripping the railings with his hands.

He nods to acknowledge he's heard me.

'Where is she?' Theo asks.

'She's been put up for adoption.'

'What the hell?' Theo is floored. 'Why weren't you kept together?'

I stare at the back of George's head, my heart squeezing as he shrugs.

Now I understand why he was so affected by the news of Ashlee and Nia's circumstances.

I take a couple of steps closer to him. 'How old is she?'

'She turns four next week. But I haven't seen her in nine months.'

'That sucks.' Theo lights himself another cigarette and offers George the packet.

George shakes his head. 'I'm too scared of getting the shit kicked out of me.'

Theo grins at him, a proper, surprising, the-clouds-have-cleared-and-the-sun-has-come-out kind of smile.

'Why did you flip out?' George asks him curiously, changing the subject.

Theo shrugs and takes a drag of his cigarette. 'Felt like it.' He blows smoke out of the corner of his mouth and stares at me.

I stare back at him.

I don't know what it is about Theo Whittington that makes me want to do this – there was also this morning on the bus, out the window – but for some unknown reason, I refuse to break eye contact.

The seconds tick by and I become increasingly edgy.

But then Theo smirks and averts his gaze and I inwardly smile at my small victory.

'When will your dad be here?' George asks me. He seems bemused.

I check my watch. 'Ten minutes or so.'

'I need more cigarettes,' Theo states.

The rain has died down so we walk with him to the high street, hanging back on the bridge while he goes into the newsagent on the corner. He's too young to legally smoke, so if he's going to lie about his age, I don't want us to have any part of it.

George gazes down at the river, swirling and surging below us.

'The water's black,' he muses. 'It's like squid ink.'

It is very dark in contrast to the brilliant green of the trees that are growing on either side of the banks. I like the analogy.

'I think it might have something to do with the iron content in the water,' I say. 'Or the peaty earth.'

George doesn't reply and I wish I'd kept quiet. I preferred his description to my explanation anyway.

He nods past me towards the newsagent. 'What happened when you guys went to his house?'

I tell him about Brandon – and Theo's mum's reaction. '*Step*mum,' I correct myself.

'She sounds grim,' George says when I've finished. 'Poor Theo.'

I've never really thought to feel sorry for him before.

He obviously doesn't get on well with his brother, either. And his dad is an arsehole.

Maybe he's different to his family.

Theo comes out of the shop, stuffing change into his

trouser pocket. I catch sight of my parents' Land Rover coming down the high street behind him and hold out my hand to flag down Dad. He waves and points at the car park opposite.

'Are you okay?' I ask Theo as we walk across the pedestrian crossing.

He seems kind of stiff.

He doesn't answer straight away, then he asks, 'Are you sure your dad won't mind giving me a lift?'

'He won't mind at all. I promise.'

Is he feeling awkward because of the incident at his home? Dad will remember it, not only because I've asked about Theo this week, but because he has a memory like an elephant.

But he doesn't bear grudges, and he certainly doesn't hold kids accountable for the actions of a family member. Theo will see that soon enough.

We reach the car park as Dad completes his U-turn. He pulls to a stop and rolls down his window.

'Hi, Dad, this is Theo. Can we give him a lift?'

'Sure.' He winces at the sight of Theo's split lip. 'That looks painful, son. Have you put anything on it?' He doesn't ask how he got it – he's seen far worse.

Theo shakes his head.

'Taken anything for the pain?'

Again, Theo shakes his head.

'Grab the first aid kit from under the passenger seat, love,' Dad prompts me. 'There's Ibuprofen in there.'

'I'll be okay,' Theo brushes him off.

'Well, let's get you home so you can put a cold compress on it. Lip cuts heal quickly, but you'll need to be careful when you eat dinner tonight. Hop in.'

I go around to the back of the car and open the rear

door, glad to see Theo looking more relaxed as he climbs in. George is next, but he seems surprised when I follow.

I guess he thought I'd sit up at the front, next to my dad. But I don't want to give him any more reasons to consider me 'other'.

9

NOW

A week after Dad's funeral, Jamie asks me to meet him in Ripon for lunch. There's something he needs to talk to me about and I suspect he doesn't want Mum to overhear.

He suggests the pub at the end of the high street and texts to say that he's found a seat in one of the two bright front rooms. But when I walk into the eighteenth-century former coaching inn, I see that he's not alone.

Jamie's face lights up at the sight of me, prompting George to look over his shoulder. I meet George's eyes with surprise and he gets up from his stool to greet me, giving me a brief hug that manages to leave me breathless, even though he barely touches me.

'What are you drinking?' he asks, his expression seeming marginally less intense than I remember.

'Oh, um, a soda water for now, ta.'

He walks straight behind the bar.

Jamie distracts me from the sight of George helping himself to a glass by patting the seat beside him in invitation.

'Now then,' he says as I sit down, giving me an affectionate squeeze.

'I didn't know George worked here.' He didn't specify which pub when he told me he worked in Ripon. This is one of my favourites and I'm not sure how I feel about him being a semi-permanent fixture.

We look over at the bar in time to see George filling a glass with the soda gun. He's already added ice and lemon.

'You'd better *hope* he works here,' Jamie replies. 'Otherwise he's about to get arrested.' He passes me a menu. 'You hungry?'

I nod, scanning the options. Three women walk in and pull up stools at the bar.

'Be with you in a sec,' I hear George tell them as he comes over and places the soda water in front of me. 'I'll catch up with you guys later,' he murmurs, disappearing back behind the emerald-green panelled bar area.

'I'll have a burger,' Jamie states, returning his menu to the table.

My attention is diverted by George taking the women's order. I thought he looked good in a suit, but that was before I saw him in casual clothes. He's wearing well-worn denim jeans and a long-sleeve dark-grey T-shirt. He nods at his customers and brushes his hand through his unruly curls as he turns away. The women exchange appreciative smiles.

I try to focus on the words written in front of me.

'No salad,' Jamie says, covering the corresponding section of the menu with his hand. 'You're fading away. Go for a pie. Come on.' He taps the menu with his finger as I give him a weary smile. 'Beef or chicken. Which one?'

'Chicken.'

He gets up and I experience a stupid stab of regret that I'm not the one to lean across the bar towards George.

'How's Emilie?' Jamie asks upon his return. 'I thought you might bring her.'

'No, Mum wanted to spend some time with her. I keep feeling as though I've forgotten something.'

In the last two years I can count the hours Emilie and I have spent apart on the fingers of one hand. I used to work at a boutique clothes shop in Hampstead, not far from our flat in West Hampstead. I studied Philosophy at university because I was unsure what I wanted to do with my life and thought it might help me find some clarity of mind. I graduated just as clueless as when I started, but I felt I'd landed on my feet at the shop. The owner pretty much left me to it, allowing me to order in all the clothes and build relationships with local designers. Recently she asked if I wanted my old position back, but I still haven't been able to bring myself to put Emilie into childcare. I know she should be going to nursery at her age – she plays with the twins who live next door, but she needs more interaction with other children. The problem is, I find it hard to let her out of my sight.

'I'm sure Carrie will appreciate the distraction of having her there today.'

'Yeah.' I miss the distraction myself. 'How are you?'

When Jamie nods, often his whole body seems to nod with him, but he has a nervous energy radiating from him today that is making him even bouncier than usual.

'Yeah, I'm grand.' He reaches for his pint of Coke and

takes a sip. 'There's something I want to talk to you about, actually.'

'Go on.'

'Your mam mentioned you've been thinking about moving back home.'

'Did she?' She and I haven't spoken about it since the funeral, but it must be on her mind if Jamie knows. 'I am, yes.'

'How serious are you?'

'I thought I might check out the nursery here this afternoon.'

'So you're *really* serious?' Jamie asks, his eyes sparking with what looks like hope.

'Put it this way, the thought of going back to London is leaving me feeling cold.'

'I thought you loved it there.'

'I used to.'

'What about Australia?'

I frown at him. 'What *about* Australia?'

'You don't think you might still go?'

'Without Theo?' I fervently shake my head, avoiding Jamie's gaze because I know his pity will set me off. 'No. Anyhow, it was his job that qualified us for the visa. I doubt Australia needs another shop assistant.'

'You were a manager, not an assistant,' he corrects me.

'Whatever. I'm nothing now.'

'You're a mother. And a great one. The way you've raised Emilie on your own these past couple of years—'

'Don't.' I touch his arm. I don't want to get emotional.

'Dani has been offered an apprenticeship at the Museum of London,' Jamie tells me as I try to swallow down the lump in my throat with a few sips of water.

'Oh, *wow*!' I almost splutter up my mouthful. This is major news. 'That's incredible!'

'It's her dream job,' he says simply, but he's not smiling.

'Do you want to go with her?' There must be loads of veterinary practices in London that would snap him up.

'How can I?' he asks helplessly. 'Dani applied when your dad was still with us. I wasn't sure it would come to anything, if I'm honest, but how can I leave now? I was already helping out a lot before we lost your dad – he did his back in a few weeks ago and couldn't rebuild a wall that had come down, and your mam twisted her ankle, so she could barely walk out to feed the herd.'

Needles of guilt prick my conscience. How did I not know this? Mum and Dad obviously didn't want to burden me, but I feel so neglectful.

'I was coming to the farm every day,' Jamie continues. 'The trees need work, the stream needs clearing, the chicken coop needs to be repaired, but I haven't had time to sort out anything. Your mam can't manage on her own. I've talked to her about reducing the herd size, but she gets upset every time I bring it up. I think she'll come around eventually, but it's all too much on top of losing your dad.'

'We'll move back home,' I say decisively. 'That way you can go to London with Dani. You could even take my flat, if you like.'

His eyebrows jump up. 'Really?'

'Yes.'

He seems relieved, but almost immediately sobers. 'You'd still need some help on the farm.'

'We can find someone,' I reply determinedly.

Jamie looks over at the bar again. This time I follow his gaze and see George facing away from us, his hip leaning casually against the bar. His T-shirt is pulled tight across his back, stretched over lean muscle, judging by what I felt when I was in his arms last week. I realise he's talking to a girl behind the bar, and when he moves aside, I recognise her: she's the younger sister of someone we went to school with, I can't remember her name. She's pretty: petite and curvy with winged eyeliner and red lipstick. Her chestnut hair is piled up into a messy bun and she's looking up at George with unmasked adoration.

'He's interested,' Jamie says.

'What?' I turn back to him, my mind still half on the image of George and that girl.

'George,' he says. 'He's interested.'

Why is Jamie talking to me about George's love life?

And then I get it. 'George is interested in helping out at the farm?'

Jamie nods. 'He'll still work here, but he reckons he can fit in the farm jobs too. That would only be okay if you were willing to help out on a day-to-day basis. I don't want to put pressure on you—'

I cut him off. 'Jamie, I said I'd do it. We'll move back as soon as possible.'

Surely he knows that, once my mind is made up, not much can change it. And it has nothing to do with George. Jamie has shouldered the responsibilities of looking out for my parents for too long. It's time for me to step up and take over.

10

THEN

It's Saturday morning and I'm standing outside the study, trying to pluck up the courage to knock on the door.

Joanne and Preston have gone with Dad to the market, Mum and Ashlee are grooming our pet rabbits, and Jamie is in the living room, entertaining Nia.

I heard George go for a shower half an hour ago, so I know he's up, but I haven't seen him yet.

After we dropped Theo home yesterday, George disappeared into the study, his makeshift bedroom. He came out for dinner and I wondered if he'd ignore me like he had all week. But when I made a joke – something stupid, I can't even remember – he laughed and gave me a surprisingly warm look.

I feel as though we've formed a tentative bond and I'm hoping to build on it.

Taking a deep breath, I knock.

'Yeah?' he calls from inside.

'It's Leah.' Nerves pulse through me.

A moment later, the door opens.

He's *so* tall. Seriously. He's like a beanstalk. He's wearing jeans and a faded black Elastica band T-shirt and his hair is still damp from the shower.

'Hi.'

'You all right?' he asks, placing one hand on the door frame and looking down at me.

He's gone a week barely meeting my eyes, and now I'm not used to this level of interaction. It feels, bizarrely, incredibly intense.

'I wondered if you wanted to come for a walk?' I force myself to look at him.

'Where?'

'Up to Brimham Rocks?'

He grabs a grey hoodie from the back of the office chair.

I guess that's a yes.

We head into the kitchen and I poke my head around the living room doorway. Jamie is sitting on the worn green carpet with his back resting against the sofa and Nia propped up between his legs. They're both taking turns to bash on a xylophone.

'Can you tell Mum we've gone up to Brimham?'

'Sure, have fun,' Jamie replies cheerfully, accenting his reply with a plinkety plonkety tune. Nia giggles and cranes her neck to look up at him.

I turn around and smile at George, but he averts his gaze, his jaw clenched.

We set off up the hill in silence. I'm racking my brain for something to say because it's not a comfortable one.

I settle on: 'I wonder how Theo is today.'

'Yeah,' George replies.

'Do you reckon he'll ignore us on Monday?'

He shrugs.

Help me out here, buddy.

'Have you ever been to Brimham before?'

He nods. 'But I don't remember much of it. I came here with my mum.'

Suddenly I wish Theo was with us. The way he and George spoke to each other seemed so natural. Why can't I get him to open up to me like that?

'I'm sorry,' I find myself saying before I've had a chance to think it through. 'I want to ask you about your family and why you're here, but I don't know if that's okay. I'm out of practice.'

'Out of practice?' He casts me a look.

'When I was younger, I always used to ask the teenagers who came here about their situations. But over the last few years, I've stopped doing that so much. I don't know why.'

'Yeah, you do. When you were younger, you didn't understand what you were hearing. Each story was just another story: a fairy tale with wicked stepmothers and big bad men. You might have been able to picture the horror, but only now you're older can you truly imagine it and know that it's real.'

I'm taken aback by his eloquent analysis. It's probably the most he's said to me in one go.

'You're right,' I say. 'I don't know how my mum and dad do what they do, to be honest.'

'Do you resent them for it?'

I want to say no, but I decide not to lie again.

'Sometimes,' I admit.

I open the field gate and let George pass through, securing it behind him. There's less mud than there was a week ago, but George shoots me a warning look as he takes a stride over a large puddle. I grin at him and follow his lead.

Mistletoe and Marigold gallop towards us, swerving at the last moment to walk the final few steps. I reach out to touch Mistletoe, but she grunts and jerks away.

'I should've brought you an apple. Then you'd let me pet you.'

'They *are* cute,' George says with a smile.

'Wait until you see their newborn cria.' I point at Jessamine, Hazel and Elizabeth, who are all expecting in June. The whole herd has made their way over to us now. 'Those three are pregnant. When alpacas give birth, it's called "unpacking".'

'Unpacking an alpaca? I like that.'

'Me too. There's not much to dislike about them.'

'Apart from when they spit,' he reminds me drily.

'Luckily, they don't do that very often.'

By now we've reached the top of the paddock. I'm self-conscious as I climb over the stile, aware that I don't have the slimmest figure in the world. I'm not exactly overweight, but I'm definitely curvy and my jeans hug my figure more tightly than I'd like them to. It's hard not to compare myself to Becky, who's pretty much perfect.

George jumps down from the second to last step, his feet making almost no sound as he lands. The ground beneath our feet is damp and spongy, almost like woodchip in its consistency. The track carves straight through the landscape and the higher land on either side is thick with brambles that come almost to head height. When it's raining, this path becomes a stream, but right now it's dry and easy to navigate.

We break out into a small wood of silver birch trees.

George runs his hand down the pearlescent white trunks as we wander between them.

'They feel like satin, don't they?' I say, copying him. 'I love silver birch trees.'

He nods, staring up at the branches overhead. They're covered with lime-green shoots.

'The first child my parents fostered was a six-year-old boy who had never seen a tree,' I confide.

Liam had been locked in his bedroom high up in a tower block flat while his parents went to work each day. He'd been so badly neglected that he had the mental age of a toddler. Mum and Dad poured their hearts and souls into helping him, and he was a different boy by the time he left us to go and live with his aunt.

George glances at me. 'Is that why they started their wood?'

'I think so.'

I don't want to mention the tree ceremony and set him off again, so I carry on walking until we reach a sandy track lined on either side with scraggy heather bushes and long tufty grasses.

'In August, this whole area is covered with pink and purple heather,' I say.

'I guess I came here in August, then. I remember the heather.'

'How old were you?'

'Seven? Eight? It was before Sophie was born. Wow,' he says as a cluster of gritstone rocks come into view.

'The main outcrop is another ten minutes or so away. This area is called Hare Heads,' I tell him. 'I love it here. Tourists don't tend to venture this far.'

'Isn't there, like, an enormous rock balanced on top of a tiny rock somewhere?' he asks.

'That's right. Druid's Idol. There's also a rock called Druid's Altar and another one called Druid's Writing Desk. People used to think that the Druids carved the rocks into these shapes.'

'Didn't they?'

I shake my head. 'They were created by over three hundred and forty million years of weather and water erosion. We did a geology walk around here once with school.'

There are small rocks balanced on top of big rocks and vice versa, big chunky slabs and rounded, bulbous creations, a couple of storeys high, that look as though they're melted out of candle wax.

I point out a large oblong-shaped rock balanced on top of a flat slab. 'I call that one Mini Druid's Writing Desk. I don't know if it has an actual name.'

'I remember there being one called the Dancing Bear,' George says.

'People have given them loads of names over the years: the Turtle, Sphinx, Watchdog, Camel.' I reel off some I remember. 'But if you come with Jamie, you'll get a different tour: Lava Lamp, Crack Head, Sheep Horse, Slug and, his personal favourite, Bell-End Rock. I won't show you that one, you'll get a complex.'

I can't believe I've said it. It's so inappropriate. I was getting carried away with the buzz I get when I make him smile, but now my face is *burning*.

There's a startled silence, and then he throws his head back and laughs.

The sound – warm and deep – is one of the best things I've ever heard.

'Come on,' I urge giddily, no longer caring that what I

said was bordering on flirty. 'You can see the farm from up here.'

George follows close behind as I climb up between the rocks. We reach a large flat overhang that juts out over the rugged land below by a couple of metres. If we look over our left shoulders, we can see all the way to the Yorkshire Dales, and straight ahead, beyond the farm, the view extends towards the Yorkshire Moors.

Below us, the land rolls away and climbs up again. The gradient is deceptive from this angle – the hills are a lot steeper than they look, as I know from climbing them. They're speckled with the yellow of wild primroses.

'That's Becky's farm, there.' I point past a field of brown-and-white cows towards a stone farmhouse with black-painted window frames, nestled in amongst some weather-boarded outbuildings. The wood on the barns is silvery in colour, not dissimilar to the grey-hued stone of the farmhouse.

In contrast, our buildings, including the open-ended shelters in the alpaca paddocks, are built from the same sandy-coloured stone. On the right of the courtyard are the barns. The nearest is the Bunny Barn where we keep angora rabbits and animal feed, and the big one behind it is the Yarn Barn, which is where we prepare the alpaca fibre and spin it into yarn. There's also a third barn further along that's used to store equipment for the farm.

The farmhouse, with its gleaming white window frames and shiny slate rooftop dappled with bright yellow lichen, is on the left. The living room looks out onto a small garden, which is enclosed by a low stone wall and bordered with white daisies. Mum spends a lot of time out there with Ashlee and Nia. It has a wooden bench that's a sun trap on clear days, plus a sandpit and a mini trampoline for the little ones.

I sit down and dangle my feet off the edge of the overhang. The rocks are the colour of concrete, but with more sparkle. They're glistening under the sun's rays.

'Do you come up here much?' George asks, settling down beside me.

'Yeah. If you can't find me at the farm, this is where I'll be.' I pause. 'Whoops. I've given away my Number One hiding spot.'

I sense him smiling, but don't look to see if he is.

'I bet you often want to get away from us lot.'

My brow furrows. 'Don't say that.'

'What?'

'"Us lot". As though I'd lump you all in together.'

'It's true though, isn't it? You're not one of us.'

It's a statement, not a question. And he's right. I don't like it, but I can't really argue with him.

'No, I guess not,' I reply.

'I'm sure that's hard for you too, though.'

I'm surprised he's conceded this. I don't know what to say so I let the silence stretch on. The warmth from the sun is soaking into my skin. Without the wind, it's almost too hot.

'Joanne seems a bit of a handful,' he says at last.

'Mm. I do a lot of reminding myself that she's had a hard time of it. I mean, I know you all have, otherwise you wouldn't be here.'

'You can ask me if you want,' he says after a moment. 'But don't feel that you have to.'

I *do* want to. But where to start?

'You said your mum...'

'Drunk-driving accident. She was the one drinking and driving.'

'I'm so sorry.'

He shrugs. 'At least no one else was hurt.'

'Did she drink much?'

'On and off. She didn't drink once she found out she was pregnant with Sophie, and I don't think she drank much before I came along, either, so I have that to be thankful for.'

He does a good job of containing his resentment.

'What about after she'd had Sophie?'

'She was a nightmare,' he replies offhandedly. 'Sophie's dad left and she lost it.'

'You and Sophie don't have the same father?'

'No. I barely know my dad – he's a total waste of space. Sophie's dad is too. Once, when Sophie was a baby, these guys came looking for him, saying he owed them money. I'm sure he was dealing drugs. They beat him up really badly.'

'Where were you?' I ask.

'With Sophie, under my bed. We barely fit. She stayed asleep, thankfully. I'd grabbed her from her cot.'

'How old were you?'

'Eleven? Mum was out, but when she came home and found out what had happened, they had a big argument and Twatface walked out. I was glad when he left, even though it sent Mum over the edge.'

'Who looked after Sophie when she went downhill?' As soon as I ask the question, I know the answer. 'You did.'

'Yeah,' he replies softly.

'I'm so sorry they separated you.'

His face creases with pain and he coughs. 'They didn't at first. We went to my aunt's, but her boyfriend...' He laughs darkly under his breath. It's so far from the pleasant sound of real humour that it sends a chill down my spine.

'What happened?'

'My family is a piece of cake,' he says, still grinning miserably. 'You've heard enough.'

'No,' I insist. 'You can tell me.'

'My aunt is my dad's sister. *My* blood, not Sophie's. Sophie's family were never on the scene – I don't even know if she has anyone else other than her dad.'

'Did social services try to find him after you lost your mum?'

He shrugs. 'I guess so, but they've had no luck. He's not fit to look after her in any case. Which left my aunt. Our grandmother is still alive, but she's in a nursing home with dementia.'

'So your aunt's boyfriend…'

'Kevin. A violent man with a very short temper,' he adds bluntly. 'The social workers believed my aunt when she told them the bruises were caused by clumsiness and kids at school.'

'He beat you up?' I hardly dare to seek clarification.

'Often. Gave me a black eye once.'

'Why didn't you say anything?'

'I did eventually, but only because he started on Sophie. If I'd known they'd put us into separate foster homes, I would have kept my bloody mouth shut.' His voice cracks. 'Sorry,' he says, pressing the heels of his palms to his eyes.

My nose prickles and I have an overwhelming urge to hug him.

My parents don't think kinship placements are always in the best interests of the child. 'Kin' could be a distant relative, a friend of the family, or even a neighbour. The child might barely know the carer, and that was the case with Liam, the boy who had never seen a tree. He was taken away to go and live with an aunt he'd only met twice. The aunt didn't even want him, but she took him under duress. Mum and Dad felt so helpless and frustrated at having no say about what happened to him. They thought Liam should have stayed with them – and he wanted that too.

'Argh,' George mutters, getting to his feet before I can act on my impulse. His eyes are red, but he doesn't look at me. 'Fun, fun, fun,' he says in a singsong voice.

I stare up at him, my eyes brimming with tears. 'Does Ashlee remind you of her?'

He nods. 'Yeah, a bit. They have similar expressions. Sophie used to get the same look on her face that Ashlee does when she's worried about something. They sound the same when they laugh too. And they're about the same age. Well, Sophie's nearly four now, but she was three when we were separated.'

'Has it really been nine months since you've seen her?'

He nods. 'My social worker keeps changing and no one seems to care enough to make a fucking meeting happen.'

His misery has mutated into anger.

'That's unlucky.' This sounds like a terrible understatement, but it's the truth. With the exception of Jamie, the others have all had the same social workers since they came here.

Jamie's has changed three times in the past five years, but he doesn't really care who comes to check on him now as he's so settled.

It sounds as though George has had an unusually high turnover of caseworkers. No wonder some things have slipped through the cracks.

'You should speak to my parents about it. They might be able to help.'

'*They* can't even keep Ashlee and Nia together,' he

reminds me, and there's an accusation in his tone that makes me feel horrible.

'Believe me, they *are* trying. Nia's adoptive parents are coming in a few weeks and I know my parents want Ashlee there for the meeting. They haven't given up.'

His eyebrows draw together. 'You mean there's a chance they might be adopted by the same couple? Why didn't you say that last week?'

'I don't want to get anyone's hopes up. I'm trying not to think about it myself. The alternative is too heartbreaking.' I clear my throat. 'You'd better change the subject if you don't want me to cry.'

He rolls his eyes.

'I'm serious. And I'm not a pretty crier.'

'Is anyone a pretty crier?' he asks.

'Becky is. She's stunning at all times.'

He presses his lips together. 'I doubt it.'

'I'll make her cry for you one day, you'll see.'

He grins and I return his smile.

11
——————

NOW

It's early July and mild, but Mum lights a fire anyway. It's been a month since Dad's funeral and this is my first night back after packing up the flat in London. I left the furniture for Jamie and Dani, plus a few other bits and pieces. They needed somewhere to live at short notice and will cover my monthly mortgage payments, so it worked out well for all of us. It's unlikely I'd get another mortgage in my position so I'm in no rush to sell.

It was surreal saying goodbye to Jamie and Dani and my friends in London. I'm close to Bronte who lives next door – she's the mum of the twins that Emilie plays with – but she and her husband have been talking about moving further out too so we might not have been neighbours for much longer anyway.

'Is Emilie okay?' Mum asks.

'She's excited,' I reply with a smile.

Bedtime took longer than usual. I thought Emilie would be shattered, but she wanted to chat.

'She asked if you could read her a story, but I didn't think we'd ever get her to settle if you did.'

'I can read to her tomorrow night. I'm looking forward to being able to help out more.'

'I'd like that too.'

We smile at each other and Mum passes me a small glass of sherry from the side table. I'm not a big sherry fan, but I chink her glass anyway.

'Cheers.'

Her eyes mist up.

'Oh, Mum,' I say gently.

'Sorry! Sorry!' She brushes away a couple of stray tears. 'I won't be like this for long, but I'm so grateful you decided to come home. The house has felt horrendously empty.' She looks around the living room. 'I've been thinking I might have to take in some boarders or open a B&B—'

'Please don't!' I'm not sure if she's even remotely serious, but I am not joking.

'I wouldn't.' She shakes her head. 'I know you need your space these days.'

I always needed space, Mum. More than I ever let on.

'How has it been going with George?' I know that Jamie has been showing him the ropes.

'Great,' she replies. 'Isn't it good to have him back in our lives? I worried about him for so long.'

Didn't we all.

Mum looks down at the glass in her hands, swirling the liquid around before taking another sip. My gaze drifts to the flames dancing hypnotically in the fireplace.

'I've had an idea,' Mum says hesitantly. 'Well, it's not my

idea exactly, but I heard about something similar when I was last in the Cracked Teapot.'

The Cracked Teapot is the café my parents set up almost twenty years ago to help teenagers transition out of care: they employ only care leavers. It can be terrifying going out on your own at the age of eighteen, but having a steady, decent job with a boss who understands what you're going through is worth its weight in gold.

Jamie did a stint there the summer before he went to veterinary school. Shauna ran it then and still does. An indomitable thirty-something with flaming red hair and multiple ear piercings, Shauna's daily duties include not only serving tea and cakes, but managing and mentoring the young people who work under her. Of her four current employees, only one is a former charge of my parents.

'Tell me,' I encourage, detecting doubt in her voice.

'I thought about running some knitting workshops,' she says. 'At the café. I'd supply the fleece and knitting patterns and people could pay to join in. We thought we could include lunch or afternoon tea as part of the deal.'

'We?'

'I was talking to Shauna and Gemma about it.'

Gemma is Shauna's girlfriend, a larger-than-life, warm and steady woman with a wicked cackle of a laugh. She works as a postie in and around Ripon.

'It sounds like a great idea, but weren't you planning to take on less?'

'I need to occupy my mind, Lee-Lee,' Mum replies. 'I have to do something. And if it's not going to be running a B&B...'

She smiles at the look on my face.

'Well, I'll help in any way that I can,' I state.

'I was hoping you might come to my first workshop.'

'Erm... I do know how to knit...'

She smiles at me. '*Obviously*. But I'll need people to make up numbers so it looks like a roaring success.'

'I'm sure it'll be a roaring success anyway, but of course I'll come – as long as it's okay for Emilie to come too? Unless she's started nursery by then... When are you planning the first one?'

'I'm hoping as early as next month. And yes, Emilie can join us. I'll teach her to knit too.'

'At three and a half? You reckon?'

'She's a bright little thing. Start her early – she might be running this place one day.'

This comment gives me pause for thought. 'Mum, I'm not sure how permanent this will be for us,' I say cautiously, looking around at our surroundings. 'I don't know what we're going to do yet.'

'I know, I know,' she brushes me off.

I let it go. The thought of selling off the herd is bad enough. If she had to give up the farm, it might well be the end of her.

The next morning, I take Emilie with me to let out the hens. She's on top of the world, running through the long grass in bright yellow wellies, a summer dress with a blue-green floral pattern on it and a knitted jumper fashioned from light silver grey – courtesy of Dahlia, if I remember correctly. Her hair is getting long now – I still haven't taken her to a hairdresser – and it comes to her shoulder blades, her natural dark-blond shade glinting with golden summer highlights.

I walk along behind her, feeling lighter than I have in a long time. I know it won't last, but right now, I'm simply happy to see Emilie happy. She was excited to move up here. I don't think she fully understands that Gramps is never coming back – it still hasn't fully sunk in for *me* – but her questions about him are becoming fewer and less distressing.

'Hello, boys!' I call to the males as we make our way past their paddock.

'Hello, boys!' Emilie mimics me, making me laugh.

I swing her up onto my hip and pause by the drystone wall as Heath comes over. Emilie reaches out, hoping to stroke his pure white nose. He sniffs her, then retreats.

'How's it going, old man?' I ask softly.

Alpacas have a lifespan of around fifteen to twenty years, so at the ripe old age of twenty-one, Heath is on his last legs.

He was one of the first crias to be born on the farm. Hazel and Hyacinth also arrived the same month, but they passed away a couple of years ago.

It was Daisy, one of our original seven alpacas, who inspired us to name our cria after plants and flowers. She was three years old when we got her, as were Derek and David. Edna, Elizabeth, Edith and Eddie were all only two. The person my parents bought them from had allocated a letter of the alphabet to their year of birth to make it easier to remember their ages. My parents decided to continue with the tradition, forgoing F and G and beginning with H when the first crias were born that spring.

Having skipped a few letters that weren't very inspiring, we've now come full circle.

I have no idea what we'll do next year, if not plants and flowers.

That's if we still have the herd.

For a moment, I imagine what it would feel like to stand

here, staring at an empty field, and I realise it would destroy me to sell off the herd too. They're like family.

I pinch the tip of Emilie's nose and she giggles. 'Let's go set those cheeky chickens free.'

We're standing on the sandbank in the middle of the stream when a dark-grey pickup truck rumbles slowly along the lane.

Emilie is stomping her boots at the edge of the water, creating splashes that make the recently released chickens flap and squawk with fright.

'If you scare them too much, they might not lay any eggs for tomorrow's breakfast.' My mind is only partly on the warning.

I watch as George cuts the engine and climbs out of his truck.

I still can't get over how grown up he looks, how *manly*... It's such a rubbish description, but it's apt.

Theo always seemed younger than his years. George looks like the thirty-year-old man that he is, and then some.

He holds up his hand in a casual wave and I mimic the gesture, my stomach a tangle of nerves as he comes to stand on the bridge.

'You've taken a trip to Chicken Island, I see.'

'It's still as resplendent as ever,' I reply, gazing up at him.

He smiles down at me, resting his forearms on the wooden railing that's permanently slippery with mildew thanks to the shade of the evergreens growing nearby. He's wearing a dark-blue shirt over a cream-coloured T-shirt with charcoal grey jeans and chunky black boots.

'You look like two peas in a pod.' He nods towards Emilie.

I glance at her, then down at myself, before laughing and shaking my head with amusement.

'I do that sometimes, and I don't even know I'm doing it.'

I'm wearing an almost identical outfit, although my wellies are dark green rather than sunny yellow, and my floral dress is more of a mossy grey. Instead of a jumper, I have on a rose grey cardie that Mum knitted for me years ago using Marshmallow's fleece. It's an old favourite: so soft and cosy and exactly what I need right now.

George is still looking at Emilie, but his expression has grown pensive. I wonder what he's thinking.

Does every little girl remind him of Sophie?

He meets my eyes. 'How did packing up your flat go?'

'Fine.'

He nods at the chicken coop. 'Have you collected the eggs?'

'Not yet.'

'I'll do it.'

'You can help us. Do you want to come and collect the eggs, Emilie?' I ask before George can speak again.

'Yeah!' she yells, stomping through the water to the grassy edge and sending two more birds into a frenzy.

George jumps down from the end of the bridge to the soft earth beneath the conifers. Emilie runs after him as he makes his way towards the coop.

I follow at a slower pace, my stomach squirming. George has to duck right down to enter the pen – as do I, although to a lesser extent – but Emilie wanders straight in and picks up a pure white feather from the ground. She lifts it up to her eyes and studies it. George casts me a smile and my jitters ramp up a notch.

Emilie slips the feather into one of the pockets on her

jumper and picks up another – brown this time – putting that into her pocket too.

'What are you going to do with those?' I ask as she reaches for a couple more.

She shrugs.

'You could make a pillow for one of your teddies,' I suggest.

She looks at me, her hazel eyes wide.

'Did you know that pillows and cushions are sometimes stuffed with feathers?' I ask. 'You can have a look at some of Nanna's when we get back.'

George opens up the door to the nest boxes and peers inside.

'Oops,' he says.

'What's wrong?' I step forward to look, expecting to see cracked carnage, considering his reaction, but I'm met instead with the sight of a dozen or so glossy-white and matt-brown eggs.

'I don't have anything to carry them in.'

'Oh. Me neither,' I reply, hyper aware of his close proximity. There's so much of him that it feels as though he's everywhere.

'I'll nip up to the house.'

'No, don't bother, we can carry them between us. Emilie?'

She looks over at me.

'Can you carry some eggs in your jumper?'

She nods and walks over, pulling out her jumper to create a dip in the middle. I pick up a couple of eggs and place them gently in the centre of her makeshift basket.

'You've done this before,' George says.

I smile. 'Yep.'

'I can carry some too.' He pulls out his own T-shirt.

I think he's overestimating how many eggs there are, but my thoughts are distracted by the sight of his flat stomach and the V-shaped muscle that runs diagonally from his hips towards his pelvis. I quickly avert my gaze and reach back into the nest box, fumbling for a couple more eggs and finding them surprisingly slippery all of a sudden.

I allocate another two eggs to my daughter and pick up four more. 'You can probably carry the last few in your hands,' I mumble, hoping George hasn't noticed me blushing.

'Hello!' Mum chirps when we arrive back. 'I've just put the kettle on. Will you have a brew?' she asks as she puts our eggs into a carton, ready to take to the Cracked Teapot.

'I should probably get on,' George replies.

He's been clearing the stream and cutting back the undergrowth alongside it, a job that Dad had been talking about tackling for the last two years.

'Don't be silly, there's plenty of time. You're not working until tonight, right?'

George nods.

'How's it going at the pub?' I ask, trying to relax into small-talk territory as I pull out a chair for Emilie.

'I need a wee,' Emilie declares, derailing the conversation.

'Come on, then.' Mum holds out her hand.

I smile after them, then glance at George to let him know I'm still waiting on an answer.

'Fine.' He leans against the wall and folds his arms as I get on with making the tea.

'Are your colleagues nice?' I'm fishing.

'Nat's cool,' he replies.

A slithery feeling coils into my gut. I remembered her name after I left the pub the last time. I used to know her as

Natalie, but George is obviously familiar enough with her to use a nickname.

'You realise we went to school with her?' I keep my voice sounding casual as I pour boiling water into the teapot.

He nods. 'Her sister Amanda was in our year.'

'That's right. You've got a good memory.'

'I didn't remember. Nat reminded me,' he admits.

I put everything onto a tray and take it to the table, nodding at the chair opposite.

'I like that your parents still have the same table,' he says.

We both wince simultaneously at the mistake. There's no plural anymore.

'Do you still take sugar?' I ask.

'One.'

I pour milk into our cups.

'Are you happy to be home?' he asks. 'Do you still call it home?'

I think about this. 'I do, although it hasn't really been home since I was eighteen. Our flat in London felt like home when Theo was with us, but it's been a long time since I've been happy there. Yes, I *am* glad to be back.'

Seconds tick by.

'Your mam told me about your prison visits,' George says quietly.

I flinch before dully replying: 'He doesn't want to see me anymore. Apparently, he finds it too hard,' I elaborate, bitterness creeping into my tone.

'Oh, *he* finds it hard?' George's eyes spark with anger, and I remember the time Dad took him to visit his own father in jail. He was even more introverted than usual when he returned.

'Going there has been difficult for me too.' I reach for the teapot.

'Let me,' George says.

Our fingers brush and I yank my hand away, feeling as though I've been electrocuted.

How can this be happening again?

When George left all those years ago, it was as though he'd ripped a hole in my heart. Theo helped to fill it, but not completely. And now I'm wearing a Theo-shaped hole and I know it'll kill me to lose any more of myself. George has the ability to break me. And I'm already so fractured.

He's still staring at me, his hand gripping the teapot, but failing to pour. I'm looking anywhere but at him.

'Leah,' he whispers, putting the teapot back down on the tray.

I break a bit more at hearing him say my name.

'I miss him,' I confide. 'But I'm also still so angry at him.'

'I get it,' he replies, and I believe him. If anyone understands what I'm going through, it's George.

At this realisation, my walls come tumbling down. 'Why didn't he listen to me? If he hadn't walked out that door...' My anger loses steam and I feel deflated all of a sudden. 'Theo always had to do things his way.' George doesn't speak and I find myself continuing: 'I just want to talk to him, tell him about Emilie and all the small things, stuff that's so easy to forget, like how she collected those feathers earlier. It's another moment that he's missed out on.'

The sound of the toilet flushing travels down the hallway.

I reach for the teapot and George goes to take over again.

'No.' I shake my head at him and begin to pour. 'I need the distraction.'

12

THEN

I'm at the dining room table on Saturday afternoon, doing homework, when Dad and the others return from the market.

I hear Dad knocking on the study door.

'Are you there, son?' he asks.

'Yep?' George calls back.

'I thought we might go to the tree nursery?'

Silence.

'It won't take long,' Dad adds.

I peer around the door frame to see him standing there, patiently staring at George's door.

'Can we go tomorrow?' George replies at last.

'It's closed tomorrow. Are you all right?'

There's another lengthy pause before the door handle turns and the door opens. I swiftly retreat as I hear George tell him, 'I'm fine, I'm in the middle of something.'

'Can I help?'

'No, I'm writing a letter. Any chance you can go without me?'

'Er, I suppose I could. Is there any tree in particular that you would like?'

'No, happy for you to choose.'

'Unless we go sometime this week after school?' Dad asks hopefully.

'I really don't mind,' George replies.

'Okay, then.'

The door clicks shut again.

'Dad,' I whisper.

He pokes his head around the living room doorway. 'Oh, hello, love, I didn't know you were there.'

'Get him a silver birch,' I say softly.

'A silver birch tree?'

I nod. 'We went for a walk earlier. He likes them.'

'Right you are.' He hesitates. 'Don't suppose you want to come with me?'

'Just you and me?'

He nods brightly.

I close up my textbook with a smile. 'Sure.'

Better make the most of a rare opportunity.

We all attend the tree ceremony on Sunday afternoon, several hours later than planned because of delays caused by one thing or another. First no one can rally George, then Joanne kicks off because she can't find her hairbrush, and then Preston falls off the quad bike. The dozy git shouldn't have been on it in the first place – Jamie was using it to do some work around the farm – so Dad has to give him a proper talking to because his actions put not only him, but *everyone* at risk. Who knows what social services would have done if he'd been badly hurt. Thankfully he wasn't.

Dad insists we all go straight after lunch, but it's clear that George's heart isn't in it as we trudge down to the lower paddock. I watch for his reaction when we reach the small silver birch sapling sitting front and centre of the others. He stands and stares, then looks at me, his lips quirking up at the corners. 'Was this you?'

'Leah picked it out,' Dad replies on my behalf.

George reaches down, picks up the shovel lying on the grass, and begins to dig.

The first thing I do when I wake up on Monday morning is check my phone to see if Becky has texted. She was feeling ill all weekend and she didn't think she'd be in today. There's no message to confirm either way, so I send her a quick one, saying I hope she's better and knowing that, if she doesn't reply, she's likely still in bed.

Sure enough, Becky's seat is empty when I board the bus, and once again, Joanne beats me to it.

I ignore her triumphant expression and slide into an empty row, almost jumping out of my skin when George sits down beside me.

I glance at him. A moment passes.

'Hello there,' I say.

'Hello there,' he replies, stretching his long legs out under the seat in front of him and folding his arms across his chest.

He doesn't put on his music, but that's all we say to each other.

Theo is leaning against the gatepost when we round the bend by his house. He's not smoking today, but as before, he locks me in a staring contest while the bus is pulling to a stop. And, as before, I win. He smirks and casts his eyes to the ground as the bus doors whoosh open.

'All right, Posh Lad?' Pete calls from the back.

'Fuck off,' Theo answers.

'Enough of that,' the bus driver growls.

Full of dread, I glance over the top of my seat at Pete, but his expression is impish, not menacing. A quick glance at Theo reveals there's no anger to be found on his face either.

So that's it, then? One punch-up and the war's over?

Theo nods at George and swings into the seat across the aisle from us. His hair is so dark that it looks black. I bet it's soft. I have a sudden image of myself making wrist warmers out of it and the thought is so ridiculous that I burst out laughing.

George and Theo glance at each other.

'Do you know why she's laughing?' Theo asks him.

'No. Do you?' George replies.

I think I'm giddy with relief that the bullying seems to be behind us.

'I will never, ever tell you,' I say at last, realising that I'd sound like a right nutter if I did.

'That sounds like a challenge if ever I heard one,' Theo replies with amusement.

That day, George and Theo hang out together at lunchtime. The three of us sit by each other on the way home and the next day it's the same. On Wednesday, I break away from some of my other classmates to join the two of them on the field at break. Our conversations barely skim the surface – there's certainly nothing profound about them – but our random banter about TV shows, bands and movies is entertaining.

By the end of the following week, I would call us friends. Becky is still off school and her illness has been confirmed as viral meningitis. It's not as dangerous as the bacterial kind, but she seems to have got a bad bout of it. The infection was contagious initially, but I visited her after school a couple of days ago, although she was too tired to talk for long.

I feel so sorry for her, but while I miss her, this time without her hasn't been as awful as it would've been if it weren't for Theo and George. And when, on Friday afternoon, Theo morosely grumbles that he doesn't want to go home, I don't hesitate to invite him back to ours.

'Your parents won't mind?' he asks hopefully.

'Not at all,' I assure him.

'Well, hello there!' Dad says buoyantly when we walk in. He's sitting at the kitchen table, nursing a mug of tea. One arm is hooked around baby Nia, who's perched on his knee, sucking on her slippery fingers.

The kitchen is warm, thanks to the always-hot Aga, and it smells delicious, but it looks as though a bomb has hit it. Mum has evidently been baking for the café, and the thick wooden countertops are cluttered with dirty bowls, the pale-blue cupboards are splattered with cake mixture, and the well-worn red-tiled floor is coated with a dusting of flour and who knows what else.

'Now then, son, that's looking better.' Dad nods at Theo's lip.

'Yeah. Thanks,' Theo replies awkwardly.

Joanne and Preston hone in on the plate of freshly baked flapjacks and Dad barks at them: 'Oi! Hands!'

Mum comes into the kitchen, carrying Ashlee.

'Hello!' she says with a big smile at Theo, putting Ashlee down.

'Mum, this is Theo.' I make the introduction.

'Lovely to meet you,' Mum says, although I'm sure, like Dad, she remembers him. 'Do you want to use the cloakroom?' She directs him into the hall while the rest of us take turns washing our hands at the kitchen sink.

When Theo returns, I try to see things from his perspective: the mess, the chaos, all these people. He must feel as though he's wandered into a madhouse.

Ashlee is regarding him warily, so I tickle her ribs and make her squirm and giggle.

'I was about to see how much she's grown,' Mum tells me, opening the larder door wide.

Names and heights are charted all the way up the wall on the left-hand side. You have to look closely to be able to decipher the messy scrawl, but we're all there – even me.

'Come on,' Mum urges Ashlee, standing her just inside the door. 'Ooh, you've grown a whole inch!'

Ashlee beams up at her as she marks the wall with a Sharpie.

'You next, Lee-Lee, you haven't been measured in a while.'

'Do we have to do this now?' I gripe, shooting a look at Theo. He's leaning against the counter and munching on a flapjack, seeming perfectly content.

'Chop chop,' Mum replies, her attention momentarily pulled away by Preston and Joanne trying to make a speedy exit. 'Where are you two going?' she shouts after them.

Joanne ignores her, but Preston calls back: 'I have to pack.'

'Fine, I'll get you later,' Mum replies, but I don't miss the pain that briefly contorts her face.

Preston is leaving us tomorrow. He has two younger siblings and one older sister who have all been in separate foster homes. He'll be the second to be reunited with his mother. The woman was grossly neglectful – addicted to drink and drugs and willing to do anything to get her hands on them, from the stories I've heard Preston telling Jamie and Joanne – but she's out of rehab now and allegedly doing well. All Preston has wanted since he came here eight months ago was to return to her. Despite everything, he loves her and he can't wait to go home.

My parents have witnessed too many failed reunions to not be sceptical about this one. They're very fond of Preston, even with all his moaning and laziness, and they'd have him back in a heartbeat if it didn't work out.

But at the same time, as long as he's happy, I know they'd be at peace if they never saw him again.

Whatever the eventual outcome, tomorrow will be hard for everyone.

Mum is still waiting for me, so I drag my heels over to the larder cupboard and stand there dutifully as she marks my height.

'There you go,' she says when she's finished, and I turn around to inspect the wall.

'Ooh, a whole millimetre,' I say sarcastically.

Mum rolls her eyes. 'Up you get, George, you're next.'

George stares at her with alarm.

'Hurry along, George,' Theo urges in an amused murmur, giving him a shove.

George glares over his shoulder at him, but does as my

mum asks, scraping his wooden chair legs over the tiled floor with a screech and unfolding his long body.

'I'm not going to be able to see over the top of your head,' Mum says.

'I'll do it.' Dad's shorter than George by several inches, but manages to make a faithful marking on the wall. 'You're the tallest of all of us, *and* I bet you've still got some growing to do,' he muses.

'Come on,' I say to George and Theo, nodding towards the door.

'Can you bring the rabbits in?' Mum calls after us as we head outside.

'Okay.'

Theo is more vocal than George was at the sight of our absolutely enormous, white, ball-shaped bunnies. George was struck dumb, but Theo exclaims, 'What the fuck?' and stares with disbelief as George steps over the low fence and scoops one off the grass.

'Who's this?' George asks me, tickling her behind her long pink ears.

'Sooty,' I reply.

He cocks an eyebrow at me.

'Jamie was going through an ironic phase,' I tell him.

'Can I pick one up?' Theo asks.

'Go for it. They're used to being handled.'

He climbs into the pen and reaches for the nearest. 'Whoa! It's heavier than I thought it would be.'

'*She*,' I correct him. 'That's Ewok.'

'*Star Wars* phase?' George asks me.

'No "phase" about it,' I retort. 'That one's Wookie.' I point out another rabbit.

He narrows his eyes at me. 'Are you named after Princess Leia?'

I laugh. 'It wouldn't surprise me. My dad has a thing for her – you can see it on his face when we watch the movies – but my name is pronounced '*Lee*-ah, not *Lay*-ah'.'

'Why do you have so many?' Theo asks, and I get the impression he's only half listening to us.

I give him a brief overview of the fleece farm as we carry the rabbits back inside and secure them in their cages.

Angora rabbits are primarily bred for their wool, which is extremely fine and softer than cashmere. Ours are Giant Angoras – glossy white and round in shape with striking pink ears and eyes. They're so fluffy that they look like big balls of cotton. It's hard to believe that they're real, let alone useful.

But although these rabbits do produce fleece for the farm, the main purpose of our bunnies is less widely known. My parents bought these animals not so much for their fur but for their therapeutic value. It wasn't until Jamie came to live with us that I realised. We only had two of them then as opposed to the six we have now, but I remember how much they would calm him after he'd had a meltdown. Jamie could go from yelling and screaming to quietly grooming the rabbits in less than twenty minutes.

It's quite hard to feel angry when you have a surprisingly hefty fluffball sitting on your knee – I know, because grooming them chills me out too.

Every silky strand they shed when being brushed or plucked is kept and put aside, ready to be carded and spun. The spinning itself – whether it's angora wool or alpaca fleece – is also therapeutic. There's something about the gentle rhythm of the wheel that seems to quiet busy minds.

It doesn't always work, though. The only child my parents have ever had to move on was a twelve-year-old boy named Connor who squeezed one of the rabbits so tightly that she had to be put down. Everyone has a threshold, and causing harm to the animals is the one thing that will push my parents over theirs. But I know that their failure to help Connor will haunt them for the rest of their lives.

'Do they need brushing now?' Theo asks as we're making our second and final trip.

'Always. You want a turn?'

He shrugs. 'Sure.'

'Let's take these two to the Yarn Barn.'

'Er, I might go and change,' George says, glancing down at his black blazer.

'Okay, see you in a bit.'

As George sets off across the courtyard towards the kitchen door, Theo follows me into the adjacent barn. It's much bigger than the Bunny Barn – a long rectangular space full of tables, drying racks and various equipment, from washing machines to spinning wheels.

Right now, it's relatively clean and tidy, with white-painted walls and a well-swept light-grey linoleum floor, but in the weeks and months to come, practically every surface will be covered with alpaca fleece.

We send a lot of our fibre away to be processed, and keep some of it here at the farm. It has to be cleaned and carded and spun into yarn before it can be used, and each of these techniques takes time.

We go to an empty table and I pass Theo a brush and an apron, settling Annie – Annie the Angora; no story there – before me on the table while I tie up my apron. Theo drapes his apron over the back of his chair instead of putting it on, an act he will soon come to regret.

'You can brush or pluck.' Grabbing a handful of oats from a container on the table, I sprinkle some in front of

Annie and Wookie and they tuck in, sitting there quite contentedly.

'Doesn't plucking hurt them?' he asks apprehensively as he watches me tug gently on Annie's fur. A tuft comes away easily.

'Not at all. They moult anyway, and if they take in too much hair while grooming themselves, they might get wool block.' I place the tuft in my left hand and pull out another, laying it with the first in a long strip.

'What's wool block?'

'It's when they swallow so much hair that it makes a hairball. Rabbits can't vomit them up like cats can, so it can be fatal. Start at the top, around her neck, so you know where you've been.'

Theo falls quiet as he gets to work.

'This is actually quite relaxing,' he says after a while.

I smile at him. 'Isn't it?'

'If my masters could see me now...' he adds darkly.

'Why did you leave boarding school?' I finally ask the question that's been on my mind.

'I didn't leave.' He pauses. 'I was expelled.'

'Oh. Why?'

'Because I was *naughty*.' He says this in a low voice, exaggerating the last word to make it sound strangely sexy. 'Disobedience, smoking, vandalism,' he continues. 'And there might've been drugs involved.'

Ah. *Okaaaay...* 'Why didn't you go to another boarding school?'

He smiles, but the humour doesn't reach his eyes. 'That was my third. Dear old Daddy had had enough. He told me I could take my education or leave it, but he wouldn't pay another penny either way. It's not like I matter to him. Acton will inherit. I'm just the spare.'

He says all this flippantly, but it clearly bothers him.

'What do we do with it now?' He shows me the hair he's collected.

'Now it has to be carded.' I pick up two curved brushes that are covered with small metal tines. Laying the hair across the top of one brush, I drag the other over it repeatedly until all of the hair is collected by the second brush. 'You're brushing the hair into fine, straight layers so they can be spun more easily,' I explain as I repeat the process. 'These are hand carders, but that machine does the same job.' I nod at the drum carder on the table next to us, which consists of two round drums, pressed up against each other and covered with tines.

'Are you guys still at it?' George asks from the doorway.

'Yep,' Theo replies. 'Mind if I have a go?' he asks me.

'Watch your fingers; the tines are sharp,' I warn as I hand the brushes over.

'Shall I put the bunnies back?' George interrupts.

'Sure. Ta,' I reply.

He picks up Annie and walks out.

I get the feeling he wasn't expecting to spend his Friday afternoon like this. He returns to collect Theo's rabbit a couple of minutes later.

'Why were you laughing?' Theo asks when George has walked out of the barn again.

He's asked me this question every single day over the last fortnight, still keen to know why I cracked up in hysterics on the bus.

'I am *not* telling,' I repeat with a grin.

There's no way I can admit to what I wanted to make out of his hair. He'd think I'm barmy.

Theo tuts and shakes his head.

'I would show you how to spin this into yarn, but I think

George has had enough bunny fun for one afternoon,' I whisper when George reappears, purposefully saying it loudly enough for him to hear me.

Theo grins over at him. George raises his eyebrows, and rocks impatiently on his heels.

'I need a smoke,' Theo declares bluntly. 'Is there anywhere we can go that's safe from your parents?'

'My parents won't bat an eyelid.' I get up and push my chair back in.

'Still, I'd rather not flaunt it in their faces.' He catches sight of himself as he stands up. His lap is covered in white fur.

'That'll teach you not to wear an apron.' I laugh at the look on his face.

'I can't wait to explain this one,' he mutters.

'What did your family say about your lip?' I ask.

He shrugs. 'They didn't notice.'

I stare at him as he pats his pocket for his cigarettes. I turn to gauge George's reaction, but he doesn't seem at all surprised.

I realise then and there that Theo may, on the surface, seem as if he has it all, but he's damaged like everyone else who comes here.

13

NOW

'T hanks so much,' I say to Robin as I reach for my door handle.

'You're welcome,' he replies in his baritone Canadian accent. 'Call me if you need a lift home, okay?'

'No, no, we'll definitely catch a cab,' I hear Becky assure him as I step out onto the pavement. 'You should get an early night.'

Through the window I see my old friend lean across the centre console to peck her husband on his bristly cheek.

I like Robin – I always have – but I don't know him well. This journey into Ripon has helped me get to know him a bit better, although I still couldn't tell you what he does for a living. Something to do with computers and finance, but Becky cut him off before he could grant my request to explain in more detail.

'Don't, we'll be asleep before we get there.'

He laughingly brushed off her ribbing.

I thought Robin was still abroad when I rang to ask Becky if she fancied going out for dinner. When I discovered he'd only returned from his business trip to Canada this morning, I expected her to turn me down so she could spend the evening with him. But she jumped at the chance to have a girls' night out.

Robin insisted on driving us. He's lovely: tall, dark and handsome. Tonight is one of the rare times I've seen him in casual clothes, and he seemed more approachable somehow: more of a cuddly giant than an imposing businessman.

He drives away and Becky and I grin at each other.

It's been a long time since I've felt excitement.

I actually enjoyed the process of getting ready this evening and Becky has made an effort too. She's wearing black jeans and a long-sleeve black lace top and has blow-dried her dark chin-length locks to shiny perfection.

As for me, I dug out my curling tongs and now my previously limp 'do has a bit of a kink to it, falling in tousled dark-blond waves to a couple of inches free of my shoulders. I'm wearing heels for the first time in ages – suede ankle boots – with a thigh-length navy shirt dress. I've put on a little weight thanks to Mum's home cooking over the last few weeks, but I know I'm still too thin. The dress helps to disguise my slight frame.

Robin has dropped us off near the cathedral and it makes for a spectacular view as we click-clack along the pavement beside the towering beauty. The setting sun is hitting the warm sandy-coloured stone of the building and making it shine a golden orange, while its myriad of tall arched windows are reflecting the light and sparkling back at us blindingly.

Across the road is the Cracked Teapot. Festoon lights

hang from the leafy tree outside, making the place look inviting even though it's dark and empty and the outdoor furniture has been packed away for the night. Twinkling fairy lights are suspended from the window frames inside too, along with a blackboard propped up against the glass, revealing the day's specials. Tomorrow's cakes will be banana and caramel, coffee and walnut and a classic Victoria sponge – I know because Mum was baking them earlier. She also made animal biscuits for Emilie with brightly coloured icing: yellow giraffes, pink hippos and green crocodiles.

I should say 'with' Emilie, but I know that my daughter was more of a hindrance than a help. Still, they looked as though they were enjoying themselves.

The warm summer air is perfumed with the scent of the roses growing in nearby garden beds as Becky and I cross over the road to the high street. The road slopes down and curves away to the right, and bunting zigzags between the old terraced buildings on either side, fluttering in the breeze.

I've booked us a table at the pub where George works, but the fact that it's my favourite place to go out in Ripon doesn't alleviate my guilt. The sad truth is, I'm itching to see him.

My butterflies spiral into a frenzy at the sight of him behind the emerald-green panelled bar. He's pulling a pint, his dark eyes cast downwards, but then he looks up and sees me, doing a double take. His initial surprise transforms into genuine pleasure. I smile at him, feeling very edgy indeed, and then Becky reminds me of her presence.

'Is that George?' she asks with surprise.

She saw him at the wake and we've spoken briefly about his return, but she didn't know he worked here at this pub.

'Yes,' I reply.

She helped pick up the pieces after he left, but she never fully understood why I was so destroyed. The spring that George came to live with us coincided with Becky contracting meningitis, and in the summer, she got her first boyfriend, so she wasn't around much. If she had been there, I doubt George, Theo and I would have got so close.

'Eh up,' George says as we walk up to the bar. He finishes with one pint glass and reaches for another. There's a man waiting.

'Hi.' I smile and prop my elbows on the polished mahogany bar top.

'Are you here for dinner or drinks?' George asks.

'Dinner, but we'll have a quick one at the bar first, shall we?' I check with Becky.

'Why not?' she replies, dragging a stool over the weathered stone floor and perching.

Natalie is down at the other end of the bar. She sees us and comes over. 'What can I get you?'

'I'll see to them,' George tells her abruptly, placing his second pint glass in front of the man and telling him the price.

She stares at him. He looks over at her briefly before coolly taking the man's card and running it through the till. She gives me a curious look, then her gaze moves to Becky and her face shows signs of recognition.

'Oh, hello!'

My friend is more familiar around here, probably because she used to visit her parents a lot more than I did.

I can hardly bear the fact that I didn't come home enough while Dad was still alive. Now it's too late to rectify my mistake.

'Hi, Natalie,' Becky chirps as I try to push these regrets

aside. I need a break from my demons tonight. 'How's Amanda?'

Amanda is Natalie's older sister, the one we went to school with.

'She's all right, thanks. Not enjoying her morning sickness much, though.'

'I didn't know she was pregnant.'

As Becky and Natalie catch up, George finishes with his customer and comes to stand opposite me, behind the bar.

'You look happy to be out and about,' he says with a small smile, proceeding to unbutton the cuffs of his denim shirt. He's wearing it open over a black T-shirt.

'First time in a while.'

He nods. 'I heard.'

'Has Mum been talking about me again?'

He shrugs. 'She worries. What can I get you?'

I tap Becky on her shoulder, interrupting her mid-sentence. 'Are we doing Prosecco?'

'Absolutely. Get a bottle.'

I smile at her command.

'You heard the lady,' I say to George as he pushes one sleeve up to reveal a tanned, leanly muscled forearm.

Becky has already returned to her conversation with Natalie.

George smiles at me and pushes his other sleeve up. My heart skitters as I see that his skin is etched with the ink of several tattoos. I can't stop staring as he gets a bottle of Prosecco out of the fridge and returns to the bar top, deftly peeling off the silver wrapper and unwinding the metal cage to free the cork.

I lift my eyes to see him watching me. Now his expression is serious.

He knows what I'm thinking.

'Do you still have it?'

'Yes,' he replies in a low voice, easing the cork out with a small pop.

I want to ask if I can see, but I've lost my nerve.

He pours out fizzing liquid into flutes and I distract myself by opening my bag and pulling out my purse.

George shakes his head. 'It's on me.'

'No, it's fine—'

'Leah,' he cuts off my protestations, filling a champagne bucket with ice. 'It's on me,' he repeats steadily, causing a shivery feeling to ripple over my entire body.

He passes one glass to Becky and she beams. 'Ooh, thank you!'

Natalie leaves us to it and Becky spins around to face me, chinking my glass.

'Cheers!'

'Cheers.'

'Enjoy your night,' George murmurs, clunking the bottle into the ice bucket and going to attend to another customer.

I feel deflated as I watch him leave us.

Becky gives me a significant look. 'Shall we take this to our table?'

I nod, silently agreeing.

'It must have been so strange to see George again,' she says when we're comfortably seated at a wooden table by the window in the restaurant area. The sill beside us is crammed with ornaments: a pottery pug wearing a suit and tie, old-fashioned bottles and books, picture frames and a globe of the world.

'It was very surreal,' I reply, knowing that the description falls well short of conveying how it really felt to discover George sitting two rows behind me at Dad's funeral.

'Have you found out where he went?'

'No. We still haven't had that conversation.'

'Seriously? I thought he was helping out at the farm.'

'He is. But I don't see that much of him.'

'You're avoiding him.'

'For my own sanity.'

Her face scrunches up with sympathy and she reaches across to cover my hand with hers. A moment later, her expression becomes thoughtful. She cocks her head to one side and whispers conspiratorially, 'If you're avoiding him, why are we here?'

I shrug and smile. 'Psychoanalyse away.'

She laughs. 'Well...' she starts.

I cut her off with a grin. 'Actually, don't. Let's talk about something else.'

Becky launches into a story about the latest naughty thing Hayden has done, and I laugh and amuse her in turn with tales about Emilie being cheeky. Our children are the main topic of conversation for the next hour or so, and we're aware of the irony, considering we're hardly ever without them and should be making the most of our freedom. But Emilie is the one thing guaranteed to make me smile, so I don't care.

'I don't know how the hell your parents managed to look after so many kids at once,' Becky says at last.

'Neither do I.'

'They're pretty special people.'

'They *are*, and they *were*,' I gently correct her, thinking of Dad.

'How's Jamie getting on?' Becky asks hurriedly, realising we've accidentally strayed into sentimental territory.

'He and Dani are great!' I'm glad she knows that I don't want to dwell. 'They're loving London life. I can't believe it. Jamie always seemed so at home in the country so the thought of him hanging out in the big city is really making me smile.'

'Are they coming back for a visit anytime soon?'

'Not for a while. I think they want to get settled there first.'

We go on to talk about the life Becky left behind in Canada, and eventually come around to discussing what it's been like for us both to move back home. I tell her about Mum's upcoming knitting workshop and she says she'd love to come.

'I won't bring Hayden, though. He'd tear the place up.'

'I have to bring Emilie.'

'I'm sure Robin would have her. He's working from home for the next few weeks. This Thursday lunchtime, you say?'

'Yes, but honestly, don't worry, she can come with me.'

No one aside from family has looked after her since – I freeze, stunned, at the sight of two tall girls, one with long blond hair and another with dark hair, ordering drinks at the bar.

Becky, seeing my expression, follows my gaze.

'Too young,' she states dismissively as George prepares their order.

She thinks I'm worried about the competition, which is insulting in itself, but she's wrong.

The blonde girl over there is Katy. Katy, who babysat for us the evening of my parents' party. Katy, who forgot to text to say that she was home safe after her taxi journey. Katy, who is inadvertently responsible for Theo walking out of our door that night in his desperation to check on her.

George glances past her and catches my eye.

'What is it?' Becky asks, now with alarm. She's realised that she failed to hit the nail on the head.

And then Katy, perhaps wondering what has caused the bartender to look so perplexed, casually glances over her shoulder. As soon as she sees me, her relaxed smile wilts.

I shakily lift up a hand to wave hello and she does the same before turning back to say something to her friend. They pick up their drinks and head in the direction of the front rooms. I reach for my glass and take a sip, forcing the bubbles down my throat.

'Hey,' Becky says with concern.

I glance over at the bar again. George is watching me intently.

'*You okay?*' he mouths.

'Leah?' Becky prompts, demanding an explanation.

'That was Katy, the babysitter—'

'Oh shit.' She exhales heavily.

I don't even need to finish my sentence.

George comes out from behind the bar and strides over, crouching at my side.

'Are you okay?' he asks again, placing his hand on my knee.

I jerk violently and he removes his hand, flustered. I know the gesture was meant to be comforting, yet it was anything but.

'That was the babysitter Theo went after,' Becky explains, and I wince, hearing his name said out loud.

Our waitress comes over. 'Everything all right?' she asks brightly, with a puzzled glance in George's direction.

He nods and stands up.

'What are we thinking about for dessert?' she asks breezily.

'Give us a couple of minutes, will you?' Becky says sharply.

I inwardly flinch and force a smile at the waitress.

'Of course.' She gives George another querying look before leaving us to it.

'I'm okay,' I tell him. 'Thanks. It was a shock, that's all. I haven't seen her since.'

'Can I get you another bottle?' He picks up the empty one, along with the ice bucket.

I shake my head, feeling too unsettled to consider it. 'But don't you stop,' I say to Becky.

'I'm all right for now.' Becky nods at George to let him know he can leave us too.

'How are you getting home?' he asks me, not moving an inch.

'Taxi.'

'I'll drive you.'

'There's no need.'

'I want to. Let me know when you're ready. It's not that busy tonight.'

I find myself nodding in quiet acceptance. George gives us a curt nod and returns to the bar.

For a long time afterwards, I'm aware of the heat from his palm on my skin.

14

THEN

The day after Preston leaves, my parents decide to take us to Fountains Abbey for an outing. They think the family time will do us good, but Joanne is having none of it. She wanted to go shopping in Harrogate with her friends, not visit 'a fucking pile of old rocks'.

'They're ancient ruins,' my dad tells her calmly.

Mum is driving and Nia is beside her in the car seat. Dad is sitting on one of the rear parallel bench seats running along each side of the vehicle, opposite me and between Ashlee and George.

'It's a UNESCO World Heritage Site,' he adds.

'Do I look like I give a shit?' Joanne asks crossly from beside me.

'Oh, shoosh,' Dad says mildly. 'Not in front of the little ones, please.'

'Sod the little ones,' she snaps, not even looking at

Ashlee, who is right across from her. 'When are they leaving?'

'Shut your face, *now*,' George says angrily, and all of us look at him with alarm, including Ashlee, who peers with trepidation around Dad.

'It's okay, son, it's okay,' Dad says soothingly, patting George's knee.

I stare at George, watching his shoulders rise and fall with obvious agitation as he glares at Joanne. On my left, Jamie is rigid. On my right, Joanne sinks down in her seat, huddling in on herself with her head bowed.

'Sorry,' George mutters, turning to stare out of the rear window.

'We're almost there,' Dad says with another conciliatory pat on George's knee.

Beside me, Jamie relaxes. I remain tense for the rest of the journey.

When we get there, we go straight to the playground.

'Can I walk on ahead with George?' I ask Dad, who nods. 'Meet you back here in two hours if you don't catch us up,' I add.

'Okay, love.'

I can't imagine Ashlee wanting to leave the playground anytime soon.

Jamie is standing nearby, giving Joanne a pep talk. He's good with her, better than I am, in any case. I want to leave them to it.

'Let's go,' I say to George.

So much for a family outing.

We walk along the winding path in silence. I can tell George is still brooding about what happened in the car.

'Don't worry about it.' I bump his arm.

'I don't like losing my temper.'

'It's the first time I've *seen* you lose your temper. Come on, you're going to grind your teeth out if you don't relax. Take a deep breath.'

He does, letting the air out of his lungs with a long exhale.

The abbey ruins come into view, stretching across acres of green grass. The hollow shells of the stone buildings are mostly without roofs, but the tower stands tall and many of the walls still contain large arched windows, including the breathtakingly big one at the Chapel of Nine Altars.

I take George straight there, leading him along the length of the abbey to the very end.

George gazes up at the enormous arched window. It's open to the elements, framing the mottled sky beyond.

'Wow,' he says.

'Awe-inspiring, hey?'

He nods.

I'm glad this is his reaction. It was Jamie's reaction too, the first time he came here. I was only about ten and more interested in climbing the walls and finding the hidden spiral staircases, but I remember him standing and looking up at this window with a look of wonder on his face. He'd never been outside the city until he came to live with us. And in the days after he arrived, he would fidget uncontrollably. He was always on his feet, bouncing and jumpy and full of pent-up energy. But that day he just stood calmly and stared.

'Henry VIII has a lot to answer for,' George says as he studies a decorative detail carved into the stone.

He's been reading the leaflet we were given at the

entrance. The abbey was destroyed in 1539 when the King ordered the dissolution of the monasteries.

'Are you interested in history?' I ask.

'A bit.'

George is quiet at school, but he takes everything in. Last week our English teacher asked him a question and it took him ages to answer. A couple of the girls near me started sniggering, but then he gave a softly-spoken, involved explanation that shut everyone up. That's the thing. He thinks before he speaks. And his voice is measured rather than slow. He's bright.

We wander aimlessly. The cellarium still blows me away: a 300-foot-long span of room with a gorgeous vaulted ceiling that somehow survived when so much else was destroyed.

Birds circle over our heads as we come out into the open air. Grasses, ferns and flowers grow out of cracks in the walls, and occasionally the sun hits us through a break in the clouds and the stone glistens in the damp air.

I spot Joanne and Jamie coming down the hill and gesture towards the river, wanting to move on before they catch us up.

'What was your last foster home like?' I vaguely remember Dad saying that this is George's fourth placement, but I was eavesdropping at the time.

'Awful,' he replies in a low voice.

'How many have you been to?'

'After my aunt and before this, a couple,' he confirms. 'They couldn't have given two shits about any of us – definitely only in it for the money.'

I know the sort of carer he means. There are three distinct types: kin, people like my parents who are passionate and resilient, and those who are, as George says, 'only in it for the money'.

My parents hate to be lumped into this third category. Fostering *does* pay, but Mum and Dad spend so much of their own money on extras, from nice food to days out like this, not to mention trees for the tree planting ceremony, that they could never be accused of rolling in it.

'Were you mistreated?'

He shrugs. 'The first placement was appalling. Our so-called foster mam made one lass stand in the corner facing the wall for four hours, wouldn't even let her go to the bog. I was only there for a few weeks until they found a more permanent placement for me. The next lot simply didn't care. There was a lad who wet the bed and they couldn't be arsed to wash his sheets, so our room stank like nothing I'd ever known. No one was told to shower – I think I was the only one who bothered, half the time.'

'How did you leave?'

'Walked out.'

'You ran away?'

'No, I just said I was leaving and wouldn't be coming back. Or I might've said, "fuck this", but I went to school and asked them to contact my social worker. I told her that I wasn't going back so she'd better move me on or I *would* run away. She took me to your place.'

'I hope you like our place better than the last two?'

He smiles at me. 'Stop fishing for compliments.'

I laugh, feeling warm inside.

We're still walking on the grass beside the river, but it's widened out now, unrecognisable from the tumbling stream by the abbey. A family of swans glides beside us, a few metres away. George watches them.

'How are you feeling about sharing a room with Jamie?' I ask.

I know my parents want the study back, but they're giving Jamie a few days to get used to life without Preston.

'Fine,' he says. 'I like Jamie, he's a good lad.'

I smile. 'Yeah.'

'I hope he doesn't mind sharing with *me*.'

'He won't. I bet you'll be better company than Preston.'

I mean it as a joke, but I feel a twinge, even as I say it. Preston cried when he left us yesterday – we all did. Joanne still had red swollen eyes at dinner.

George gives me a curious look. 'What's the deal with Jamie's family?'

'He has eight brothers and sisters, half from different fathers. Five of his younger siblings have been adopted – Jamie hasn't even met three of them. His mother has learning difficulties and struggles to parent, but she keeps getting pregnant.'

She was only thirteen when she had her first baby.

'Does Jamie ever see her?'

I shake my head. 'Not in a while.'

When Jamie was taken into care, his mother kicked up such a fuss, but she hasn't turned up for a single one of his foster review meetings. At the same time, she's refused to give her permission for him to go on holiday with us in case it meant he'd miss one of her allocated visitation days. As a result, we basically stopped going on holiday, even though she's cancelled the visits more than she's attended them.

Jamie hasn't seen her in almost a year, but I don't think he minds – he's certainly not pushing for a meeting.

'What about his siblings?' George asks.

'He's in touch with his two older brothers, but you'd

have to talk to him about that,' I reply uneasily, partly avoiding the question.

Jamie isn't like George. When he came to us, he was in a terrible place. His home had been so chaotic and he was living in poverty, literally starving. He was so malnourished and skinny that he looked *my* age, not almost three years older. He used to eat his meals so fast that he'd throw them up afterwards, and he hoarded food too: stole it out of other children's bags at school and even shoplifted. He wouldn't think twice about eating anything edible that had fallen on the floor.

The teachers didn't understand – they hadn't had nearly enough training to know how to support him – and when the headteacher brought up the possibility of exclusion, Mum and Dad fought tooth and nail for Jamie to get the extra help that he needed. It's hard to believe any of this when you see him now.

It took him a while to get used to the peace and quiet at home, though. And then he *did* get used to it and the thought of having to go back to his own home again gave him nightmares. Jamie wanted to leave that life behind, *had* to, for his own sanity.

'Actually, maybe don't,' I say, changing my mind.

I doubt Jamie will want to talk to George about his siblings, and I don't think George will want to hear what Jamie has to say.

'Okay,' he replies, and I sense that he understands.

We've reached the landscaped Georgian Water Garden now and we cross over an old stone bridge that is coated with thick bright-green moss. Below us, the river stretches on, the man-made edges now dead straight and pristinely manicured. In the distance, there are two moon-shaped ponds and a round lake, complete with a central white neoclassical statue. But here, the landscape climbs steeply before us and visible amongst the thick forest of trees is a pretty round rotunda. The view is awesome from up there, but I'm not sure we have time to climb up.

'Uh-oh,' I say as it starts to rain. 'I didn't bring my raincoat.'

'Neither did I,' George replies.

'I'm sure it'll pass soon. The weather forecast said no rain.'

Up ahead, a stone grotto has been built into the hill. The incline around it rises so steeply that the roots of conifers are protruding from the dirt.

'They look like octopus tentacles,' George says, nodding at the tangle of roots.

He's right: one of the tree trunks has been cut away, giving even more of an impression of an octopus with an elongated body.

'You and your squid analogies,' I say with a smile. 'First there was the inky colour of the River Nidd, and now you've found your octopuses.'

He says nothing at first, and then he gives me a sidelong look, a twinkle in the depths of his dark eyes. 'I'm a man of many molluscs.'

I laugh loudly and he grins, making my insides bubble and fizz.

'Is English your favourite subject?' I ask.

He nods. 'Yeah. I've always liked it.'

The light pitter-pattering all around us suddenly breaks into a full-on pounding.

'Argh!' I squeal, taken by surprise.

'Over here,' George says, running towards the grotto.

We stumble into the small cave. It's damp and dark, but it's sheltered, and there's a small bench seat. We sit down and stare out of the toothy stone opening at the rain hammering down.

'I spoke to your dad about Sophie,' George says.

'What did he say?'

'He reckons he'll be able to organise a meeting.'

'That's brilliant!'

'Yeah. I hope she's okay. I dread to think what she's been going through after my experiences.'

'It's easier to place younger kids,' I reassure him. 'Her social worker probably had more options. *Nicer* options.'

'I wish she could've come here with me.'

'I wish she could've too.'

'I wondered if, maybe, when Ashlee and Nia leave – *if* Ashlee is adopted too – whether your parents might agree to take her.' He says all of this stutteringly, his voice full of uncertainty.

'That would be *amazing*,' I effuse.

He looks at me, his expression brightening with hope. 'Do you reckon it could happen?'

'I don't see why not. I'll ask my parents too, if you like.'

His relief is palpable and I feel a twinge of panic. I don't want to get his hopes up.

But why *wouldn't* my mum and dad take Sophie too?

I try to think of something else to say, some way to change the subject, but all I can think is that I'm cold. The rain has dampened my jeans and jumper. George is wearing black jeans and another band T-shirt – Pulp this time. His arms are bare, but I can't see any goosebumps.

'Aren't you cold?' I ask.

'No, I'm all right.' He glances at me. 'Are you?'

'A bit.'

'Come over here, then.' He jerks his head to indicate that I should edge closer, but he doesn't move himself.

I slide along the bench until we're almost, but not quite, touching. We're near enough that I can feel the body heat flowing from his skin.

'Have you seen Pulp live?' I ask with a nod at his T-shirt.

'Yeah, at the Leeds Festival last year.'

'Brill! I've never been to a festival.'

'No?'

'I've never even been to a gig.'

He looks surprised.

'Becky wants to go to Leeds this year, but my parents think I'm too young.'

'Jamie could take you? We went with my friend's older brother and a bunch of his mates. Or your parents could? I can imagine your dad, having a bit of a boogie.'

I laugh and he smiles.

'My parents don't have a lot of spare time.'

He gives me a sympathetic look, which is completely unexpected.

'But Jamie might be up for it,' I say with renewed hope. 'Who else did you see?'

George comes to life as he talks about music: Muse, The Strokes, the White Stripes, the Dandy Warhols... He has a lovely voice, all warm and deep, and right now he's more animated than I've ever seen him. I've edged further away so I can look at his face.

'Honestly, it was the best weekend of my life,' he says.

'Maybe *we* could go this summer?' I say with sudden excitement. 'You, me, Becky, Theo *and* Jamie?'

He nods, but he's lost some of his earlier energy, and I feel a little crushed at the realisation that he probably believes that his best memories are behind him, before his mother died, while he still had his sister, a permanent home and friends he'd grown up with. I can't imagine how it must have felt to be ripped away from it all.

'Do you miss your friends?' I ask as my enthusiasm for our last topic wanes.

He hesitates before nodding. 'I was part of a big group, though. I wasn't really close to anyone in particular. I'd say we were *mates* rather than friends. I haven't spoken to anyone in a while.'

'Oh. So you don't have a best mate?'

'Nope.'

'Maybe *I* can be your best mate,' I say jovially, elbowing his ribs. 'Theo and me. And Becky, when she's better.' I say Becky's name a bit reluctantly and feel a familiar pang of guilt.

Becky will like George and Theo, when she gets to know them, but I don't love the thought of that happening. She's so self-assured and funny – much more popular than me and always has been. I haven't minded. I love her and I love feeling warm under the glow of her affection. But sometimes, if I'm being honest, I feel overshadowed by her. Her personality is so sunshiny and attractive that I can't help but feel smaller in comparison.

With Theo and George, I don't feel small. I'm kind of enjoying having them to myself for a bit.

'Yeah, maybe.' George gives me a smile and I edge back in towards his body heat.

We fall silent. The rain is still coming down, but it's not as heavy. I'm strangely reluctant to leave our tiny shelter.

'Have you ever had a girlfriend?' I ask out of the blue.

'Not proper ones. We didn't kiss or anything. I'm not sure they really count. Have you?' he asks. 'Had a boyfriend, I mean.'

'No. Becky fancies Martin.' My stomach drops. 'Oh, shit,'

I gasp. 'Please don't tell anyone. I can't believe I just told you that!'

George laughs under his breath. 'I won't.'

I'm genuinely shocked that I've broken her confidence. Why did I tell him? Did I want him to think that she's unavailable?

He nudges my knee with his. 'Don't worry about it.'

'I feel so bad.'

'I can tell.' He leans against me, giving me what is supposed to be a gentle arm bump, but he doesn't fully move back to his starting position afterwards. The whole left-hand side of my arm is now brushing against his.

I don't move away either.

We fall silent, and I start to become aware of the clean-linen smell of him, his musky deodorant, his warm skin. The air around us begins to feel charged and I can't stop thinking about the place where his bare arm is touching mine. Is he as aware of it as I am? Where we were comfortably talking before, now I can't think of a single thing to say.

I hear him swallow.

Jamie appears in the jagged opening and we jerk apart. 'What are you dozy buggers doing, squirrelled away in there?' he asks with a grin.

'It was raining,' I exclaim, jumping to my feet and heading outside.

'I know. Joanne and I got soaked. It's stopped now, thankfully.'

The four of us make our way back to my parents together, but my head is only half on our conversation. The other half can't stop thinking about how it felt to be with George alone in the grotto.

15

NOW

It's close to eleven by the time George has dropped Becky home after our night out at the pub. She and I did stay for dessert. We were determined to end the evening on a high note.

'Thanks for this,' I say to George when we're back on the lane leading to our farm. 'You didn't have to.'

'I wanted to.'

We reach the farm and he begins to swing into a parking spot.

'Stop!' I cry as his headlights sweep over the lower paddock.

He slams on his brakes and we both jolt forward.

'What?' he gasps.

'Sorry, just...' I point at his tree, shining satiny white in the darkness.

'Oh. I know. It's grown so much.'

'I can't believe you got a tattoo of one.' The tree inked onto his arm is a silver birch.

He nods. 'After all that fuss about the tree ceremony, turns out I wanted to keep part of it with me when I left.'

'We still haven't talked about that,' I say quietly.

His *leaving*.

'I know.' He sighs. 'You haven't asked.'

'I think I'm asking now.'

Alcohol has lowered my defences.

George pulls on the handbrake and turns off the ignition. His headlights cut out and the night engulfs our view. 'What do you want to know?'

'Where did you go?' *When you ran away…*

'Leeds first, to Sophie's foster family's house. But I was too late: she'd already left for Devon.'

That was where he'd learned her adoptive family came from.

'How did you get to Leeds?' I've always wondered.

'I climbed into a car boot up at Brimham Rocks when some people were leaving. They had a Leeds United sticker on the window, so I hoped they were heading there. Unfortunately, they went to a tiny village somewhere on the East coast, and then I got stuck in the boot and no one heard me banging until the next morning.'

I can scarcely believe what I'm hearing. 'You could have *died!*'

'I was in a state, Leah. I wasn't thinking.'

'How did you get to Leeds from there?' I hardly dare ask.

He sighs. 'Well, I didn't have any money on me, so to start with I walked and tried to hitchhike, but when no one picked me up, I'm afraid I broke into a house and stole a wallet from a sideboard.'

He notes my shocked reaction and averts his gaze. I don't

think he can bring himself to look at me.

'What if you'd been arrested?!'

'Like I told you, I wasn't thinking.' He sounds morose. 'I was single-mindedly trying to get to Sophie. But when I got there – train, in the end – she'd already left. I had just enough money for a ticket to Devon, so I headed straight there.'

It's traumatising to think of fifteen-year-old George going through all that.

'Why *did* you leave us so suddenly? It's something I've never understood. You didn't take clothes or money or *anything*.'

He didn't even take his iPod – I could've listened to his songs till my ears bled. I probably would have, but one day it simply stopped working.

'Don't try to make sense of it,' he mutters.

The car falls silent. But there's still so much I want to know.

'What did you do when you got to Devon?'

'I got a job washing dishes at an Indian restaurant in Dartmouth. The owner took pity on me and let me sleep in a back room. He kept me off the streets. Over time, I scoured the county, but never found her.'

'You didn't go back into the system?'

He shakes his head. 'Nah, I was done with that.'

'Did you stay in Devon?'

He nods. 'Then one day I saw that article about your parents and their so-called "Foster Farm". Stumbled across it online.'

'You wrote to my parents...'

'And they replied.'

'They *replied*? How did they get your address?'

'I wrote it on the back of the envelope.'

I feel as though I've been winded. I didn't think to ask my parents if George had included his personal details – the card only had his message. I can't believe that, by default, he's been in my life for the past two years.

Not that I would have had the emotional strength then to face that fact.

'Did you write to them again?' I ask.

'A couple of times.'

'And you never asked them for *my* address?'

And they never mentioned it?

No wonder he seemed so familiar with Mum at the funeral.

'Leah, I'm sorry,' he says in a gruff voice. 'I asked after you and your mam told me what had happened to Theo. I wanted to contact you, but I didn't think you'd want to hear from me.'

'What made you think that?' I realise I'm raising my voice, but I can't help it.

'After the way I left.' He sounds frustrated. 'And when you and Theo became a thing... I don't know, I thought you'd moved on; you wouldn't want a blast from the past.'

'Wait. When are you talking about? When Theo and I became a "thing", as you put it?'

He looks out of his window at the night beyond.

'*George.*'

'I kept tabs on you,' he reluctantly admits.

'What do you mean?'

'This is going to sound stalkery.' He hesitates before confessing: 'I friended Becky on Facebook.'

'You *what*?!' I turn to face him.

He rakes his hand through his curls, looking uncomfortable. 'Not under my real name. I created a fake profile.'

'Why didn't you friend *me*?' I squawk.

'I didn't want you to know it was me, and you would've seen through it. Becky used to say yes to everyone.'

It's true, she did.

He sighs. 'I knew that you and Theo went to London together. It was obvious that you guys were happy. And at some point, I had to let you go and move on myself. So I deleted my account.'

A lump swells in my throat. The thought of him checking up on Theo and me hurts. The thought of him deciding not to reach out to us hurts. It hurts because I know *he* was hurting.

'I wish you'd got in contact.'

He doesn't comment.

I brush away a stray tear.

'When you say you moved on... Were you happy?' *Did you meet someone else?*

'Yeah, sort of.' He casts me a small smile and then his face falls. 'Hey, I didn't mean to upset you,' he says huskily, reaching out with his hand before retracting it. He folds his arms across his chest instead of touching me and I ache for the missed contact.

'Why did you come back now?'

The silence stretches on. He's staring straight ahead. The trees are cut-out shapes in the starry sky.

I wait, and finally it comes: 'I guess I felt as though there was unfinished business.'

'Unfinished business?'

'I wanted to tie up some loose ends.' He glances at me again, his dark eyes glinting in the moonlight. 'I *tried* to move on. I didn't say I succeeded.'

'Do you— Did you— Is there anyone else in your life?'

'A girlfriend, you mean? No. Not anymore.'

'Was it— Was it serious? Did you break up recently?'

Why can't I speak properly?

'About six months ago.'

He hasn't answered the first part of my question.

'What happened?'

'I don't know, Leah. This is probably a conversation for another time.'

'Oh, sorry,' I say with embarrassment. 'Yes, you're right. It's late.' I pick up my bag from the floor. 'Ta for the lift.'

'Can I make a suggestion?' George asks.

I nod stiffly.

'Write to Theo.'

I stare at him.

'Write to him. Tell him about the little things, the things that he's missing out on. Write to him, the way I used to write to Sophie. I didn't know if she'd ever get my letters, but it made me feel better to put it all out there in any case.' He scratches the top of his head. 'Sorry if I'm overstepping the mark.'

I shake my head quickly. 'No. It feels good to talk to you again.'

He looks relieved.

'Goodnight, George.' I open the door.

'Hang on.' He swings his own door open and jumps out. He's around at the passenger side in seconds.

'You didn't need to do that,' I say, but I accept his hand anyway and a fizzing warmth travels up my arm as he helps me down from the cab. I let go of his hand reluctantly, not objecting when it becomes clear he's walking me to the front door.

'See you tomorrow,' he says when we reach it.

Do we hug goodbye? Kiss?

In the end we do neither. But my pulse continues to race as I close the door behind me.

16

THEN

Becky is back at school on the Monday after we go to Fountains Abbey. It's a shock to see her sitting on the bus – she hasn't been in touch since Saturday morning.

'Surprise,' she says weakly, as I walk down the aisle towards her. My smile is ever so slightly a mask, as I feel quite torn when George slides into what became my new regular row over the last couple of weeks.

'How are you feeling?' I ask as I sit down, ignoring Joanne, who stomps past Becky to a seat at the back.

'Absolutely knackered,' she replies grouchily, smoothing her hand over her long dark hair. It's tied up in a pristine high ponytail and she still looks beautiful, even though there are dark circles under her eyes and she's lost weight that she definitely didn't need to shift.

'Why are you in?' I ask, mystified.

'I'm so bored at home,' she moans. 'But don't expect me to be good company.'

'Okay. I'm glad you're here.'

'What's new?' she asks. 'Has Martin asked after me again?' she whispers.

'Not since the week before last,' I whisper back. 'But he's been much more subdued than usual, so I'm sure he's missed you,' I add hurriedly.

This seems to pacify her. She rests her head on my shoulder.

'I'm sorry I've been ill,' she murmurs sleepily. 'I hope you weren't too lonely.'

I stare at the back of George's head, a fresh wave of disappointment pulsing through me.

Last night I couldn't sleep because I kept imagining this journey to school. I was planning on asking him if he'd play me a couple of the songs by the bands at the festival. I know he still brings his headphones and iPod to school, even though he hasn't listened to music while we've been sitting on the bus together.

When Theo boards, I feel another pang. He sees that I'm with Becky and smiles, giving me a small wave. I wave in return before he swings into the seat next to George.

'Is he speaking now?' Becky looks taken aback.

I shrug. 'Yeah, sort of. We've sort of become friends,' I say awkwardly.

She stares at me. '*How*?'

She sounds almost accusatory, and I can't really blame her. We have spoken while she's been off ill and I went to see her last Wednesday after school, but, I don't know, I kind of thought she might feel left out if I told her I was forming bonds with people in her absence. So I've let her lead our conversations and text exchanges.

I fill her in about Theo's scrap with Pete and how George and I went after him. I play it down, but realise I've probably done this a bit too much because she stiffens when I mention that Theo came over on Friday after school.

'I'm not sure you've missed me at all,' she teases, but her smile is shaky and I know she needs reassurance.

'You've got to be kidding,' I say vehemently. 'I've missed you *violently*. I'm so glad you're back.'

'Don't get used to it. The doctor said I'll probably have a "patchy return". I think I'm going to be so tired after today that I might not be in for the rest of the week.'

I *hate* that I don't hate the sound of this.

At lunchtime, I ask Becky if we can go and sit with Theo and George on the field, but she needs persuading. I realise that it's probably the first time I've taken the lead in making friends, and I suspect this has thrown her, but she agrees eventually, mostly because I point out that it might make Martin jealous.

I'm nervous as we make our way over to them. When the sun breaks through the cotton wool clouds, it's got real heat to it, and Theo is currently lying on his back with his arms behind his head and his face up to the sky.

George, on the other hand, watches our approach, his dark eyes giving away no clue as to whether he's glad to have our company.

'Hi,' I say.

'Oh, hello.' Theo smiles and props himself up on his hands.

'Can we join you?'

'As if you need to ask,' he teases, pulling up a handful of daisy-strewn grass and throwing it at me.

'Steady with the hay fever irritants,' Becky says drily, sitting down.

'Neither of us gets hay fever,' I tell Theo hastily as my stomach twists, but he doesn't seem fazed by Becky's cool attitude.

'Are you feeling all right now?' George asks Becky, setting the conversation on another course as I collect a few daisies together and attempt to make a chain.

Theo copies me.

'A bit.'

'This one's been moping.' He nods at me.

'Aw.' She seems mollified.

I smile at her. 'I told George that we want to go to Leeds Festival this summer. He went a couple of years ago.'

'Did you?' She perks up. 'Who was headlining?'

'The Strokes.'

'The White Stripes are headlining this year,' Theo says, threading a daisy through the stem of another.

'Oh, I *love* them!' Becky exclaims. 'We *have* to go,' she says to me. 'You've *got* to persuade your parents.'

'George suggested we ask Jamie to take us,' I reply.

'Shall we *all* go?' she asks excitedly, her attention moving from George to Theo. 'We could get a whole group together!'

'I'd be up for it,' Theo replies, handing me his chain so I can connect it to mine.

I smile at him and glance at George.

George nods. 'Sure.'

Becky *beams*.

I let out the breath I hadn't known I was holding. I don't mind that Becky will forever think that this was her idea – as long as it happens, I don't mind at all.

. . .

'Hello, you lot,' Mum calls cheerfully when we arrive home after school on Friday. Through the open door to the living room, I can see a stack of Life Story books out on the coffee table. Mum must've been updating them.

These are the memory books that are started by social workers and passed onto foster carers to continue with. They're supposed to preserve the memories of children in care and record who might've been important to them at different stages in their lives, from their parents to their foster families. One day in the future, when they're ready, they'll have these books to look through and help make sense of their pasts.

'George, I've washed your sheets and made up your bed, but you need to take your things upstairs, okay?' Mum says.

'Okay.' He nods and heads for the study, but she stops him. 'There's no rush. Have something to eat first. Ivan wants to talk to you too.'

'What about?'

'Here he is,' she says as Dad walks into the kitchen.

'Ah, George, I finally got hold of your social worker today.'

He's been trying all week, but, and I quote: 'That woman is always in bloody meetings!'

'She promised to call Sophie's social worker first thing on Monday to see if we can get you two together. I'll keep chasing.'

'Thank you,' George replies gratefully.

I did speak to my parents about Sophie coming to live with us if Ashlee and Nia leave soon. Dad said we'd have to wait and see how the land lay, but he didn't seem opposed to the idea.

'Have some banana bread,' Mum urges. She's made a fresh loaf.

'No, thanks. I want to get my room sorted.'

'Do you need any help packing up?' I call after him as he heads to the study.

'Nope, everything's ready; I've just got to take it upstairs.'

After I've eaten and caught up with my parents, I go and get changed out of my uniform. As I exit my room, I see Joanne sitting on the floor of hers, holding Ashlee's teddy, Dolly.

I pause in the doorway. 'You okay?'

She jolts and casts Dolly aside. 'Yeah, fine,' she snaps.

'Where's Ashlee?'

'How should I know?' she replies, getting up and slamming her door in my face.

Nia's adoptive parents are coming for a visit in the morning. I'm glad Dad's taking Joanne to the market with him as I can't imagine her helping Ashlee's cause if she's here.

Jamie pokes his head out of his room. 'Psst!' He jerks his head back over his shoulder, indicating that I should follow.

I do, stopping short at the sight of George lying on what used to be Preston's bed, his headphones in, his eyes closed and his foot tapping. He already looks at home.

Jamie closes the door behind me, and when I next look at George, his eyes have opened. He takes his headphones out.

'What's up?' I ask Jamie, wanting George to know that he brought me in here – I wouldn't encroach on his personal space otherwise.

He nods towards the girls' bedroom.

'School photos today, that's why she's in a mood. That and the thought of Nia and Ashlee leaving.'

I let out a sharp laugh. 'You're joking, right?'

It's his second claim that I take issue with. I understand why she'd be irritable about school photos. Joanne is not allowed to be photographed because her identity has to remain a secret. Understandably, she doesn't want to be reminded of her precarious situation.

Jamie shakes his head, deadly serious. 'I'm not joking. It's all bullshit, all that stuff she says about wanting the room to herself. Ivan told her she could have the study, but she wasn't interested. She *likes* being in with the little ones – she's only lashing out because she can't stand the thought of losing them.'

I narrow my eyes at him dubiously.

'I'm not kidding. It's a front. I caught her crying last night. She's devastated about Preston going. Can't handle goodbyes, not like you and I can. She's put up this shield around herself, but you forget that she's only a kid. Barely thirteen. She's got major attachment issues – pushes us all away because she thinks we're going to leave her too. We need to look out for her.'

I sit down on the end of George's bed, feeling flummoxed. I don't realise I'm actually sitting *on* George's bed until he edges away from me, grabbing a pillow to prop himself up against the wall. Only then do I feel self-conscious.

'Why would she have a problem with it being school photos day?' George asks, baffled.

Jamie explains.

'Who's a threat to her?' he asks.

I almost want to cover my ears with my hands, but I resist.

'Her mum's a schizophrenic drug addict. Used to take Joanne's bus money and make her walk four miles to and from school every day. She was really violent and aggressive, but Joanne reckons she could handle her; it was her mum's boyfriend who was the problem. He's a predator. He kept trying to give her lifts to school, and was texting her lewd messages and photographs. He turned up at her school, looking for her, after she was taken into care. She was moved here for her own safety, but she had to leave behind all her mates.'

'Christ,' George says.

'I didn't know,' I murmur, horrified.

'I feel bad for telling her to shut her face in the car the other day.'

'Don't worry about it,' Jamie replies to George. 'But we need to look out for her now, okay? Do what we can to cheer her up.'

George and I nod.

The following morning, Jamie goes with Joanne and Dad to the market, while I stay behind and help Mum get Ashlee and Nia ready for their visit.

'What should Ashlee wear?' I ask Mum.

'You choose, love. Maybe leggings and a T-shirt?'

I avoid white, knowing it's likely to get grubby between now and when Anita and Ollie, the couple in line to adopt Nia, arrive at 10 a.m. A lot can happen in an hour.

'What do you want me to do when they come?'

'I'd love you to stick around,' Mum replies. 'If you do some colouring or something with Ashlee in the kitchen, they'll get to see her without it being too obvious.'

'I can't believe we're actually trying to get rid of her,' I murmur, my throat thickening.

'Neither can I,' Mum replies in a similarly husky voice. 'Can you find George? It would be good if he's on hand too.'

'Is he in his room?'

'I think he's downstairs.'

I find a note from him on the kitchen table.

Gone up to Hare Heads, it says in neat handwriting that has a slight slant to the left.

I call up to Mum.

'Ooh, would you walk up with Ashlee and bring him back?' she asks eagerly, appearing at the top of the stairs. 'The three of you could come back after Anita and Ollie arrive. That would look quite good, actually. As long as you don't wear Ashlee out too much!'

'You're so devious,' I tease.

'Anything to get the best for my kids,' she replies with a grin.

Ashlee's legs don't carry her uphill very fast, so it takes us almost half an hour to reach the rocks. But with Mum's plan in place, we've got time to kill.

'Hey,' I say to George when we finally arrive at the overhang. I've carried Ashlee the last part of the way and now I put her down with a groan and hunch over, huffing and puffing. She mimics me, which is hilarious – even George can't help laughing.

'What are you up to?' I ask him.

'Writing.' The pages of his notepad flutter in the wind.

'Homework?'

'No, a letter.'

'Oh. Who to?'

'Sophie.'

'I didn't know you wrote to her.'

He looks down at his pad. 'Often. Hopefully one day she'll read them.' He lifts his head and nods towards Ashlee. 'I thought Nia had a visit this morning.'

'She does.' I explain Mum's plan.

'So she wants me to come and play happy families?'

His tone is neutral, but I have no idea if he minds.

'Exactly,' I reply truthfully.

'Okay.' He sighs and gets up.

'Really? Thank you.'

'Anything to help,' he says drily.

I look past him to see a car coming along the lane. 'Oh no, they're early! Quick!' I pick up Ashlee and scramble down the rocks.

'Careful!' George calls out, sounding panicked. 'Let me take her.'

'Are you sure?'

'I'm sure. Is that okay, Ashlee?' he asks. 'You want a piggyback?'

'A piggyback!' I exclaim, trying to get her excited.

Ashlee smiles shyly and I put her down on the edge of a rock, while George passes me his notepad and faces away.

'One, two, three, UP!' I lift her onto George's back.

'Let's go!' he yells, and my heart swells as he jogs off down the path.

I don't mean to look, but I can't help noticing the words written across the top page of George's notepad:

Dear Sophie,
I miss you, little one.

My eyes fill with tears. The wind carries them away, along with the sound of Ashlee giggling.

17

NOW

I t's late Wednesday afternoon, a few days after my evening out with Becky and my late-night conversation with George. I've been thinking about what George said.

I stare down at the notepad in my hands. A blank page, except for two words: *Dear Theo*.

When Theo went back to boarding school, I wrote to him all the time, but now there's so much to say that I don't know where to start. Maybe that's my opening.

Dear Theo,

We used to write all the time, but now there's so much to say that I don't know where to start. I guess I'll start with here and now.

I'm up at Hare Heads, sitting on our rock with my legs dangling over the edge. The grassy paddocks of the farms are spread out before me, but behind me and all around, the heather is out, a rolling sea of pinky purple amongst the vivid green fern fronds. It's the middle of August and I wish you were here.

I saw Katy the other day – it was a shock. I can't stop thinking about where we'd be and what we'd be doing if she had simply sent us a message to let us know she was safe. Would we be sitting on a sandy white beach in Brisbane, building sandcastles with Emilie? Would you be creating a masterpiece with fortress walls and seashell towers and letting her knock it down? I bet that you would.

It feels so surreal to think that we should be on the other side of the world right now. But instead, she and I are here at my childhood home in North Yorkshire, and oddly, it doesn't feel wrong at all.

I wish you could see Emilie. She loves it here. She collects the chicken eggs every day along with as many stray feathers as she can lay her hands on. Mum's going to teach her how to knit a mini cushion for one of her teddy bears. Emilie is loving spending more time with her. I think it's really helped Mum to have the diversion since Dad's death too. She'd probably go back to fostering, given half the chance...

As I write, the subject of George presses down heavily on me. I have no idea how to put into words that the boy I loved is back in my life when the man I married is agonisingly absent.

It doesn't help that I saw George drive in a while ago.

I've been half watching from up here as he's loaded gear from the back of his truck onto the quad bike. Now he's standing in the lower part of the paddock adjacent to the girls, staring up at a big horse chestnut tree. The underside of the tree is dead straight and perfectly manicured, thanks to the girls sometimes being allowed into that paddock to graze.

George walks over to the quad bike and pulls on a helmet, then grabs some equipment before disappearing under the tree. Soon afterwards, the sound of a chainsaw carries towards me on the breeze.

I sit up straighter with alarm.

Dad rarely used a chainsaw himself, and he wouldn't let Jamie anywhere near one. Tree work is for tree surgeons, *not* for amateurs.

I quickly sign off my letter to Theo, telling him that I love him and that I'll write again soon. Stuffing the pages into an envelope, I scribble his name across the front, then hurry back down to the farm, feeling bad about not managing to give my husband my full attention.

George is halfway up the tree when I reach him and my heart is in my throat as I watch him carving his way through a branch. He appears to be wearing a safety harness, although where that came from, I have no idea. I don't want to distract him and risk causing him harm, but I'm not sure how to get his attention without shouting. Thankfully he saves me from my dilemma and the chainsaw splutters to a silence.

'George!'

His face appears around the side of the bough he's sitting on. 'Hello.'

'What are you up to?' I don't mean to sound cross – he's only trying to help.

'I'm taking off some of the dead branches. They're a hazard to the girls if they graze in here.'

'I'm worried you're going to chop a limb off.'

'I know what I'm doing,' he replies patiently, disappearing back behind the branch.

'We can call tree surgeons in! Please come down.'

I hear his low deep chuckle. 'Leah. I really do know what I'm doing.' He sounds amused. 'I'm a trained forester.'

'You're *what*?'

'I worked for Forestry England before I came here.'

Excuse me while I scrape my jaw off the ground.

His face reappears. 'You thought I'd been stuck behind a bar all this time?'

Yes, I did. Not that it mattered, *but I had assumed...*

'Why didn't you tell me before?'

He shrugs. 'It hasn't come up.'

'Did you work there for long?'

'About five years.' He glances down at me. 'Shall we talk about this later? I'd like to crack on before the wind picks up again.'

'Oh, sure.' I walk away, my cheeks flushed.

The chainsaw restarts.

Mum will be gone for at least another hour so I get on with feeding the herd. We have thirty-seven alpacas now – twenty-four girls and thirteen boys – but we'd probably have double that if my parents had stuck to only selling yarn and alpaca products. They had to accept that they wouldn't always be able to cope with the size of their growing herd, so their main income in recent years has come from breeding and selling cria. I know it pained Dad and will continue to sadden Mum to say goodbye to any of the animals, but they go to good homes – my parents have always made sure of it.

I feed the boys first and then the girls, wandering

amongst them and dispersing buckets as I go. Mum likes to feed each animal separately to make sure they all get their fair share. It's a bit of a hassle, but they're so low maintenance generally that it feels like the least we can do.

Bellflower is more interested in playing with Bramble than eating. I pause, staring at them.

'You're very deep in thought.'

The sight of George, hanging over the drystone wall, makes me jolt. He has a slight sheen on his brow and his long-sleeved checked shirt is rolled up to his elbows, revealing a light coating of sawdust on the brown hairs of his muscled forearms.

'I'm wondering why Bramble is so much bigger than Bellflower.'

'Is she pregnant?'

'She can't be. I mean, we tried to mate her last month, but she wasn't having any of it.'

George raises an eyebrow.

'They spit if they're not interested,' I explain.

He looks amused. 'That's one way of saying "no", I suppose.'

Alpacas can fall pregnant at any time of year, but we mate ours in July so they're born the following June when their mothers will have had the benefit of feeding on lots of lovely spring grass.

'They also spit if they're already expecting,' I say. 'But I don't understand how she could have mated. She looks about six months gone.'

'Could she have escaped?'

'They have been known to get out via the field gate if someone has left it open – tourists sometimes stray from the footpaths. But that doesn't explain how she got into the boys' paddock.'

'One of the drystone walls did have a weak point...' George says thoughtfully.

I remember Jamie saying that now. 'In the boys' paddock?'

He nods. 'I helped to rebuild it.'

'Did you?' I ask with surprise. I really hope my mum is paying him well. 'Goodness me,' I murmur, reaching out to stroke Bramble's super-soft neck. 'Have you been looking for love?'

Her big dark eyes stare back at me unwaveringly.

'I guess we'll find out who the lucky boy was in a few months.'

'How will you tell?'

'The cria often take on characteristics of the father.'

I start to gather up empty buckets. George comes through the gate to lend a hand. I don't resist his help, even though I can manage on my own.

'Have you finished chopping back the dead wood?' I nod towards the horse chestnut.

'Yep. I still need to clear it, but I'll come back tomorrow to do that.'

'I hope you're keeping an accurate log of your hours.'

He doesn't reply.

'George?'

He shakes his head, setting off down the hill. 'I don't want payment for this.'

My mouth falls open as I hurry after him. 'You've got to be kidding. You are *absolutely* getting paid. You've been paid for the work you've done so far, right?'

Again, silence.

'George!' I'm horrified. 'I need to have a word with my mother.'

He looks sheepish. 'She keeps asking for my bank account details.'

'Bloody hell! *Give* them to her.'

'I make enough at the pub. I want to help.'

'No. That is completely unacceptable.' I realise I'm using my 'telling off Emilie' voice and check myself. 'You didn't do all that training for nothing.' We reach the barn and return the buckets to the shelf.

'Do you want to come in for a brew?' I ask.

'I've got a shift at the pub,' he replies reluctantly. He stares down at me for a long moment. 'Are you up to anything tomorrow night?'

'No. Why?'

'I've got the evening off. Maybe we could catch up.'

'That would be nice,' I say with a smile.

Later I beat myself up about how easily I agreed to spend a whole evening with him. But the truth is, I'm lonely and craving adult company, even more so after my night out with Becky. I've spent the last two years giving Emilie almost a hundred per cent of my attention. Is it so awful that I want to spend time with my old friends? With *George*?

However much I rationalise it, I can't shake my feelings of guilt. I hope Theo will forgive me.

18

THEN

'Seriously, feel how soft it is.' I offer a big handful of snowy white fibre to Theo. 'It's like cuddling cloud.'

He takes it from me dubiously and his dark eyebrows shoot up. 'It really is.'

It's weird having Theo here without George. Dad has taken George to visit his dad in prison, but I didn't realise that was happening when I invited Theo over to work on our art projects. We're studying portraits. Theo is sketching me, I'm supposed to be drawing George and George was supposed to be doing Theo, but before George left this morning, he said Theo and I should just draw each other instead. He said he'd ask Jamie to sit for him when he got home.

I didn't like seeing George so subdued. He was surprisingly upbeat when we returned to the farm yesterday for Anita and Ollie's visit. We stayed in the kitchen for most of it, drawing pictures with Ashlee and letting her go between us and Mum and Nia, who were in the living room.

I liked Anita and Ollie, despite everything. To my surprise, Ashlee seemed to like them too. She's normally very shy around new people, but she was keen to show them her artwork.

It was completely obvious what we were doing, Mum said afterwards, but she didn't think that was a bad thing. '*It'll give them something to think about,*' she said with certainty, while waving brightly as their car drove off down the lane.

Ashlee's social worker plans to get in touch with them on Monday. We'll have to wait and see if anything comes of it.

It's a dazzling sunny day and the thought of sitting inside at the dining room table doesn't appeal to either Theo or me, so we've decided to walk up to Brimham Rocks.

Mistletoe comes up to Theo as we make our way through the girls' paddock.

'Hello,' he says.

Her dark eyes stare at him inquisitively and her ears flick backwards before coming forward again. She cranes her long neck towards him and sniffs. He reaches out to pat her and she jerks away, trotting off towards Marigold.

'They were born last year,' I tell him. 'It was Marigold's fleece that you felt earlier. That's her there. And that's her mum,' I point out Ivy.

As if sensing we're talking about her, Ivy wanders over, coming right up close to Theo's face. He doesn't even flinch. Tentatively he reaches out. Ivy sniffs his face and makes a small humming noise. Theo's hand connects with her neck and a smile tilts the corner of his lips.

I'm kind of astonished. 'She doesn't normally let strangers anywhere near her.'

'She can probably sense that I like animals more than I do people.'

'Maybe you should do Ivy's portrait,' I joke.

He smiles at me. 'You're not getting out of it.'

'Come on, then.'

We head to the same big flat rock that I took George to. This time, though, Theo and I face each other, rather than the rolling landscape.

He's wearing a faded grey T-shirt with black jeans and looks so different out of his school uniform.

'Who's going first?' I ask.

'Let's go at the same time,' he replies, getting his pad out of his bag.

'Really? How will that work?'

'Ask me to pause if you need me to,' he says casually, and then to my surprise, he starts to sketch.

'Hold on, I'm not ready yet.'

'Take your time,' he murmurs, his pencil working quickly over the paper and his eyes darting up to my face and down again.

I'm nervous as I turn to a fresh page of my own. It feels disconcerting to be under scrutiny.

I focus on sketching the shape of Theo's face. His hair is helping. It's falling in its usual dark slash across his forehead, meaning I could probably get away with only doing one eye, the one that's not obscured. Every time he glances up, his hair swishes aside and navy blue glints at me.

His hair isn't as dark under the sunlight. Sometimes it looks like it's black, but now it's a very dark brown.

'Did your mother have dark hair?' I ask, breaking the intense silence.

Theo's pencil jars to a stop. He nods abruptly, his eyes flicking to mine and sliding away again. 'Yeah. I look like her.'

'Do you remember her?'

'Not as much as I'd like to,' he replies in a low murmur, still sketching away.

'You were six when you lost her?'

He nods, pressing his lips together at the memory.

'When did your dad remarry?'

'When I was seven.'

'Oh.'

'Yeah. He doesn't fuck around.' He snorts, back to his usual caustic self. 'Actually, it turns out he *did* fuck around. Last Christmas, Sylvie, my wicked stepmother, dropped in that she and dear old Daddy were celebrating ten years together. The bastards had the nerve to toast each other over the roast turkey.'

My mouth drops open. 'He was seeing her when your mum was still alive?'

'While my mum was battling cancer. Yep.' He says this nonchalantly, but I can't imagine how much hurt he's carrying.

'Is that why you acted up at boarding school?' I've long since stopped drawing, but Theo is still at it.

He laughs. 'The reason I got expelled?' He shrugs. 'I was done with it anyway. Sick of the rules and regulations. I needed a change of scene.'

'When did you start boarding?'

'When I was six.'

'The same year your mother died?'

'Straight after,' he mutters.

I'm horrified at the thought of Theo being sent away to school as a six-year-old while he was grieving the death of his beloved mum.

He breaks me out of my daze by nodding at my pad. 'How are you getting on?'

'I haven't done much yet.'

'Show me.'

I turn the pad around, squirming. I'm not the best artist in the world. He nods and carries on drawing.

'Can I see mine?'

He shakes his head.

'Oi! That's not fair,' I protest.

'Who said life was fair?'

I roll my eyes and sweep my light-brown hair over one shoulder. We're sheltered from the breeze here and the sun is surprisingly strong today.

'Can you put it back where it was.' It's a command, not a request, but I oblige him, lifting my long, slightly wavy locks to fall down my back.

'You must see a lot of shit around here,' he says. 'Mine can't be the only sob story you've heard.'

'Far from it. Doesn't make any of it easier, though.'

'You don't ever find yourself getting a bit immune to it all?'

'I can't imagine ever being immune to it, although I know people can get compassion fatigue. Mum and Dad have had real issues with the occasional social worker. Don't get me wrong, many of them are incredible. But they're all so overworked and underpaid – Mum knows because she used to be one. She thinks that if young people start becoming just another case number, care workers should quit and do something else.'

'Keep still a minute,' he says.

I freeze.

'Lift your chin a bit...'

I try to follow his direction. He leans forward and stares right into my eyes, his gaze shifting only a minuscule amount as he sketches. I almost have the feeling he's looking through me, rather than at me. There's no connection – he's focused on his work.

He has very long lashes. His eyes are so dark blue. They're really stunning, actually.

Just as I think that thought, his pencil pauses.

The two of us stare at each other, not moving a muscle.

My cheeks begin to warm and I avert my gaze.

He laughs under his breath. 'I won that one.'

My eyes shoot back to him. 'Are you having staring contests with me?'

'Come on,' he gently reproaches me. 'Don't pretend you're not aware of it.'

I smirk and reposition my pencil. I feel his gaze on me and when I glance up, he's grinning. He turns the pad around.

'Holy shit,' I murmur, snatching the pad from him so I can study his drawing properly. It's really good, like, *unbelievably* good.

'Theo, this is amazing. How the hell did you learn to draw like this?'

My sketch in comparison is laughable. I've barely got the shape of his face down – he's done shading and everything. I'm blown away.

I glance up, waiting for his answer.

He shrugs. 'My mother used to paint. I guess I got it from her. My father doesn't approve. He said I could take Art A level over his dead body.'

I frown. 'Did you do Art at boarding school?'

'Oh, plenty,' he replies with a grin. 'I did a lovely piece all over the outside of the gym wall just before I left.'

'You graffitied? That's so naughty!'

'I bet you've never done a naughty thing in your whole life,' he says in that low sexy tone of his.

I blush and look down. 'My parents have enough to deal with without me adding to the burden.'

'So you have to be the good girl?' I glance up to see that his brow has furrowed. He's no longer joking about. 'That must be tiring.'

I shrug. 'I'm naturally pretty well behaved. The thought of graffitiing all over the gym wall...' I laugh. 'What did you draw?'

He grins evilly. 'A couple of my masters with great big dicks coming out of their foreheads.'

'No!'

He shrugs. 'Not very original, but it felt fucking great to do it.'

'I'm not surprised you got expelled!'

He laughs. 'Yeah, no, neither am I.'

'Is it so bad having to go to our school?'

'It's all right,' he says. 'To be honest, I'm just killing time until I work out what I'm going to do.'

'Do you have any idea what that will be?'

'Getting as far away from my family as possible.'

'You're moving to Australia then?' I ask with a smile.

'Wouldn't that be great?' He stares up at the clear blue sky. 'Hell, yeah, I'd do that in a millisecond.'

'You'd better marry an Aussie girl.'

He raises an eyebrow at me. 'Know any?'

'No, but I'll keep my eyes and ears open.'

'Sounds like a plan. Maybe I'll meet one at university.'

'Do you know where you want to go?'

'I'd love to go to the RCA.'

'The RCA?'

'The Royal College of Art – it's in London.'

'Awesome.'

'Yeah, but I have to find a way to get myself there as "Daddy" won't pay. What about you?'

'I don't have a clue.'

He nods at my drawing. 'Maybe not Art.'

I whack him over his head with my pad. I do it softly, but he bats it away and squawks as though I've hit him with a cement block.

'Give it here,' he says with a smile, holding his hand out.

I pass him the pad.

'Let's swap over. The light is better from where I'm sitting.'

'Kind of you to make excuses for me,' I say as we stand up and switch positions.

'Or you could give up and do George later,' he says. 'I don't have all day.'

'How rude!'

'You know that about me already.'

That afternoon, I stand in the corridor and knock on Jamie and George's bedroom door.

'George? Are you in there?'

He got back from visiting his father in prison an hour ago. Dad said he was very quiet on the way home – he doesn't think he'll want company.

'George?'

Still no answer.

I open the door. The room is empty.

Mum comes along the corridor, carrying Nia.

'Do you know where George is?' I ask.

'He went outside.'

'Did you see in which direction?'

'Towards the stream? The lower paddock? I'm not sure. Ouch,' she says as Nia grabs a fistful of her hair.

'Okay.' I close his door and go downstairs to pull on my wellies.

George is not by the stream or the chicken pen, nor is he with the boys in the lower paddock. I find him in our small wood, leaning against the big old oak that was here long before any of us.

He looks over at me as my boots crackle through the path of fallen twigs.

'Hi,' I say gently, coming to a stop in front of him.

He's balancing a notepad on his lap and is holding a pen in his left hand. The page is half full of his handwriting. Another letter to Sophie, I presume.

'I thought you were doing your Art homework.'

'No.'

'You know it's due tomorrow?'

He shrugs and gazes up at me, his expression bleak.

'Are you okay?'

He shrugs again, more half-heartedly.

I almost ask if he wants to be left in peace, but something makes me sit down next to him instead.

Neither of us says anything as we listen to the rustling of the leaves overhead.

I shift slightly and my shoulder brushes his. He doesn't move away.

After a while he closes up his notepad.

'Sorry, I didn't mean to disturb you.'

'S'all right,' he mumbles. 'I didn't feel like writing anyway.'

I nod at the pad. 'Any more news on when you're seeing her?'

'Your dad thinks the week after next.'

'Finally!'

'Yeah. I thought I'd pass the letters on then. Even if she doesn't read them until she's older, at least she'll have something to remember me by.'

'That sounds good.' I pause before saying, 'I'm guessing today didn't go so well.'

'When does it ever go well?'

I sigh. 'I've never been to a prison before.'

'You're lucky then.'

'What's it like?' I ask.

'Big. Cold. Full of terrifying people. Not a place I ever want to end up.'

'Do you want to talk about it?'

'There's not much to say.'

'Was he mean to you?'

He hesitates. 'No. He was indifferent, which is probably worse. He was late, so we only had five minutes. He couldn't even be arsed to look at me. I hate him,' he says through gritted teeth.

'You don't have to go there again,' I tell him heatedly. 'He might be made up of some of the same cells as you, but that doesn't make him worth your time. Who gives a shite about biology?'

I feel some of the tension leave his body with a long exhale. I rest my chin on his shoulder and he tilts his face towards me. I grind my jaw on his shoulder.

'That tickles,' he says with a laugh, wriggling out from under my chin.

I grin and lift my head to meet his eyes.

He gives me a small smile then leans forward again and sniffs my hair.

'Your hair smells of strawberries.'

My stomach feels strangely fluttery all of a sudden.

'Want to do my portrait?' I try to keep my voice sounding light as I edge away. It felt as though we were sitting too close.

'What?' He looks bewildered.

'For Art. I did a totally crap job of Theo's earlier. You can do me, if you like. Get it out the way.'

He rests his head back against the tree trunk. 'I think I'm going to stay here a while longer.'

'Do you want me to bring your art stuff down here?'

He hesitates, his expression becoming a tiny bit hopeful.

'Lazy git,' I say with a smile. 'I'll be back in a tick.'

I set off towards the farm, amused.

George and Theo are so different, I think to myself later, once George is in the swing of sketching me.

Theo has a confidence about him, a devil-may-care attitude that a lot of girls would find attractive. George is confident, but he's quiet with it. Steady. He's not cocky.

He's been working away for a while and, as time has gone on, his expression has grown more intense. He's deep in concentration, and right now his eyes are tracking the lines of my lips. I don't think he's aware that I'm watching him. His chin is tucked down, his eyelashes lowered. He lifts his gaze and meets my eyes. A moment passes. Then another.

This is not a staring contest. It's something else.

Heat spreads within my chest, and then he tugs his eyes away.

'That'll have to do.' He casts the pad aside.

I pick it up, feeling jittery. It's not a *bad* depiction, but it's not terribly good either. My hair is a tangled mess – accurate, but hardly flattering – and my cheeks and eyes look flat and unappealing, but he's got the shape of my face down and my lips are better than I'd expect them to be, sort of heart-shaped.

'Cool.' I glance up to find him watching me. 'How are you feeling now?'

He shrugs.

'I know something that will cheer you up.'

'What?'

'I'm going to show you how to make good money.'

'Eh?'

'You're going to sell the most brilliant scarf at the market and it's going to pay for your festival ticket.'

'I'm going to sell a scarf,' he repeats slowly. He stares at me, then shakes his head as I grin at him. 'No. No,' he says. 'You're not teaching me how to knit.'

'I am,' I say.

'You're not.'

'I am. Come on, mister, come with me.' I reach down and grab his hand, and my pulse speeds up at the feeling of his palm pressed against mine, even as I put all my weight into my heels and try to pull him up.

He laughs and obliges me. I let go of his hand reluctantly and we set off back to the house, my heart jumping like a jackrabbit in my chest.

All week, I'm distracted. By Friday, I've accepted that I have a crush on George. Despite threatening a 'patchy return', Becky has only missed a couple of days of school since coming back. One of those days was yesterday, and the thrill I got sitting next to George on the bus was ridiculous.

We've spent at least a small part of every evening this week sitting side by side in front of the fire on the living room floor. I've been teaching him how to knit, and even though he's been rolling his eyes and complaining, I *know* it's a front. I *know* he likes being with me. His low laughter is literally my favourite sound on earth at the moment. I could live to amuse him.

Last night, our knees were touching and neither of us moved away. I was so aware of the heat of him – I felt like my skin was on fire, as though the warmth was travelling right into my bloodstream and making me feel light-headed. And then Mum came into the room and we both jerked our legs away from each other. He wouldn't have done that if he hadn't felt *something*, if he hadn't felt guilty.

That's the thing. Even if he *does* like me, nothing can happen. I can't have a relationship with someone who's in my parents' care. If Mum and Dad found out, they'd probably have to move George on, and the thought of him having to leave us – let alone because of me – is completely unfathomable.

But unfortunately, my crush feels more powerful *because* it's forbidden.

I haven't told Becky that I like him. And despite the fact that we've hung out with Theo and George most lunchtimes, she hasn't guessed.

I've decided to keep my cards close to my chest for now. I kind of enjoy having a secret that no one else in the world knows. And I don't fully trust that Becky wouldn't stir things up, even if only a little. That's something I can't risk, not when George's place in my home is at stake.

. . .

'Why were you laughing?' Theo asks me in honeyed tones on our way into Art.

I chuckle and give his shoulder a shove, in higher spirits than usual because this is our last lesson before we break for half term. 'I'll never tell,' I reply.

One day I'll crack. I don't care anymore if he thinks I'm a weirdo – he knows me, he can think what he likes. But I am quite amused by this game we're playing. I can't believe we're still at it, all these weeks on.

Theo throws his arm around my shoulder and says in my ear, 'I'm going to win this one.'

'You're so competitive.' I pat his chest good-naturedly.

He winks at me and trails off to go to his table. It's only then that I realise George is right behind me.

'Hi,' I say.

'Hi,' he replies shortly, not quite meeting my eyes.

'You okay?' I ask.

'Fine.'

He doesn't sound fine.

He drops into the seat next to Theo, while I go and take mine beside Becky. The room is set up in a semi-circle of tables, all facing a central table which is usually cluttered with still life stuff. Theo and George sit a couple of tables away from Becky and me, but we're partially facing each other.

The lesson begins. Mr Edwards is talking about the portrait homework that we handed in on Monday, walking amongst our tables and handing back our marked work. I'm still distracted by George, wondering why he seemed offhand when he came into the lesson. Could he be jealous? Does he mind that Theo and I are so easy together, that Theo can throw his arm around my shoulders?

I can't imagine George ever being that casual with his gestures.

I'm looking at him as I'm thinking all this, so when he flicks his eyes to mine, the sudden contact feels like an electric shock. He immediately averts his gaze, and I do too, but then I find myself being drawn back towards him, and he must feel the same way because our eyes meet again. This time the contact lasts for one, two, three long, incredibly intense seconds – enough to make me feel shivery and hot – and then Mr Edwards reaches their table and we both jolt to our senses.

'This,' he says, looking down at Theo with a proud smile, 'is one of the best student portraits I have *ever* seen.' He glances over at me and gives me a meaningful nod as he places Theo's portrait on the table in front of him.

Our classmates crane their necks, some getting out of their seats to look. There are murmurs of appreciation and a few people look over at me.

I squirm in my seat, and, for the first time since I've known him, Theo blushes.

George leans over towards Theo and stares down at the piece of paper. There's something about the set of his shoulders that makes him look stiff.

He slides back to his previous position, facing straight ahead.

'Sit down, sit down,' Mr Edwards says, returning to retrieve Theo's portrait. 'I'll show you.'

He walks amongst the tables, proudly displaying the piece of work.

'Whoa,' Becky says aloud, her eyes wide with astonishment. She turns to look at me as Mr Edwards moves on. 'You must be Theo's muse.'

I pull a face at her, squirming under the spotlight. A couple of classmates overheard her and now they're sniggering. George seems to be steadfastly avoiding looking at our table. Mr Edwards continues handing out the remaining portraits, not saying much. He places George's drawing of me down in front of him, and as soon as he moves on, George flips the page over. Theo doesn't seem to notice, too overwhelmed and discomfited by the praise from his teacher and classmates to pay attention, but my stomach twists at the sight.

'Do you think Theo fancies you?' Becky asks me on the bus.

'No!' I hiss, sinking down into my seat. 'Don't, you'll make it awkward.'

'All right, I'm just *saying*,' she replies slyly. 'Do *you* fancy *him*?'

'What? No!'

'Why not? He's hot.' She waits a while before asking, 'Don't you think?'

'He's good-looking, but I don't fancy him.'

'I might ask him to draw *me*,' she says with a snigger.

'Go ahead,' I mumble.

'Are you sure you wouldn't mind?'

'I thought you liked Martin.'

She looks smug and I realise I've failed her test.

George is striding towards the house, faster than I can walk at my normal pace. I'd have to run to catch up with him, but I'm not sure I should. I'm expecting him to disappear straight upstairs, so I get a shock when I find him blocking the kitchen doorway, his back to me.

'Oi,' I say, giving him a push.

He steps forward and gives me a strange look over his shoulder. It's then that I see my parents standing in the middle of the kitchen, hugging. Mum lifts her face from Dad's shoulder. Tears are streaming down her cheeks, but she's smiling.

'Hey,' she says in a husky voice.

'What's wrong?' There's dread in the pit of my stomach as I watch Dad dry his own tears. He's turned his face away, but it's obvious what he's doing.

'Nothing's wrong,' Mum replies.

Jamie and Joanne arrive, both of them stopping short.

'Are Ashlee and Nia okay?' Jamie asks, panicked.

Mum nods. 'They're both fine, love. Nia's still asleep and Ashlee's in the living room, watching telly. Her social worker just called. Anita and Ollie want to adopt her too.'

I burst into tears. Mum comes straight over to give me a hug, but as her arms fold around me, her whole body shakes with emotion. The two of us clutch each other desperately and proceed to silently sob our hearts out.

We're so *so* happy for Ashlee and Nia, yet at the same time, absolutely devastated at the thought of losing them both.

Mum releases me, and as I blow my nose, she goes to give George a hug. He's standing there uncomfortably with his head bowed, but he lets her embrace him.

Dad pulls away from Jamie to comfort Joanne – tears are streaming down her face, but as soon as she's in Dad's arms, she starts to wail loudly.

I hurry into the living room, turning to shut the door and startling at the sight of George right behind me. He looks upset too – his eyes are shining and his nose is red – but he follows me into the room, gently closing the door behind him.

Ashlee is sitting on the sofa, her eyes fixed on the television. She seems completely unaware of what's going on in the kitchen.

'Hello, Ashlee,' I say brightly.

'What are you watching?' George asks, also endeavouring to sound cheerful.

'*Teletubbies*,' she replies, unable to tear her gaze away from the action on the box. George sits down on one side of her and I sit down on the other, and as I rub Ashlee's back, I can't stop the tears from slipping down my cheeks. She doesn't notice, but George does. His warm hand closes over mine and my heart jumps at the feeling of his fingertips curling into my palm. I turn to look at him, but his gaze is fixed on the TV. My eyes travel over his side profile, from his brown curls to his dark eyelashes and his straight nose. And then he slowly tilts his face in my direction and lifts his eyes to meet mine. The intensity in his dark depths steals my breath away.

We snatch our hands away from each other as the door bursts open.

'Hello baby,' Joanne says, coming into the room and sitting on the carpet in front of Ashlee.

'I'm watching *Teletubbies*,' Ashlee tells her distractedly.

'My favourite is Dipsy,' Joanne says, still rubbing away a perpetual river of tears.

'I like Laa Laa,' Ashlee replies.

'Oh, Laa Laa's ace,' Joanne agrees hoarsely.

The sight of her pain brings on a fresh wave of my own. I get up and go into the kitchen to find a tissue. Jamie, Mum and Dad are in the dining room, talking. As I'm drying my eyes and blowing my nose, I hear the kitchen door open and close behind me, and when I turn around and peek back into the living room, George is no longer on the sofa.

I hurry out of the kitchen door and see him stalking up towards the high paddock. The sight of his shoulders shaking makes me step up my pace, and suddenly I'm running up the grassy hill towards him.

'George!'

He spins around, his cheeks wet and his eyes glistening. 'Will Sophie's foster parents care as much as that when she's adopted?' He points towards our house. 'Is she going through that right now and I'm not there?' His voice is raised and full of emotion. 'Who's going to adopt *her*? What will they be like? Will she call them Mam and Dad and *what the fuck*, Leah?' he gasps, almost tearing his hair out. 'How can I let her go like that?' His eyes are wide with disbelief that this is happening to him, to his family. 'I have to find her. I *have* to stop this! She can't be adopted. What if I never see her again?' He breaks down into full-on sobs.

I can't bear to see his pain – I feel it as though it's mine. I've *got* to help him. *We've* got to help him. Ashlee and Nia will have each other through life. George and Sophie should have each other too. Isn't it more important that Sophie has a brother, a big brother who she loves and looks up to, than a new mum and dad who she's hardly ever met? *Isn't* it?

Oh God, I don't know! Ashlee and Nia will have a mother and father who will love them and care for them, support and help them through every stage of their young lives. They'll be dedicated to their upbringing, protect them at all cost. Isn't it too much to ask that of George? His own life has barely got started – he's a boy, not a parent. He should be allowed to live for himself, not for his little sister. Isn't that why the courts made the decision they made? It's all such a minefield.

I step forward to comfort him, but his body goes rigid beneath my palms. He pulls away.

'I need to be by myself for a bit,' he says gruffly.

'George,' I choke out.

'I'll be all right,' he tells me over his shoulder.

I stand on the grass and watch him walk away.

Anita and Ollie come for another visit the very next day. Mum and Dad are doing everything they can to accommodate them, wanting them to form as much of a bond as possible with Ashlee and Nia before they go to live with them. Dad wants to be there for the visit this time, so after dropping Jamie, Joanne and George to the market, he returns home.

I'm glad George has gone with the others – glad for his sake, not mine. I don't think he could handle seeing this process through, not when he's linked it so strongly to what's happening with Sophie.

Anita and Ollie pay much more attention to Ashlee than they did last week, and while I struggle to hold back my tears, it does warm my heart to see their shared looks of affection and excitement. They're clearly blown away by the fact that they'll soon be a family of four. While it's nowhere near official, my parents and the girls' social workers are confident that the courts will support the decision for Ashlee and Nia to go to the same family.

In fact, Mum is so confident about this, that she tells Ashlee that Anita and Ollie are going to be her new mummy and daddy. Ashlee goes along with this quite happily, having no real understanding yet of what this means. Anita and Ollie both get a bit tearful when Ashlee repeats the words: 'My new mummy and daddy?'

'That's right, darling,' Mum says. 'That's daddy there.'

Ollie holds open his arms to Ashlee.

'Nia's mummy and daddy too?' Ashlee asks Mum, not going to Ollie. He doesn't seem to mind, dropping his hands and continuing to smile.

'Absolutely,' Mum says.

Ashlee grins and tickles Nia's tummy, making the whole room laugh, along with her baby sister.

19

NOW

'Talk to him, *please*,' I implore Mum before going upstairs to say goodnight to Emilie.

George has just pulled up in his truck. We're off out to a pub near Masham for dinner. Mum will read Emilie a bedtime story after I've gone, but first I want her to speak to George about payment for the work he's been doing.

I hear her let him into the kitchen as I enter Emilie's bedroom.

'Night, night,' I say softly. She's lying in bed, watching her revolving bird-themed nightlight go around and around in circles.

I stay with her for a while, chatting about her day, until Mum comes to take over.

'Any luck?' I ask after giving my daughter one last kiss.

She shakes her head and shrugs as if to say, '*What can I do? I tried!*'

I huff with annoyance and stomp downstairs, glaring at George.

He gives me a funny look. 'All right?'

'You can*not* work for free,' I hiss as we go outside.

He groans. 'I've had all this from your mam! I *want* to help.'

'Why?'

He opens his truck's passenger door for me and goes around to the driver's side.

'Seriously, why?' I persist as he climbs in. 'You don't owe us anything, if that's what you're thinking.'

'Actually, I *do*,' he says firmly, buckling up and putting the truck in gear.

'It was my parents' *job* to look after you. You don't owe them for that. Looked after children don't owe any adult *anything*.'

He glances at me as he drives down the farm lane. 'Do you know what your dad said to me when I first came to your place?'

'What?'

'Before she left, my social worker warned me to be good. Your dad turned to me and whispered, "No, son, we'll take you as you are." Do you know how much that meant to me?' he asks. 'I'd come from three places where no one gave a shit and then your dad said that. At first, I dismissed it, convinced myself that it was just something he said to everyone. But he *meant it*, Leah. He meant it.'

'Of course he did.'

'And I threw it back in his face by running away without so much as leaving a note. He and your mam must've been worried sick. I *know* they were. They told me.'

'You were only trying to do what you thought was right.'

'No, I *knew* it was wrong. But I was so inside my own head at the time that I didn't care who I hurt. I didn't even call later when things had settled, I just buried it and tried to forget all about you.'

I stare out of the window, feeling faintly sick. 'Well, you've more than paid them back with all the work you've done in the last few weeks. I think you should let it go now.'

'No,' he states firmly. 'I want to do this for your mam. In your dad's absence, it's the least I can do.'

I look at him. 'But when will it stop? When your guilt subsides?'

Is that when he'll go back to Devon? When he feels he's paid his penance?

'I don't know. Please, though, leave it for me to decide.'

I return to staring out of my window at the fields cast in sunshine.

Is this the loose end he was talking about tying up?

Or is there more to his 'unfinished business' than that?

It's a gorgeous summer's evening, balmy and still: perfect weather for sitting outside a pub by the river.

George goes to the bar while I find us a table at the water's edge. He returns with a gin and tonic for me and a pint of what looks like lemonade for himself.

'Are you not drinking?' I ask.

'I never drink when I'm driving.'

'Not even one?'

'No.' His reply is curt.

I'm tense as I lift my glass. 'You must be furious with Theo.' I can't help but say it.

'It's not my place to be angry,' he mutters.

'*I'm* angry.'

'I know you are.'

'It's okay if you're angry too.'

He stares into his pint glass.

'I wrote to him, like you suggested.'

He lifts his gaze. 'Yeah?'

'Two letters and counting.'

I wrote again to him today, had an absurd urge to tell him about Emilie's potty training and the silly things she sings to herself when she's doing a Number Two.

Our daughter is random.

'How did it feel?' he asks.

'To get it all out?'

He nods.

'Kind of good.' I shift on my seat. 'I haven't told him about you yet, though.'

'No?'

I shake my head.

'Why not?'

I shrug and reach for my drink.

The sun has come out from behind a low-lying cloud, basking George's face in golden light. His brown eyes have become more caramel-hued. He's still staring across the table at me.

'How mad was he at me for leaving?' he asks.

'He was more upset than mad. He cared a lot about you, and he knew I did too. It made it even harder for him to be away.'

'Away?'

'In Italy.'

He cocks his head to one side, puzzled.

'Theo's dad sent him to Italy to live with his aunt. He

went to boarding school there. Becky didn't have any of this on her Facebook page?'

'No.' George looks knocked for six.

'He came to tell us, but you'd already left. We tried so hard to find you.'

'I'm sorry,' he whispers, dragging his hand across his mouth. 'I had no idea.'

'He left the same day you did.'

20

THEN

I t's half term, and even though we have no school for the next week, there's so much to do on the farm. The herd has now been shorn, but the alpaca 'blankets' still have to be sent away to be processed. First they have to be skirted, which means all of the 'vegetable' matter has to be removed. In other words, the pooey bits and other impurities have to be picked out. We have twenty-six animals, so that's a *lot* of fleece to get through.

Mum has her hands full with the little ones, Jamie has his A levels coming up, so he's got loads of revision to do, and Joanne point-blank refuses to do the 'dirty stuff'. It was hard enough to get George to learn how to knit, so I'm not expecting much help from him either.

On Monday morning, I head downstairs, preparing to get stuck in, when I hear Dad on the phone in the study. He sounds cross, which is so rare for him, that it causes me to eavesdrop.

'This is completely unacceptable,' he says. 'No, she was supposed to call me herself first thing, and now you're telling me she's on holiday?'

Movement in the kitchen redirects my gaze. George is standing at the door, listening. We share a look of apprehension.

'She said she'd try for *Wednesday*! That's *this* Wednesday! I was calling to find out a time.'

'Sophie,' George says to me quietly.

'Can anyone else help?' Dad asks. 'I've got a young man here who simply wants to see his sister, the sister he was separated from almost a year ago. *That* should be a priority here, not a bloody holiday.'

I bite my lip, listening intently.

'Oh. I see. Well, I'm sorry for her. But this poor lad has already been through three social workers. Do you understand what I'm saying? At this rate, his young sister will be adopted and he won't have even had a chance to say goodbye.'

I realise I'm holding my breath.

'That would be much appreciated.'

Dad ends the call and comes out of the room, stopping short at the sight of the two of us.

'I'm sorry,' he says resignedly to George, ushering us both into the kitchen. 'I'm afraid your social worker has had to take a bit of a break for mental health reasons. A new one will be appointed to you soon.'

'And my meeting with Sophie?' George asks through gritted teeth.

'We'll make it happen,' Dad assures him. 'Not this week, maybe not next, but soon.'

I jump out of my skin at the sound of something smashing on the tiled floor: a mug. Rage has contorted George's face and his body is racked with tension, his chest rising and falling sharply and his hands clenched into fists at his sides.

'All right, son,' Dad says calmly.

'No, it's *not* fucking all right!' George yells, grabbing another mug from the countertop and hurling that at the wall too.

'George!' I gasp with shock as it ricochets off and broken crockery scatters everywhere.

He storms towards the door, wrenching it open.

'Leave him, Leah!' Dad shouts as I hurry after him. 'Give him some space!'

I ignore him. 'GEORGE!'

He's striding fast along the lane, away from the farm. I have this overwhelming feeling that, if I let him go, I'll never see him again. The thought is so hellish that I run, catching up with him at a bend in the road and spinning around to try to halt his progress.

'Move!' he commands, his dark eyes flashing with fury.

'No. Stay,' I beg, sidestepping to block his path.

'Get out of my way.'

'Please,' I gasp, placing my hands on his chest.

He smacks them away and butts right up against me, completely invading my body space.

'Get out of my fucking way,' he growls at me with cold hatred.

Ice floods my veins.

'What the *fuck* is going on?'

I spin around at the sound of Theo's voice. He's standing in the lane behind me, looking appalled.

'George is upset,' I tell him.

'I can see that, but why the hell is he taking it out on you?'

George turns his face up to the sky and lets out a strangled scream. It rips out of him, full of frustration and anguish and fury.

He turns and sets off towards the lower paddock and I run after him.

'LEAH!' Theo shouts, before following too.

George comes to a stop at his silver birch sapling and proceeds to try and pull it from the ground.

'*Please*,' I cry.

He's sobbing: scary, heart-wrenching and out-of-control yelps. He seems unhinged, his face red, veins popping in his neck.

Theo stands beside me, dumbstruck, as I cry and beg. And then my dad appears, just as George yanks his sapling free of the rich peaty earth.

'Go inside, Leah,' Dad says with quiet but absolute authority as George falls to his knees, his head bowed, the fight gone out of him. 'Take Theo with you.'

This time I don't argue. This time I do as I'm told.

'And I thought *I* had problems,' Theo says flatly as I make us tea.

'What are you doing here?' I ask him bluntly.

'Went for a walk.'

'That's a long walk.'

'Nowt else to do,' he replies in a monotone.

'You sounded Northern then.'

'I *am* Northern. Not my fault I had my accent beaten out of me at boarding school.'

'I hope you don't mean literally.'

He shrugs.

I *really* hope he doesn't mean literally.

'You should've called for a lift. Dad would've picked you up.'

'Looks like your dad has got other things on his mind.'

'Yeah,' I agree morosely.

'What happened?'

I fill him in as we drink our tea in the living room. When we're up to date, his comment from earlier comes back to me: '*And I thought I had problems...*'

'How are you?' I belatedly think to ask. 'You didn't have plans for half term?'

'Nope, but Acton's in Monaco and my father and Sylvie are no doubt having a lovely time in Italy,' he replies drily.

'Oh. You didn't want to go with them?'

'I didn't even know they were going until Saturday when Bart took them to the airport.'

'What?' I let out a small disbelieving laugh. 'Your dad didn't tell you he was going abroad?'

'Nup,' he replies sardonically, picking up a skein of rose grey yarn from the basket next to the sofa. He freezes when he sees that one end is attached to a knitting needle.

'Careful,' I say. 'That's George's scarf.'

The edge of his mouth curls up as his blue eyes dart towards me. 'George is knitting a scarf?'

'Well, not all that willingly. But if he can sell it at the market, it should pay for his festival ticket.'

'I need to get in on this.'

'I can't tell if you're being sarcastic,' I reply after a pause.

He grins at me. 'Why were you laughing?'

He slips the question in so casually, but I don't miss a beat.

'I will never tell.'

He returns my smile, but his is not as carefree as it usually is.

'It's good to see you,' I say, sobering. And I *am* glad of his company. Dad is still with George and I have no idea if he's managed to calm him down.

'It's good to see you too,' Theo replies quietly, holding my gaze.

I smile and look away, feeling oddly edgy. 'Have you got the house to yourself this week, then?'

'Yeah. Want to come over for a house party?'

'Really?'

'Well, no, but... You could come over for a movie night?'

'George too?'

'Sure,' he replies after a slight hesitation. 'And Becky, if you like.'

'He wasn't going to hurt me.'

I feel a wave of nausea when Theo averts his gaze, not quite convinced.

I hate the thought of Theo thinking badly of George, not with everything that George is going through.

'He kept asking me to get out of his way, and I wouldn't.'

'I did *not* like hearing him speak to you like that,' he says gravely, and it's the most serious I've ever seen him.

I change the subject.

A couple of days later, Dad drives George, Becky and me over to Theo's house. I haven't spoken much to George since his meltdown. He was very quiet when he returned to the house with Dad. Theo and I were out in the Yarn Barn so we missed him and Theo left soon afterwards. It was probably a good thing that Mum gave the phone to George rather than me when Theo called earlier. It gave the two of them a chance to clear the air.

It feels completely different visiting the Whittington residence now that Theo is a friend. I stare out of the window as Dad turns into the gate, driving slowly along the winding road surrounded by open fields. A herd of deer are lazing under the shade of a big oak tree. I would've missed them if it weren't for the stag horns spanning majestically above the long grass.

'Bloody hell,' Becky murmurs from beside me when the house comes into view.

Built out of cream-coloured stone, with a myriad of windows reflecting the late afternoon sun, the large Elizabethan mansion is almost too breathtaking for words. The gardens are also out of this world: a yew hedge has been sculpted into interesting rounded shapes, and the rose garden before it is in full bloom, bursting with colour.

George, in the front, is silent.

Dad crunches to a stop on the gravel drive. The heavy wooden front door swings open and Theo comes out.

'Don't you have staff to open the door to visitors?' Becky teases.

'I've given them the night off,' Theo replies with a grin.

I *think* he's joking.

I lean forward to say goodbye to Dad, giving him a peck on his cheek. He's picking us up at eleven tonight, which is about the latest he'll stretch to these days.

'Have fun!' he calls from his open window as we make our way up the wide stone steps.

'Ta,' George replies, while Becky calls back: 'Bye, Ivan, thanks for the lift!'

Theo stands aside to let us in as Dad waves and drives away.

'Have you been playing pool all by yourself?' Becky asks, seeing the long wooden stick Theo is holding.

'Snooker,' he replies.

'Ooh, *snooker*,' she says. 'La dee dah.'

Theo rolls his eyes at her and shuts the heavy door behind us with a solid clunk. 'I'm not being a twat. There's a difference. Can you play?' he asks George.

'Only pool.'

'Snooker's easy to pick up.'

We're standing in a huge hall, with highly polished darkwood panelled walls. A double staircase winds up the stairs behind us, and above it, a large oil painting hangs on the wall. It features an opulently dressed man with a stern face and a grey wig.

'I'm up for a game,' I say.

'Can we have a tour of your house first?' Becky asks.

'Er, sure,' Theo replies equably.

He doesn't take us everywhere, but he does show us his bedroom. It's enormous, with dark wooden antique furniture and a four-poster bed that may be in keeping with the four-hundred-year-old-plus house but is completely alien in a teenage boy's room.

Becky seems spellbound by the surroundings, but I feel cold. While Becky bounces on Theo's bed and George studies another oil painting of an ugly old ancestor, I go and stare out of the huge window at the fields.

'I love your view,' I say to Theo softly. 'You can see for miles.'

'The window is my favourite thing about this room,' he replies. 'It's the *only* thing I like, actually.'

I glance at him. 'It's a really nice house.'

'Is it? I'd rather live at yours.'

'It's a little crowded at the moment,' I whisper with a smile.

He shrugs. 'I'd sleep in the Yarn Barn.'

'Yarn Barn or Bunny Barn?'

'Bunny Barn, actually. Fuck, I'd sleep in with the alpacas if that were my only option.'

I laugh and he grins at me.

'What are you two whispering about?' Becky asks.

'Come on, let's go to the Games Room,' Theo says instead of answering her. 'You and George against Leah and me.'

George turns around and looks at us. I have a funny feeling in the pit of my stomach as we make our way downstairs.

21

NOW

'Tell me about your job at Forestry England,' I say to George as we sit in the early evening sunshine outside the pub by the river.

'What do you want to know?' he asks.

'What did you do there? How did you get the job?'

'Well, I used to help grow and shape and care for forests, conserve homes for wildlife and build walking trails and things like that. As for how I got the job, I went from washing dishes to working in a garden centre, and from there to a tree nursery.'

'Really?' I smile at him.

He nods. 'One day we had to deliver a bunch of trees to this big country house. I got talking to the groundskeeper – Ernie – and we hit it off. He was in his late seventies and very sprightly. Crazy salt-and-pepper hair and a big handlebar moustache. A real character,' he tells me with a smile. 'He said a position had come up on the estate and asked me if I wanted it.'

'How old were you?'

'Seventeen, but everyone thought I was older. Ernie took me under his wing. Trained me up, taught me about trees and the various diseases to look out for, and eventually he encouraged me to go back and finish my schooling.'

'Did you?'

He nods. 'It was hard work, but it paid off. Once I got the qualifications I needed, I could apply to work for Forestry England. Ernie was behind me the whole way.'

'He sounds amazing.'

'He is. We're still close.'

'Does he know about your history?' *About us?*

He nods. 'Over time, I told him everything. He was the one who encouraged me to come back here, actually.'

'To tie up your loose ends?'

'Mm,' he replies shortly, picking up one of the menus he brought back from the bar.

I do the same and we fall silent.

The air is filled with the sound of chatter from the nearby tables and cars passing over the arched stone bridge. Sunlight is hitting the bridge and making the trees and grass look brilliantly green next to the dark water.

A memory comes back to me.

'The water is like squid ink,' I say, smiling across the table at him. 'I'm a man of many molluscs,' I add, quoting his words back.

He groans and hides behind the menu as I crack up laughing.

'I can't believe I said that,' he moans.

'It was funny!' I insist.

'I was trying to be,' he admits.

'It wasn't *all* bad, was it?'

'Of *course* it wasn't.' He puts the menu down. 'I was in a bad place with what was happening with Sophie, but some parts of it were good. *Really* good.' He scratches his arm, reminding me of what's hidden beneath his shirt.

Impulsively, I reach across and take his wrist, pulling his arm across the table so I can study his tattoos. They're very simple line drawings, each tattoo standing separately from the others. There's a compass, with only the N marked on for North, I realise with a smile; an ink pen; and a silver birch tree.

'This is beautiful,' I say of the last one, glancing up to find him watching me. 'Wait, what is *that*...' I push the rolled-up sleeve of his dark-green shirt further up his arm and can barely believe what I'm seeing. 'You got an *alpaca* tattoo?' My eyes are wide with delight. It's only an outline of the animal, but it's instantly recognisable.

He nods, giving me a bashful smile.

'Did you do them yourself?'

He chuckles. 'No, they were done by a professional.'

'I was only asking because they're unfussy, not because they look amateur. I like the simplicity of them.'

He pulls his arm away and reaches for his pint glass.

I down the last mouthful of my gin and tonic.

'Same again?' he asks.

'I'll go. And we should probably order. It gets busy here.'

'Do you know what you want?'

'The chicken. You?'

'Bangers and mash.' He gets up from the table.

'I'll go,' I repeat, edging out from the bench.

'My shout.' He bops me over the head with the menus and strides across the beer garden.

I watch him go, amused.

He returns with another gin and tonic for me. 'Is this okay? I forgot to ask what you wanted, but I can get you something else if you'd prefer.' His glass of lemonade is still half full.

'I was going to switch to soda water,' I admit, but take a sip of my gin and tonic anyway. 'Thanks for this, though. It's only because I didn't want to drink alone. What are you like drunk?' I ask curiously.

He smiles. 'Um... Happy?'

'Really?' I love the sound of this. 'When can I see you blathered?'

George shrugs. 'I don't know. You'll have to come for a few with me in Ripon sometime.' He frowns. 'But then you'd have to catch a taxi.'

'That's okay.'

'No, I should be the one to do that.'

'Why?'

'It's more...' He thinks for the right word, before settling on: '*chivalrous*.'

'*Chivalrous*?' I bark out a laugh. 'Do we live in the Dark Ages?'

'You know what I mean,' he mutters.

'Why don't you come to the farm one night for dinner, then?' I ask with a grin. 'Next Saturday after Mum's knitting workshop? We could give you a lift back to ours.'

'I work Saturdays,' he says with regret.

'Sunday, then? I could pick you up.'

'Are you sure?'

'Yes.'

He returns my smile with a nod. 'Okay.'

I'm curious about something. 'Why *are* you working at the pub instead of Forestry England?'

'There's nothing available in this area. They have my CV.'

'So you're staying in North Yorkshire permanently?' My heart has sped up.

'At least for a while. I'm technically on sabbatical, so I can go back to my job in Devon if I need to.'

I do *not* like the sound of that.

'Do you still have a place in Devon?'

He nods.

'What's it like?'

'It's nice. Only small, but right by the sea. It's an old fisherman's cottage.'

'Do you have any photos?'

'Um...' He reaches into his pocket and pulls out his phone, then hesitates, pushing the device back in his pocket. 'They're a bit buried. I'll find them another time.'

Is he being deliberately evasive?

'Have you rented it out?'

'Er, sort of.'

I frown at him.

'My ex is there right now,' he explains.

They were living together?

'Did you co-own the house?' Is this why he doesn't want to show me photos? Because she's in all of them? Exactly how serious are we talking?

He shakes his head. 'No, it was mine. She's looking for somewhere else, but I don't want to rush her.'

'What's her name?' I don't know why I've asked. I don't even want to know, but it seems wrong to reduce her to a 'she'.

'Annie,' he replies.

'We used to have an angora rabbit called Annie.'

He laughs under his breath. 'I know.'

'How long were you together?'

'A couple of years. We lived together for one of those, but broke up a few months before I came here.'

'You're not running away again, are you?'

He looks shocked and then affronted. 'Absolutely not!'

'It's none of my business if you are.'

'We broke up because my heart wasn't fully in it. Ernie had been telling me for years that I needed to come back here and make peace with you all. Annie knew that too.'

'So she's back in Devon, waiting? Waiting for you to make peace with us so you can go back to her and get on with your life?'

I realise too late that the gin has already taken effect. My defences are down again.

'I don't know what I'm going to do yet, Leah.' George's eyes flash at me and I experience a strange thrill. 'But I can't see Annie and me ever getting back together. We want different things. She wanted to take our relationship to the next level; I didn't.'

'Marriage?'

'She wanted a baby, but I can't give her one. Not that I *can't*... I mean, everything's working down there. I just... *can't*.'

'You're not ready?'

'I'll never be ready. I don't want kids of my own.'

I don't know why this news hits me so hard that I feel oddly winded. What's changed in him? He wanted to parent Sophie when he was still a child himself... Did he grow up and realise he didn't have the capacity to be a dad after all?

At that moment, our food arrives.

'This is kind of a heavy discussion we're having,' he says lightly, or at least, trying to sound it, once the waiter has left us to it.

'Yeah. Sorry about that. I'll let you eat in peace.'

'Anyway,' he says. 'Annie and I are not getting back together.'

I don't know why he felt he had to repeat that part, but I can't ignore the wave of relief I felt when he did.

22

THEN

I'm lying in bed, listening to the wind and rain lash my window. I can't get to sleep – my head is too full of George. He's like an impossible problem I'm trying to solve.

He seemed to be all right when we were at Theo's house last week. We went three more times during half term and had so much fun, playing snooker, exploring the grounds without fear of Theo's uptight family sticking their noses in, and raiding Acton's video collection to watch movies that were way too old for us (*Kill Bill: Volume 1* and *The Silence of the Lambs*).

I can't imagine how Theo felt to be abandoned by his family during the school holidays. I think he genuinely appreciated our company. He was probably the happiest I'd ever seen him: on top form, quick and witty, and yet still his usual self-deprecating self. He cracked Becky and me up, and he made George laugh at times too, but I could tell George's mind was elsewhere. Theo and Becky wouldn't have known anything was up. George put on a decent show, and this week at school, he's also been fine around them, but at home, it's a different story. He has been *incredibly* distant with me.

I've tried to make conversation with him, but from the second he steps off the bus to the second he steps back on again, he gives me one-word answers and keeps to himself. I have to keep reminding myself that I've literally done *nothing* wrong.

It's hard to pinpoint exactly when things changed between us. Was it when he lost his temper in the lane and screamed? Or did he start to pull away before that? My mind keeps returning to the moment in Art when he saw Theo's portrait of me. Is he embarrassed or jealous? Either way, I hope he gets over it soon.

I really wanted to speak to him tonight. When we got home from school, Dad pulled him aside to say that his new social worker had managed to arrange a visit with Sophie. Mum told me that much while they were in the study, talking it through. George went out for a walk afterwards and only came back in time for dinner, disappearing into his room straight after. Jamie told me he was listening to music with his headphones on. I could picture it: eyes closed, totally introverted and shut off to the world and everyone in it.

I'm feeling a bit pissed off about it now, but only because I'm frustrated. I care about him and I want to help.

With a huff, I throw my covers off my bed. It's almost one a.m. and I feel wide awake. We've got a Maths test tomorrow so I could really do without being an insomniac right now. I decide to go to the bathroom – more for the want of something to do than because I need to. I open the door to the sound of the stairs creaking and look to see that George and Jamie's bedroom door is slightly ajar.

I find George in the living room, sitting sideways on the sofa and staring out of the big picture window. The heavy curtains are wide open to the stormy night beyond.

'Hi.' I speak up over the sound of the rain.

George jumps and turns to look at me in the doorway.

'Sorry,' I apologise for scaring him. 'I heard you come downstairs. Couldn't sleep. You?'

'Same.'

I quietly close the door behind me and go to sit at the other end of the sofa. He looks awkward, pulling his knees up to his chest. He's wearing pyjamas, but they're effectively shorts and a T-shirt, so it's not a big deal. I feel underdressed in comparison. I'm also wearing pyjama shorts, but my top is a vest and I have no bra on underneath. I mimic his body position, hugging my knees to my chest. No way am I leaving now to go upstairs and get my dressing gown.

'Are you okay?'

He nods and returns his gaze to the window. It's so dark, we can barely make out the raindrops streaking the glass.

'I should probably go back to bed.'

'Please talk to me,' I say. 'I feel like you're avoiding me.'

'No, I'm not,' he snaps, scowling at me. 'It's not all about *you*, you know.'

I don't even try to mask my hurt.

His expression creases into contrition. 'I didn't mean that,' he whispers.

'*Talk* to me,' I plead, my nose prickling as I stretch my hand across the top of the sofa cushion towards him.

He lets out a long heavy sigh and stares at the basket next to the other sofa containing our scarves in progress.

'Have you got a date for a meeting with Sophie?' I ask.

He nods. 'Wednesday the twenty-third of June. Your dad says I can have the day off school.'

'That's good.' It's still the week after next, but at least there's a date in the diary.

He looks weary. He looks *sad*.

'Isn't it?' I ask.

He shrugs.

'*George*,' I implore.

He blinks quickly. I move my hand to his bare knee and he jolts. His skin is warm.

'Her social worker doesn't think it's a great idea,' he reveals slowly.

'What do you mean?' I ask with a frown.

'Sophie's social worker,' he explains. 'She said Sophie is about to be adopted by a "*truly lovely couple*",' he says bitterly, adding, 'Apparently she's doing really well.' There's no bitterness when he says this last part – he simply sounds matter-of-fact. He blinks again, rapidly. 'She thinks that seeing me might upset her.'

'Well, *tough*,' I snap crossly. 'They should have let her see you sooner, then.'

He lets out a small laugh. 'She's more important than I am, Leah.'

'Bullshit!' I erupt. 'You're *both* important. This is bollocks, George. You need to be able to say goodbye to her.'

He buries his face against his knees and emits a stricken sob.

My heart contracts. We were foot to foot, but now we're knee to knee and I move even closer until the lower half of our legs are pressed together. I take his face between my hands. His shoulders are heaving and in a far-off part of my brain I register how unexpectedly soft his hair is.

'I don't want to say goodbye.' He lifts his head to stare at me, his expression distraught. 'She's my *sister*. I looked after her for *three* years. She's mine!'

I brush the tears from his cheeks. 'I know. It's so unfair.' His tears keep on spilling from his dark eyes, and he continues to look right at me as I wipe them away.

My heart is overwhelmed with compassion for him. I want to take his pain away, would do *anything* to dispel some of his hurt. The most powerful urge to kiss him overcomes me. In the moments that follow, I picture myself doing it, imagine myself pushing his knees apart and sliding over him, our chests flush against each other as our lips connect. And then reality hits and I recoil, shocked to my core that I almost did something that could propel him out of my life for good.

Abruptly George jumps up from the sofa. He stares down at me, breathing heavily, and then he stalks from the room without a word.

My heart hammers in my chest as I listen to his footfall on the stairs, but I stay on the sofa for a good half an hour longer, reeling from the thoughtlessness that almost led me down a path to losing him.

———

George and I barely speak at all after that; we don't even make eye contact. If distance is what he wants, distance is what he gets because I'm terrified that my parents or Jamie or Joanne might suspect that my feelings for him go further than friendship. Even at school, I avoid him, hoping that I might be able to gradually shift my frame of mind to a platonic place.

I'm unable to get the thought from my head that the

compassion that I experienced, the emotion that made my heart feel as though it was going to burst... It felt a lot like love.

But while my relationship with George is on dangerous ground, my friendship with Theo couldn't be easier. He makes me laugh like no one else can.

Becky is off ill again when George goes to see Sophie at her foster home in Leeds, so it's only Theo and me together at school that day. On the bus on the way home he asks me if I'm okay.

'I'm worried about George,' I reply. 'He's been really stressed about this meeting.'

'What time's he coming home?'

'I don't know.'

'Want me to come over for a bit?'

I smile at him. 'You just want to see a baby alpaca.'

He nods, grinning. 'I totally want to see a baby alpaca. Are you going to deny me?'

'I could never deny *you*, Theo Whittington,' I reply dramatically.

'Well, *that's* good to hear,' he says in that low meaningful voice of his, his blue eyes twinkling.

Last night, Jessamine gave birth to a snowy white cria. Theo declares her the cutest thing he's ever seen.

She *is* unbelievably adorable with her long wobbly limbs, big dark eyes and small ears that flick this way and that. We've walked up to the girls' paddock to see her.

'Shall we carry on to Brimham?' Theo suggests.

I glance back at the farm, but there's no sign of the Land Rover. Dad drove George today – we should be able to see them returning from up at Hare Heads.

'Sure.'

When we reach the stile, I climb over and check the farm again.

Theo follows my gaze. 'He's lucky to have you,' he says.

'Who?'

'George. You can't even walk five paces before seeing if he's back yet.'

'You can call George a lot of things,' I reply drily. 'Lucky is not one of them.'

I take a last look at the farm before it disappears from view. We continue on in silence.

We're almost at the silver birch wood when Theo says, 'He *is* lucky. I'm lucky too. I don't know what I would've done if you hadn't come after me that day.'

'George came after you too,' I remind him.

We're walking in single file along the narrowest part of the track. Tall bramble bushes line the path on either side.

'Yeah, but I feel like it was mostly you. I think George was following *you*, not me.'

I frown at him over my shoulder. 'Why do you say that?'

His mouth twists at an odd angle. 'Don't you think he likes you?'

My heart jumps and I stumble, scratching myself on the prickles.

Theo's hand shoots out. 'Mind yourself!'

I dart away from him. 'What, like *likes*?'

He nods.

'No!' I exclaim, facing forward as my cheeks heat up. 'No way. We're friends. That's it.'

'So *you* don't like *him*?'

'No!' My voice jumps up another octave. '*Definitely* not! Oh my *God*!'

Don't protest too much, Leah...

'Okay. Well, that's good,' Theo says casually as we come out into the wood.

'Why is it good?' I know I should leave it alone, but I can't.

'I don't think he's a great fit for you.'

'In what way?'

He lifts an eyebrow at me and sets off along the track towards the first crop of rocks.

'I'm only asking because I'm curious!' I exclaim.

'You're too kind. And after what I saw in the lane a few weeks ago, I'd be scared he might hurt you.'

'What? *Physically*?' I'm shocked. 'George would *never*! He was *upset*, not *violent*. I've never seen him lift a finger in anger towards *anyone*. Unlike *you*.'

He blanches. 'I would *never* hurt a girl.'

He's appalled and I immediately wish I could take back my words.

'I know you wouldn't.'

He digs into his pocket for his cigarettes. He lights one and walks a few paces away from me, then climbs up onto a boulder.

He looks older than usual, even though he's technically dressed in a school uniform. He's wearing black trousers and a white shirt, rolled up at the sleeves and unbuttoned at the collar. He left his blazer and tie with his rucksack down at the farm.

'I'm sorry, Theo,' I say, pushing my toe into a molehill. The peaty earth is richer and darker than coffee. 'It wasn't your fault that Pete started on you.'

He makes his way out onto another rock close to Mini Druid's Writing Desk. I feel so bad as I follow him up. I can tell I've hurt his feelings.

He's looking down at a dip in the rock that's half filled with rainwater.

'It's shaped like a love heart,' I say with surprise.

'I know.'

'I've been up here so many times, but this is the first time I've noticed it.'

'See the edges...' Theo points with his shoe. 'If it had even a tiny bit more water in it or a tiny bit less, it would just be a blobby puddle.'

'Well, today it's a heart,' I state.

He looks at me, and a moment later, he presses his lips together, suppressing a smile. 'It's a sign from the gods,' he says, trying to keep a straight face.

I laugh with relief at the return of his sense of humour and he turns away, walking out to the overhang. With a jolt, I hurry after him, realising I haven't checked to see if Dad and George have returned. I look down at the farm, but there's still no sign of the Land Rover.

Theo finishes his cigarette and bends to stub it out on the rock, placing the butt beside the charred mark.

'I'll take it with me when we go,' he says as he sits down.

'That's very conscientious of you,' I tease, settling beside him.

He shrugs. 'It's beautiful up here. It should stay that way.'

'This is where I want my ashes to be scattered.'

'That's a bit morbid,' he grumbles.

'I disagree.'

'I'll be buried in the *family graveyard*,' he says sardonically. 'So yeah, maybe this *is* better.' He sighs. 'I do love it here. I'm going to miss it when I move to Australia.'

I laugh. 'With your Aussie wife that you're going to meet at The Royal College of Art?'

He smirks. 'Exactly.'

'It was funny when everyone saw your portrait of me.' I keep thinking about our classmates' faces when Mr Edwards showed his drawing around. 'They were all so blown away. You're proper talented. Becky wants you to sketch her.'

Theo lets out a small snort that sounds like derision.

'You wouldn't?'

He shakes his head. 'I've no interest in drawing Becky.'

'Why not? She's stunning.'

'She's predictable.' He glances at me. 'I'd draw you again, though.'

I know it's wrong, but I get a thrill when he says that.

His hair lifts in the wind, near-black strands floating away from his face. Maybe it's what he's wearing, but with his sharp eyebrows and angular features, he looks more like a Dark Prince than ever.

'You want to know why I was laughing?'

His blue eyes sharpen. 'Are you going to tell me?'

'I might do... Actually, I don't know if I can.'

'You're such a tease! Why not?'

'I'll sound like a psychopath.'

His eyebrows jump up and he looks absolutely delighted. 'Oh, now I *really* want to know.' He reaches over and pokes my ribs. 'Tell me.'

I squawk and he does it again.

'Okay! Okay.' I take a deep breath. 'Your hair.'

'Yes?'

'It always looks so shiny.'

He looks amused. 'Right...?'

'I imagined myself making wrist warmers out of it,' I blurt.

He stares at me, his eyes wide and his mouth slack, and then he throws his head back and howls with laughter.

I collapse into giggles.

'That is some seriously scary *Silence of the Lambs* shit, Leah.'

'I know! I told you I'd sound like a psychopath!' I reach out and touch his hair. He freezes, amusement caught on his face. 'It is *so* silky,' I say with amazement.

He's still laughing, but not as much as before.

'Fuck me, you're funny,' he says, with a look of such fondness that it makes my heart swell.

'You make me laugh too.' I shove his arm good-naturedly and glance down at the farm. 'They're back!' I gasp at the sight of the Land Rover. 'Quick, come on!'

I know when I walk into the kitchen, huffing and puffing from running almost the whole way back, that the meeting with Sophie did not go well. Mum and Dad are in the kitchen, talking, and they both look grave.

'Where's George?' I ask, panting.

'He went for a walk,' Dad replies wearily. 'Hello, Theo.'

'Hi,' Theo replies, uncomfortably.

'Do you know where? Is he okay? What happened?'

Dad sighs. 'I'm sure he'll tell you all about it when he's ready, love, but I think he might need some space right now.'

'If he does, we'll leave him be.'

'Give him half an hour or so,' he insists.

'Fine.' I look at Theo and jerk my head towards the door. 'Come on, we'll wait in the Bunny Barn.'

Halfway across the courtyard, I duck left. Theo jogs after me. 'What are you doing?'

'I think I know where he'll be.'

'But your dad said—'

'What, *you* always do what you're told?'

'I thought you were the good girl,' he gripes.

'Not today.'

We find George under the big old oak tree in the wood.

He stares at me bleakly as I approach, his knees drawn up in front of him and his head resting against the trunk. His eyes move past me to Theo and he shifts and straightens.

'Hey,' I say cautiously as we both go to sit down.

He looks as though he's been crying – his face is patchy and red – but his eyes are dry.

'Hey,' he mumbles.

'Are you okay?' Theo asks with concern.

George shakes his head, his bottom lip wobbling. Unthinkingly, I reach out and hook my arm around his knee. Theo pats George's other knee. George doesn't move.

'Did you see her?' I ask.

He nods and looks down.

'Was she okay?'

'She was grand,' he replies gruffly.

'What were her foster parents like?'

'Nice. They were nice.' He swallows. 'She seemed happy.' He pauses. 'I don't know if she remembered me.'

My heart squeezes.

'I was thinking that she didn't,' he continues. 'But a few times she looked at me for a bit longer and seemed to be thinking about it. Mostly she was acting like a happy little kid, showing me her toys and wanting to play. But then, when I went to leave...' His Adam's Apple bobs up and down again. 'She had a meltdown,' he says. 'And refused to say goodbye.'

I hug his knee and two fat tears spill from his eyes. My heart is breaking for him.

'Did you give her the letters?' I swipe my own tears away.

'I gave them to her foster parents to pass on to her adoptive parents. I don't know if they'll give them to her straight away or wait until she's older.'

'*Surely* you can still see her after she's adopted!' Theo snaps with a sudden burst of frustration and anger.

'It'll be up to her adoptive parents,' I explain gently.

I can tell he wants to fix this. But it's not that simple. Many adoptive parents start off thinking that they'll be fine with their adopted son or daughter having a relationship with their biological family, but when it comes down to it, if things are going well, they might wonder if it's worth the risk of upsetting them.

'They live in Devon,' George says. 'Her foster parents said they have a house near the sea. They were going on about what a great life Sophie was going to have. Lots of fresh air and sandcastles on the beach.'

I can't speak. My throat is too swollen. He's talking in such a matter-of-fact way – there's no bitterness, only acceptance.

I tighten my hold on him.

'This is a joke,' Theo spits, getting to his feet. 'How can they do this? How is this fair?'

'It's not fair,' I murmur, resting my chin on George's knee.

'There must be something we can do,' Theo says.

'There's nothing we can do,' George replies starkly, looking up at him.

I lift my eyes. George glances down at me and we hold each other's gaze for a long moment.

'You could write to the adoptive parents.' Theo starts

pacing. 'We *all* could. We'll convince them that George and Sophie shouldn't be separated. We'll—'

'Thank you,' George interrupts him. 'Ta for being here.' He meets my eyes again. 'I don't know what I'd do if I didn't have you two.'

'You'll always have us,' I say in a husky voice. 'We'll help you get through this.'

The sound of a car makes us turn our heads to see a dark-blue Range Rover coming along the lane.

'That's my father.' Theo sounds shocked. He tears away from us, trying to flag his dad down.

Theo never calls his dad for a lift – if he doesn't walk, it's the groundskeeper, Bart, or even one of my parents who will drive him.

But for some reason, Edwin Whittington is here.

I watch as the blond giant of a man gets out of the car. Dad has come out into the courtyard, but Edwin point-blank ignores him, furiously beckoning Theo over with a murderous expression on his face.

Theo walks to the car with his head bowed. I remember that his bag and blazer are in the house so I run up the hill, trying to catch him in time, but the Range Rover is already on its way back down the lane.

'Your bag!' I shout.

Theo stares at me through the window. He doesn't seem older now: he looks young and pale.

I feel ill as I watch the car drive out of view.

23

NOW

I t's Saturday afternoon, a week after my dinner with George at the pub by the river. Mum, Emilie and I are at the Cracked Teapot, setting up for Mum's first knitting workshop.

Shauna and her team are still serving customers out at the front – the café is by the cathedral in Ripon, and the town is heaving with tourists – but we've taken over the back room and gone a bit bonkers with bunting. Mum is expecting ten people, three of whom only booked yesterday: twin twenty-something sisters who thought it might be a nice surprise for their mother's birthday. Becky and I make up another two of the numbers. The rest are legit customers.

Last week, Gemma, Shauna's down-to-earth girlfriend, came over to the farm for a photoshoot – turns out she's an amateur photographer as well as being a postie.

Mum had roped in Shauna, Emilie and me to be

photographed wearing alpaca items of clothing over our own clothes: scarves, headbands, cardigans, skirts and jumpers. Shauna and Emilie were natural models, but I took some coaxing before I could relax into it. It helped when I told myself it didn't matter what I looked like because the clothes and accessories were the main focus, and the backdrops were spectacular too. We shot on the lime-green fields amid different coloured alpacas, and up on the rocks at Hare Heads with our hair blowing in the breeze. Shauna looked especially striking with her multiple ear piercings and her long flame-coloured tendrils falling free of her loose plait.

We also did some pictures on Chicken Island with the stream flowing at our feet, and on the bench seat in Mum's flower garden, which currently looks as though it's been caught in a snowstorm thanks to the number of white daisies growing around the border.

The photos came out better than I expected. I was kind of amazed, actually. The filter Gemma used gave the shots a summery seventies feel, and the daisies she'd asked us to wear in our hair also added to the retro look.

Mum had the photographs made up into postcards which are now pinned to corkboards on the walls. Many items of clothing are here, hanging on rails in a delicious palette of light and dark greys, chocolate browns, cream, fawn and black liquorice. There are also big baskets of skeins of yarn in multiple shades. It all looks so professional and I'm full of pride for Mum and how much work she's put into this.

A knitting pattern comes included in today's workshop price, so when customers start to arrive, Mum takes their tea or coffee order and urges them to browse the designs so they can choose what they'd like to knit. Today she'll help them to cast on and show them how to get started, but they'll finish their designs at home.

Becky studies the postcards with amazement.

'Flipping 'eck, Leah, you look like a model!'

'I felt so awkward.'

'You don't seem it.'

'Thanks.' I try to accept the compliment, knowing she means it. If she'd made this sort of fuss when we were younger, I would have been embarrassed.

'I love this dress. Where's it from?'

She's talking about the burgundy dress I have on under a knitted grey bolero. I'm wearing the same outfit today with high heels.

'I got it from the boutique I used to work in.' It was made by a local designer.

I think I used to spend half my salary on clothes. It was quite nice to put them on again for the shoot. I haven't had much of a chance to dress up in the last couple of years, and not much of an inclination to bother, either.

The afternoon is nothing short of a success. Everyone's eyes go as wide as saucers when Shauna and her team bring through afternoon tea – tiered vintage-style plates full of sandwiches, mini cakes and scones – and it's heart-warming to hear the happy chatter as people get stuck in. Mum gives everyone discount cards to pass on to their friends, and everyone leaves promising that they'll spread the word, with a few already talking about coming back in a couple of weeks, just for the fun of it.

As Shauna closes up and Mum, Becky and I set about cleaning, we hear the jingle of the bell over the door.

'We're closed!' Shauna shouts, then she laughs and

exclaims, 'Hello, you!' in such a warm voice that Mum, Becky and I look at each other before all at once heading towards the front room.

We hear Jamie's voice before we see him.

'What are you doing here?' Mum gasps, running through the café to sweep him up in a hug. Dani is hovering behind him.

'We couldn't miss your debut,' Jamie replies, before disgruntledly adding, 'Well, actually, turns out we *could* miss it. There was an emergency at work. Sorry we're late.'

'Never mind, never mind,' Mum waves him away. 'I can't believe you drove all this way from London!' Her cheeks are pink.

'It's so good to see you,' I say as I hug them both.

'We're only here for one night,' Jamie tells me regretfully.

'Where are you staying?'

'Royal Oak. George says there's a room free.'

'You've got to be kidding, why wouldn't you stay with us? The spare room is all made up.'

It used to be Jamie's room anyway, but now it has a big double bed in it. He rarely uses it. Jamie doesn't drink – mainly because he doesn't like the taste, not because he has particular issues with alcohol – so never minded driving home after an evening at the farm.

With Jamie and Dani's help, we have everything packed up and in the car in less than fifteen minutes. Becky doesn't have to rush back to Hayden, so she suggests we go for a drink at the pub to celebrate Mum's success. That way, Jamie can let George know that they won't be using the room after all. Gemma and Shauna already have plans so can't join us.

My stomach is a tangle of nerves as we walk along the high street, Jamie carrying a perky Emilie on his shoulders.

Dani leads the way into the pub, holding the door back for the rest of us.

I'm full of anticipation as I enter, expecting to see George behind the bar. Instead, there's a young blond guy serving customers.

'Grab that table,' Jamie instructs us as one comes free by the window.

'I thought George was working tonight,' Mum says when Jamie comes back with a bottle of Prosecco, an apple juice for Emilie and two small bottles of elderflower fizz.

'Not till later,' he replies, opening one of the soft drinks and pouring it into a glass of ice. 'The lad behind the bar says he's upstairs, but he's going to give him a shout and let him know we're here.'

The rush I feel scares me.

Jamie passes one of the elderflower fizzes to Dani. She's not drinking? Mum notices too.

He opens the Prosecco next and pours Mum, Becky and me each a glass.

'I'm driving so I can only have one,' Becky tells the table.

'Me too,' Mum says.

'I could,' I offer.

Mum shakes her head. 'I'm fine, love. You don't get out often enough.'

'Neither do you,' I point out.

'I'm going to Veronica and William's tomorrow night,' she reminds me.

I was invited too, but only as an afterthought. Becky and Robin aren't going to be there – they've got theatre tickets. Mum seemed pleased to hear that I'd already made plans with George. Suddenly he appears at the doorway leading to the upstairs rooms. I sit up straighter, watching as he scans the room before alighting on us. He smiles and comes over.

Jamie jumps to his feet to embrace him. 'Now then, fella, how are you?' he says amiably.

'Grand. You? How's it going in London?'

'Pull up a pew and I'll tell you all about it.'

'I will do, I'll just grab a drink first. I don't start work for another forty-five minutes.' George places his hand on Mum's shoulder in greeting. 'Everyone else okay?' he checks, making sure our glasses are full. I lift my flute at him and feel a flutter inside my stomach at his extra warm smile.

My eyes track his path to the bar. I think he's just got out of the shower, judging by his damp hair. His curls are more defined than usual. He stands in front of the bar, like a customer, and places his order with the blond guy.

I pull my attention away, and a minute later, George returns, taking the stool beside Jamie. Jamie is telling us about the veterinary practice where he works in London.

'About the most excitement I've had since I've been there was when a man brought his pet snake in. Otherwise it's all cats, dogs and guinea pigs.'

'Aw, no alpacas?' I ask.

'No farm animals at all, but at least the hours are more predictable. No more being called out at midnight.'

I'm so proud of him. I wonder if he would have become a vet if it weren't for Dad. I'd like to think so, but he went through plenty of wobbly patches at school. I remember hearing Dad say to him more than once, 'Come on, son, you need to work a bit harder. Don't give up.' And when he was worrying about the way his exams were going: 'Come on, son, of *course* you're going to get into vet school. Even if you don't get the grades this time, there's always next year. Don't give up. You *will* do this!'

Dad fought for him all the way. Jamie barely scraped through his exams to get the grades he needed, but once he was at vet school, his confidence soared and he sailed through.

Grief is an unpredictable beast. Sometimes it strikes out of the blue, and other times it lays dormant, waiting to catch you unawares.

I blink back tears at the memories of Dad as George reaches for the bottle of Prosecco.

Mum covers the top of her glass with her hand. 'I can't, I'm driving.'

'Dani and I can take you lasses home,' Jamie offers. 'Collect the car later.'

'Or I could drive it over tomorrow evening?' George suggests. 'I'm insured to drive any vehicle.'

'What's happening tomorrow evening?' Jamie asks with interest.

'George is coming for dinner,' I tell him.

'Ace.' Jamie seems pleased.

'Go on then, I'll have another,' Mum decides. 'I feel like celebrating.'

'How did it go?' George asks, topping up her glass and mine.

Becky dutifully sticks to her one.

As Mum recounts the day, Emilie starts to get wriggly. I pull her onto my lap for a hug, pressing my lips to the top of her head.

I glance up to see George studying us, a contemplative expression on his face. He averts his gaze.

I'm still thrown by the fact that he doesn't want kids, that his relationship broke down *because* of it.

It occurs to me that, if things had worked out differently, if George hadn't run away, if I hadn't ended up with Theo... my daughter would not exist.

I feel sick at the thought.

I might have regrets – and some of them might be huge – but I wouldn't change anything about the path that led me to becoming Emilie's mother.

Later, on the way to the car, we pass a post box. I surreptitiously pull my letters to Theo from my handbag and slip them in.

I still haven't written about George. But I will. I definitely will.

24

THEN

After Theo's dad came to collect him on Wednesday afternoon, he didn't return to school for the rest of the week. When I've called, his phone has gone straight through to voicemail, and his text messages remain unanswered.

George has been in a dark place of his own. He's attended school physically, but mentally, he's been an empty shell.

I've been going out of my mind with worry for them both, but trying to hide my feelings from my parents. It was Jamie's eighteenth birthday yesterday, but he wanted to hold off celebrating properly until after his exams. He's been stressed out about how they're going, and Joanne keeps breaking down about Nia and Ashlee leaving us next month. My parents have their hands full.

What I need is to be able to vent to my best friend about

what's happening, but Becky and I are in a weird place right now. She's 'so tired' all the time, and a bit over the 'melodrama', as she calls it. She insisted on spending the tail end of last week up on the high field watching the boys play football at lunchtime. Martin was one of those boys and all she could talk about was seeing him at Amanda's birthday party. It was last night and I had no interest whatsoever in going – George and Theo weren't invited – so I used Jamie's understated birthday meal as an excuse.

Becky hasn't come out and said it, but I'm pretty sure she's angry at me for putting the boys and my family first. I feel very separate from her right now.

Theo is back on the bus on Monday, and I watch him board with such a wave of relief that I momentarily forget to listen to Becky's mammoth recount of the party on Saturday night. She and Martin snogged and she can't believe I missed the occasion. She's now worried it was only a one-off and will be in no mood to have to repeat herself to me. There's no way I dare to get up and go to speak to Theo, even though I want to.

I catch up with him on our way to form group.

'We brought your things in with us,' I tell him hurriedly. 'Mr Balls is looking after them.'

'Yeah, thanks,' he says. 'I got your text messages.'

'Why didn't you reply?' I ask with a frown. 'I've been worried.'

'Sorry,' he mumbles, averting his gaze. 'My father confiscated my phone – I only saw them when I left the house this morning.'

'Are you okay? I've been so worried.'

He gives me a small smile. 'You've already said that.'

I shrug at him, feeling hurt. 'Well, I have.'

He pulls me to one side of the corridor. 'I'm all right,' he says, leaning his shoulder against the wall and facing me. 'My dad was pissed off because it was Sylvie's birthday on Wednesday and we were supposed to be going out for dinner. He was angry I forgot.'

'Is that all? Why weren't you in school on Thursday and Friday?'

He winces. 'I wasn't feeling well.'

'What was wrong with you?'

He shrugs and shakes his head, his lips pulled down at the corners. 'I don't know. I just felt off.'

'Well, I'm glad you're back,' I say, going on to tell him about Hazel and her cria as we walk the rest of the way together. 'Come over after school – he's even cuter than Jessamine's baby, and that's saying something. I reckon he's a "Periwinkle".' I glance at him when he doesn't respond. 'What do you think? Are you up for it?'

'Yeah, maybe.'

'You don't sound so sure.'

'I'll tell you why later,' he replies as the bell goes.

I risk Becky's wrath to sit with Theo and George at lunchtime. George clearly has his mind on other things, barely engaging with our conversation at all, until Theo tells us that his father has banned him from 'ever setting foot on our land again'.

'What?' I gasp.

George's jaw drops.

'He said he'd put me back in boarding school,' Theo reveals, letting out a small laugh.

'What? No!'

He smiles miserably. 'Can you believe it? After swearing he'd never pay another penny towards my education, as soon as I seem remotely happy, he threatens to send me away again. He really is an arse.'

I can imagine his dad coming to this decision. There are far too many prejudiced parents in the world who worry that their precious offspring might be in danger by mingling with a child who's in the care system.

'What will you do?' I feel nauseous.

'Sod him,' he replies with a shrug. 'He's away half the time anyway, and Bart has my back. Dad'll never know.'

Still, the thought of losing him has me reeling. I'm so fond of George *and* Theo. They've had such different upbringings, but they have many things in common: both lost their mothers prematurely, and both have fathers who are indifferent to them. George's father isn't there for him at all; Theo's father wants to control him. George has lost Sophie; Theo has no relationship with Acton. Neither have parents who love them unconditionally.

My parents might not be there for me as much as I'd like them to be, but at least I feel loved by them.

Ever since Jamie came to live with us, it's been a family tradition to go to Lightwater Valley, the local theme park, on the first day of the summer holidays. It's something he and I look forward to months in advance, and our enthusiasm rubs off on everyone else in the house. In previous years we've all flown out of the car, laughing as we've hurtled towards the nearest rollercoaster.

For weeks, Joanne has been saying it's the only thing that will cheer her up, and even Ashlee, who has no idea what a theme park is, has been shouting 'Yay!' whenever Lightwater Valley has been mentioned.

I wanted to ask Mum and Dad if Theo could come with us, but there's not enough room in the car. He's spent so much time at our house recently that Dad has joked he'll have to kick Jamie out so Theo can move in. Jamie knows he doesn't mean it. My parents always offer to give Theo a lift home and he usually takes them up on it. While it's not their place to get involved in the affairs of other families – at least, *unofficially* – I sense they feel as protective of Theo as they do of some of the teenagers who have come to live with us.

So far, Theo has managed to pull the wool over his dad's eyes – he got to see out the school term with us, in any case – but I'm scared that it's only a matter of time before his dad finds out he's been disobeying him.

I should be feeling happy and relieved on the morning of our excursion – school has broken up and I'm free for the summer – but this year, everything has a dark cloud hanging over it.

Becky is now going out with Martin and is so deep in his pockets that we've barely spoken at lunchtimes, let alone seen each other outside of school. I'm sure she bears a grudge against me for being emotionally unavailable to her, but it goes both ways.

Ashlee and Nia are leaving us in a few days and Joanne has been really struggling, Jamie is fretting because he thinks he messed up a couple of his exams and won't get into veterinary college, and my parents are wrapped up in comforting them both while trying to hold it together emotionally themselves.

As for George... George is just... quiet. Ever since going

to see Sophie a month ago, he's retreated into himself. I'm worried about him, but when I ask if he's okay, he repeats that he's fine.

In the car on the way there, Jamie makes it his mission to pep us all up. 'Come on, you lot. This is our last outing together as a family of eight – let's make it a day that even a three-year-old might remember.' He nods at Ashlee. 'You got your camera, Carrie?' he calls up to Mum in the front.

'Sure have!' Mum chirps back.

'Let's fill up those Life Story books, lads and lasses! Lightwater Valley! Yeah!' he cheers, fist-pumping the air.

'Lightwater Valley!' Joanne echoes, to everyone's surprise.

'Yay!' Ashlee shouts back with glee, clapping.

And that's the way we play it. All of us get on board. I've never seen Joanne laugh and smile so much in her life. It might be an act to begin with, but soon our enthusiasm becomes real. We manage to temporarily suspend our fear and sorrow to try to make it the best possible day for the little ones. Mum and Dad stay with Ashlee and Nia the entire time, but Jamie, Joanne, George and I alternate riding the big kid rollercoasters and taking them on the baby rides. None of us want to miss out on Ashlee's adorably infectious giggles.

George and I ride our last rollercoaster of the day together – it was the longest rollercoaster in the world, when it was built – and seeing him look across at me, laughing with abandon as I scream, makes my stomach flip even as it bottoms out. I'm giddy with affection for him and when the ride ends, I do something uncharacteristic: I turn and step up against his chest. It's not a hug – our arms are at our sides – but we're flush to each other and my forehead is resting on his shoulder. After a moment, he lays his cheek against the top of my head.

It feels natural for all of three seconds, and then my heart begins to race. He smells clean and lovely and I know I need to put distance between us. But it's so, *so* hard.

Just as I'm about to wrench myself away, George's arms slip around my waist. Wild horses couldn't stop me from wrapping my arms around his neck and holding him tightly in return.

I'm pretty sure I'm in love with this boy.

It's the sound of Jamie calling our names that jerks us apart, but we sit next to each other in the car on the way home, and I'm incapable of speech. I feel as though I've been plugged into a socket – my blood is charged and I'm fizzing with electricity. I can't think about anything except for the feeling of George's leg pressed against mine.

Two days later, reality hits. And what a heavyweight punch in the guts it is.

Saying goodbye to Ashlee and Nia is one of the worst things I have ever had to do.

It's different with teenagers. Teenagers, you know, will remember you. Even though it hurts, even though it's painful to no longer see them at the breakfast table or on the bus to school, there's every chance that you'll hear from them again from time to time.

But with Ashlee and Nia, this could well be it. Their adoptive parents have no obligation to keep in touch with us. In fact, they probably won't. Ashlee and Nia have formed such a strong bond with my parents – especially my mum – that for them to see her, or any of us again anytime soon, may only confuse them. It will be hard, these next few weeks and months. Everything in their young lives is changing, and while Anita and Ollie will no doubt shower them with love and attention, there will be times when they'll miss my mum acutely.

I know it's this that distresses Mum more than anything else: the thought of Ashlee or Nia crying out for her in the night and her not being there.

Although she's smiling brightly as she hugs first Nia and then Ashlee goodbye, her whole body is trembling with emotion. I feel hollow inside, as though someone has carved a huge chunk out of my heart. It was hard enough holding Ashlee's small body to mine for the last time, but seeing Mum like this upsets me on a different level.

She keeps it together as we stand side by side in the courtyard to wave goodbye. The girls don't understand what's happening – certainly not Nia and definitely not Ashlee, who sticks her tiny hand out of the window and wobbles it this way and that while her little voice calling 'Bye!' becomes harder and harder to hear.

But as soon as the car rounds the bend in the lane, we fall apart. Mum and I clutch each other as we cry, while Dad literally has to pick Joanne up off the ground. I'm aware of Jamie hugging George, but when I finally break away from Mum's embrace, George is no longer with us.

I find him in his usual place, down by the oak tree, with his head in his hands, and his whole body heaving with quiet sobs.

If it hurts this much for me to let Ashlee and Nia go, I can't believe how much pain he must be in, knowing that his own sister is about to be cut from his life, possibly forever.

'I have to see her again,' he says fervently, lifting his face to look at me. 'That *can't* have been the last time I see her. I *have* to see her again. I have to say a proper goodbye.'

Sophie is moving to Devon with her adoptive parents in less than a fortnight. When we speak to Dad about arranging another meeting before then, he promises that he'll try.

But I know my dad. He does not look hopeful.

In the days after Ashlee and Nia leave us, George's anger bursts back into flame. Theo is there when he punches his knuckles raw up at Brimham. We're sitting together on the overhang when George suddenly flips out, jumping the couple of metres to the ground and laying into a rock as though it's made of rubber. No amount of my begging can get him to stop, and Theo won't let me climb down to him, although I want to.

That night I lay in bed, replaying the incident over and over in my head. George's anguished yelps, Theo's stark expression, the way he held me back protectively, worried for my own safety.

Afterwards, he took George for a walk, just the two of them. I stayed on the rock, crying my heart out.

The week before Sophie is due to leave her foster parents, I find out what they must've discussed when they were alone – and I'm not at all surprised they kept it from me. I'm furious.

George wants something permanent to mark the pain he feels in losing his sister, and if it's not going to be scars caused by punching rocks or other self-harm, it'll be her name etched onto his skin.

At boarding school, Theo had a friend who inked his own arm with a skull and crossbones. His friend got expelled, and even though Theo didn't have anything to do with it, the fact that he was there while his friend performed the act was another black mark against him.

George is far too young to get a tattoo done legally by a professional – you have to be over eighteen – so Theo, in all his wisdom, has offered to do it himself.

I am simmering with anger and anxiety as I lead the way alongside the stream to a glade that's far enough away from the farm that we won't be disturbed. I seriously considered telling my parents what we were up to, but I knew both boys would find a way to do what they wanted regardless. George's mind is made up, and I don't want to be his enemy.

The air is heavy with the scent of wild garlic and the earth smells damp and mossy as we settle on some rocks amongst the leafy ferns. The sunlight streaks through the silver birch trees overhead, hitting our faces in a flickering dance.

I've packed baby wipes, antiseptic wipes and Ibuprofen. George agrees to the antiseptic wipes, but turns down the pills. He wants to feel the pain.

Theo has already sterilised the needle. It's a longer than normal one – I don't know where he got it – but he's strapped it to a wooden tool so he can hold it like a pencil. He also has an inkpot and a biro – the latter to create a template to trace over with the needle. George has rolled his T-shirt up as high as it will go and cleaned his skin with the antiseptic wipe, but when Theo goes to write Sophie's name below his shoulder, George stops him.

'What?' Theo asks, biro poised.

'I want Leah to do it.'

Is he out of his mind?

'Just the writing part,' he says with a short laugh at the look on my face. 'Please,' he adds.

'Yeah,' Theo agrees, getting up and passing me the pen. 'Your handwriting is much nicer than mine.'

I hesitate, but only briefly. Turns out I do want to be a part of this madness after all.

I sit down next to George, so close that my knees are pressed against his side.

'Cursive?' I ask. 'Or capitals? What do you want?'

'You decide,' he says in a low voice, lifting his clear brown eyes to meet mine.

'I think cursive,' I murmur, staring back at him.

He nods. I hold his arm steady, stretching his skin so I can write as smoothly as possible. As soon as I touch the pen to his arm, he tells me to hang on.

'Little one,' he says. 'Not Sophie. Write "*Little one*" with a capital L.' He swallows. 'It's what I used to call her. It's how I talked to her in my letters.'

I remember seeing it on his notepad. It's how we referred to Nia and Ashlee too.

I nod, forcing down the lump that's formed in my throat, and get to work.

He watches me the entire time that I'm penning the words, and there's something oddly sensual about it. I feel incredibly edgy, but I'm also very aware of Theo standing over us. I can't imagine how much tension there would be if George and I were alone.

When I'm done, I blow on the ink, making sure it's set. George inhales sharply and his eyes meet mine for a long, goosebump-inducing moment before I get up and let Theo take my place.

Theo dips the needle in the ink and pierces George's skin. George's jaw is clenched, but pain flits across his forehead with every jab of the needle. Theo repeats the process, tracing the letters prick by prick, while I clean off excess ink with the baby wipes until, finally, it's done.

George takes one last look at the words etched across his inflamed red skin before rolling down his T-shirt sleeve.

'Not a word of this to your parents,' he warns me seriously.

I shake my head, his silent accomplice.

25

NOW

'Where's your mam?' George asks when I let him into the kitchen on Sunday evening.

'She's gone to the Nortons for dinner.'

'Oh.' He seems surprised, placing one of the big boxes from the knitting workshop on the kitchen table. He's driven here in Mum's car, as planned. We left everything in the boot overnight. 'I thought she'd be here too.'

'She already had the invitation. Don't worry, I might not be able to cook as well as she can, but I promise I won't give you food poisoning. Drink?'

'Let me grab the other boxes from the car first.'

'I'll give you a hand.'

'I can manage.'

He disappears out the door and I go to stir the ragu that's simmering on the Aga hotplate.

A couple of trips later, he comes into the kitchen with a fabric tote bag and a big bunch of sunflowers.

'They're lovely. Are they for Mum?' I ask.

'No, for you. Well, both of you, I suppose, but you, seeing as she's not here.'

I laugh lightly and take them. 'Thank you.'

'Sorry, that came out wrong. I was thinking of you when I bought them.'

I glance at him, feeling my stomach flip.

He gets Mum's car keys out of his pocket. '*These* are for your mam. I have a couple more things too.'

He lifts a box of chocolates out of the bag, plus a bottle of Prosecco, a bottle of red wine and a six-pack of Theakston's.

'We're going to be mashed!' I exclaim.

He laughs. 'I wasn't expecting us to drink it all tonight.'

'Oh, we are definitely making a hole in this stuff. I told you, I want to see you drunk.'

He looks around. 'Is Emilie in bed?'

I nod. 'She went down half an hour ago. Hopefully she'll stay that way till morning. Which of these magnificent beverages will you start with?'

'I'll have a bitter,' he says. 'You?'

'Prosecco, all the way.'

He opens the bottle and deftly fills a flute for me, judging the bubbles so they don't spill over.

'You are very good at that, you know,' I say. 'Are you *sure* you haven't been working behind a bar all these years?'

He lifts an eyebrow at me.

'I suppose you're used to pouring Prosecco for Annie.'

Did I really say that?

'And your other girlfriends, no doubt.'

And *that*?!

He laughs quietly. 'There haven't been too many of those. No one serious, in any case. What about you?'

'There's only been Theo for me.'

He reaches for a bottle of Theakston's, cracking it open.

Did I imagine him flinching?

'You want a glass?'

'No, this is grand.' He lifts it to knock against mine.

'Cheers. Let's go through to the living room. Dinner won't be long. I hope you like Italian.'

'I do.'

George is wearing dark-grey trousers and a white shirt with the sleeves rolled up, hanging loose over another white T-shirt underneath.

I wonder what his tattoos look like in winter – do they stand out more against paler skin? Right now, he's honey-coloured, tanned from spending time outdoors.

I lift my knees up onto the sofa so I can face him. It's a warm night, so my feet are bare – earlier I painted my toenails in coral pink polish and now I realise the colour unintentionally matches the T-shirt knotted at my waist. I'm wearing skinny black jeans.

George looks around the room, his eyes coming to a rest on the basket of yarn by the fireplace.

'Remember how I taught you to knit?'

He smiles and nods. 'I never did finish that scarf.'

'I finished it for you.'

'Did you?'

'Yeah. I think there were more tears in it than fibre at one point. I still have it in a box somewhere.'

His brow creases and his fingers flex. I have a funny feeling he'd like to reach out and touch me, but I laugh lightly before he can act on it.

'So much for going to the festival. Becky managed to go. She went with Martin. Do you remember him?'

'Yeah, they started going out before I left.'

'They were together for a couple of months, but broke up at the end of summer. Straight after the festival, actually.'

'That'll teach her for not inviting you.'

'Oh, she invited me,' I reply flippantly. 'But I was in no mood to go without you and Theo.'

Martin calling things off with Becky was what brought us back together in the end. She realised she did need her best friend after all. Comforting her took my mind off my own heartache. We were close again by the end of September.

We chat for a while and then I go to put the pasta on.

George gets up from the sofa and joins me in the kitchen. 'It smells amazing.'

'It's Theo's aunt's recipe,' I disclose automatically.

'Oh, right.' He sounds surprised.

'Did you know Theo's mother was Italian?' I decide to continue on this course.

'No?'

'Neither did I. His aunt was his mother's sister. Claudia. Theo got on well with her. She taught him how to cook, in fact.'

And he, in turn, taught me, once we were living together.

'I'm still reeling from the fact that he went to Italy,' he says.

'He liked it there, despite how much he hated to leave this place.'

'So you two stayed in touch? Well, *obviously* you did.'

I nod. 'We wrote and spoke on the phone. He came home for the longer school holidays so we'd see each other then.'

'Shall I open the bottle of red?'

'Go for it. I might stick with Prosecco.'

He sorts out our drinks while I drain the tagliatelle. We carry everything through to the dining table.

'This room feels so empty,' George says as we sit down. 'Didn't we have nine people around this table at one point?'

I think aloud: 'Mum, Dad, you, me, Jamie, Joanne, Preston, Ashlee and Nia. Yep, nine.'

'Do you ever hear from any of them?'

I nod and pick up my fork. 'Preston returned to us, unfortunately. I mean "unfortunately" for *him*, not us. His mum went back into rehab.' I twirl some pasta around my fork, already regretting the messy food choice. 'Did you know Dani is his sister?'

'No!'

'Yeah.' I smile at his surprise. 'She came back with him the second time. She was seventeen, so we only had her briefly. Preston went to live with her eventually. He runs a doughnut stall these days which he takes to various markets around North Yorkshire. He always did love going to Masham with Dad.'

I sigh and George gives me a sad smile.

'Joanne went on to become a social worker,' I reveal.

His eyebrows jump up.

'And then she quit and became a primary school teacher.'

'Ah.'

'She got married and divorced and married again, and now she and her second husband are expecting their first baby together. He seems nice. We went to their wedding last year in Wales.'

'Is that where they live?'

I nod.

'What about Ashlee and Nia?'

I shake my head and pick up my napkin. 'Their father was eventually caught and convicted for the murder of their mother so at least we knew he was no longer a threat to them.' I pause before asking, 'Are you in contact with *your* dad?'

'No. As you once said, just because he's got some of the same cells as me, doesn't make him worth my time. I decided enough was enough and stopped all contact. I'm sad you've never heard from Ashlee and Nia, though.'

'Me too. I still hold out hope that one day they'll look through their Life Story books and decide to get in touch. It's hard to believe that Ashlee is eighteen now.'

'Or that Sophie is nineteen.'

'You really never got any leads on her?'

'No.'

'It's probably a stupid question, but have you looked for her on Facebook?'

'On and off, but I don't even know her last name.'

'Do *you* have a Facebook page?'

I've searched for him a few times over the years, but not in a while.

He confirms what I thought. 'No.'

'What if she tries to look for *you*?'

He shrugs, then puts his fork down and reaches for his wine glass.

Has he really given up on ever seeing her again?

'I don't want to overstep the mark,' I say gently. 'But it wouldn't have to be a big thing: just your name and photo, and you could mention her in your bio.'

He nods. 'Yeah, that makes sense. I guess I just don't want to get my hopes up again.'

'That's understandable.'

We move onto lighter topics after that, and the more he drinks, the more relaxed he becomes. By the time we've finished dessert, we're two thirds of the way through two bottles of booze. I'm feeling light-headed but happy, and George seems very chilled on the red.

We take our glasses through to the living room, just as Mum arrives home.

'Hello, you two!' She beams at us from the doorway, her cheeks flushed.

'Who gave you a lift?' I ask.

We heard the car pull up, but earlier she was insistent on walking back across the fields.

'Robin. He and Becky came back a short while ago. Oh, I tell you what, their place is going to be *lovely*.' She perches on the arm of the sofa opposite. 'Veronica and William gave me a tour. They're starting to think *they* should have the barn conversion and give Rebecca and Robin the farmhouse.'

'Really?'

'Yes. Veronica hates the stairs. So do I, after my fall. Maybe it's something we could think about—'

'What fall?' I interrupt with alarm.

'When I twisted my ankle.' Mum waves away my concern. 'But maybe we *could* think about converting the Bunny Barn for me one day. You could have the house for your family. I only mean if you decided to stay!' she says at the look on my face. 'Oh, never mind. I'm drunk. I'm going to bed,' she adds brusquely, getting to her feet. 'Night, night. George, there's the spare room if you don't want to bother with a taxi. *I* wouldn't.'

'Night,' he calls after her with amusement, before meeting my eyes. 'I've never seen your mam blathered before.'

'Looks like she had a great time.'

I'm pleased. I know she's still finding it hard without Dad – incredibly so at times. Socialising with their old friends must really bring his absence home.

'You *could* stay,' I say. 'I bet Mum'd do us a fry-up in the morning if you did.'

'Benefits to living at home, eh?'

'*Loads* of benefits.'

'Bit worrying about her fall,' he muses.

I nod. 'I knew she'd hurt her ankle, but I didn't know she'd done it falling down the stairs. We could do with a second railing on the other side of the wall to give her something else to hold onto.'

'I could put one up,' George offers.

'You're already doing so much.'

'I don't mind. I'd like to.'

'Thank you,' I say sincerely. 'It's nice that you want to look out for her.'

'Not only her.'

I meet his eyes for a long moment before glancing away and tucking my hair behind my ear. George leans forward and brushes a stray strand away from my face. My breath catches.

'Sorry,' he mutters, withdrawing. 'I've wanted to do that all night.'

So *this* is what he's like when he's drunk, I think, dizzily.

'Gah,' he says quietly, scrubbing his face with his hand.

Smiling, I reach forward and pull his hand down. He shyly rests his arm along the back of the sofa.

'I still can't believe you got an alpaca tattoo.' I lean closer to study his ink. 'Do you have any others? Or only the ones I've seen?'

'I don't know which ones you've seen.'

'Your silver birch, your ink pen and your compass,' I reel off.

And 'Little one', of course, although I haven't seen that one for many years. I can't quite bring myself to look at it again tonight.

He runs his hand up his arm to the inside of his bicep.

'You've got one there?' I ask. 'What is it?'

He looks at me, a funny smile on his face. He shrugs. 'It's under my shirt.'

'So take off your shirt. You've got a T-shirt on underneath.'

'I don't know, Leah,' he mumbles, scratching his chin and looking embarrassed.

Oh God, I *love* him drunk!

My face must've lit up with glee because when he looks at me, he laughs a little.

'I must be mad,' he says as he shrugs his shirt off.

My eyes widen at the sight of him. Frankly, he's a work of art *without* his tattoos.

He slowly turns his toned, tanned arm over to show me the sloping scrawl stretched around the inside of his bicep.

I shift onto my knees, trying to get even closer.

'What does it say?' I'm intrigued as I take his arm and hold it steady. 'It looks like Ye Olde English.'

He chuckles. 'Actually, it's Middle English, not Old English – if you want to be pedantic,' he adds, gently mocking himself. 'It's Chaucer. "As an ook cometh of a litel spyr".'

I gape at him with delight, and once more his cheeks warm.

'It's the origin of "Mighty oaks from little acorns grow",' he explains self-consciously. 'Spyr is a sapling.'

My breathing spikes and he holds my gaze. Goosebumps

shiver over his arm and with a jolt, I let him go, returning to my previous position on the sofa. He slides his arm back into his shirt.

'You've got memories of us etched all over your skin,' I whisper, staggered, as he finishes putting his shirt back on.

'You've always been with me,' he replies earnestly, meeting my eyes.

My heart trips and stumbles.

This is too much. Too intense. I try to think of another topic, something lighter to ease the tension.

All I can think of, in my stupor, is, 'Shall we crack open the chocolates?'

I get up and go into the kitchen, feeling unsteady. I should probably stop drinking. Filling up the kettle, I glance through to the living room. George is sitting on the sofa with his feet planted firmly on the floor, his hand cupping his chin and his eyes on the wall opposite.

'Actually, do you want a coffee?' I call through to him.

He starts at my question. 'Er, sure.'

'Can you grab the coffee jar from the larder cupboard?' I ask when he comes through.

He crosses the room while I try to focus on clearing my head. Fat chance. I'm ludicrously tipsy. I look over after a while to see George staring at the inside wall of the larder cupboard. He's found the height chart.

'We never did paint over them,' I say as I walk over to join him.

'There are so many,' he replies with amazement, tracing his fingers over Ashlee's name.

'I know. There's barely enough room for Emilie.' I hesitate, but the words are coming out whether I want them to or not. 'Does Emilie remind you of Sophie?'

'No. She reminds me—'

'Of Theo,' I finish for him.

'No.' He glances at me. 'She reminds me of you.'

'Oh.'

'She takes after Theo too, but mostly it's you. She has your hazel eyes and your dark-blond hair. And your smile...' He searches my face, then his eyes come to rest on mine. 'She's lovely.'

'Oh,' I say again, feeling heat creep up my body. 'Look, you're still at the top.'

I don't know how many more times I'm going to be capable of switching our conversation back to lighter territory.

'Dad said you still had some growing to do,' I add with a pang. 'He was right. Hey, we should mark you on again now!'

He laughs down at me.

'Come on, Dad would've liked that.' I hurry away and dig a marker pen out of the drawer. 'Up against the wall,' I command.

He lifts an eyebrow at me teasingly.

I roll my eyes and push him backwards, my stomach somersaulting at the feeling of his hard chest beneath my palms. *What he must look like with his shirt off...* I shake my head quickly, trying to expel the thought. His back hits the larder wall and I step up on my tiptoes.

'I don't think I'm going to be able to reach. I don't have shoes on.'

'I noticed,' he says in a low murmur.

'Seriously, I can't see over the top of your head.'

He very slowly bends his knees and slides down the wall.

I stare at him and then crack up laughing.

'I think that defeats the purpose,' I say when I've recovered.

The light level is low, but his eyes are definitely sparkling.

He straightens up again as I drunkenly look around for something to stand on. I use my foot to shift a four-pack tin of tomatoes into place. Stepping up onto them and standing on my tiptoes, I'm almost high enough to see over his head and mark the wall. When I wobble, he steadies me.

Whoa...

His hands are on my waist and his thumbs are pressing into the bare skin beneath my knotted T-shirt. With my hand resting on one of his broad shoulders, I pull the pen's lid off with my teeth. Every nerve-ending is standing to attention as I lean in.

My breasts press firmly against his chest and I both feel and hear his sharp intake of breath as I mark his height on the wall. Withdrawing a minute amount, I discover that his gaze is fixed on my lips.

I lower my heels down and put the pen lid back on, but I don't step off the tins or move away. He doesn't remove his hands from my waist either.

We're looking at each other now and time is stretching on. He reaches up and brushes the edge of my mouth with his thumb. My lips part on a breath and I know he wants to kiss me.

And *oh, I want him to...* In that moment, I want it so much.

But I'm drunk and so is he. Neither of us is thinking straight.

'Am I part of your unfinished business, George?' I dare to ask.

He blinks at me.

'If Theo were here, would you have come back?' I whisper.

He closes his eyes and his hands on my waist go slack. The kettle begins to show signs of whistling and the spell is broken. I step down from the tins.

But George grabs my arm before I can walk away.

'Do you still love him?' he asks, his expression tortured.

'I'll never stop loving him,' I reply honestly.

His brow creases with pain and he lets me go with a nod, accepting my answer. I cross the room and remove the kettle from the hotplate as it begins to screech.

26

THEN

A second meeting with Sophie is not going to happen. At least, that's what Dad is telling George. Her social worker doesn't believe that it's in her best interests – she leaves for Devon tomorrow.

When George comes out of the study after talking this over with Dad, he catches my eye and nods towards the stairs. I follow him up, but he goes into my room, not his, closing the door firmly behind us.

'I'm going to see her,' he tells me, his jaw set with determination.

I sit down on my bed and stare up at him in dismay.

'Come with me,' he implores.

'George, *no*. I don't think you should go.'

'I'm going.'

'Just think about it a while longer.'

'It's all I've *been* thinking about, Leah!' he hisses. 'I can't shake the feeling that it's all wrong! I haven't fought enough for her. *I'm* her family. I haven't even met those people and yet I'm going to allow her to go and live with them?'

'Her social worker said they're nice,' I try to reassure him.

'Sod her social worker! I wouldn't trust her as far as I could chuck her! They'd say anything to get a kid off their books.'

'That's not true.' A horrible feeling settles over me as a thought occurs to me. 'What are you planning to do when you get there?'

He doesn't answer.

'George!' I'm appalled. 'You can't take her!'

'She's *mine*!' he shout-whispers.

'LEAH! GEORGE!'

We stare at each other with alarm at the sound of my mum calling up the stairs.

'Yes?' I call back.

'Theo's here!'

My shoulders slump. I get up from the bed and go to the door. 'See you downstairs in a minute?'

He nods, his eyes flaring.

Theo isn't in the kitchen.

Mum nods towards the courtyard: 'He didn't want to come in.'

I don't have time for this right now!

My chest is tight with exasperation as I walk outside and look around. Theo is up by the girls' paddock. I stomp up the hill towards him. *Maybe he'll be able to help me convince George*, I tell myself. Then I see Theo's face and stumble.

He must've been *bawling* to look this way: all red and

patchy and swollen. He breaks down again when he sees me, his shoulders shaking violently as he drags his hand over his mouth. I run the rest of the way.

'What's wrong?' I ask him. 'Tell me!'

'I'm going to Italy tomorrow.' He can hardly speak for crying.

I don't understand. 'On holiday?'

'No. To live.'

'*What*?'

'Can we walk?' He nods up the hill towards Hare Heads.

I glance back at the farm, wondering where George is.

'For fuck's sake, Leah!' Theo gasps.

I shoot my head around to look at him. His eyes are wide and distressed.

'Just this once,' he begs tearfully, nodding behind me.

I realise what he's getting at. He wants me to give *him* my full attention.

I nod and let him lead the way.

By the time we reach the overhang, his eyes are dry, but he still looks utterly despondent.

'Talk to me.' I take his wrist and pull him down to a sitting position on the rock.

I let him go, but he swipes my hand, holding it in his lap. My heart skips a beat, but I don't pull away, even though the unusual contact makes me jumpy.

'My father told me a while back that he was considering sending me to a boarding school in Europe,' he reveals in a constricted voice.

'Why didn't you say anything?'

'You guys are going through so much already, I didn't want to be another burden.'

'Theo, you're our *friend*. You'll never be a burden.'

He tightens his grip on my hand.

'What's this about Italy?' I'm almost too scared to ask.

'My aunt – my mother's sister – lives in Milan. My father has got me into St Louis. It's a private school.'

'But...' I'm shocked. 'You don't even speak Italian!'

He lifts a shoulder. 'I do, a bit. My mother was Italian. She wanted me to be brought up bilingual, so she spoke to me in Italian when I was young. I learnt it at boarding school too.'

'I never knew that.' How am I so ignorant about him? About his family? 'So you're going to go and live with your aunt?'

He nods. 'For the rest of the summer, then I'll be at the school. My father says he'll allow me to study Art only under these conditions.'

My throat closes up. He's really leaving us?

I grab his other hand. 'I don't want to lose you.' My voice chokes out the words.

'I'll be back at Christmas,' he replies. 'Hopefully.'

Why is this happening? 'Does your dad know you've been coming here?'

He nods. 'He knew all along.'

'So he's trying to take you away from us?'

He nods again, his eyes filling with tears.

'Oh God. No!' I pull my hands away from him and get to my feet.

'Leah,' he calls as I walk out past Mini Druid's Writing Desk. I come to a stop at the hole in the rock. There's no water in it today, but I can still make out a vague heart shape.

'Leah,' Theo says quietly from behind me.

I turn around and pull him into a hug. 'I don't want you

to go,' I say against his neck. It's all too much, too hard. George seems to be on a crazy path that is pulling him further and further away from me, I'm missing Ashlee and Nia and can't bear to see my mum's pain, and I feel alienated from my best friend. Theo was the only one making me smile... And now he's leaving too.

He holds me tightly as I cry. He's so warm and solid. Comforting. I feel safe in his arms. The thought quiets me in a strange way, but I have no desire to step away from him. When he loosens his grip on me, I feel a stab of disappointment, but he cups my face between his hands and gently makes me look up at him.

He stares into my eyes steadily. Even when rimmed with red, his are *so* blue. They're mesmerising. I don't want to look away.

And then he slowly brings his mouth down to mine.

I inhale jaggedly a split second before our lips connect, taken by surprise. But then something happens: a warmth bursts from my heart and my whole body tingles as his lips begin to move.

I kiss him back. And it feels good... until my mind begins to race.

I'm kissing Theo. But I love George.

I break away, confused. Theo's brow knits together and he goes to step away, but I don't want that either. I pull him back in for another hug, burying my face against his shoulder. His body is tense, but soon he relaxes and holds me in turn.

'Write to me,' he whispers.

I nod against him, tears spilling from my eyes. I can't believe he's leaving.

. . .

I hold Theo's hand as we walk back down to the farm. It feels surreal, but I want to keep him close for as long as possible.

Theo wants to say goodbye to George, but George is nowhere to be found. He's not in any of his usual places and after we've been searching for half an hour, I start to worry. Surely we would have seen him if he'd come up to Brimham?

Theo doesn't have long before Bart comes to collect him, so Jamie takes the quad bike to search further afield. He returns none the wiser.

I'm a mess as Theo writes a note to George while Bart waits in his car. I can't believe this is happening. George is going to be so sad when he realises that Theo is another person he can't say goodbye to. Where *is* he?

I break down again as Theo and I hug goodbye. Anxiety is gnawing away at me and I'm so worried about George that I'm not fully in the moment. I know I'll beat myself up about it later.

Another two hours pass and I'm out of my mind. Is George already on his way to Sophie?

When he doesn't come back for dinner, I crack, telling my parents what he had planned. I feel like I could throw up as Dad, horrified, hurries out to the car.

It's after midnight before he returns – alone. He drove to the home of Sophie's foster parents and spoke to them, but there was no sign of George.

Mum calls the police. They come at three o'clock in the morning and wake up the whole household, asking us to get out of our beds so they can search our rooms to make sure he's not hiding anywhere.

We stand in the corridor, Jamie and I, while Joanne sits on the floor, half asleep.

'Has he taken anything?' I ask Jamie.

He shakes his head. 'Not that I know of. I'm sure he'll come back in the morning.'

But he doesn't.

As the days turn into weeks and the weeks into months, I begin to think that I'll never see George Thompson again.

27

NOW

I wake up with a parched throat and a stonking headache. Memories of last night come back to me and I place my palm on my forehead and stare up at the ceiling.

Clearly George is unfinished business for me too.

I *really* need to write another letter to Theo.

How would he feel, if he could have seen us last night? I still remember the look on his face when he saw me holding George's card the night of my parents' party. He wasn't here to witness the full extent of my devastation after George left, but he knew how broken I was, and I definitely don't think he welcomed the idea of George coming back into our lives.

I sit up and grab my notepad from the bedside table, along with a glass of water. Downing half of the latter's contents, I return it to the tabletop and put my pen to paper.

Dear Theo, I write. *I have to tell you about George.*

No, I can't. Not yet. I cast the pen and pad aside and climb out of bed.

George *did* stay over in the end – not because he wanted to, but because he couldn't get a taxi. He rang for one while I made coffee. We drank our drinks in near silence and then I told him I needed to call it a night and suggested he did the same. He didn't argue, but it was awkward as we went into our separate rooms.

I can hear Mum downstairs with Emilie. She told me yesterday that she'd get up with her. I hope she didn't regret offering after having a few drinks herself. It's only seven thirty, in any case. Sadly, my body clock is not wired for sleep-ins anymore.

I have a shower and get dressed very gingerly, wondering how George's head will feel this morning. He's bigger than I am, though, I bet he can handle his alcohol.

Then again, he seemed pretty drunk last night. I inadvertently smile at the memory of his reserve tumbling away, how sweet and open he became when he'd had a few. Then I remember his thumbs on the bare skin of my waist and his dark eyes fixing on my lips, and uncontrollable jitters explode in my stomach.

I leave my room and creep past his, wincing with every creak of my footsteps on the stairs.

'Good morning,' Mum says warmly when I appear in the kitchen. 'You're up early. I thought you were having a lie-in?'

'You can go back to bed if you like?'

'No, I'm up now. Did George stay over?' she calls through to me as I go to say hello to Emilie. She's watching telly.

'He did,' I call back, giving Emilie a kiss on her forehead. 'There was a ridiculous delay for a taxi so it made sense.'

'First Jamie and Dani and now George,' she says with pleasure as I wander back into the kitchen and pull up a chair, thanking her for the cup of tea she's poured from the pot. 'It's lovely having a full house again. It's like having my kids back.'

I smile at her as she comes to sit down beside me.

'I've actually been wondering,' she says.

Uh-oh. I know that scheming look.

'Did you hear George saying he needs to find somewhere else to live?'

I nod and slurp my tea. I heard him mention it on Saturday night when we were at the pub, although I was distracted with a wired Emilie at the time.

'How would you feel about him taking Jamie's room? *His* old room?'

I gawp at her.

'I know you don't want a boarder,' she says quickly. 'But it's *George*. He's not just *anyone*, and I thought it would be a way to get past this issue he has with being paid. Something to give him in return.'

I get up and hunt out some Paracetamol, my mind spinning.

'Not on an empty stomach,' Mum reprimands me. 'Pop some toast in. I'll do you a fry-up when George comes down.'

We both freeze at the sound of doors opening and closing upstairs. *He's awake!* My heart begins to gallop.

'Think about it,' she whispers. 'But wouldn't it be nice to have a man about the house again?'

I snort. 'You're so old-fashioned.'

'Well, I *would* like it,' she mutters. 'I'm very fond of George. Aren't you?'

I nod, carving through the loaf of bread on the chopping board and trying to steel myself against the sucker-punch of grief I feel every single time I do this.

Making toast always reminds me of Dad these days. He somehow managed to slice the bread to exactly the right thickness, every time. I guess he had enough practice, over the years, with all those breakfasts he used to do. What I wouldn't give to come downstairs and still see him standing here at the counter...

'He's so different to how he was.' Mum is still talking about George.

'I don't think he's *that* different,' I argue.

'Oh, he *is*.' She dismisses my comment. 'He's much more mellow. I hope he sticks around.'

My insides lurch of the thought of him walking out of our lives again. It's a distinct possibility.

'You'd better hope a job comes up at Forestry England in North Yorkshire then.'

'Surely something will sooner rather than later. He can't enjoy being stuck inside. Do you think he'd go back to work on an estate?'

I shrug. 'I don't know, you'd have to ask him.'

'I will.' Mum hesitates, then opens her mouth, and closes it again.

'Spit it out,' I say with a laugh as my toast pops up.

'Nothing. I don't mean for George,' she continues over the sound of me buttering. 'But I heard Bartholomew is retiring.'

'Morning,' George says from the doorway.

I jump. With the noise of my knife scraping, and us talking, I didn't hear him come down the stairs.

'Good morning!' Mum says brightly, getting up to make him a cup of tea.

I carry on buttering my toast with the single-mindedness of a lunatic. I can't look at him.

'Did I hear you say Bart is retiring?' George asks.

Turns out I *can* look at him after all, and holy hell, he's even more attractive with day-old stubble. His white T-shirt is creased and looks slept-in and his hair is sexily dishevelled. I want to run my fingers through it.

His attention is focused on Mum.

'Yes,' she replies. 'They'll be looking for a new groundskeeper. But I'm sure you're not interested,' she adds hastily, with a worried glance in my direction.

'Hell, no. I couldn't work for people like that.'

He acknowledges my look of relief with a small smile before accepting the tea from Mum.

I don't think I'm the only one finding it difficult to maintain eye contact this morning.

'Do you see much of them?' he asks either or both of us.

He sounds rough.

'No. Theo disowned them years ago,' I reply, popping a couple of Paracetamol out and offering the packet to George. He takes it with a grateful thanks.

I prefer to say Theo disowned his family rather than the other way around. The fact is, Theo's father and brother stopped speaking to him when he went to art college. He got into the RCA, which was an achievement in itself, and then Theo's dad refused to help with his tuition.

So Theo sold his grandfather's carriage clock – an antique that had been in the family for years. It was Theo's to sell – his father's father had left it to him in his will – but Edwin and Acton considered it an unforgivable act.

Perhaps if he'd gone on to become a world-renowned artist who they could boast about to their friends, they would've felt differently. But instead Theo used his degree to become a secondary school Art teacher, a job he thrived at.

'They don't have a relationship with Emilie?' George

asks, leaning against the counter and raising his cup to his lips.

I shake my head.

'Right, fry-up!' Mum claps her hands.

'Please don't go to any hassle,' he says. 'I should get going.'

'You stay right where you are,' Mum commands.

'In that case, how about I bring in the eggs?'

'Oh, that's a good idea,' Mum agrees. 'Why don't you take Emilie with you. Get her away from the TV.'

I stiffen, but George doesn't seem fazed by the suggestion.

'Want to come and collect the hen eggs with me, Emilie?' he asks from the living room doorway. 'We'll see if we can find some more feathers for your cushion too.'

'Okay,' she agrees quite happily, getting to her feet.

My heart contracts as I watch her take his hand and trot after him out the door.

'*She reminds me of you... She's lovely.*'

Mum smiles at me when they've gone. 'He *would* make a wonderful boarder,' she says. 'Promise me you'll think about it.'

I doubt I'll do anything else.

I hear my mobile phone ringing as George is preparing to leave. I've taken Emilie to the toilet so I call out to Mum to ask her to answer it.

'It's Sally!' she calls back.

'Can you take a message?'

I will Emilie to hurry up so I can find out why my lawyer is calling me at this time on a Monday morning.

'What did she say?' I glance from Mum to George, who's

standing by the door with a strange look on his face. 'Was it about the parole hearing?'

'That's not for a few more weeks,' Mum says gently, confirming what I already knew. The date is etched in my brain.

'What, then?' I demand to know.

'He's asked to see you.'

My stomach has tied itself up in knots as I wait on the cold plastic chair in the Visitor's Hall. So much has changed in my life since I last came here back in April. I've lost Dad, moved home, and found George. I can scarcely believe he's waiting in the car park. He offered to drive me here, and Mum urged me to take him up on it. I didn't have the will to resist.

One by one, the guards bring in the prisoners, a sea of grey jumpers filtering out across the room. They settle themselves on chairs separated from friends and family by low tables.

I see him and my heart claws its way up my throat as a prison guard brings him towards my table. He looks better than last time. There's more colour in his cheeks and he's not as thin. He's had a haircut too, a neat trim around his ears.

He sits down across from me. 'Thank you for coming,' he says in the raspy voice I've got to know.

'I was surprised you asked me,' I admit. 'I thought you were finding it all too hard.'

'I was,' he says. 'I'm sorry.'

I nod and swallow. 'At least you'll be out soon.'

His eyes fill up with tears. 'I'm sorry about that too.'

'Please don't cry,' I whisper. 'You'll set me off.'

Too late.

'I'm sorry, I'm sorry,' he repeats, as we both brush our tears away. 'I wish it were him coming up for parole, not me.'

I don't want to cry, but it's impossible to stop.

I wish it was too...

'I still don't know how I'm going to carry on without them,' he adds, his shoulders shaking as he begins to sob with silent tears.

I let out a choked gulp.

This is why I had to stop coming. I only intended to come the one time: for closure, because I wanted to forgive him and try to move on. But it felt cathartic to see his pain so I kept coming back. Eventually he asked me to stop because *he* found it too painful.

I understand. He lost his wife and the mother-to-be of his baby girl, only one month shy of being born.

I lost my husband.

Theo was taken from me when Carl, the slight blond man in his thirties sitting opposite, crashed into Theo in a head-on collision between Harrogate and the tiny village of Killinghall. Carl had been drinking and was over the limit, as was Theo, although just barely, but it counted in Carl's favour when he was sentenced. The courts also considered the far worse punishment that Carl had suffered in losing his wife and unborn child. He hadn't drunk *that* much and was only driving because his wife was tired, but it was enough to alter his judgement on the narrow country road.

'I hope you're okay,' he mumbles. 'I hope your little girl is growing up strong and healthy.'

'She is,' I say on a sob.

'And I hope you can move on too and be happy again one day. Find love, you know?'

I've found it, I think inside my head. I just don't know what to do about it.

George sees me coming as I walk towards him, wiping away my tears. He jumps out of his truck and hurries around to the passenger door, opening it up for me, but I throw myself against his chest instead.

He rests his face on the top of my head as I cry.

'I'm sorry. I'm sorry, Leah,' he murmurs, holding me tightly.

He couldn't understand why I wanted to come, why I ever considered visiting the man responsible for the death of my husband. Mum never got it either. In fact, the only person who supported my decision was Dad.

I cry even harder. Will I ever stop missing him?

When I finally calm down enough to retreat, I see that I've sobbed tears into George's T-shirt.

'Whoops,' I say in a muffled voice, placing my hand on his solid chest and looking up at his face. I can feel his heart thudding beneath my palm. He still has his hands on my hips.

He gazes down at me, his brown eyes shining with emotion. Without asking, without even thinking, I run my hand up his left bicep and push the sleeve of his T-shirt over his shoulder. The words '*Little one*' stare back at me in blurred ink.

Theo's handiwork.

George pulls me back into a hug.

I slide my hands up his broad back and along his neck, pushing my fingertips into his hair. It's so soft.

I could make wrist warmers out of it...

Memories of Theo in his late teens and throughout his

twenties hit me in one blinding blow. He used to tease me about my 'psychotic tendencies' relentlessly, but the best reaction, the one I remember the most, is him at fifteen, sitting up on the overhang at Hare Heads, howling with laughter when I admitted to him why I had laughed on the bus.

I don't know who lets go first, but George and I step away from each other at the same time.

We're quiet as he drives me back to the farm.

28

NOW

The next big hurdle in my life, not to mention Emilie's, comes early in September when Emilie begins nursery.

She enjoyed her first two short introductory sessions when I sat in the staff kitchen, on hand in case she needed me. But now it's time for her to go it alone and I'm struggling to keep it together as I walk her across the car park. I want to pick her up and carry her, hold her to me tightly and never let her go, not hand her over to a group of adults we barely know, however nice they may seem.

There are other parents milling around, chatting to each other. They seem like a nice bunch and hopefully, in time, I'll make friends with some of them, but right now the most I can manage is a nervous smile.

'Hello, Emilie!' Cath calls cheerfully as we approach the nursery doorway.

Cath is Emilie's key worker, the person assigned to look after her while she's at nursery. She's in her early forties and has a kind disposition. I had a good feeling about her when I came here for Emilie's settle-in days and Emilie took to her immediately.

'Hello!' Emilie replies. 'I've got my yellow wellies on,' she adds proudly, outstretching one foot and pointing her toes.

I had to wash the mud off them before we left home because she was insistent on teaming them up with her navy and pink polka dot dress. She's also wearing a light-grey jumper that I knitted for her myself, wanting her to be as snug and cosy as possible today.

'Ooh, they're very sunny,' Cath says. 'And you have a matching yellow hairband too.'

Emilie looks delighted as she reaches up to touch it.

'Hello, Emilie's mummy,' Cath says warmly.

'Hello.' I try to sound upbeat.

'Are you ready to come inside and play Tap Tap again?' Cath asks Emilie.

Emilie nods, her hazel eyes growing round with excitement.

Before I can ask what 'Tap Tap' is, Cath adds, 'Say a quick goodbye to Mummy, then.'

The nursery staff encourage parents not to linger, and even my own mother advised me to make drop-offs speedy to lessen the chance of Emilie getting upset, so I try to keep this in mind as I crouch down and fold my arms around her small body.

The thought of her crying and clinging to me is horrendous. I want to do the right thing by her, but I'm finding it hard to let her go. There's a lump in my throat and tears are stinging the back of my eyes as she begins to withdraw. I fight the urge to clutch onto her more tightly and instead release her with a kiss to her forehead.

'Have fun, darling. See you soon.'

'Bye, bye, Mummy!' Cath says brightly.

Emilie waves at me with one hand, while Cath takes her other hand and leads her into the nursery. I straighten up, and through blurry vision, become aware of a blonde woman of about my age standing nearby.

She gives me a sympathetic smile. 'First day?'

I nod, swiping away a tear.

'It gets easier.'

'I hope so.'

Emilie is already absorbed in her game with Cath. I drag my attention away from them and give the kind stranger a shaky smile before heading back to the car and bursting into tears. Today is such a milestone. Theo should be here and it hurts so much that he's not.

Becky has arranged to meet me at the Cracked Teapot to take my mind off things. Hayden is with her parents at home.

I'm grateful to have the company.

'Aw, Lee,' she murmurs as she swoops in for a hug. 'She'll be okay, darling.'

'I know. She's happy. But I can't believe my baby is growing up so fast.' I'm rooting around in my handbag for a tissue.

Becky puts one in front of my face. I take it and blow my nose loudly.

'I mean, how did that *happen*?' I ask in a strangled-sounding voice. 'Not so long ago I was all she had. Now I've gone and handed her over to a bunch of nursery staff. It feels so strange and wrong, like she's no longer mine and mine alone. She belongs to the world now. Does that sound weird?'

Becky shakes her head. 'I'm yet to go through all that, but I believe you when you say it feels wrong. It's not, though. It's right. It's the way it should be. She needs to meet other kids, learn to depend on other adults. Socialise. It'll do her good.'

'I know.' I nod. 'I know.'

'It'll be okay,' she assures me, pressing her hand to mine.

'I know.'

If I say it enough, maybe I'll start to believe it.

Emilie is perky as anything when I go to pick her up, a proper cheeky chatterbox who can't stop telling me about what she's been up to for the last three hours. She's run out of steam by the time we get home, though. It was an effort to keep her from dozing off in the car.

By 7 p.m., my perfect angel has conked out. I sit by her bed for a while, watching her rotating bird nightlight cast dancing shadows across her face. The sound of a car on the lane and the headlights glinting at the edge of the window frame have me finally leaving her room and going downstairs.

'Are you expecting anyone?' I ask Mum as I go into the kitchen and peer out of the window.

'Oh, it's George!' I say with a thrill of anticipation at the sight of his truck. He's still sitting in the driver's seat, staring straight ahead.

What's he doing?

I open the door and his head shoots towards me, his eyes round with an emotion I don't recognise.

'What is it?' I ask with a mixture of alarm and curiosity as he climbs out of the truck and comes inside.

'It's Sophie.' He drags his hand across his mouth. 'She's contacted me.'

'What? On Facebook?'

He nods. 'She's read my letters. She's seen her Life Story book. Her adoptive parents have told her all about me.'

I've never seen him like this before, so nervous and full of hope and yet very clearly overwhelmed.

I step forward and give him a hug, only to find that he's shaking.

'She still lives in Devon.' He pulls away from me. He seems agitated, as though he can't stand still. 'She lives in Kingswear, right near Dartmouth. It's only about ten miles from my place,' he adds in a shocked whisper.

'What's this?' Mum asks, coming into the room.

As George fills her in, a wave of darkness folds over me, along with the strangest feeling of calm acceptance.

But *of course* I was going to lose him again. I've known it all along, deep down.

He'll go back to Devon. I'll stay here. We're on separate paths that the universe has set us on. We've always been on separate paths.

I push these thoughts from my head, wanting to concentrate on him, on the fact that he's found his sister after all these years.

'George, that's amazing,' I say when Mum has relinquished him from her embrace. She leads him through to the living room. 'Come on, lad. Come and have a stiff drink.'

'I can't, I'm driving,' he protests unsteadily.

'Oh, hush, you can stay over.'

He doesn't argue, sitting down on the sofa. He looks utterly shell-shocked.

'I can't believe it,' he murmurs.

'Have you replied to her?' Mum asks.

He nods. 'I gave her my number.' He digs into his pocket and pulls out his phone. 'Her message was dated a few days ago, though. I don't check very often so she might not see it for a while.'

'Sit down with him, Leah. I'll get him a drink,' Mum commands.

I climb onto the sofa next to George, right up close to him with my knees pressing against his legs. He almost absentmindedly hooks his arm around my knees, but doesn't look at me.

A black hole is expanding inside me. I'm trying to ignore the emptiness, but it's hard. It feels a lot like grief. I'm grieving George's loss before I've even had him. Again.

'Will you come with me?' he asks abruptly. 'To Devon. When I go to meet her for the first time. Will you come with me?'

I stare at him. Does he remember that he asked me to go with him once before? And then he left without a word?

'Emilie too,' he says quickly, misreading my hesitation.

I nod. 'Yes. Yes, I'll come.'

He looks relieved. Mum returns with a sherry for him which he accepts without question.

'Mum, get him a beer,' I chide gently. 'You're the only one who likes sherry in this house.'

'Right now, I'd drink anything.' George knocks back half a glass and winces.

Mum rolls her eyes good-naturedly and tuts at me on her way out of the room. She returns with one of the cans he brought when he came for dinner.

'Anything I can get for *you*, madam?' she asks me haughtily, giving me a curtsy.

I laugh at her and shake my head. 'No, I'm fine.'

'Well, bugger it,' she says. 'I'm opening a bottle of champagne. I think this calls for a celebration.'

George and I smile at each other as she flounces from the room.

'And we should celebrate today anyway!' she calls back.

'What happened today?' George asks me with confusion.

'It was Emilie's first day at nursery.'

'Oh! How did it go?'

I nod. 'She had a great time. I was a bit of a mess, though.'

'I'm sorry,' he says tenderly as he turns towards me. 'Are you okay?'

'Please, George, don't worry about me. This is momentous.' I nod at his phone.

'Yeah. I can't believe it.'

'Wait, do you have access to *her* Facebook page?' I think to ask.

He nods.

'Can I see her?'

He unlocks his phone. It's still open to the Facebook app. He clicks on Sophie's icon and passes the phone over, craning his neck to look over my shoulder.

Tears unexpectedly prick my eyes. 'She looks like you.'

She has long wavy brown hair, maybe a shade or two lighter than her brother's, and brown eyes, with a strong nose and an oval-shaped face. Her smile is what really makes her stand out, though – she's smiling in every photo, all white teeth and beaming. She's with friends in most of the shots, but there's one with her adoptive parents, I presume, a man and woman in their late forties or early fifties perhaps. The man is ruddy-faced with brown-grey hair and deep laughter lines spanning from the corners of his eyes. The woman has dark hair and a warm smile. They're at a restaurant, from the looks of it, and in front of the three of them, on the table, is a birthday cake with a large lit Number 18 candle. It must've been taken last year.

I turn to George and press a kiss on his shoulder. 'I'm so happy for you,' I whisper as Mum comes back into the room with two filled champagne flutes. 'Will you have a glass too, George? Don't make Leah and me drink it all. You've seen us tipsy.'

'Yeah, I have,' he replies with a grin. 'I'll stick with bitter.'

I whack his arm and pass Mum his phone. 'Have a look, Mum, she's beautiful.'

Mum takes the phone and sits down on the other side of George, scrolling through the photos.

As George smiles and nods and agrees with Mum's spoken-aloud thoughts, it occurs to me that he must've driven straight here after discovering Sophie had replied. *We* were the ones he came to, the ones he wanted to share this with. It should make me feel happy, but I know only too well how fragile bonds can be. If I'm not careful, I'll find myself hanging on by a fine thread when they snap.

29

NOW

A little over a week later, shortly after Emilie finishes nursery on Friday afternoon, George drives us down to Devon.

Mum offered to have her granddaughter for the weekend, but I thought Emilie would enjoy the mini break. It's been a long time since I've taken her to the seaside.

'Annie's gone to visit her sister and family so we'll have the house to ourselves,' George reveals an hour into our journey.

Why didn't he tell me this earlier?! I've been stressing all week about it. I'm not ready to meet his still-too-recent-ex, let alone stay with her in the home they shared together.

'How many bedrooms is the cottage?'

'Only two,' he replies. 'So yeah, that wouldn't have worked.'

'I hope she didn't mind.'

'No, she offered. She said she'd make up the spare room for you too, but we'd better check that she has before we carry Emilie in.'

I'm hoping Emilie will stay asleep. It's a six-hour journey, but we plan to break it up with dinner and coffee breaks along the way so it'll be late by the time we arrive.

It's eleven when we finally roll into the tiny village of Torcross on the south coast of Devon. It's dark, so I can't see much outside the window, but when George returns to tell me that the cottage is unlocked and our room is indeed ready, I climb out of the car to the sound of waves crashing against the shore.

I realise as I cross the road with my sleeping daughter in my arms, that the sea is *right there*, and a few moments later, as we walk down an alleyway between a cottage and a restaurant, it becomes clear that George's fisherman's dwelling sits practically on the beach.

We climb up three steps to reach a patio, and then he has to duck his head to enter through the front door. Inside, the space is so small that it makes George seem even taller than usual. He's switched on a table lamp so I can see where I'm going without the room being flooded with light. He leads us up the stairs and opens a door to the right of the landing. The spare room is neat and tidy with a double bed taking up a large chunk of the space. George has already turned down the covers so I'm able to slip Emilie straight into bed. She stirs but continues to doze. I changed her into her pyjamas and brushed her teeth at our last motorway stop.

Back downstairs, George has switched on the lights properly and now I can see signs of a woman's touch *everywhere*. In the throws over the cream-coloured sofas, on the floral-patterned cushions, in the pastel artwork hanging on the walls...

'It wasn't this girly when I lived here,' George tells me, as though reading my mind. 'I'm a man of minimal tastes.'

'A man of many molluscs,' I tease.

He cuffs me over top of my head, his lips pursed.

'Drink? Brew?' he offers when I've finished laughing.

'Just water, I think.'

The kitchen is simple and clean, albeit tiny, with white cupboards, a wooden countertop and a table by the window. The fridge is plastered with magnets and photographs. I wander over to study them, feeling uneasy at the sight of a very pretty twenty-something with flyaway light-blond hair and blue eyes in several of the pictures. There are other people too – men and women and a couple of young children who may be Annie's niece and nephew, but I'm hazarding a guess that the blonde is Annie.

Then I see a picture of her with George, both of them sitting outside in the sunshine. It's a selfie, which he's taken from the looks of the angle. I don't know why this makes it so much more painful to see. They're both smiling and they seem carefree, joyful.

Even though George hasn't lived with her for several months, Annie still has a picture of him on her fridge.

Is this a woman who wants him back? Is she keeping his bed warm for him until he ties up his loose ends and comes to his senses?

'Here you go.' George jarringly interrupts my thoughts as he passes me a glass of water.

I have a feeling he's been standing there, watching me.

'Do you still love her?' I blurt out the question before remembering that he asked me the same thing about Theo.

He frowns and shakes his head. 'We broke up ages ago.'

'Then why does she still have a photo of you on her fridge? You look so happy together.'

He shrugs. 'We still *like* each other. Just not in *that* way.'

Tonight he's sleeping in the bed they shared. I detest the thought.

'When I told you that I still loved Theo...'

He cuts me off. 'It was a stupid question. Of course you still love him. I'm sorry I asked.'

We call it a night soon afterwards – George is exhausted after the long drive and tomorrow will be a big day – but I lie in bed for ages next to Emilie, staring up at the ceiling and wondering how my heart will withstand another fracture.

———

We're meeting Sophie at the Kings Arms in Strete, which is only a few miles from Torcross. George knows it well, but it was Sophie who suggested it because she loves its amazing clifftop location and pub garden overlooking the sea. Her parents are coming too.

George is a bundle of nerves all morning. I came downstairs with Emilie after what turned out to be a bit of a lie-in for us both to find him already showered and dressed and sitting on an armchair by the window. He seemed lost in thought, but he jumped to his feet at the sight of us.

He was jumpy at breakfast too. Eventually I suggested we go for a walk to blow off some steam.

The view from his place is astonishing. There's only a narrow road and a low wall separating the cottage from the shingle beach, and beyond that is the sea, silvery grey in the morning light. It's a hazy September day, which promises to be warm later, but right now, at ten thirty, it's still relatively cool.

There are some huge blue-grey rocks on our right at the end of the beach and beyond it the land climbs up to a clifftop. George points out the location of the Start Point Lighthouse.

We turn left, trudging across the thick bed of smooth multi-coloured pebbles. A road runs adjacent to the beach, and as we come out from behind the cottages, restaurants and cafés lining the shore, I realise that there's a stretch of water parallel to the other side of the road too: a freshwater lake, according to George. Birds dance in the air above it and beyond are green hills, flowing upwards to a pale-blue sky.

'This place is absolutely breathtaking.' I'm not trying to talk him into staying, but why would he ever want to leave?

'Yeah, I was lucky to get the cottage when I did. It belonged to a friend of Ernie's who passed away. Ernie put me in touch with the solicitor handling the sale. It was a bit of a steal, but it needed a lot of work.'

Ernie is the groundskeeper who helped George train to be a forester. George wants me to meet him later today.

'Do you miss living here?' Turns out I'm a glutton for punishment.

'I mean, I liked it while I was here, but if you gave me a choice between living by the sea or in the middle of a forest, I'd choose trees every time.'

'Right, that's it, we're selling the alpacas and planting trees.' I'm trying to sound light-hearted.

He smiles sideways at me. 'I wouldn't change a thing about your place.'

'No?' *Convince me.*

'No. I love spending time there. Coming back...'

'Yes?' I prompt when his voice trails off.

He shrugs. 'Coming back felt a bit like coming home. I know that's mad. I barely spent any time there.'

'It's not mad.' Actually, his confession floors me. I make a snap decision. 'Mum said you're looking for somewhere else to live.'

He nods. 'I don't mind working at the pub, but I need to get away from it after my shifts.'

'She suggested you take the spare room at ours.'

'Oh.' He shoots me a look.

Is that a positive reaction?

'She loves having you around,' I continue. 'And she thought it would be a good way of offsetting some of the work you've been doing.'

'I'd still pay rent,' he says gruffly.

'You'll never get her to agree, but... does that mean you're keen?'

His brow furrows. 'What do you think about the idea?'

'I love it,' I admit.

'Mummy, look!' Emilie interrupts us. She's been running on ahead, oblivious to the conversation we're having. Now she's bending over something on the ground. I step up my pace and go to see what she's found.

'A jellyfish! Don't touch it in case it still has a bit of sting left in it.'

'That's a moon jellyfish,' George says, joining us.

He crouches down and turns the creature over with the end of a long stalk of seaweed so Emilie can have a closer look. He talks her through the jelly's anatomy in that deep measured voice of his, and my heart is full as I watch them.

But then I come down to earth with a bump.

George doesn't want to be a father.

Even if he decided to stay in North Yorkshire and move away from this place and, now, the sister he's spent years searching for... Even if he and I ever manage to move our strange, charged friendship into romantic territory... How could I even contemplate forging a future with a man who doesn't want children in his life?

The pub is enchanting from the outside, painted cream with a slate roof and wrought-iron detailing. We arrive first – George was so on edge that we set off early – and find a table outside in the garden. The view is out of this world, stretching across the sea for miles. It's sunny and warm so I'm glad I remembered to plaster Emilie with sunscreen.

After setting my daughter up with crayons and a colouring book and helping her to get started on her choice of picture, I look across the table at George. He's gazing out at the water, his brow pulled together in a slight frown. His brown hair is glinting under the sun, his curls taking on an almost golden hue. My attention drifts from his perfectly straight nose to his full lips and I have a surreal moment when I remember that we almost kissed. He chooses that second to look at me.

We stare at each other in silence. His eyes have become treacle-like in the sunshine.

He is *so* gorgeous.

'What are you thinking?' he asks in a low murmur.

I shake my head quickly and take a sip of my Diet Coke.

And then George's head turns towards the pub and he goes rigid. His sister – his sister! – is making her way between the wooden bench tables, closely followed by Jude and Roy, her parents.

She's so tall! She's taller than her parents by several inches and is strong and healthy-looking. George is already on his feet so I stand up too, my heart in my throat as Sophie beams and runs the last few metres. She embraces George and I feel a rush of emotion as his arms come around her. They hug each other tightly and then she pulls away and stares up at him, beaming from ear to ear. He's knocked for six as he gazes down at her.

She must be around six-foot tall, but he's taller still, of course: six foot four and a half inches, going by the new marking on the larder wall.

I make my way around to the other side of the table to say hello.

There's something desperate about Sophie's hug with me. It's as though she can't believe what's happening and wants to hang on tightly until she knows it's real.

George goes to shake Sophie's father's hand, but Roy pulls him in for a hug instead, as does Jude. They both embrace me in turn before saying friendly hellos to Emilie, who's still very much focused on colouring in her bunny.

'I feel as though I already know you,' Sophie says to George once we're settled around the table.

George has moved to sit beside me so he and Sophie can speak face to face.

'I mean, obviously I *did* know you once, but my memories of that time are few and far between. It was all those letters that you wrote to me. Mum and Dad gave them to me along with my Life Story book when I was fifteen and going through a bit of an identity crisis.' She casts her parents an apologetic smile. 'I read them over and over. I wanted to try to find you back then, but I was scared. I wasn't sure if you'd still want to know me after all this time, or if you'd be the person I'd built you up to be inside my head.' She grins. 'I can tell that you are.'

George blushes. 'I'm glad to hear that. I hope it's true.'

'I bet I'm different to how you remember me?' she asks.

'Completely,' he replies with a smile. 'No, that's not true. Not completely. You were chatty, full of beans... Not always, but when we were alone, and sometimes with Mum.'

'Not with my dad?'

George shakes his head. 'Not with him. He wasn't...'

His voice trails off, but Sophie fills the gap in his sentence. 'He wasn't a good guy. I read about him in my Life Story book.'

'I see,' George says, as Jude and Roy nod with solemn agreement.

'I'm so glad you finally joined Facebook!' Sophie seems to be leaving the subject of her biological parents behind for now.

I'm sure she and George will discuss them again in time, perhaps when it's just the two of them.

'I'd been checking on and off for about a year,' Sophie says, 'and then, suddenly, there you were!'

'That was Leah's doing.' George casts me a sidelong look of affection.

'Well, I'm very grateful.' Sophie gives me a warm smile. 'It's not as though I wasn't happy before. These two are the best parents I could ever wish for.' She wraps an arm around her dad, who's sitting beside her. 'But I always had this feeling that something was missing.' She pauses. 'I know that you looked after me a lot when I was little.'

George nods. 'I tried to.'

'Thank you.' She reaches across the table and squeezes his hand.

'You're welcome,' he replies quietly, sincerely. 'I never wanted to be separated from you. I searched for you for a long time afterwards.' His eyes are shining as he gazes across the table at his sister.

'I'm glad you found me.' Sophie's expression matches

the emotion in his. 'Well, actually, I found you,' she adds abruptly, grinning. 'But I can't wait to get to know you again!'

George laughs lightly. 'I'm looking forward to getting to know you again too.'

It's a joyful afternoon. Sophie is a breath of fresh air: kind, confident and spirited. She's very talkative and there's rarely a gap in the conversation so it never feels uncomfortable. George doesn't say anywhere near as much, but I can tell that he's completely and utterly smitten – it's written all over his face.

We say goodbye after a couple of hours, happily accepting the invitation to come via their home for a cup of tea on our way back up north.

After buckling Emilie into her car seat, I climb into the front of the truck and smile across at George.

He shakes his head at me, speechless, before putting the truck into gear. It's a while before he can talk, and even then he keeps falling quiet after a few sentences. I think he needs time and space to process all this, so I don't attempt to make aimless conversation.

Ernie is retired now, but he still lives in the old cream-stone gatehouse on the estate, along with the lad who took over from George. It's this lad who answers the door to us, an affable freckly faced man in his late-twenties called Freddie. After he and George enthusiastically greet each other, Freddie disappears into the kitchen to make a pot of tea.

George takes me through to the living room to meet Ernie.

George explained to me on the way here that Ernie lost his son, a soldier, in the Iraq War, and his wife a year later following a long illness. He says that when they first met, Ernie struck him as someone with a lot of love to give and no one to give it to, which is probably why Ernie took him under his wing in the first place.

I adore him instantly. He's just as George described with crazy salt-and-pepper hair and a big handlebar moustache, but he seems stiff when he gets up from his armchair by the window and comes over to greet us. To my surprise, he homes in on me first, a wide grin on his weathered face and a look of pure delight in his eyes.

'So *this* is the one that got away!' he exclaims.

George groans and I laugh, even as my cheeks flush.

George proclaimed Ernie sprightly when they first met, but although he might not fit that physical description anymore, he's certainly still chirpy.

'Who's this then?' he asks, grinning down at Emilie. 'You must be Emilie,' he adds before I can introduce them.

George must've already told him about her. I'm dying to know how much he said.

'Would you like a biscuit?' Ernie asks her.

Emilie nods eagerly.

'I'm coming!' Freddie calls through from the kitchen.

'Sit down, sit down,' Ernie commands, returning to his armchair by the window. His view looks out onto the thick rough trunks of towering pine trees. The light spilling down through them is minimal, even on a sunny day.

George, Emilie and I settle on the sofa.

'How are you, lad? How did the meeting go?'

As George tells Ernie about Sophie, I take in our surroundings. The living room is warm and cosy, with a fire-place that still has charred logs in the hearth, and chequered blankets and throws slung over the well-worn chairs. A glance through to the kitchen tells me it hasn't been updated in probably fifty years, but it looks clean and tidy.

It's strange to think of George living here, but it helps in an odd way too. I'm starting to be able to piece together his journey after he left us.

'He wasn't much of a talker when I met him,' Ernie says to me after Freddie has returned with tea and chocolate chip cookies. 'But once I got to know him, and once he started, you couldn't get him to shut up! It was all Leah this and Leah that.'

'*Ernie*,' George chastises him grumpily.

'Shoosh, lad.' Ernie waves him away. 'Life's too short, enough of the nonsense.' He catches my eye and holds my gaze. 'You know that only too well, don't you, love?' His tone is gentler. 'I do too. Don't waste it.'

George interrupts to talk to Freddie about the work he's been doing on the estate and Ernie lets the subject go, but I feel his eyes on me often over the next hour. I'm bizarrely not too discomfited by his scrutiny, and when we come to leave, he gives me a brief tight squeeze and repeats in a whisper, 'Life's too short.'

I squeeze him in return.

'Sorry about that,' George mutters on the drive back to his cottage.

I can tell he's embarrassed.

'Don't apologise for Ernie, I want to adopt that guy as my grandfather,' I declare. 'I'm so glad he was there for you.'

'Me too.'

'He raised a few questions, though,' I admit with a perplexed glance across at him. I look over my shoulder at Emilie before returning my eyes to George.

I plan to get to the bottom of it later.

George shifts uneasily and drives on.

That evening we have takeaway fish and chips out on the patio. It's only big enough to have three chairs lined up in a row, so we face the sea rather than each other, and are so famished, having barely touched our food at lunchtime, that we eat without saying much.

When I take Emilie upstairs for a bath, George sits at the end of his bed, chatting to me through the open door while she splashes about in the bubbles. Afterwards, he offers to read her a story, and I'm taken aback both by his suggestion and her eagerness to agree.

I go downstairs and top up my wine glass until I'm called back up for a bedtime kiss.

'Night night, Emilie,' George says sweetly from the doorway after he's moved aside to let me in.

'Night night, George,' she replies adorably.

He smiles at me before leaving us to it.

I don't know what to make of his behaviour.

When I get back downstairs, George is standing in the middle of the room, tapping on his phone screen. 'Seven Nation Army' by the White Stripes spills from a speaker near the TV.

'This song!' I exclaim. 'It really reminds me of you. I think it was on almost every one of your playlists.'

'You listened to my iPod?' he asks with a cocked eyebrow.

'Until it died on me. Why you didn't take it with you? Were you initially planning on coming back?'

'No. I knew I was going for good.'

I pick up my wine glass from the sideboard and sit down on the sofa, confused.

'There's so much I still don't understand,' I say. 'And after what Ernie said...'

'Don't listen to Ernie,' he grumbles as he sits down beside me.

I turn to face him. 'But I *wanted* to listen to him. You're such a closed book.'

'And you're not?' He frowns at me.

I'm flummoxed. 'No! I don't think I am! I feel like you should be able to read every emotion that's plastered across my face.'

'I thought I could,' he replies after a while.

'What did he mean when he said that *I* was the one that got away?'

He gives me an exasperated look. 'Come on, Leah,' he snaps.

'No! It makes no sense! *Did* you have feelings for me?'

'Of course I bloody did! I was in love with you!'

My heart crashes against my ribcage. 'But *you* left,' I whisper dazedly. '*You* were the one that got away.'

He scratches his head, frustrated, and takes a large gulp of his wine. I wait for him to speak, hoping that the alcohol will loosen his tongue, the same way it's loosening mine.

'I thought you felt the same way about me,' he says, not meeting my eyes.

'I did.'

I'm stumped by the dark look he shoots me. He's disbelieving, angry even.

And then realisation dawns on me and the blood drains from my face.

'You saw Theo kiss me, didn't you?'

His jaw twitches. A moment later he nods, a single, curt,

brusque nod, before throwing the remainder of his wine down his throat. He gets up abruptly and stalks into the kitchen, refilling his glass.

I feel quite ill.

'I'm sorry,' he says tersely, coming back through with the bottle. 'I know I need to get over it,' he adds as he tops up my glass. 'I didn't want to talk about it – it's in the past. But sometimes it hits me out of the blue and I'm just so fucking baffled.' He sits back down. 'I knew you liked Theo, but I thought your feelings for him were platonic. At least, I thought that *most* of the time, when I was thinking straight and not riddled with jealousy,' he adds grouchily.

'My feelings *were* platonic,' I insist. 'He was a friend – *just* a friend. *You* were the one I had *feelings* for.'

It's clear George doesn't believe me. After years of rejection from his parents and other adults who were supposed to care for him, he thought I'd rejected him too. No wonder he fled.

'George, Theo was upset,' I say. 'He came to tell us both that his dad was sending him to Italy. We walked up to Hare Heads to talk and I knew he wanted my attention because usually I was divided, worrying about you, but he was in such a state that day that I decided to put him first.'

'So you kissed him?' He sounds bitter.

'No, he kissed me,' I reply. 'And yes, I kissed him back. But I was crushed about him leaving. Nothing else happened between us for another year and a half.'

He reels backwards. 'What?'

'We stayed friends. But after you left, I was a wreck. There was no way I could think about being with anyone else. I mean, I couldn't imagine falling for anyone ever again, but that's teenagers for you,' I say wryly.

'I saw pictures of you with him on Becky's Facebook page that New Year.' He still doesn't trust what I'm saying.

'Hugging, right? Not kissing. Theo was my friend. That's all. But when he came home for Christmas the *following* year, I started to see him differently. He said he'd always had feelings for me.'

'That much was obvious,' he mutters with only a trace of resentment.

'But you were the first boy I ever loved,' I say quietly.

George has been sitting on the edge of the sofa with his jaw clenched and his elbows resting on his knees. He's been staring at the floor, but as soon as I say these words, he turns his head to look at me.

'I chose *you*,' I whisper.

He stares at me and I can practically see the cogs in his brain turning.

'And *you* left *me*,' I repeat, tears filling my eyes.

He looks stricken and then, suddenly, incredibly weary. 'I don't think I can handle this, Leah. After everything that came afterwards, everything I went through... And I'm not saying it wasn't hard for you too,' he adds hastily. 'But now you're telling me it was all a big misunderstanding? That's too much.'

I brush my tears away. 'I'm sorry, but I don't have any regrets. I know it was awful, and I can't imagine how you must have been feeling if you walked away from Hare Heads and climbed into the boot of a stranger's car.' I'm breathless with pain at the thought of him doing that, at the thought of him hurting so deeply at seeing me kiss Theo that he put his life at risk. 'But if you hadn't left, I wouldn't have got together with Theo and I wouldn't have Emilie. And I loved Theo, George. Not at first, I promise you, not at first, but, God, I loved him,' I say with a tearful smile.

I loved him so much that I followed him to London when he went to art college. Throughout most of our twenties, it was just the two of us. After such a hectic childhood, growing up in a houseful of troubled teenagers, we were free. Free of his family, free of mine – a thought that always comes with a pang of guilt – but we thrived on it. We had fun together. We made each other laugh. And when I fell pregnant by accident, Theo proposed to me and told me he wanted to spend the rest of his life in my company.

We went through rocky patches – his love wasn't infinite and unwavering, and I know for a fact that he had at least two Italian girlfriends while he was at school in Italy – but we always made it through.

And I can't regret it.

'Would you really change it all?' I ask George. 'If you could go back, I mean.'

'I don't know,' he admits, still hunched forward. 'When I remember how I was at fifteen, I can see I was on a destructive path. Maybe if I'd stayed, I would have blown things with you anyway.'

'Nothing could have ever happened between us,' I state.

He glances at me, his eyebrows pulling together.

'If my parents found out that we were in a relationship – a potentially sexual one,' I add with a blush, 'they would have had to move you on. Can you imagine social services hearing about it? There was no way I could risk anything happening between us. I was *terrified* that I'd lose you.'

'There were so many times that I thought you liked me and then you'd retreat.' Only now does he comprehend what was really going on. 'I thought you were blowing hot and cold on me.'

'No!' I pull my knees up onto the sofa so I can face him

properly. 'I wanted to kiss you more than I'd ever wanted to kiss anyone.'

I still do…

He mirrors my body position and regards me for a long moment. Then he reaches over and takes my hand. He holds it from beneath with my palm facing upwards, his thumb resting on my inner wrist. He drags his thumb back and forth and everything zeroes in on his touch. He's staring at my hand, I'm staring at his thumb. Butterflies are going berserk in my stomach, but I'm *still* terrified that I'm going to lose him.

'I'm scared,' I confide shakily.

The movement of his thumb ceases, but his hand is still cradling mine.

He cocks his head to one side. 'Why?'

'I know I should be used to saying goodbye – I've had enough practice over the years – but with you it's different. The thought of losing you again terrifies me.'

'Why would you lose me?' he asks with a frown.

'This house, it's incredible.'

'I'll sell it or rent it, but I won't live here again.'

'Seriously? Your job at Forestry England?'

'It's only a matter of time before something comes up in North Yorkshire. I can wait.'

I pause. 'What about Sophie?'

'I'll get to know her over the phone and via Facetime and we can visit each other. My relationship with you is more important right now.'

My heart is filling with hope, but there's one more obstacle, and for me, it's by far the biggest.

'Emilie,' I whisper.

'Emilie?' He looks mystified.

'You don't want to be a dad.'

'What on earth made you think that?' His voice has jumped up an octave.

'You don't... You said... You said you don't want children,' I stutter.

'I said I didn't want children of my *own*. Leah,' he says firmly, edging closer. He stares at me intently. 'I *do* want to be a dad. I want to have a *big* family. But I don't want to bring any more children into the world when there are already so many who need love and care. I'd like to do what your parents did: foster – *and* adopt. I want to look after kids who don't have anyone else, and love them unconditionally. *That's* what I plan to do with my life. *That's* what's important to me. But Christ, I *adore* Emilie. Don't think that I don't want to be a father figure to her, because I absolutely do.'

Now emotion chokes up his voice and we both move at the same time. He opens up his arms to me and I slide across the sofa, trying to get as close to him as possible.

'What a pair we are.' He sniffs against the top of my head.

I laugh, feeling high with the most exhilarating sense of relief.

George pulls me even more firmly against his chest and I soak up the feeling of the steady beat of his heart thudding against mine.

My face is pressed against his warm neck and I breathe him in, feeling heady at the scent of clean cotton and pine-scented shower gel.

Eventually I lift my head to look at him. His eyes stare back at me, so dark and dilated that they look almost black in this light.

I bring my hand to his jaw and trace my fingers across his rough stubble.

His gaze drifts down to my lips, hovering there for a few seconds, before rising again to meet my eyes.

And then his hand cups the back of my neck and our mouths come together at last, my pulse tripping as our lips part. Shivers roll down my body in waves as his tongue entangles with mine. The kiss becomes more passionate, more fervent, more uncontrollable... *More, more, more...*

He kisses me harder, deeper, and the ache I'm feeling builds and builds until I'm a tightly coiled bundle of nerves.

But do I want to have sex with him in the cottage his ex-girlfriend still lives in? The tiniest hesitation on my part has him breaking away.

'You okay?' He searches my eyes.

'I don't want to stop. But I'm not sure we should do this here.'

He looks around the room, puzzled, before he understands.

'Ah,' he says, with a sigh. 'That's okay. I've waited half my life for that kiss. I can be patient for whatever comes next.'

30

NOW

The next morning, George and I are careful not to confuse Emilie with displays of affection. She and I beat him downstairs, but he follows soon afterwards, saying hello to Emilie before greeting me. He has that shy, slightly bashful look about him, which makes me reticent in turn. But when Emilie is seated at the kitchen table, tucking into her choice from a cereal multipack, he gently skims his thumb along my waist, leaving a fizzing heat trailing in its wake.

While she's distracted, I lean in and brush my lips against his neck.

He breathes in sharply and takes a small step away from me.

'I thought we might go to a different beach this morning,' he says. 'One with sand so we can build some castles.'

'Yay!' Emilie cries, kicking her feet against her chair with excitement.

I grin at George and he smiles at me, letting out a quiet sigh filled with longing.

I'd like us to have more time to ourselves before we tell Mum or anyone else about our budding relationship, so we agree to keep things between us a secret.

The week after we return from Devon, we hardly see each other.

George has to make up for the shifts he didn't work while we were away and I spend most of my time while Emilie is at nursery at the Cracked Teapot, trying to build a simple website for Mum's knitting workshops.

After repeated encouragement from me, George accepts Mum's offer to move in. He'll leave the pub at the end of the month. Mum is predictably thrilled.

It's occurred to me that if – or rather, *when* – George and I finally take our relationship to the next level, it's probably going to happen under her roof, which is nauseating or thrilling, depending on my frame of mind. I have wondered if we should make the most of our privacy while George still has a room at the pub, but for some reason, the thought of heading upstairs with him there doesn't sit well with me.

It's not that I'm not crazy for him – I want him desperately and feel slightly insane at the realisation that I'll soon get to see him first thing in the morning and last thing at night – but something is holding me back. I'm simply too afraid to face up to it because I know what needs to be done.

It's another case of unfinished business.

· · ·

When Theo died, his father got in contact with me to dictate the funeral arrangements. There's a church on the Whittington estate – and a lovely one at that – but the thought of putting my beloved husband in the cold ground and leaving his gravestone in the care of people who treated him with so little love and respect while he was alive felt wrong. I also worried that they'd somehow make it hard for me to visit him – they've made no effort to get to know Emilie and I'm fine with that. They're not good people and her life is full without them. But I believe Edwin would get a sick kick out of holding all the cards. He made Theo feel powerless when he was younger and I couldn't bear to be at his mercy over my husband's final resting place.

So I had Theo cremated. And his remains are still in an urn at the back of my bedroom cupboard.

I know people would think I'm morbid, so Mum is the only one aware of this – everyone else thinks I've already scattered his ashes, Theo's scandalised family included.

The thing is, Theo is still with me, metaphorically *and* physically. I haven't fully let him go.

It's been two and a half years since he died and it's time. I know that. But the thought of climbing up to Hare Heads and setting him free on the wind makes me want to claw my heart out with agony.

Mum has told me I'll feel lighter once it's done, but the idea of doing it at all is so horrendously painful to me that I keep resisting.

Now that George is coming to live with us, it simply doesn't feel right having them under the same roof, so to speak.

·   ·   ·

'Can you look after Emilie for me this morning?' I ask Mum on the morning of what should have been Theo's thirty-first birthday.

She sees the urn in my hands and then looks at my face.

'Oh, Lee-Lee,' she murmurs, enfolding me in a hug.

I cry into her shoulder. I've shed so many tears already and I haven't even left the house.

'Do you want me to come with you? And Emilie?'

'No. I'd prefer to do this alone.'

It pains me, but Emilie doesn't remember Theo and I can't imagine any benefit to her seeing what her father's body has been reduced to. One day, I'll tell her that Hare Heads is his special place and perhaps it will be somewhere she'll go to think about him or talk to him.

It's a crisp autumnal morning. The bramble bushes are bursting with plump blackberries, glistening like beads of caviar amongst mint-green leaves. I brush between the feathery ferns that come almost to my shoulders, and climb up onto the rocks before walking out onto the overhang.

For a while I simply sit there, cradling the urn in my arms as I look across the vibrant green fields at a yellow tractor rumbling away in a far-off paddock, carrying black-plastic-coated hay bales to the barn for safekeeping.

Memories of Theo begin to play out in a long film reel inside my mind, jumping endlessly from one thought to the next.

I think about him meeting me up here when he came back for Christmas a year and a half after leaving: the day I saw him as, not second-place to George, but someone I loved in his own right...

'What is going through that mind of yours?' Theo asks.

We've walked out to the overhang, but it's too cold and damp to sit down.

'I hope you're not contemplating turning my hair into wrist warmers again,' he adds, narrowing his eyes at me.

I laugh. 'No, I've got some of those now, thanks. I could do with more socks, though.'

'You nutter,' he says with a grin, gently punching my arm. 'I do still want to know what you're thinking, though. You've had a funny look on your face all morning.'

His expression has grown serious and I blush, averting my gaze. I have *been staring at him more than usual. Trust him to notice.*

'I don't know,' I mumble with a shrug. 'There's something different about you. It's freaking me out a bit.'

Now he full-on grins at me. 'Different? In what way? Have I got better looking?'

I raise my eyebrows sardonically. 'You've always been good-looking, Theo, but you don't need me to tell you that. I'm sure you get more than enough of an ego boost from... What's her name? Francesca?'

I haven't really forgotten Francesca's name. He told me about her at the end of October when he called for a rare phone chat, casually slipping in the fact that he had a new 'friend' he'd been hanging out with.

'Friend, my arse,' I said at the time. 'You've been snogging her, haven't you?'

I was staggered by how jealous I felt when he laughed off my comment instead of denying it. It played on my mind relentlessly afterwards. It's still at the forefront of my thoughts almost two months later.

He looks down. 'I haven't seen her in a while.'

'No? Why not?'

He shrugs.

'She's not your girlfriend?'

'No,' he replies in a low voice, staring at me directly.

I hold his gaze for as long as I can, but break eye contact first, turning towards the view.

'You're different too,' he says from behind me.

'In what way?'

He lifts a lock of my hair away from my neck and I shiver, still facing away from him. I'm nervous as he steps closer, his hands resting on my hips.

'You seem... edgy.'

I freeze. 'I am a little on edge,' I admit.

'Why?'

I'm reluctant to explain why I no longer feel at ease in his company. The truth is, he's not different. I am. My feelings for him have shifted since the summer. Maybe even before that, although I wasn't quite ready to accept it after what had happened with George.

It's taken me a long time to separate Theo from George and the pain I felt when George left, but last summer, that connection finally severed. I felt like my old self again. No, better than my old self: I don't remember ever laughing as much in my life.

But Theo and I also had a lot of heart-to-hearts, confiding in each other about our families and our anxieties. The thing about him is he listens actively – when you're speaking, all of his attention is on you. He made me feel like the centre of his universe and, I'll admit, I loved it.

I missed him intensely when he returned to boarding school. It took me long enough, but I had finally stopped taking him for granted and realised what a truly special person he is. I found myself daydreaming about him relentlessly and it became very clear that my feelings for him were no longer platonic. I hoped he might feel the same way.

So when he called and sort of admitted to having a girlfriend, it threw me.

'Do you want to know what I'm thinking?' Theo asks.

I nod and turn around. We're toe to toe, standing so close, his hands still on my hips. I stare into his twilight eyes and my heart flips.

'I'm thinking that I still like you,' he tells me earnestly. 'As much as I ever have. No. More. I've always liked you, Leah. And not just as a friend.'

I breathe in sharply, my stomach cartwheeling. 'I like you too.'

'As a friend?' he asks.

'No.' I shake my head. 'More. Much more.'

He grins. 'Really?'

I nod.

'So... if I kiss you now, you won't make me wait another year and a half before I can kiss you again?' he asks, his eyes sparkling.

I laugh. 'Definitely not,' I reply, tilting my face up to his.

My heart was full to bursting that Christmas. Things progressed very quickly between us and I lost my virginity to him just before he returned to Italy. We spoke almost every day for the next year and a half, and when he finally graduated from boarding school and returned to the UK, he vowed to never again let his father or anyone else come between us.

He was my person and I would have followed him anywhere. I almost followed him to the other side of the world – Australia was his dream, not mine, but I was willing to go along with his wishes, even though my parents were shattered at the thought of us moving so far away. It's hard to imagine how I could ever have contemplated leaving my family. Being here with Mum again and seeing Emilie thriving on the farm has made me realise how special my childhood was.

In some ways, I can see now that Theo came between my parents and me. He'd make the occasional jibe about how busy they always were or how much they depended on Jamie. I don't blame him – when we were younger, he'd watched me grow increasingly frustrated. There was only so much I could take: *I* hadn't chosen to foster, my parents had, yet I was suffering all the same.

Once, when I was seventeen, I returned from Becky's to find that Emma, fifteen, had a knife to my mum's throat. I called the police, but Emma fled before they came.

Mum was in pieces afterwards – Dad was at the market so I had to put her back together again.

But Emma came back, even after all that. She was so aggressive and abusive that I hated to be in the house with her. I wanted to move in with Becky. I was so sick of coming home and having no idea what I was walking into.

By the time I turned eighteen, I was ready to leave.

Theo made me think that we didn't need my family and that they didn't need us. I know he loved my parents, but he was still struggling so much, even to the day he died, about how his own family had failed him. I think he wanted to keep Emilie and me close. He wanted us to himself. We were *his* people.

I close my eyes and try to picture his face.

I see him in the sunshine on a long white stretch of beach in Brisbane, building a sandcastle for Emilie and letting her knock it down. It was the holiday we'd taken to decide if we could live there, and he spent time visiting the high schools in the area.

I see him standing up here, behind Mini Druid's Writing

Desk in the middle of winter, asking me to marry him. He'd come up the evening before and filled up the hole in the rock with the right amount of water to make it heart-shaped. It had frozen over in the night, so when we came up here together, he asked me to close my eyes before placing the engagement ring on the ice and bending to one knee.

I see him at the table with Jamie and Dani at the party shortly before he died, his face lit by the flame of his cigarette. I remember the déjà vu I experienced, how I felt as though I'd tumbled back in time.

And then there was the feeling of his hands on my waist in the car.

And the worry on his face because he cared about Katy getting home safely.

In my head I can't help but play back the recurring nightmare I have where I step in front of the door and tell him, 'No. You will *not* do this,' before taking his car keys and hiding them away.

But I didn't stop him. He left. And shortly after he was gone.

Now it's time to let him go again.

Very slowly, I unscrew the cap on the urn.

The sight of the coarse grey dust within makes me break down in sobs. Is this really all that's left of my beloved husband?

No. *He lives on in Emilie*, I remind myself.

I get to my feet, tears streaming down my cheeks, and walk to the edge of the overhang.

'Goodbye, my love,' I whisper.

I let the dust flow.

· · ·

I'm lying on my bed, still unable to stop weeping, when Mum knocks on my door.

'Darling?'

'Come in,' I reply in a choked voice.

I sit up in disbelief when I see what she's carrying. She has my letters to Theo, wrapped in a pink ribbon.

'Shauna passed these on to me,' she says, placing them in my hands.

I look down at the name scrawled across the front: *Theo White*. He changed his surname to mine by deed poll, had no interest in Emilie being a Whittington, and he didn't want to be different from us either.

There's no address, or stamp. I sent these letters off into the universe via random post boxes in Ripon – I didn't expect them to come back to me.

'Gemma spotted a couple when she was emptying the post,' Mum says. 'She passed them on to Shauna. They weren't sure what to do with them – you'd clearly posted them for a reason – but she's kept an eye out for them since. I don't know if they're all there.'

'I should have scattered the pages on the wind,' I mumble, looking down at the bundle.

'Don't,' Mum pleads. 'Don't throw them away. And please don't stop writing to him either. Put them in a box and keep them safe. One day you might want to give them to Emilie. I think she'd like to read about the things you wanted to tell her father.'

I blink back tears, but nod at her.

I'm not ready to emerge from my room yet, so when she leaves, I lie there for a while remembering some of the things I've told Theo over the last few weeks, about Emilie, about Mum, even about that hussy alpaca Bramble who snuck off to have sex and is due to give birth in a few months.

But I still haven't told him about George.

I open my bedside table drawer and pull out my notepad. I've written several letters since, but the one I started is still there at the top. *Dear Theo, I have to tell you about George...*

I put my pen to paper and take a deep breath.

He's back in my life and I desperately want to feel happy. The problem is, I don't know if you'd be at peace with it or not.

He's different to the boy we knew when we were fifteen. You were both my beautiful broken boys, but you grew up and so did he. I think you'd like him now. Mum has described him as more mellow and she's right. He's calmer, more dependable, and he wants to be with me. He's willing to sacrifice so much to make that happen.

He adores Emilie and he's good with her. She likes him too. Right now, he's just George. But in the future, there's a possibility that she'll think of him as a father and I hate the thought of that hurting you.

I wish she remembered you, Theo. It's the one thing I really struggle with. I keep your photograph in her room and she knows you're her daddy. I'll continue to talk about you often, whether George is with me or not. I'll keep your memory alive. I promise you that.

I love you, Theo. I will always love you. And even though I set you free on the wind today, you're still with me in my heart and always will be.

Leah x

31

NOW

George moves in at the end of September. He gave his notice at the pub after we returned from Devon and they've already released his room to hotel customers, but in hindsight, I wish we'd waited a bit longer.

I'm still upset about Theo and I think I need more time to process everything. I'm grieving for my husband all over again and that's something I want to do in private.

I know George would be horrified if he knew how I was feeling, so I try to put on a brave face. But he sees through it, and barely an hour after he's taken his bags to his room, he's cornering me in the kitchen.

'Are you okay?' he whispers, his hand on my hip.

I'm torn between needing to run away and wanting to kiss him senseless.

I nod. 'I'm okay. It's okay. Please don't worry.'

'Is this too soon?'

He's very, very concerned now, and I'm inwardly kicking the hell out of myself for causing him to have doubts.

'No,' I try to reassure him as Mum comes back into the room.

He hunts me out later. I'm in the Yarn Barn, spinning from the cloud – that is to say, I've simply broken apart the lock structure of some alpaca fleece with my fingers and what I'm left with is a big 'cloud' of soft fluffy fibre. There's more inconsistency when you spin it into yarn this way, pinching, pulling and sliding to create a twist that will be drawn onto the bobbin. It requires more concentration, which is exactly what I need right now.

Unfortunately, my concentration breaks when George pulls up a chair and sits down in front of me.

I sigh as the twist tears apart and I have to reconnect it.

'I'm getting seriously freaky vibes from you, Leah,' he says. 'Have you been avoiding me since Devon?'

'No.'

'Are you sure?'

I peek up at him and realise my vague reassurances are not going to cut it. His jaw is set, his dark eyes disquieted.

'Maybe a little,' I whisper.

He looks crushed. 'Why?'

'I'm sorry.'

'Don't be sorry, but please tell me the truth.'

I can't. If I say he's moved in too soon, he'll be mortified and will probably move straight back out again. I'll never get him to come and live at the farm. And I really, *really* do want him here in the long term. I could've just done with a few more weeks to properly lay Theo to rest.

'Will you trust me?' I ask.

He stares at me apprehensively. He's wearing a white T-shirt and scuffed jeans and a wave of longing overcomes me.

Christ, he wears his clothes well...

'I want you,' I say, and then I'm instantly wide-eyed with surprise that the words spilled out of me so easily and without filter.

His eyebrows jump up, but in a good way.

I let my instincts lead me out from behind the spinning wheel. He unlinks his hands and looks up at me as I stand in the space between his legs.

We stare at each other, and then he very slowly brings one hand behind my knee.

My breath hitches at the feeling of his palm heating my bare skin. I take his face in my hands and bring him towards me, cradling his face tenderly against my stomach. He wraps his arms around my waist and holds me.

And that's all we do.

Without me having to tell him, he understands that I need to take it slow.

The weeks that follow are deliciously torturous, full of covert looks and clandestine brushes of our fingertips on each other's skin. It's the most exquisite foreplay I could imagine.

One morning, I exit my bathroom as George exits his, and the sight of his bare chest and nothing but a towel wrapped around his waist makes me stop short.

My eyes travel over every inch of his naked flesh, taking in his broad shoulders and his chest with its dark smattering of hair, and, *holy hell*, the V-shape that forces my gaze from his hips to his happy trail.

And he just stands there.

I assume he's indulging my need to stare, but then I realise he's soaking up the sight of me in turn.

I'm also wearing nothing but a towel: my dark-blond hair is damp and falling in a tangle around my shoulders, and my skin is glistening with the shimmery body butter I've applied.

I can barely breathe as his gaze roves from the swell of my breasts to up past my neck and mouth, eventually resting on my eyes. He gives me a darkly warning look and, in the space between his legs, the towel kicks out. He very slowly shakes his head at me and goes into his room, locking the door behind him.

He doesn't come out for some time, and the thought of what he's doing in there makes me feel slightly insane.

But the gradual build-up to what is certain to happen one day soon is exactly what I need. The chains of my grief are loosening as my fixation with George climbs to dizzying heights, and before long I know I'll be free to take things further without the burden of guilt.

With George living at the farm, the work is more than manageable. Alpacas are so low maintenance anyway, but it's great to have an extra pair of hands, and I've loved seeing him spending more time with Emilie.

He's still going to the pub every day and I've been knitting children's clothes that will go on sale at Mum's next workshop, which takes place in a few days. She's had five so far, and they're going from strength to strength, so much so that she's had to put on an extra session for a group of women from a book club who recently read *The Friday Night Knitting Club* by Kate Jacobs. They thought it would be fun to do something different together.

Part of my reason for setting up a website for the workshop was to highlight the idea of special days out for groups of friends, so I'm thrilled. Mum's fortnightly Saturday afternoon workshops will continue to tick over with some of the same people attending each time, but this is a good way to expand. And she loves hosting these sessions. I've attended every one and it's a joy to see how much pleasure she gets from building people's confidence and watching their skills develop.

On Friday night, when we arrive home after her book group session, Mum and I open a bottle of Prosecco and settle on the sofa to celebrate her ongoing success.

George is still at work.

'Honestly, you look like you were born to do it,' I say, chinking my glass proudly against hers.

'No. I enjoy it, but I wouldn't say I was born to it.' She smiles at me. 'I was born to parent, that's the truth. I was born to foster.'

'George wants to foster one day,' I find myself telling her.

She nods. 'I know. He talked to me about it.'

I'm no longer surprised that they have heart-to-hearts. I like that he's comfortable enough to open up to her. It occurred to her, a couple of weeks ago, that she still had his old Life Story book somewhere. She managed to hunt it out from a filing cabinet in the study and they went through it together, just the two of them.

'What did you say to him?'

'I told him that anyone who feels that they might be even remotely interested in fostering should pursue the possibility. But if it's not the right thing for him, there's plenty more he could do in a wider sense.'

'Like setting up another coffee shop that only hires care leavers?'

The Cracked Teapot is all about helping teenagers transition out of care.

'Possibly, but there are other ways. He could volunteer at a youth club or mentor a teenager. I used to hate it when we lived in London and people complained about addiction problems in their area. "Don't complain, *do* something!" I wanted to shout. Get involved in the community, find out where the problems are, *why* there's a problem, and try to work out how you can help. Stop living for comfort and care. Even giving support to another foster family is worth its weight in gold. Do you remember when Ashlee and Nia landed on us with next to no notice and I was run off my feet?'

I nod.

'Do you remember how Veronica came over that day with a homemade casserole that she'd prepared for her own family and gave it to us instead?'

I shake my head, my nose beginning to prickle.

'What she did meant so much to me. She didn't want to be a foster parent herself, but she was able to support *me*, and that helped. Social workers need support too: a shoulder to lean on, an ear to listen. It all helps the bigger picture. It really does take a village and we can all do a bit more.'

'I'm worried George wouldn't be able to cope when the children come to leave him.'

'He'd pull the strength from somewhere,' Mum assures me. 'He'd have to. People used to say to me, "I don't know how you do it. I couldn't do it; I couldn't say goodbye." But you can and you do and it hurts and it never stops hurting. But it's not meant to be easy. These kids *need* someone to care for them and hurt for them and never want to let them go. Someone *has* to. *I* had to. Your dad and I both did. It was our calling.'

I'm overcome with emotion at hearing Mum speak so passionately. We don't often talk about it.

'I know it was hard for you at times, Lee-Lee,' she says to me as tears roll down my cheeks. 'And I'm sorry about that. But I hope you understand. Now that you have Emilie, I hope you understand.'

'I do.' I nod and her eyes well up too.

'Fostering is the best thing I have ever done with my life,' she states fervently.

I believe it.

George comes home at eleven, as we're calling it a night.

'You're back early,' Mum says with delight.

Usually we're fast asleep by the time he returns, knackered after Emilie-induced early mornings.

'It was surprisingly quiet tonight,' he replies with a smile, and I realise there's an unusual energy radiating from him. 'I have news.'

'What is it?' Mum and I ask in unison.

'A job at Forestry England has come up. They want me to go for an interview on Monday.'

'Oh George, that's fantastic!' Mum cries as my heart leaps. 'Here in North Yorkshire?'

Now my heart lurches, but he replies with a yes and it soars again.

'I'm off to bed, but sit down and have a drink with Leah,' she urges. 'You should celebrate.'

'I haven't got the job yet,' he says with amusement.

'Oh, but you will.'

I admire her confidence.

George ducks out to use the bathroom, but before Mum heads upstairs, she whispers to me: 'I've been thinking. Maybe Emilie should call George Uncle George, like she does Uncle Jamie?'

'Mum, *no!*' My response is loud and absolute.

She looks surprised at my overreaction.

'No. "George" is fine,' I add more evenly.

She accepts what I'm saying with a shrug and an 'Okay', but I hope she doesn't think too much about it later.

Now I understand why Jamie and Dani always stress that they didn't have feelings for each other when they lived under the same roof. They weren't technically foster siblings at the time as Jamie had already left for university, but their paths crossed when he came home for the holidays, as he always did.

I'm still reluctant to tell Mum that George and I have history. There's something... I don't know... *icky* about it.

George comes back with a bitter from the fridge and the bottle to top up my glass.

'Mum just suggested Emilie call you Uncle George,' I whisper, closing the living room door and pulling a face.

He mirrors my expression and I giggle, going to sit down beside him on the sofa.

'Hello,' I say, knocking my glass against his bottle.

'Hello,' he replies, holding my gaze with his dark eyes.

He looks so hot in his dark-green shirt, layered over a plain white T-shirt. He's got his extra well-worn denim jeans on too. It's a style I'm familiar with: understated, yet cool. I like his clothes very much, but after what I saw a few days ago outside the bathroom, I'm getting increasingly eager to see him out of them.

I know he won't make the first move, though. It has to

come from me. We've reached an unspoken understanding and he won't act until I show him I'm ready.

Right then and there, seeing him sitting a foot away from me with his arm draped over the back of the sofa and his foot resting casually on his knee, not to mention the bottle being pressed to his lips, I *do* feel ready.

I close the distance between us. His outstretched arm is behind my shoulders, but it comes around me now as he pulls me closer. His body is so warm and solid, his arms so strong and capable. He looks down at me, a smile tugging the corner of his lips.

He takes another swig from his bottle and I stare at his mouth, mesmerised.

We're only inches away.

He lowers his drink and stares at me until the air leaves my lungs, then he turns and puts the bottle down on the side table and I'm pressing my glass into his empty hand, silently asking him to do the same with mine.

A moment later, I'm straddling his hips. I slide my palms up his hard chest and he digs his fingertips into the small of my back and edges me closer. The heat of him is spreading *everywhere*. I am *aching* for him, and judging by what I'm beginning to feel beneath me, I believe the feeling is mutual.

Desire burns in his eyes and I slowly bring my mouth down to his. It's all the permission he needs.

32

NOW

The next morning, George finds me at the kitchen sink, rinsing out Emilie's cereal bowl. Mum and Emilie left a moment ago to go and collect the eggs. He comes up behind me and wraps his arms around my waist, pulling me flush against his chest and pressing a kiss to my neck. We don't speak for a while, we simply stand there, enjoying the feeling of being so close.

'I love you,' he whispers in my ear.

I twist in his arms so I'm facing him, my back against the counter. His brown eyes stare down at me, dark and intense.

'I love *you*,' I say solemnly. 'I've loved you for half my life.'

I loop my arms around his neck as he brings his mouth down to mine, and our kiss is full of the words we've said to each other.

'Oh!' Mum exclaims from the doorway.

We jerk apart. George turns away and I blush and cover my face with my hands, peeking at my mother guiltily through my fingers. I feel like a naughty teenager.

Out of the corner of my eye, I see Emilie through the window, skipping about in the courtyard, so at least she's oblivious.

'I forgot the basket,' Mum explains, as George finally turns around to face her, looking sheepish. 'Is this why you didn't want Emilie to call him Uncle George?' she asks me, cocking an eyebrow.

I nod.

'Fair enough,' she says with a knowing grin, grabbing the basket from the table. 'Emilie and I will be at least ten minutes. As you were,' she says as she walks out the door.

George and I look at each other and laugh, both slightly mortified. And while I feel a twinge of disappointment that our secret is out in the open – it was quite a thrill sneaking around – I'm mostly relieved that I no longer have to lie to my mother. I'm still a good girl at heart.

George and I talk about it with Mum later, after Emilie has gone to bed. He and I are on the sofa opposite Mum, sitting apart, and I've confessed that I don't know how to play things where my daughter is concerned.

'I bet she doesn't even bat an eyelid,' Mum says. 'Children are so adaptable at that age.'

'Do you think so?' I need reassurance. I don't want to do anything that will hurt or confuse her.

'If this is serious between you—'

'It is,' George interrupts. 'Leah's it for me.'

I flash him a tender look, reaching over to take his hand.

'George is it for me too,' I say softly, holding his gaze

before turning to see Mum regarding us both with fond affection.

'Then don't hide it from her,' she repeats gently. 'The sooner this becomes her new normal, the less confused she'll be.' She gets up and walks to the door. 'And maybe we need to start thinking about converting the Bunny Barn for Nanna sooner rather than later!' she adds merrily, disappearing into the kitchen.

George and I take Mum's advice, and the next morning, when he comes down for breakfast while Emilie is still sitting at the kitchen table, I make a point of going straight over to him and giving him a quick kiss on his lips.

'Good morning!' I say brightly, glancing over at Emilie to check her reaction.

She's seen us, but she returns to eating her cereal without a fuss.

'Good morning, Emilie,' George says, squeezing her shoulder.

She looks at him as he sits down.

I dare to hope that Mum is right and that she'll accept this as her new normal without even questioning it.

'Are you my daddy now?' she asks George.

Oh, *shit*!

He looks at me, but before I can speak, he answers her.

'There are different types of daddy, did you know that?'

She shakes her head.

'Theo is your real daddy. You have a photo of him in your bedroom. He will *always* be your real daddy and he loved you very, very much. Your Gramps was *not* my real daddy, but he was a bit like a daddy to me when I lived here a long time ago. He loved and protected me, just like he loved and protected your Uncle Jamie. He was a *really* good dad,' he says seriously as pressure builds behind my eyes. 'I would like to try to be that sort of dad for you. I will love and protect you and I want you to always feel safe with me. If you're ever scared about anything or if you ever need help, you can come and find me and I'll look after you. Is that okay?'

She nods and grins at him, looking thoroughly pleased with his answer.

I blink back tears, and when George meets my eyes, doubting himself, I nod and smile, trying to convey that what he said was absolutely perfect.

Jamie and Dani are coming to spend Christmas with us, so ahead of their visit, George and I decide to make our fluid sleeping arrangements permanent. We move most of my belongings out of my room and into his so we still have a degree of separation from Mum, but with the way she's eagerly talking about a barn conversion, it really may only be a matter of time before we have the house to ourselves.

George is working most days at Forestry England now, having secured the job at his one and only interview, so he's not at home on Friday afternoon when Jamie and Dani arrive.

We're all sitting around the kitchen table having tea and Christmas cake when he does appear, and as usual, I'm the first person he kisses, followed by Emilie: lips for me; top of the head for her. By the time he reaches Jamie, my foster brother is positively beaming. We've told Dani and Jamie about our relationship on the phone, but seeing is believing and no one could doubt the love between us.

The thrill of keeping our relationship a secret is incomparable to how it feels to be tactile with George in public. It's a pure joy to be able to walk down a high street hand in hand, or sit side by side at the pub with his arm draped around my shoulders. We've also got together with Becky and Robin a few times – Robin and George get on well and I'm sure it's a friendship that will only strengthen with time.

Mum is beside herself that night with all of us around the table – I haven't seen her this happy in a long time. The Christmas decorations are up and fairy lights are twinkling on the tree. The mantelpieces are decorated with fresh-cut pine and the room smells of forests and vanilla, thanks to the row of tealights flickering prettily on the table.

This will be our first Christmas without Dad, and while these firsts are bound to be tough, it helps to be surrounded by loved ones. It was Emilie's fourth birthday last week and I missed him desperately on that day too, as I did Theo. I wrote about it in a letter to Theo, telling him about the giant unicorn cake Mum made and how Emilie's eyes grew so round when I helped her cut into it and jellybeans spilled out of the middle. We invited some of her playmates from nursery over for a party, along with their parents. I've become friendly with the blonde woman who spoke to me kindly on Emilie's first day. Her name is Rosie and we often go to the café together, sometimes with the kids too. Emilie and Rosie's daughter Isla get on well.

Dani raises her Diet Coke into the air. She isn't drinking again, nor did she drink at the pub back in August after Mum's first knitting workshop. Mum and I speculated then that there could be a number of reasons for it, but felt it was rude to ask.

'So, you may have noticed that I'm not on the booze,'

Dani says, putting the glass back down before continuing. 'I made a decision to stop when we moved to London. I know that I have a problem with alcohol and I really don't want to turn out like my mum, so I've been going to meetings.'

Mum reaches across the table and covers her hand, supportively. 'I am very proud of you, darling,' she says seriously.

'Dani thought she'd better clear that up before you jumped to the conclusion that she's pregnant,' Jamie chips in.

'Well, I did wonder,' Mum admits with a smile.

Jamie coughs. We all look at him. His face breaks out in a grin.

'You're not?' Mum gasps.

Dani nods, beaming. 'Twelve weeks. We had the scan this morning.'

'Oh, I'm so happy for you!' Mum exclaims, jumping to her feet to hug them both. George and I immediately follow suit.

The next day, on Christmas Eve, Bramble, our little minx of an alpaca, goes into labour. Usually alpacas 'unpack' without a fuss, but Bramble struggles.

'It's as though she knew I was coming up for the weekend,' Jamie says, getting his veterinary bag out of the car. He never goes anywhere without it.

Jamie soon determines that Bramble's cria is facing the wrong way, and after trying to unpack her without success, he has to perform an emergency caesarean or risk losing both mother and baby.

I can't watch – I'm not great with blood – but George stays with him the whole time, helping wherever needed.

Unfortunately, after going through so much trauma, Bramble rejects her offspring, a dark-brown boy who is the spitting image of Blackthorn.

'You found your old friend again, didn't you?' I say to poor, exhausted Bramble.

She and Blackthorn were born the same week and used to play together all the time before he was moved into the boys' paddock.

'Don't worry, we'll get you together again in the spring,' I promise.

Right now, though, we have to take on the responsibility of bottle-feeding her cria. Emilie wants to help, so I decide to let her have a later bedtime than usual. It's not as though she'll be able to sleep anyway, with the excitement of Father Christmas coming.

Mum brings the bottle out to the barn. I'm sitting on the straw-covered ground with Emilie in between my legs and the cria on her lap. Bramble is resting in the stall beside us.

Emilie is cradling the cria like a baby. I show her how to hold the bottle and her face brightens with delight as he begins to suck.

Mum smiles at me. 'She's a natural.'

'I'm not going to be able to get her away from the barn after this,' I say.

My daughter will make this cria her own – at least until he goes back in with the herd, and then he'll no doubt have a few aunties who will take him under their wing.

As I look down at Emilie's face, lit with wonder, I know that this is another moment that I'll be writing to Theo about. My letters to him have become almost diary like. I've taken Mum's advice and will put them somewhere safe until the day that Emilie might like to read them. It will be her Life Story book of sorts.

'What shall we call him?' I ask Emilie now, before looking up at Mum. 'Were there any more "G"s left to choose from?'

We've already had Geranium, Gerbera and Gladioli this year.

'Gardenia, Goosefoot, Gillyflower... Or we could do Gerry for another type of Geranium?'

'Do you like the name Gerry, Emilie?' I ask her.

She screws up her nose. 'I want to call him Teddy.'

I glance up at Mum as a memory of Ashlee comes back to me. 'A teddy named Dolly and an alpaca named Teddy. All we need now is a dolly named Alpaca and we'll be sorted.'

Mum laughs. 'Whoever said life made sense? Teddy it is.'

On Christmas morning, we take a family walk up to Brimham. The silver birch trees have shed the last of their leaves so there's no more russet-coloured confetti to rain down on our heads as we pass through the wood. Emilie loved it up here in the autumn.

While Uncle Jamie chases her between the withering ferns, and Mum and Dani take their time catching us up, George and I walk out to the overhang.

A few weeks after George moved in with us, I came clean to him about scattering Theo's ashes. He claimed he was glad to have somewhere to go to think about him too, but I reassured him that this space up on the rocks belongs to *all* of us. It always was and always will be somewhere to go to get away from it all, to simply sit and appreciate nature. It was never my intention for it to all be about Theo. He seemed glad to hear that.

But now, as we sit down, side by side on the dry, cold rock, I know that we're *both* thinking about my husband.

I lean against George and he wraps his arm around my shoulders, pulling me close.

'I love you,' I say, pressing a kiss to his jaw.

'I love you too.' He takes a deep, shaky breath. 'Do you think he'd be okay with it?' he asks. 'With me?'

I nod. 'I think so. Yes, I do.'

But if I have any doubts, a few minutes later, they're extinguished. As we make our way out past Mini Druid's Writing Desk, via the hole in the rock, I look down to see that it has frozen over with water to just the right amount.

And it's as though Theo himself is sending a message of love to us straight from his heart.

EPILOGUE

Neither then nor now...
...but sometime in the future

'I thought I'd find you here,' I say, handing George his tea.

'Hey you,' he replies with a smile up at me. 'Thank you.' He takes the reusable cup and pats his lap, opening his arms to me.

The ground is damp so I accept his invitation, snuggling into his warm embrace. We stare up into the bare branches of the big old oak tree.

I passed his silver birch just now, running my hand along the satin-white trunk as I always do when I'm seeking out my husband. He doesn't have many hiding spots, but this is by far his favourite.

To our left and right, spanning both lower paddocks, is one of his many achievements. Alpacas don't need much land to graze on – a paddock each is more than enough – so we moved the boys up to the field adjacent to the girls, and, with help from the Woodland Carbon Fund, expanded our wood across the lower land.

We have a broad variety of species, from silver birch and wild cherry to western red cedar, willow and oak, plus a collection of conifers. A more diverse forest is a more resilient forest, George says, so ours will be better equipped to defend itself against pests, diseases and the threat of climate change in the future.

We've called it Ivan Wood, after my father.

George and I won't live to see it grow to maturity, and neither will Emilie, but we created it with the youngest generation in mind, and all of those who'll come after.

'I'm looking forward to tomorrow,' I say to George.

'Me too,' he replies with a sideways smile.

Sophie and Jack are visiting with their newborn baby. They met at university in Leeds – Jack is a lovely local boy who made it his mission early in their relationship to show Sophie practically every inch of Yorkshire. She grew to love it almost as much as he did and now they live in York permanently. We see them whenever we can.

I still vividly remember the look of elation on George's face when Sophie told him she was coming to study here. He never had to feel guilty about choosing North Yorkshire and me over Devon and his sister because she moved to be closer to him anyway.

We still make it down to Devon for the occasional holiday, although Ernie, sadly, is no longer with us. George sold the cottage years ago, but it wouldn't have been big enough for us these days anyway. The effort to secure larger accommodation is worth it: a break by the coast does the whole family a world of good.

Jamie and Dani are also coming this weekend. They left

London when their first baby was born as Dani had finished her apprenticeship and Jamie missed the country. They live on the outskirts of Ripon with their four kids, the eldest of whom, Josh, takes after his dad. He comes whenever Jamie attends to the herd. Only last week, Teddy had to have an abscess cut off his toe. Emilie was in a state – she still considers Teddy her baby – but Josh sat with his dad the whole time, passing him the scalpel and helping him to clean up Teddy and bandage his foot afterwards. He's a chip off the old block, that's for sure.

'Suppose we'd better get back inside,' George says, kissing the cold tip of my nose.

I reply by tilting my face up to his, and he rewards me with a sweet, gentle kiss on my lips. We withdraw and smile at each other.

We have to make the most of these quiet moments, when it's just the two of us.

We walk arm in arm back up to the farmhouse, talking about the weekend and what it has in store.

George's eyes widen when we enter the kitchen and he sees what I've been up to.

'I almost forgot that it's Friday,' he says with glee at the sight of the chocolate cake on the table.

'Can't miss cake day,' I reply with a shrug.

It's a weekly tradition. Fridays are for cakes; Sundays are for roast dinners. Junk food night may strike at any time of the week, depending on what's going on in our lives. I try to prepare healthy meals wherever possible, but sometimes my limits are stretched, and on those days, takeaway comes in very handy. No one complains, as you can imagine.

'You're Supermum,' George says.

'That's what I used to call *my* mum,' I tell him.

'Did you?'

'Only in my head. She was pretty fantastic, though, wasn't she?'

The sound of voices in the courtyard cuts off any answer he was going to give me.

The door flies open with Emilie, fourteen, leading the charge, shouting back over her shoulder at thirteen-year-old Logan to, 'Pack it in, you git!'

'Oh, Emilie,' I want to say. *'Be patient with him. He'll get there.'*

But I don't interfere. This girl can handle herself. She's trouble at times, like her father, but she has a big heart. We love the bones of her.

Logan follows her in, slamming the door behind him.

'Mind yourself,' George says mildly, opening the door back up again.

Logan looks as though he's going to storm from the room, but then he sees the cake on the table and hesitates.

'Why don't you go wash your hands and help yourself,' I say gently, rubbing his back.

When Logan's harassed social worker brought him to us last month, and left, telling him to behave, George said, only loudly enough for Logan and me to hear, 'Don't listen to her, son. We'll take you as you are.'

And we do. We take them *all* as they are.

Here come the little ones now, although they're not so little any more. Hayley and Maysie joined our family when they were seven, but they're already halfway through their first year of secondary school. They're identical twins and you can usually hear them coming a mile off, talkative as they are.

Finally, bringing up the rear is Dillon, a quiet twelve-year-old who has been with us for four months.

'Is it okay if Hayden comes in?' he asks me uncertainly,

and I peer behind him to see Becky and Robin's eldest hovering.

'Of course it is,' I say to Hayden, passing him the phone as he comes inside. 'Call your mum and dad so they don't worry.'

It means the world to us that Becky and Robin don't merely *allow* their children, Hayden and Gina, to play with ours, but actively encourage it. Becky thinks it's good for them, that it teaches them compassion.

I agree with her. While my childhood was challenging at times and I didn't have my parents' attention as much as I sometimes needed, I wouldn't change it. It made me who I am, taught *me* compassion. I want the same for Emilie and hope that one day she'll understand and forgive me for not always being able to put her first.

The kitchen is a hive of activity with hands being washed, drinks being made, school bags unpacked and chocolate cake devoured. It's the best kind of chaos.

'They're so lucky to have you,' a mother at school said to me the other day. I'd gone in for Parents' Evening and Dillon's mother had failed to turn up, even though she'd assured us that she would be there.

Dillon was so worried about her. His father is abusive, but his mother won't leave him. She's very young; spent her own childhood in care.

I wanted to reply, 'This boy was taken from his mum and dad without warning. He was separated from his siblings, his pets and all his toys. He had to leave behind his bedroom, his house, his garden, his school, his classmates and everything he knew. And then he was brought to a strange house and expected to slot in with a new family. Do you know how terrifying that must've been? How anxious he must be feeling? All he wants to do is go home. He's *not* lucky. The very least we can do is try to ease some of his pain while he's with us.'

But I held my tongue, as I so often do.

George still works part-time at Forestry England, and, without Mum to help out these days, I have my hands full at the farm, but both George and I find time in our busy schedules to volunteer at the local youth club. George also visits schools to talk about his experience and try to educate young people and teachers. We strongly believe that we need to reframe the way we talk about people in care. We're sick of hearing struggling parents being described as the scum of the earth, simply because they find it hard to live in a way that most of us take for granted. They need support and they need education, and a whole lot more understanding.

As Mum once said, it takes a village, and there is more that we all can do.

She really was a Supermum.

I gaze out of the kitchen window at her home on the other side of the courtyard. She was so excited the day she moved in. I'd sold my flat in London and George had sold his cottage in Devon, and we'd used the proceeds from both sales to update the farmhouse and convert the barn. The building's structure was already sound, formed from sandy-coloured stone with a shiny slate rooftop, as with here at the house. George replaced the big barn doors with windows and glass doors, and we brought in a building crew to do the internal works, plastering and whitewashing the interior to a clean, fresh, clutter-free space: one bedroom and an en suite bathroom, plus an open-plan kitchen and living space. Mum was *thrilled*.

I grab Maysie and Hayley before they can disappear. Although a lot older than Ashlee and Nia were, they reminded me of them when they first came to us. Both so timid: a raised voice would send them into hiding and they'd go rigid every time you tried to hug them. But they've come so far and I'm ecstatic that we were able to adopt them.

I once asked Mum if she and Dad had ever considered adopting Nia and Ashlee. She replied that they had wanted to, very much, and would have adopted Ashlee in a heartbeat if the situation with Nia hadn't worked out. But ultimately, they knew that it was the teenagers who were more critically in need of loving, caring placements. By giving up a room to Ashlee and Nia, she wouldn't have been able to help Dani, Emma, Nikita, Catherine, Tisha, to name but a few.

It's been about twenty-five years since Ashlee and Nia left us, but I still look for their faces in strangers on the street and hope we might see them again one day. Occasionally I daydream about them coming back to say thank you to the woman who went out of her way to keep them together.

Hayley and Maisie look up at me expectantly.

'Go get Nanna, would you?' I say. 'She's going to miss out on cake.'

They run across the courtyard, calling her name. She comes out of the door, her dear old face lit with love as she scoops them up in her warm embrace.

Was a Supermum, *now* a Supernanna.

Mum is still so involved with the children and young people that come to us. She's taught them how to knit and spin and even went out to buy three more Giant Angoras. They live in a hutch now, behind the Yarn Barn, and Mum looks after them. The hills are hard on her joints these days, so I do the lion's share where the alpacas are concerned. But she'll still take the herd boxes of apples and will spend time making sure each and every one of them gets a bite.

I remember someone once rudely asking Mum how much she got paid to foster. She gave them a vague answer about it being enough, but later, when George and I were going through the fostering process and discovered that we would still need to put in a lot of working hours to get by, she told us: 'You may never be rich *financially*, but your lives will be enriched with love and laughter. There is nothing more rewarding than seeing young people grow, heal and find hope.'

What a beautiful sentiment that was.

And she was right.

It's Mum's birthday this weekend, which is why Jamie and Dani are coming to raise a glass – albeit a non-alcoholic one. Shauna and Gemma are popping over too, and Dani said Preston hoped to come say hi after he's finished up at the market.

I try not to associate Mum's birthday with the anniversary of Theo's death, but it's not always easy. Instead I try to remember him on *his* birthday, when Emilie and I will walk up to Hare Heads and sit for a while, chatting about anything and everything. Although I try to have mother and daughter time with Emilie more often than my parents did with me, this is the one day a year I'm guaranteed to get her completely to myself and vice versa. George always does something to entertain the clan while we're gone.

This weekend also reminds me of Dad, and last night I dreamt of him, as I often do. I dream about talking to him, about giving him a hug, about him saying kind words to me or one of my children – he's never, ever angry in my sleep, just as he rarely was when I was awake. But last night, I simply dreamt that I came downstairs and that he was standing at the counter, buttering toast. He turned around and saw me.

'Don't worry, love. Everything will be okay,' he said, and then he offered up his toast with a smile.

A NOTE FROM THE AUTHOR...

If you are new to my writing, thank you very much for reading this book – I hope you enjoyed it! If, however, you've read my books before, you probably know by now that I find it hard to let my characters go, and many of them pop up in future books so we can see what they're up to, hopefully without giving too much away to new readers.

Someone I Used To Know has only a very small nod to the characters from *Thirteen Weddings*, my eighth book, so there are no spoilers here. But if you'd like to learn more about my novels and characters and receive some free short story sequels, visit www.paigetoon.com and sign up to my newsletter #TheHiddenPaige – the next time I send out an email, you'll be able to click to read past editions.

In the meantime, I'm including a couple of chapters from my 2020 release, *The Minute I Saw You*, which is a summery love story set in a picturesque English riverside setting of Cambridge and Grantchester – my hometown!

I can't wait to hear what American readers think about my books, so if you'd like to come and say hi, I'm on Twitter/Facebook/Instagram @PaigeToonAuthor

Lots of love, Paige x

READ ON FOR A PREVIEW OF...

THE MINUTE I SAW YOU

C *hapter 1*

Hello, hello...

There's a good-looking man standing on the pavement outside the window. He's talking on his mobile and his eyes are hidden behind sunglasses, but a slight frown is detectable on his brow.

When he turns toward the window, I see that his short dark hair is longer on top and sun-lightened to more of a caramel shade. It's swept back from his forehead in a retro almost-fifties style.

He ends the call, shoves his phone into his pocket and disappears from view, only to reappear a second later when he pushes open the door to the shop.

'Good morning!' Abbey chirps, and we both sit up straighter as he takes off his sunglasses. 'How can we help you?'

'I have an appointment at eleven forty-five.'

While Abbey checks her desktop screen, he looks my way, a polite smile fixed in place.

'Hello,' I say, tucking a stray lock of hair behind my ear.

'Hi,' he replies, his folded sunglasses swinging from between the tips of his thumb and forefinger.

Blue eyes...

'Sonny Denton?' Abbey asks, snapping his attention back to her.

'Yes,' he confirms.

Sonny? His name is retro too.

'It's been over two years since your last eye test?'

'Must be.'

'Can I get you to fill out this form and check your details?' She hands over a clipboard with paperwork attached, before adding, with a nod in my direction: 'Hannah, our dispensing optician, will be with you shortly.'

I indicate the black leather seat inside the bay window opposite my desk. In the time it takes for him to walk the few metres across the room and sit down, Abbey and I have furtively cast each other cheeky grins.

That's the last time I'll dare to look at her for a while. A similarly hot client came in earlier this week and she enthusiastically licked her lips the moment his back was turned. Unfortunately, he spun around to ask her something, catching her in the act. I nearly choked on my tea.

Thankfully, this all went over the boss's head. Umeko, the optometrist, owns this place. She's kind and clever and has high standards that, quite understandably, she expects us to maintain. I've only been here for a few weeks so I'd rather not lose my job just yet, thanks.

It's not uncommon for young people to come in here – Umeko's is a small independent practice with a stylish (albeit slightly on-the-pricey side) range of eyewear that tends to appeal to a more designery crowd. We're based in Newnham, a suburb of Cambridge and only a short walk south-west of the city centre. Our road and the ones nearby are lined with neat Victorian terraced houses, but this is a semi-detached red-brick corner building that we share with the pharmacy next door. There's a lovely little delicatessen across the road and a hairdresser a few doors down. It's a nice part of town and only a twenty-five-minute walk from the village of Grantchester, where I'm currently living.

Abbey and I spend most of our working days in the bright and airy front room. Abbey's desk is up against the back wall. My desk is to the right, separated from Abbey by a central corridor and facing the bay window. Glasses displays are dotted all around.

Along the corridor are two consultation rooms, one occupied by Umeko. It's my job to carry out pre-screening tests in the second room before handing clients over to Umeko for their main consultation. It's where we'll be headed as soon as Sonny has finished filling out his form.

'All set?' I ask as he gets to his feet.

'Yep.'

I take the clipboard, giving it a quick once-over before glancing up at him. 'You're a photographer?'

'Yes.'

He's tall, but not toweringly so – six foot? A good head-height higher than me, and he's wearing a denim shirt layered over a white T-shirt with slim-fitting charcoal-grey chinos.

'That's cool,' I comment, noting two other important pieces of information: one, he lives in Barton, which is a ten-minute drive away, tops; and two, his date of birth places him at thirty-two. 'We've got a couple of tests to do before you go through to Umeko. I'm sure you remember how it goes from the last time you were here.'

Avoiding Abbey's gaze – I'm not taking any chances – I lead him down the corridor and into the first room on our right, inhaling a hint of spicy aftershave as he passes by.

'Are you wearing contacts today?'

'Yes, monthlies. I brought solution with me.'

'Great. Can you take them out?'

His eyes are *so* blue. Azure blue, I'd call them. They're startling against his dark lashes.

'Have a seat and pop your chin on the rest,' I say when he's ready.

After taking pictures of the back of each eye, we switch

to a second multifunctional machine so I can do a quick reading of his prescription.

'Have you worked here long?' he asks.

'Only a few weeks.'

'What happened to Mr Grumpy?'

He's leaning back in his chair, smirking and gently swivelling from left to right.

'If you're talking about Bernard – and I wouldn't like to presume – then he's moved up to Scotland to be closer to his ailing parents.'

He grins. 'Can't say I'll miss his halitosis.'

'You haven't got up close and personal with me yet.'

No, no.

No, no, no, no, no.

Those words did not just leave my lips.

Except, from the look on his face, it appears that they did. His eyes have widened, not to mention his grin.

'I did *not* mean that the way it sounded.'

He laughs with delight, and despite my embarrassment, the sound makes me feel jittery.

'One last test,' I say through gritted teeth.

'Is this the videogame one?' he asks hopefully, sitting up straighter.

'You're thinking of the visual fields test.'

'Yeah, you press a button every time a wiggly line appears around the edges.'

'All the boys like that one,' I say with a smile. 'But no, I'm afraid it's the pressure test.' It assesses for risk of developing glaucoma. I lower the machine into its tonometer setting. 'We'll start with your right eye. Keep looking straight ahead with your eyes wide open.'

He flinches as three puffs of air are blasted into each eye.

The procedure doesn't hurt, but it's not particularly pleasant either.

'That's me done for a bit.' I gather together the printouts with the retinal images and test results. 'I'll go and see if Umeko is ready for you. Are you okay to wait here for a moment?'

'Yep.'

Umeko is sitting at her desk, tapping away at her keyboard.

'Sonny Denton is here to see you,' I tell her.

'Aah, Sonny,' she says with a smile, taking the paperwork from me.

'Has he been a client for long?' I try not to sound too interested.

'Since he was a teenager,' she replies, scanning the information before her. 'His father does our accounts,' she adds.

Umeko has been living in the UK for going on forty years now, but her Japanese accent has not faded much with time. Though she's in her early sixties, she looks a good ten years younger with smooth, unlined skin and barely a grey strand to be found amongst her jet-black locks. She always wears her hair in a sleek topknot at work, but I've seen her socially on many occasions and when it's loose it comes halfway down her back.

It's like mine in that respect, except where her hair is as straight as a pin, mine is wavy: light-brown and streaked with natural highlights. I also wear it up for work, but it's a messy bun at the best of times. Sleek topknot it ain't.

After listening to Sonny and Umeko greet each other like old friends, I head back to my desk and flash Abbey a grin. She picks up a magazine and fans her face, making the wispy strawberry-blond strands that have fallen out of her high ponytail fly away from her round cherub face.

'*How* hot?' she whispers.

'Shh,' I reply, but I'm grinning. 'Apparently he's been coming here for years. You've not seen him before?'

'No.'

She's only been here for twelve months so that figures.

Umeko's previous practice manager was a bossy matronly type who took retirement at the age of fifty-three. She trained Abbey up before she left. Abbey worked alongside Bernard and wasn't sad to see the back of him. She thinks it's no coincidence that Umeko went on to hire me, a second younger, livelier member of staff – Abbey's twenty-six and I'm twenty-seven.

I continue filing NHS forms, but it's hard to get stuck into it when I know Sonny won't be with Umeko for long.

Sure enough, he's done in fifteen minutes.

Umeko sees him to the front room. 'Have a wander, see what you like the look of,' she encourages.

'Can I get you a tea or coffee?' I ask him. 'Latte? Cappuccino?'

We have a fancy coffee machine in the kitchen.

'A latte would be great,' he replies.

Umeko and I have a quick handover chat while I make his drink. It's all very straightforward – he mostly wears contact lenses but prefers to use glasses when he's photo editing at his computer, sometimes late into the night.

When I return, Sonny is trying on a pair of metal-framed glasses in front of the mirror.

'I like those,' Abbey says as I place his coffee on my desk.

'They're a bit light in colour, I think,' he replies. 'A bit too bling.'

'Are you after metal frames?' I ask.

'Yeah, but I'd prefer more of a mid-gunmetal shade.'

'Have a look at the Kilsgaards,' I suggest, directing him towards a stand hosting several of the Danish brand.

'This is exactly the colour I was talking about.' He picks up a pair and puts them on, checking his reflection.

'They look great,' Abbey remarks admiringly.

'They do,' I agree. 'You should try these too.' I pass him a pair, not wanting him to feel pressured into deciding too quickly.

We encourage him to peruse the other stands, but he ends up going back to the Kilsgaards, settling on the first pair he tried on.

'I've got to nip to my sister's.' Abbey reminds me. Her sister is having work done on her house nearby and Abbey promised to let one of the tradesmen in. 'Can I get you another coffee before I go?' she offers as Sonny and I head over to my desk together.

'No thanks, this one is still warm,' he replies, taking a sip.

'Do you want to put those on again,' I suggest when Abbey has left, turning the small mirror on my desk towards him. 'They really suit you,' I reiterate. Most of what he tried on did, to be fair. 'Can I check the fit?'

'Sure.'

He leans closer to me across the narrow desk space. He smells *amazing*.

There's the slightest trace of abrasion under my thumbs as they rest on his cheeks and give the frames a wiggle.

The corner of his mouth tilts up, but he hastily presses his lips together, trying to suppress a smile.

I bite my lip, trying to straighten my own face. His humour is having a contagious effect.

'Sorry,' he apologises.

'It's okay,' I murmur, running my fingers along the

length of the arms of the glasses to make sure they're long enough to sit properly on his ears.

Once again, his lips twitch.

'Sorry, sorry,' he mutters adorably as we full-on grin at each other.

'Lots of people get the giggles,' I reassure him as I complete my checks.

'I didn't get the giggles with Bernard,' he comments drily and a thrill darts through me.

'Right, now I need to take some measurements.' I pick up a marker pen. 'Look at me again.'

He stares straight into my eyes as I mark the spot where the centre of his pupil aligns with the lenses. I am far more aware than usual of this particular client's close proximity, but I'm focused on the task – it's important that the strongest part of the prescription marries up with his eyeline.

'You have very unusual eyes,' he says in a low voice as I finish with his second eye.

'Do I?' I reel back slightly as I reply, but in truth, I know I do. They're a strange, almost-golden colour, flecked and circled with green.

'Yeah, you do.' His gaze is unwavering.

I raise one eyebrow at him. 'You can take them off now.'

I am pulse-racingly aware of him watching me as I measure the dimensions on his glasses with a ruler and input the relevant information into the computer. By the time we're ready to discuss lens options, my heart rate has thankfully been restored to normal.

'Who makes the lenses?' he asks.

'Zeiss,' I reply. It's an astute question for a photographer. 'Do they do your camera lenses?'

He nods. 'I've got a few by them.'

'What sort of photography do you do?' I ask conversationally.

'Fashion, mostly.'

'Where? Here?'

'No, all over. Amsterdam, London, New York. I live in Amsterdam,' he explains, then, noting my look of confusion, adds: 'I used my parents' address on my form.'

'Aah, okay.' So he's *not* local. *Interesting.* 'One of my friends moved to Amsterdam a few months ago. I need to get over there this summer.'

'You should. It's an easy weekend break.'

'When do you go back?'

'Two weeks tomorrow. Hopefully these will be ready in time.'

'You leave Saturday the twenty-fifth?' I check my online calendar.

'Yep.'

'That should be fine. Shall we make you an appointment to come in the day before you go?'

I'll need to fit his new glasses and make any adjustments, so it's not simply a case of him dropping by to pick them up.

'Sure.'

'Same sort of time?'

'Perfect.'

'Not that I'm suggesting you should go anywhere other than this excellent establishment, but why don't you get your glasses in Amsterdam?'

'I like Umeko. I've been coming here for years. Even Bernie Bad Breath couldn't keep me away,' he adds with a smirk.

I laugh and turn the computer screen towards him. 'Okay, so we're looking at a total of...'

He doesn't baulk at the price.

'What are you up to while you're here?' I ask casually as he gives me a credit card. 'On holiday or working?'

'Catching up with my family for Easter, then back to work.'

'Do you come home often?' I ring up the amount.

'Not as much as I should.'

I wonder if he has a girlfriend in Amsterdam. He's not wearing a wedding ring.

'That's us all done,' I say with a smile, handing him his card. His fingers brush mine as he takes it, causing a strange heat to prickle up my arm.

'Thanks. Guess I'll see you in two weeks.'

'I guess you will.'

We're both still grinning as he walks out the door, and then he casts one last look over his shoulder at me before disappearing from view.

I bring my hands up to my face and find that his aftershave has lingered from where I touched him. I'm strangely reluctant to wash my hands, but the next client will be here at any minute and I'll have to go through that entire process all over again.

I have a feeling it won't be as memorable.

CHAPTER 2

'Today's the day,' I say out loud with a grin at the reflections staring back at me from the mirrored cabinets mounted on the wall. Snatching up my toothbrush, I proceed to brush my teeth, but it's hard to keep the smile from my face.

It's Friday, April 24. Sonny is due to come in and collect his glasses at midday.

'I wish I'd booked him an appointment for this morning.' I twirl my hair up into a bun and secure it with bobby pins, then pick up my silver bracelet from the edge of the basin and fasten it around my wrist.

My smile falls when I walk into the bedroom and see Bertie sprawled out on the bed. 'Oi! Naughty!'

My uncle's black Labrador stares up at me with doleful brown eyes as I click my fingers.

'Come on, down you get.'

Bertie eases her weary bones into a reluctant standing position and slumps onto the rug. I scratch behind her ears and her tail wags appreciatively. She knows we're headed from here to the kitchen for breakfast, so she doesn't bother to lie down again.

My uncle, Charles, is on a round-the-world cruise until the end of September. I'm housesitting his cottage and, happily, Bertie comes with it. At twelve years old, she's a bit long in the tooth, while Charles is eighty and not getting any younger himself. He'd always wanted to travel, but his wife couldn't think of anything worse than being stuck on a boat with hundreds of strangers. June suffered with seasickness, general antisocialness and also, sadly, heart disease, as it turned out. She passed away a few years ago, but Charles only recently agreed to fulfil his lifelong ambition on the condition that I return to the UK to take care of things for him. I didn't mind too much – I was in India when he called, but I've been floating around for a while now. I didn't know how ready I was to come home until Charles asked me to.

Bertie's claws click and scratch against the red floor tiles as she follows me into the cosy kitchen and drops to her haunches in front of the always-warm Aga.

Only one small window looks out onto the nearby street, with a vista that reaches straight past June's roses lining the white picket fence. The green bushes are already bright with pops of colour, from pastel pinks and yellows to luminescent oranges and cherry reds. The month of June is when they really come into their own, though – *our* June used to fill this place with vases full of them.

Pouring kibble into Bertie's bowl and switching on the kettle, I set about making myself tea and toast before taking a seat at the kitchen table. Outside it's sunny with only a few clouds drifting across the pale-blue sky.

'Perfect weather for walking to work,' I muse, and Bertie's tail thumps in response.

She knows she's coming with me. Robert, Umeko's retired husband, takes care of her during the day. He and Charles are good friends, having met at university many, *many* moons ago. Robert likes Bertie's company, Bertie likes his, and Charles can relax knowing his old girl isn't going to be lonely. It's a win-win situation.

As I pull on my old frayed denim jacket over my navy staff uniform, Bertie dances around my legs, almost knocking me over in her excitement to leave the house. She reminds me of the puppy she once was, panting and delirious as I grab her red lead from the coat hook and attach it to her matching collar. Opening the door, we step out from under the thatched porch into the cool spring air. The lawn is cast in shade and laden with dew so I'm careful to stick to the garden path as Bertie tugs me towards the gate.

A car turns into the drive. It's Evelyn, arriving for work. She's the therapist who rents the room attached to Charles's home. I say attached, but it's actually set within the original cottage layout and used to form part of the living room, which is substantially smaller now. It has its own private access at the side of the building, granted by the council before they listed the place.

I give her a wave and she responds in kind, as warm and approachable as ever. She's in her late fifties now and her bob is tinged with grey, but when I first met her it was platinum blond.

She disappears down the side of the cottage to the back where she parks each day.

Bertie and I pass two pubs on our way to the rural footpath that leads into town – Grantchester has four within a hop, skip and a jump from each other. Right now, the windows look onto dark, empty rooms and the outdoor tables are damp and unwelcoming, but it'll be a different story if this weather holds through the weekend as it's supposed to.

The grass is too long and wet to walk down by the river, but I catch glimpses of the water occasionally, glinting in the early morning sunlight.

Eventually we break out of the green fields onto the residential roads. I look left and, sure enough, there she is again: the girl from the next-door pharmacy.

Laughing, I come to a stop and wait for her.

'Right, that's it,' she calls as she approaches. 'If we're going to keep meeting like this, we need to be properly introduced.'

This week has been so strange. Not only have we continually crossed paths on our ways into work, we've also found ourselves leaving at the same time. It hasn't made a difference if I've been five minutes early or five minutes late – we have been on *exactly* the same timetable. It was getting so ridiculous that yesterday I waited inside the doorway of Umeko's for a few seconds before daring to step out onto the pavement. I almost jumped out of my skin to see her doing the same thing at the same moment. We stood there, facing each other with dumbstruck expressions on our faces, and then we both cracked up laughing like a couple of nutcases.

'I'm going to the supermarket,' she said at last, tears of laughter making her green eyes sparkle as she pointed in the opposite direction.

'Okay, see you in the morning!' I called after her as we went our separate ways.

'I'm Hannah,' I tell her now. 'And this is Bertie.'

'Hello, Bertie,' she says warmly, bending down to give her a proper pat. 'And hello, Hannah,' she adds, grinning up at me. 'I'm Matilda.'

'Nice to finally meet you.'

She's in her early thirties, at a guess, with dark hair that comes to her shoulders. Her features are slightly pixie-like, with high cheekbones and a sprinkle of freckles dusting her small, upturned nose. She's pretty.

'Where do you live?' I ask.

'Selwyn Avenue,' she replies, straightening up and jabbing her thumb over her shoulder. 'You?'

'Grantchester.'

'Nice. Have you been there for long?' We walk on together.

'About six weeks. I'm looking after this cheeky monkey while my uncle's away.'

'She's gorgeous,' she says affectionately, stroking Bertie's head again. 'I've always wanted a black Lab.'

'You can't get one?'

'My boyfriend and I work during the day so it wouldn't be fair. What do you do with Bertie?'

We carry on chatting until we reach our building. I learn that Matilda and her boyfriend were on holiday in Sri Lanka over Easter, which explains why we haven't crossed paths until recently.

'See you at five o'clock,' I tease, coming to a stop outside Robert and Umeko's front door. They live in the apartment directly above the practice and their entrance is on the right of the building.

'Or maybe even at lunchtime!' she replies with a comedy wink.

I laugh and knock on the door. By the time Robert has made his way down the stairs to answer it, my thoughts have become once more preoccupied by what else is happening at lunchtime...

Abbey heads out for her break, leaving me alone in the shop to wait for Sonny. His appointment is minutes away and my stomach is overrun with idiotic butterflies.

It was that comment about my eyes that did it, and the last look he gave me over his shoulder. I'm not imagining it; he was attracted to me too.

Yes, I know he's leaving for Amsterdam tomorrow.

But there's always tonight.

I smile to myself then quickly rearrange my features, aware that insanity is not a typically appealing personality trait.

It's been a while since I've felt any sort of chemistry with a man so it's easy to get caught up in this minor distraction. After today, I'll be back to my humdrum reality and there will be no more cause to daydream.

I sigh, drumming my fingertips on the table. I bet he does have a girlfriend in the Netherlands. She's probably a tall, stunning model that he met at a photo shoot.

Okay, now he's late. But he *is* coming. Abbey called him yesterday to confirm the appointment.

The door opens and a jolt ricochets through me.

It's him. He's dressed in black jeans and an army green T-shirt.

The next thing I notice is that his head is down.

'Hi!' I welcome him brightly.

'Hey,' he mumbles.

His eyes remain fixed on the floor, but I can see that he's wearing glasses.

'Take a seat. I have your new glasses here for you,' I say genially, pressing on.

He walks over and pulls up a chair, but continues to avoid my eyes. His whole demeanour is totally different. This is not a man who's interested in me at all, I realise, with a stab of disappointment. I've misjudged the situation entirely.

I pass him his stylish new glasses case, hoping for a sign that he might be pleased, but his face is impassive.

Maybe he's embarrassed. I mean, his behaviour before – all that smiling and staring into my eyes – was a little intense. Perhaps he felt disloyal to his girlfriend and is trying to make amends.

That's probably it, I realise with a sinking heart as he takes off his old glasses. Now I feel like a fool too.

I had planned to launch into chatty small talk, intending to ask how his Easter was and what he's been getting up to in Cambridge, but the circumstances have tied my tongue.

He opens the case and extracts the Kilsgaards.

Wait. *Are his hands shaking?*

'Can you try them on?' Perplexed, I push the mirror towards him.

Something is definitely off. His hands *are* shaking. In fact, *he* seems shaken. Is he ill?

He turns his face towards me without looking at his reflection. His eyes remain lowered. It's clear that there will be no smiling today.

'I need to check the fit,' I prompt, and he obediently and perfunctorily leans towards me across the desk.

There's such a strange atmosphere in the room. I'm full of tension as I reach out to touch the frames.

He hasn't shaved for a couple of days, judging by the length of his stubble. My thumbs brush against his cheek-bones as I check the fit of the glasses, confirming that the arms sit comfortably over his ears. I give the frames a wiggle to ensure they're steady and won't slip off his nose.

'I'd like to make a small adjustment to one of the nose pads,' I say, and he takes off the glasses and hands them to me.

This time, he doesn't watch me as I work.

'Are they pinching your nose?' I ask when he puts them on again.

'No.'

'How's your vision?'

'Fine.'

'Can you have a look around the room,' I prompt. 'Is everything clear? Can you read what that poster says?'

He swallows and nods.

'Do you want to check the mirror?'

He shakes his head and takes them off. I stare at him and he swallows again as he returns the glasses to their case.

'Sonny?' I ask worriedly. 'Are you okay?'

Suddenly he looks straight into my eyes, and what I see chills my blood. He stands up abruptly, shoving his chair back in his attempt to get to his feet.

I'm in front of him before I even realise. 'Sonny?'

'They're fine,' he mumbles, his gaze once more averted.

'What's wrong?'

Another shake of the head. He picks up his old glasses and puts them on. 'Nothing. Are we done?'

He looks at me directly then and another jolt goes through me. His eyes have filled with tears.

I'm shocked, but my overriding emotion is concern. However, before I can say another word, he sidesteps me and stalks out through the door.

ALSO BY PAIGE TOON

In order of release…

Lucy in the Sky

Johnny be Good

Chasing Daisy

Pictures of Lily

Baby be Mine

One Perfect Summer

The Longest Holiday

Thirteen Weddings

The Sun in Her Eyes

The One we Fell in Love With

The Last Piece of my Heart

Five Years from Now

If You Could Go Anywhere

The Minute I Saw You

Novellas:

Johnny's Girl

One Perfect Christmas

A Christmas Wedding

Young Adult:

The Accidental Life of Jessie Jefferson

I knew You Were Trouble

All About the Hype

ACKNOWLEDGMENTS

I always thank my readers first and this time is no different. Actually, it *is* a bit different, because I feel the need to thank you – and every blogger, bookstagrammer, booktuber and reviewer – even more this year than ever.

I'm hoping that by the time this book comes out, we should be emerging into the light following a long journey through a dark Covid 19 tunnel. I've had more messages from readers than ever during this pandemic and it has lifted me up so much, hearing how my stories have helped you to find some escapism. Whether you're new to my books or have been reading them since *Lucy in the Sky*, thank you for picking up this one. *Someone I Used To Know* was my most emotional book to write and I hope it connects with you too.

If you're interested in finding out more about fostering or adoption, please visit nfpaonline.org/foster.

There are a lot of incredible charities out there for children and young people and hopefully you will feel compelled to support them. I will be raising money for Action For Children and Become, a charity that supports children in care and young care leavers by doing auctions of signed copies of my books so please keep an eye on my social media channels if you're interested in bidding: Twitter / Facebook / Instagram @PaigeToonAuthor.

Huge thanks to everyone at Simon and Schuster UK for everything they do for me and my books, but especially Suzanne Baboneau, who has always given me the freedom and encouragement to write the stories that I love to write (you might think this is a given, but believe me, it isn't). Thank you also to Judith Long, Jessica Barratt, Sara-Jade Virtue, Pip Watkins, Gill Richardson, Dominic Brendon, Joe Roche, Amy Fulwood, Richard Vlietstra, Amy Fletcher, Hayley McMullen, Rachel Bazan, Maddie Allan, Francesca Sironi and Anne O'Brien.

Thank you to Penguin Random House in Australia and the team there, especially my publisher Ali Watts, and Sofia Casanova and Abby Wilson.

And thank you to all my foreign publishers who help my stories to reach so many lovely readers around the world, in particular S. Fischer Verlage in Germany.

For their insight into fostering and the care system, I can't thank the following people enough: Alison Barker, Joanne Hainsworth, Fiona Campbell and Lucie Martin – and my friend Sarah Horsborough who put me in touch with these amazing women.

For help with my alpaca research and for inspiring certain ideas, including Carrie's knitting workshop, huge thanks to Tracy Birch. Visiting Tracy's herd of gorgeous alpacas was one of the most fun things I have ever had to do for research! Check out purlalpacadesigns.com if you'd like to see some of the inspiration behind Carrie and Leah's knitwear, and if you're ever visiting Cambridgeshire, you might even like to attend one of Tracy's workshops.

The Cracked Teapot was also inspired by a real-life coffee shop in America that only employs care leavers – I thought this was such a great idea that I wanted to shout about it from the rooftops.

I've come across a few coincidences in my time as an author, but I was amazed to discover that there actually is an alpaca farm near Brimham Rocks. I just want to stress that everything relating to farms and farmers in the area is one hundred per cent a figment of my own imagination and not based on any real people or events. I met a couple of farmers while I was doing my research and they were incredibly friendly and helpful. Brimham Rocks is one of my favourite places in the world and there's no way I've done it justice, so I hope one day you'll get to see it for yourselves, if you haven't already. Check out National-Trust.org.uk/brimham-rocks for more information.

A very special thank you to my friend Kimberly Atkins. When I told her the idea for this book, she replied, 'Oh, I thought you were going to say this...' I immediately decided to take the story in a different direction and I am so pleased I did: this book literally would not be the book it is without Kim and I am incredibly grateful.

Thank you also to these lovely friends who read early drafts and helped to pick up errors: Jane Hampton, who always goes above and beyond, Femke Cole, Katherine Reid, Georgie Barnes, Katherine Stalham and Rebecca Banks.

Lots of love to my parents Vern and Jen Schuppan, and my brother Kerrin and his family. They all live half a world away in Australia, but the coronavirus pandemic has made that distance feel even further. Much of the emotion I felt while writing this book came from missing you.

Thank you to my parents-in-law, Ian and Helga Toon who helped with various aspects of this book, not least introducing me to so much of stunning Yorkshire. But above all, I'd like to thank them for giving me their son, Greg. Together with our children Indy and Idha, I cannot think of anyone else I would have rather spent months and months holed up at home with – I love you all so much.

ABOUT THE AUTHOR

Paige Toon grew up in Australia, America and England following her racing driver dad around the globe. A philosophy graduate, she worked at teen, film and women's magazines before ending up at celebrity title *Heat* as Reviews Editor. She left in 2007 to have a baby and has been writing books set in sun-drenched locations around the world ever since. She now lives in Cambridge, UK, with her husband and two children. Her novels have sold over 1.5 million copies worldwide.

For more information about Paige's books and characters, visit www.paigetoon.com and sign up to her free newsletter #TheHiddenPaige.

Paige loves to hear from her readers so say hi on Twitter, Facebook and Instagram @PaigeToonAuthor.

facebook.com/paigetoonauthor

twitter.com/paigetoonauthor

instagram.com/paigetoonauthor

Made in the USA
Columbia, SC
04 August 2021

42940580R00231